A

A NOVEL

PERFECT
VICTIM

ROBERT W. CHRISTIAN

Ten|16
PRESS

www.ten16press.com - Waukesha, WI

THE DEMON SIGHT SERIES

Be sure to pick up the first book in the series!

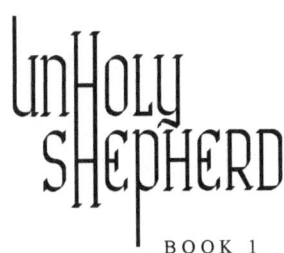

BOOK 1

"This is a complex, well-paced mystery that blends paranormal and horror with believable characters and setting...This taut book is good enough to share shelf space with crime writers Daniel Silva, Lisa Jewell, and Stephen King."

> —7th Annual Writer's Digest Self-Published eBook Awards

"...A powerful paranormal crime story..."

> —D. Donovan, Senior Reviewer, Midwest Book Review

"The thrilling plot and climax compelled me to eagerly continue reading until the last page"

> —Online Book Club

For my father,
my first fan.

"What nature does so blindly, slowly, and ruthlessly, man may do providently, quickly, and kindly. As it lies within his power, so it becomes his duty to work in that direction."

Francis Galton

tHE USS *WytHE*, 1946

The icy waves of the North Atlantic beat against the sides of the ship as Private Xavier Norman leaned against the rail, gazing west past the forward gunwale. Ahead, some two days away, was home. Behind was a part of his life he hoped would continue to fade the farther away he got.

The sense of duty to his country that had compelled him to leave college and enlist in the armed forces had been swallowed up by the horror of all that he had witnessed. When he had landed in the Mediterranean some three years earlier, he was told the campaign up through Italy would only take a few months, that the Krauts were on the run and wouldn't offer much resistance. All that talk proved false. Although the Italians surrendered almost immediately, the Krauts decided to hold fast instead of falling back, and he'd watched as day by day the progress they made north was counted in bodies instead of miles. Sometimes he wondered why he'd been spared when so many of his comrades were left to rot. Many were the nights when he thought a bullet to the head would have been a welcome release from lying in the cold rubble of so many ancient cities they'd bombed to holy hell.

Norman pulled a pack of cigarettes out of his pocket and popped one in his mouth, almost laughing as he did so. He hadn't been a smoker when he left home, and even now he didn't find much enjoyment in it. It was simply another habit he'd picked up in the trenches with his platoon, a way to keep his hands from nervously fingering a knife or gun. It also kept him from popping too many of the pep pills that were circulated like candy through the army. He never found out what was in them, but they had the effects of a pot of coffee all at once, just like some of the older troops had told him they would. Now that it had been several months since he'd taken one, though, he had begun to notice a marked improvement in how he slept.

"Got a spare one?" a deep voice asked.

Norman turned to find a man wrapped in a heavy, olive-green jacket standing a few feet behind him. He recognized the man instantly as Sergeant Alfred Bennington. The sergeant was famous among the crew of the ship. The story was that he was one of the last POWs returned to the Allies after Berlin fell the past May. They said he was a survivor of the Black March and was barely alive when his prison camp was liberated. His state of health had required him to stay in Europe far longer than anticipated. Somehow, he never complained.

"If you think I looked bad," Norman had overheard Bennington say while he was holding court with some of the younger soldiers a few weeks prior, "you should see what the damn Krauts did to those poor Jewish bastards. I saw the bodies. The reports don't do it justice. Makes me sick just thinking about it!"

The double and triple portions of food and the concoction of medications he'd been given had returned the vigor to his voice and body—not to mention adding some thirty pounds back to his frame—but Norman could still see the dark shadows of his cheekbones underneath his taut skin. He wondered if the man should be smoking, but he couldn't find it in him to deny the request of someone who had suffered so much, let alone one who outranked him. He pulled out another cigarette, lit it off his own, and handed it to the sergeant.

"Ah, that's the stuff," Bennington said after exhaling a long puff of smoke into the night air. "Thank you, Mister . . ."

"Private Xavier Norman," he replied, straightening himself up and offering the officer a salute.

Bennington laughed and stuck out his hand instead. "No need to stand on ceremony anymore, Norman. I'm pretty sure we're all just people now. No better, no worse."

Norman relaxed himself a little, shook the other man's hand, and leaned back on the rail, though he still felt a certain sense of intimidation speaking so casually with a war hero he'd heard so many stories about. He opened his mouth to speak but found words lacking.

Bennington seemed to have a sixth sense and began for him. "So tell me a bit about yourself, Norman. You look too healthy to have been in any of the POW camps. Why are you just going home now?"

Norman flicked some ash into the ocean. He'd asked himself that same question for nearly a year. "I was part of Arrowhead during the Italian campaign, the 141st. It was harder fighting than it was supposed to be up the peninsula. When we captured Rome and heard the northern advance was bogged down after Overlord, we figured we'd roll up from the south and squeeze Berlin ourselves." A snort escaped his lips.

"Wasn't the case, though, was it? I didn't set foot in Germany until five weeks after the surrender."

"Hell, even I was there by then!" Bennington grunted. "What took you so long? And why stay? I mean, I was in no condition to go home, but what kept you around these last nine months?"

"I volunteered as part of the occupation force. Don't really know why. It's not like I don't have a life to go home to. I guess I just felt that after all the shit I went through in Italy, I should at least hang around and see things start to get put back to rights."

"I can appreciate that," the other man replied, blowing a stream of smoke out of his nose and throwing the used cigarette butt into the ocean. "I would have liked to go to the trials up there in Nuremberg, but they wouldn't let me. Don't know what all the fuss is about. Those vitamins they got me on make me feel fantastic."

Bennington then looked over his shoulder and surveyed the deck as though he were checking to make sure they were alone. The night was quiet except for the occasional sigh of the ocean breeze. Once the sergeant seemed satisfied that it was only the two of them on deck, he reached down into his coat and brought out a bottle of dark liquor.

"Liberated from France on our way out," he explained, reading Norman's quizzical expression. "They had it in the officers' mess. Supposed to be over a hundred years old."

"What is it?" Norman asked.

"Cognac."

"And you think it's okay to take it from the mess?"

"I'm an officer, aren't I?" Bennington pulled the cork out of the bottle and sniffed at the mouth before taking a large swallow and offering the bottle to him. "Besides, I'm a hero.

You've seen how I'm treated around here. No one would dare say something even if they did see us."

Norman still wasn't sure, but the ferocity of the sergeant's logic convinced him to reach out and take the bottle. He took a tiny mouthful and sputtered as he swallowed. He'd had things that tasted worse but nothing that burned like that. Bennington laughed as he grabbed the bottle and threw back another swallow.

"All that time in Italy turn you into one of those frou-frou wine sippers? Or maybe that was your first drink of a man's beverage?"

"I've had liquor before," Norman said defensively. "I like manhattans."

"That shit's too sweet for me. Real men drink it straight, and the more spurs it's got, the better!"

"Gimme that." Norman's hand shot out and snatched the bottle from Bennington. If the story of his time in combat hadn't turned him into a man in the eyes of the sergeant, surely this would button up his chidings. He tipped the bottle back and let the liquor pour down his throat, taking two large gulps. He handed the bottle back to the other man and pounded his chest. It was on fire, but he did his best not to make a face. He wanted to look as tough as possible.

Bennington laughed and offered him a jovial salute as he took the bottle back. The older soldier sat himself down on the deck next to Norman and leaned back against the rail. Uncomfortable with standing over a superior officer—even one who insisted they were equals—Norman sank down on his backside as well. The two men passed the bottle back and forth as they traded war stories deep into the night.

The bottle was getting low when Bennington straightened himself up and turned to Norman. "What are you going to do when you get back?"

He'd asked himself that same question more than once. Norman's thoughts immediately turned to Mary Brightborn. She'd be a year out of high school by now, and though they had never actually discussed it, there seemed to have been an understanding between them since before they were teenagers that they'd one day marry. They had been each other's first kiss—by the river outside of town when he was fifteen and she twelve—and she had only grown more beautiful as the years went by. He'd written several letters during his time in Europe. Her responses had never reached him, but he hoped she was still waiting for him when he got back.

"I think I'll head home and see about a girl first," he told the sergeant. "Then, once that's settled, I think I'd like to finish college and maybe go to law school. I think I could do some good as a lawyer, helping the little people and all."

"That's a pretty idealistic view of the world," Bennington scoffed. "But good luck to you, I suppose. Who knows, maybe it will work out just as you think."

Norman looked over at the other man. His voice and demeanor had changed. The jovial look on the face of the man who had offered him a drink just a few hours ago had been replaced by a paranoid stare. He seemed to be trying to keep himself under control, but his hand was twitching as he reached into his pocket and pulled out something before putting it into his mouth and swallowing. Norman didn't have to guess what it was.

"So what about you, Sarge?" he asked, trying to break the

tension. "What are you going to do when you get back to the States?"

"There's nothing for me back there. I'm no good in peacetime." His hand went back into his pocket, and another pill disappeared down his throat.

"Are you sure you should be taking that many pills, sir?"

Bennington's breathing had become more rapid, and Norman knew all too well what too many pills could do to a man.

"Why shouldn't I? Doctors prescribed them to me, didn't they?" Bennington tipped the remaining cognac into his mouth. What was left in the bottle was a far smaller quantity than Norman remembered.

The sergeant must have been drinking when he wasn't looking. He had already outdone Norman two to one on drinks as it was. A prickle ran up the young private's spine, akin to the feeling he'd get before an ambush in the streets of some Italian town. He got to his feet to assess his physical state. The swaying of the deck seemed to have doubled since he sat down. Not a great sign.

Bennington followed suit and leaned on the rail. He stared out at the ocean for a moment before hurling the empty bottle into the darkness. As he turned back to Norman, it was clear that he was making a concerted effort to keep his face smooth, even kind. But the private still saw the wild fervor in his eyes that had begun to grip his sanity.

"What do you think of that woman down in the hold?" he whispered. "The one with the little boy?"

Norman was taken aback by his question but knew instantly who Bennington was talking about. In addition to a cadre of soldiers, the ship was taking about a dozen refugees to America. The woman he was talking about stood out among the rest. First of all, she was stunningly beautiful—blonde hair, piercing, blue eyes—but she was also the only person on board with a child, a boy no more than three. She didn't say much, and when she did, she only spoke French. In fact, on the one occasion he had overheard her introduce herself to anyone, she simply called herself Ms. French.

"You mean the French woman," Norman blurted out.

"Bah!" spat the sergeant. "So I see she fooled you too. That woman is no more French than I am a Chinaman!"

"How do you know? I've heard her speak French."

"Speaking a language doesn't mean you belong to it, son. She speaks French all right, same as me. Which is to say like a five year old. And she's got a funny accent to it too, which I don't expect you to pick up. But I've heard it before. It's the way the Krauts speak it—all harsh, like they got a hair ball stuck in their throats."

"Well, what about it? So she's German. Obviously, she doesn't want to live there anymore, so what's the harm?"

"She's the enemy! You don't give the enemy free entry into your country! And she's not the only one. I heard whispers while I was recovering. We didn't get all of the high command after they surrendered. Barely half of them are facing trial, they say. Some of 'em got away before it was all over, down to South America or Africa. And some of them"—Bennington's face contorted in anger—"some of them our own government is bringing into the country. Top men, with full pardons after everything they did for that evil bastard. Does that seem right to you?"

Norman couldn't answer. The sudden ferocity of the sergeant's words put him completely on his heels. Bennington was now pacing back and forth and grumbling to himself, as if he either didn't remember he'd asked him a question or else didn't care what the answer was. After a moment, he stopped and turned his head back to Norman.

"I should just go down there and kill them," he said excitedly, stepping over to Norman and grasping his collar with shaking hands. To the private, he seemed almost gleeful at the thought. He pulled a pistol from inside his coat and tapped it on Norman's cheek, beginning to speak again to the sea air. "Yes, that's what I'll do. I'll show them that they can't just let those damn Nazis into our country. Give them an inch, and they'll take everything. I'll be given a medal for this."

Bennington turned and, as if Norman had suddenly gone invisible, pulled another pill from his pocket, swallowed it dry, and began to creep toward the staircase that led belowdecks. Norman, his head still foggy from a combination of the drink and the sergeant's declaration of his intentions, took a moment to gather himself before racing past the other man and setting himself firmly in his path.

"Sarge," he said carefully, "you're not thinking clearly. Why don't we get you down to bed and forget about this? You're talking about killing a woman and a child for Christ's sake!"

"Kraut's a Kraut," Bennington growled. "And the only good Nazi is a dead Nazi."

The sergeant moved to one side, trying to get past Norman, but the excess of drink made him move slower than the younger man. Norman put himself between Bennington and the stairs again and managed to snatch the sergeant's pistol out of his hands. He raised it to chest height and aimed it at Bennington. The barrel wobbled unsteadily.

"The war's over, Sarge," he said, trying to hide the uncertainty in his voice. "Don't do anything you're going to regret."

"The war isn't over so long as any of those damn Nazi bastards are breathing."

"I don't want to use this, but I will if I have to."

Bennington sneered at him. "You don't have the guts, *Private*. But maybe you're right." The sergeant reached behind his back and pulled out a cruel-looking knife. The blade looked nearly a foot long and was as wide as a man's wrist. He continued to speak, though now he seemed to be talking to his new weapon. "Maybe an up-close and personal killing is the ticket. This little beauty hasn't knifed a Kraut in almost two years. I could drag it across that little shit's throat and make his mother watch. Then I'll put it right through her heart."

His eyes lit up at the idea, and he took a step forward. Norman planted his feet and cocked back the hammer of the pistol. Bennington stopped short and spread his arms in mocking reverence.

"You think you can actually do it, kid?" he asked. "Go ahead, then. Shoot!"

Norman faltered. He lowered the gun.

"That's what I thought." Bennington stepped forward and moved him to the side with the back of his blade. "Now stay out of my way and let me do what I need to do."

"Sarge," Norman whispered, "please don't."

"You don't know what they did to me!" the sergeant shouted, sticking the tip of his knife under Norman's chin.

"The starvation. The beatings. Never knowing if the next day would be your last! They did everything they could to break me!" His eyes narrowed. "But they didn't get the job done, did they? And now, I get to have my revenge."

At that, Bennington grabbed the front of Norman's coat, pulled him away from the stairs and behind him, and turned to go belowdecks. Norman had only a moment and reacted in the only way he knew how. He raised the sergeant's pistol and fired. He hoped the bullet would only wound the other man, but, whether guided by fate or the drink still coursing through his veins, it buried itself in the middle of Bennington's back. He fell forward on the threshold of the steps and didn't move.

For a moment, every sound around him disappeared, and Norman was left alone with his breathing—coming in gasps—in his ears. Slowly the image of the dead sergeant came back into focus. A dark pool of blood was beginning to seep out from under the body, and at once he became aware of the shouts of men and the sound of footsteps rushing up from below. The gunshot had been heard, and in moments he'd be surrounded by other soldiers who would see only the sight of a war hero gunned down and a lowly private standing over the body, gun in hand.

I can explain. But will they listen?

He didn't think they would. And in any case, at best he'd be dragged before a military tribunal when, once judged guilty, his life would be over whether he was executed or not. The footsteps were getting closer. He had to decide.

Norman backed up to the ship's rail and hoisted himself up to sit upon it. He looked east. The sun hadn't yet broken the horizon, but he could see the subtle purple hew in the sky above the water that signaled dawn wasn't far off. He looked west. Somewhere out there, Mary was still asleep in her bed. He closed his eyes and said a silent prayer, imploring God to find her someone who would take care of her and give her the life that he had wanted to. Finally, he looked down one last time at the body of Sergeant Alfred Bennington, the man who wanted to continue the war. He'd stopped him from doing that, at least.

Shame that the boy and his mother will never know what I did for them, he thought as he put the pistol to his temple.

A PERFECT VICTIM

ONE

The waters of two lakes reflected the pine groves at the base of these mountains in perfect symmetry. Between the two bodies of water, the young Colorado River flowed in a widening valley, emptying into the larger of the two lakes before gathering momentum and continuing its journey southwest toward Utah and Arizona. Ranger Alec Tyce pulled off his Stetson and mopped his brow with the back of his arm. The late-July sun beat off his neck as he looked over the edge of the cliff into the valley below. Despite the heat, he smiled. He never got tired of this sight.

Tyce shifted in his saddle to ease the pressure on his right thigh. He reached down and ran his hand over his jeans. Through the denim he could feel the old scar, about three inches long, pushing against the fabric. Despite the doctors' recommendations and the discomfort it sometimes brought him, he couldn't resist riding Digger on his trail checks around his corner of the park. The black-speckled Appaloosa could go to so many more places than an ATV or truck. That, and he liked someone to talk to during the lonely periods of his day. The horse seemed to understand him more than most people. Tyce had just begun with the park service when they had brought him in to replace another horse that they were putting out to pasture. He was the first one to ride the new horse, and in the near decade since, they had been nearly an exclusive team. It was the best partnership.

Not that he was averse to socializing with a human partner, but the budget for the park kept the staff of rangers smaller than it had been for the last several years. Fortunately, the impending turnover in the White House might free up some more federal money and make their lives easier. He wasn't worried about that for himself. With his salary and military disability pension, he lived comfortably enough in his Granby cabin, with plenty left after child support to put away some money for Aly's college tuition. He'd have a little more to put away for himself if she went to CU like he wanted, but she had her heart set on going out of state. She'd narrowed down her choices to TCU, Baylor, and Oregon. He didn't know if he could abide her becoming a Bear, but at least she wouldn't become a Cornhusker. His girl had *some* sense, he thought with a smile.

Digger nickered and swished his tail. He was getting bored standing still in the sunshine. At middle age for a horse, having celebrated his fourteenth birthday last month, he was still full of vigor, preferring galloping around the bases of the mountains to mingling with the mares in the corral by headquarters.

"Take it easy, boy," Tyce said, patting the horse's neck. "We'll get moving in a few minutes." Three swift shadows passed over him and forced Tyce's eyes skyward. He placed a hand up to his eyes and squinted, searching the skies for whatever had caused them. It wasn't long before he marked the three black shapes whirling in the air over the river. As he looked, the shapes were joined by still more, maybe half a dozen, flying out of the west. Turkey vultures, he decided. There must have been something dead in the valley. And he figured it must have been big if it was attracting so many of the carrion birds.

Tyce reached into his saddlebag, pulled out his binoculars, and with them searched the riverbed for the animal. He found the spot where the birds were beginning to make their landing and saw what looked like a large bundle partially submerged in the water. At the distance he was, Tyce couldn't tell what kind of animal it was, but he decided to check it out regardless. There were ongoing field studies on the elk herd in the park, and if it were a tagged animal, the researchers would probably want to know so they could quickly recover and examine the carcass. Also, a stray head of cattle would sometimes wander in from a nearby ranch. The owner would want to be told if that turned out to be the case.

He pulled out his radio and placed the receiver to his mouth. "Base, this is Tyce. I'm down at Checkpoint Delta and got a downed animal by the riverbed. Scavengers are on-site, but I'm gonna go down and have a look anyway. Will advise once I've assessed. Over."

"Roger that," the radio operator's voice crackled back. "Take care down there, Tyce. Over and out."

The ranger put his radio back on his belt and gently nudged Digger in the sides. He estimated that he was a little less than a mile off from his destination, but the winding trail that he'd have to take would put him beside the carcass in an hour or more. He heeled the horse a little harder, and Digger sped from a walk to a quick trot.

The terrain would quickly get uneven and dangerous for his horse to ramp up into a full gallop, so despite Digger's fervor to go faster, Tyce kept a smooth pace toward the river. He needed to guide the horse off the overlook in the opposite direction first and then circle wide to the east. Within a quarter mile, he found the path that he was looking for and turned Digger again toward the vulture frenzy. The path wound in a zigzag pattern, descending slowly into the valley. Eventually the path spilled out onto the riverbed, some five hundred yards north of his ultimate destination. The summer water level was such that a four-foot drop was needed to get from the path to the shore. The ranger urged his horse on, and they took the small drop with ease. He then turned Digger south toward the carcass.

The horse's hooves crunched along the stony shoreline of the river as Tyce approached. The vultures all looked up in unison, and some directed a raspy hiss toward the interloper. Tyce reined Digger to a stop about fifty yards away and jumped down off the horse. He shook out the cramp in his thigh and carefully began to navigate the slick stones. Then he stopped short. The birds had ceased their feeding to continue eyeing him, but that wasn't the sight that caused his feet to go still. Now that he was closer, he saw what could only be outstretched human fingers on the shore.

Tyce reached down to his hip and pulled out his pistol. Raising it into the air, he squeezed the trigger and fired off a single round. The sides of the valley intensified the sound of the muzzle blast, and this sent the vultures into the air in an eruption of black feathers. Once the mass of birds was clear from sight, the form of a person came fully into view.

Tyce crept close enough to stand over the body. Some of the skin had been eaten away by the birds, but he didn't note any other obvious signs of predation. The face of the corpse was relatively intact except for the eyes, which the vultures must have taken. He stared into the fleshy holes, wondering what color they might have been. But the lack of eyes wasn't the only thing missing from the body. There were no clothes to be seen anywhere.

He'd been working in the park long enough to have seen a couple of bodies of lost hikers or kayakers recovered from the elements. They all still had on their clothes. Whoever this person was, he could only tell two things for sure: it was a man, and he didn't die in any natural way.

Not wanting to touch the body—but still wanting to learn more—Tyce knelt down next to the torso. He ignored the water soaking through his jeans at the knee and continued his examination. The man's face was cut and bruised, but there was no trace of blood. It must have been washed away due to its time in the water. There were many other purple bruises all over the legs, arms, and torso, as if the man had been beaten by multiple assailants. Tyce finally decided that the man must have been murdered, though he admitted to himself that he should have seen it immediately.

Expanding his search around the corpse, he could see no footprints in the sand and stones besides his own, so he wondered where the body had been dumped. He turned his eyes to the north, toward the source of the Colorado. It must have come from somewhere in that direction, but how far was anyone's guess. He was about to get up and grab his radio when he saw something else.

There was a thin, red line down the middle of the dead man's torso, starting near the bottom of the breastbone and ending just above the pubic area. Tyce hadn't noticed it at first, but a tiny breath of wind had come and rippled the skin around it. He grabbed a nearby stick and gingerly poked at it. The line gave way, and the stick disappeared inside the body. He gently drew his hand to one side, and the stomach opened into a yawning cavity. He couldn't see any internal organs inside. The sour smell of decay hit his nose, and Tyce drew himself back as he came to a full awareness of just what it was he was doing. He looked down at his hand after taking two steps back and noticed that he was still holding the stick. The tip was covered with a black goo. He felt himself gag, and he tossed it into the river in disgust.

Too curious.

Tyce bent forward to steady his head and regain his composure, all the while cursing his lack of professionalism. He grabbed at his belt, drew out his radio, and did his job.

"Base, this is Tyce," he said. "I'm down along the Colorado about a mile as the crow flies northwest of Checkpoint Delta. I've got eyes on that carcass."

"Roger that. What's your report?" the operator's voice came back.

"Base, please be advised," Tyce answered, drawing a deep breath. "We're going to need the county medical examiner and a possible airlift. We've got a human corpse."

TWO

Agent Owen Samuelson sat at his desk in the Denver FBI office, staring at the open file on his desk. It was only a little after ten in the morning, but his eyes had already crossed and the words on the page blurred, signaling a need for coffee. Owen pushed himself away from the desk and turned to the table behind him, which had on it a small electric coffee pot and an assortment of ground beans. One of the perks of his near-decade-long service to the bureau: he didn't need to walk to the break room for refreshment.

The aroma of the fresh brew revitalized and reenergized him before he even took his first sip from the ceramic mug. With the warmth of his beverage flowing through him, Owen sat back down at his desk and continued poring over his case, the murder of a young woman by the name of Shelly Lindstrom. He put her medical examiner's report to one side, having read it over at least a dozen times, and began to peruse the family statements, looking for anybody in her life who may have wanted to do her any harm.

His review was interrupted by the chime of his desk phone. Owen looked over to the display to note the extension the call was coming from and see if he could let it go to voice mail.

Unfortunately, it displayed the number of Bob Auger, agent number one. He had to answer. Owen reached over and hit the button to allow the call to be heard on speakerphone.

"This is Samuelson," he said. "What can I do for you, sir?"

"Samuelson," the boss's voice came through the speaker, "my office. Double quick. And bring that file you're working on."

"Yes, sir," he responded.

Owen got to his feet, straightened his tie, and strode out of his office with his case file tucked under his arm. The tone of Auger's voice was serious. A sour feeling began to rise in his stomach as he navigated the building's hallways, knowing he was going to have to give the boss an update on the Lindstrom case. He hadn't made any significant breakthroughs since he had taken control of the investigation two weeks ago, and he could feel the eyes of each agent on him as he strolled past the line of offices. He had over three dozen closed homicides in his FBI career, but he still felt insecure anytime he had an open case on his hands.

Shelly Lindstrom. This one was befuddling him. The way the body was found was too macabre to be a random slaying. The problem was, there were no other homicides in the area or even the national database that seemed to fit the method of operation. As much as he wanted to work this case from the angle of it being a serial murder, he couldn't as of yet. Not until another body dropped, anyway.

There's a rosy thought.

Owen knocked on Agent Auger's office door, waited for a few seconds, and then turned the knob and went in. The older agent was facing away from him, grimly looking out the window.

"We wanted to see me, boss?" he said as he entered the room.

Auger turned around and cleared his throat. "Yeah, Samuelson," he said, sitting in his desk chair and motioning to one of the chairs in front of Owen. "Have a seat."

Owen slowly sat in the chair. He set the case file on his lap and waited patiently for the dressing down he believed he was about to receive. Instead, Agent Auger calmly folded his hands on his desk and began to speak softly.

"Agent, give me the rundown of the Lindstrom case," he said.

Owen was slightly taken aback by his boss's frankly casual request. Auger should have known about as much as he did. But he couldn't be insubordinate, so he opened the file to reference it and began his synopsis.

"Shelly Lindstrom," he began, "thirty-two years old, single white female, found dead on Thursday, June 5, washed up on the north shore of Grand Lake. The body was stripped naked, and ME's report puts time of death late on the previous Sunday or early Monday. Large volumes of ketamine were found in her bloodstream, potentially a sign of a fatal overdose." He looked up from the case file.

"But?" Auger prodded.

"But, the victim had apparently had her lungs, heart, and all other major organs removed, making a full tox workup impossible. Her time in the water would also make fingerprinting or DNA analysis inaccurate."

"Something else was missing from the body."

"The skull had been cut open, and the brain had been removed. The incision around the skull was clean, and there was no brain matter left inside the skull, so it's almost impossible that it was broken open by natural causes and eaten by animals."

"So what would you say that could indicate?"

"Killer is taking trophies?"

"Could very well be. And we have no leads and nothing in her life—past or present—that would offer up a good suspect?"

"No, sir. By all the accounts of her friends and family, she was well liked. Clean past. Was salutatorian of her high school class, graduated summa cum laude from Kansas, got her MBA from Brigham Young, and worked as an investment manager for one of the top fiduciaries in Denver. No known conflicts with any of her coworkers, and her customers unanimously loved her. No boyfriend in the picture as far as anyone knew either."

"What about the ketamine?"

"That's another weird thing. The street name for it is Special K, and it's become a sort of club drug over the last few years since it's fallen into relative disuse by the medical profession as an anesthetic. Trouble is, she had no history of drug abuse. And her friends say she usually volunteered to be DD when they'd go out."

"And we know it wasn't used to sedate her for a sexual assault because?"

"Because there was no sign of any sexual activity, and the rape kit came back clean. It's a mystery as to why anyone would want to kill her."

"Well here's the thing, Agent," Auger said. "It might not be such a mystery."

"How so, sir?" Owen asked, confused.

"Well first, remind me what Shelly Lindstrom was doing in the forty-eight hours before she was killed."

"She was doing her weekend service for the National Guard," he replied, opening the case file and finding the pages dealing with that weekend. "According to the members of her platoon, they were doing search-and-rescue drills. Most of their work was done on the Colorado, kayaking and aquatic retrievals there, and on the lake. The platoon broke around four on Sunday afternoon, and that was the last time anybody saw Shelly. Local uniforms took all their statements and checked alibis. They all appear to be solid."

"Okay," said Auger. "Do me a favor and read off the names of the rest of the platoon."

Owen found the page that had the names of the other twenty-three members of Shelly's platoon and began to read them off aloud.

"David Bowers, Fay Crookshank, Michael Driver, Peter Grant, Sean Harris, Mandy Hogan, Benjamin Jennings, James Kennedy, Shelly, Erik McMannis, Christopher Niemann—"

"Stop right there." Agent Auger opened his desk drawer and pulled out another file folder. He tossed it on the desk. "Have a look."

Owen grabbed the folder and opened it. He didn't have to read past the first words on the top page to understand.

"Christopher Niemann?" he said, looking up at Agent Auger.

"Found in Rocky Mountain National Park," his boss confirmed. "A park ranger on his rounds found him by the section of the river between Shadow Mountain and Granby. Read the report."

"Naked, thin slit from sternum to pelvis, organs removed," Owen read aloud. "Ketamine in system. Body believed to have been in the water between twenty-four and forty-eight hours. Victim is believed to have been dead before entering the water. Preliminaries on fingerprints and DNA have come back with nothing." Owen looked up at his boss.

Auger was staring intently back at him. Both men knew what this meant.

"We might have a budding serial killer on our hands," Owen said.

Auger nodded in agreement, folding his hands under his chin. "I want you to take this one as well and combine it with the Lindstrom case," he told Owen, closing the file for him and pushing it to the edge of the desk.

"Yes, sir," he replied and began to get up, thinking he was being dismissed.

"Hang on a second, Agent," Auger said.

"Sir?"

"You're going to be taking a partner with you."

"Of course, sir, I expected to take Turnberry with me."

"Yes, you'll be taking Turnberry, as usual—and Navarro for that matter—but it's not them I'm referring to."

"I'm afraid I don't understand."

Agent Auger got to his feet and paced around the side of his desk. He made his way close to Owen and lowered his voice. "It's not a good look to have two National Guardsmen from the same platoon murdered within two months of each other. The governor wants the case to be closed quickly, and so do the bosses in Washington. I've just gotten a call from the deputy director, and we have our orders. In order to expedite the case, we're going to use some outside help. Now, I don't have to tell you that we're going to need to keep this quiet. We don't need any press on this. You and the boys have got six hours to get your effects together and be ready to grab the chopper. You'll be making a detour up to Wyoming before you head to the other side of the mountains."

Owen felt his heart sink. He'd read the memo that had circulated around the office some four months ago, detailing a new experiment the bureau may undertake over the next few years. Being a believer that it was solid police work that brought criminals and killers to justice, he didn't hold such superstitions in high regard. In his opinion, the fantastical had no place within the FBI.

"Sir, I don't know if—"

"No buts," Agent Auger interrupted. "Go get Dreamer."

╬HREE

The morning light streamed through the open window as Maureen rubbed the sleep out of her eyes. Like every day for the last four months, she contemplated staying in bed, but like every day, she decided to get up.

The property that Father Patrick and his friends had set her up with was an old farmhouse on a dead-end road in the middle of Wyoming. There were plenty of acres for her to roam and a beautiful view of the mountains. She hadn't experienced a true winter here yet, and if she had her way, she never would. The memories of Sycamore Hills, Waseca, the deal with Agent Layton, and Manny haunted her almost as much as her dreams used to. She promised herself within the first week after she arrived that she would move on the first chance she got. It was easier said than done.

She had the run of the house and the barn, but the nearest town was almost thirty miles away, and while there were plenty of horses and all-terrain vehicles on the property, there wasn't a proper car to be found on-site. She got a grocery delivery once a week from Natalie Archer, the owner of the property. How she and Father Patrick knew each other, she never found out, but she never took any money for the food and whiskey that she brought Maureen, and so the five grand that the priest had left her was almost entirely intact. Sometimes she stayed to talk, so Maureen at least learned that Natalie lived at another farmstead three miles down the road. She had inherited it from her father after his death some seven years before. In fact, the family owned all three of the properties that stood along the east side of the road that extended north from the main highway, leasing the middle of the three to a rancher who raised prize beef cattle.

Natalie was not the only member of what she had come to call Father Patrick's inner circle. Her son, a tall, young man in his early twenties named Avery, would come out to the farm most afternoons with two or three of his friends. They were older men, though none could have been much older than Maureen herself. Of these, she'd only caught the names of Ernest Oliveira, a quiet, dark-haired man with a thick mustache and a scar over his right eye, and Iggy Tran, a short, slight man with a heavy accent. When these men and others arrived, they went instantly to the barn. During her first week there, Avery invited Maureen to join, and she found herself taking part in some type of martial arts training. The men were very skilled in boxing and wrestling, and she surmised that they were simply enthusiasts who must participate in local tournaments. Or maybe it was just the easiest way to stay in shape in the middle of nowhere. Whatever the case, they were serious about their activities and rarely took it easy on each other or her. Over time, however, she'd taken to it and made the training a key part of most of her days. It beat sitting around.

Maureen pushed her bedsheets off of her and swung her feet onto the hardwood floor. It creaked under her weight as she rose to her feet and shuffled over to the ancient wooden dresser that held her entire life. She pulled off the tank top she'd been sleeping in and tossed it aside. She opened the top dresser drawer, fished out a clean sports bra, and pulled it on, then squatted down to open the lower drawer to get a pair of shorts and a T-shirt. As she rummaged through her options, her hand brushed across a half-buried piece of red fabric. She pulled it out and held it open in front of her to reveal the logo of the St. Louis Cardinals.

She held the shirt up to her nose. Manny's smell had faded since she took it on her last night in Missouri before the feds scooped her up and sent her to her stint in prison. It was the last time she'd gotten laid. The last time for a lot of things, actually. She hadn't tried to send him any letters after she relocated, and the letters from Father Patrick told her that he moved up to St. Louis and took the job with the bureau that Layton offered him after they had brought down Father Preston and rescued the little Naismith boy. Trying to find a way to contact him was out of the question. She could never explain the way she vanished from Sycamore Hills. Besides, she was sure the FBI would have told him about the deal by now. She hoped he was well. Sometimes she even allowed herself to believe he had moved on and was happily dating someone new. She felt less selfish that way. Better that than imagining him pining for her return, which wasn't likely to come.

She tossed the shirt back into the drawer, selected one of her plain, white ones, and pulled it on before stepping into a pair of shorts. She gathered her hair into a ponytail and grabbed a baseball cap off the top of the dresser, putting it on as she walked downstairs. She decided she would go for a walk up into the foothills that began at the border of the farm's back forty and led toward the distant mountains.

Maureen emerged onto the wooden porch and faced the midmorning sunlight. The air was already hot and promised to get hotter as the sun continued to rise. She trudged down the packed-dirt path that led from the house and past the barn and then circled back north. In most places, the path was hardly discernible from the surrounding sea of brown dust and yellowing prairie grasses that gathered in thick patches. She had memorized the way over time, though, and even if she eventually strayed off it as it climbed higher, she would never find herself out of sight of the house.

After what she believed must have been more than an hour of hiking, Maureen came to a familiar outcropping. Here, she rested for a bit. Some days this was as far as she would go, choosing to sit on one of the flat-topped boulders and gaze south and east. Oftentimes, she would reflect on the past year. Her six months in Waseca were fairly uneventful, aside from the unsettling revelation her dreams provided: that one of the guards was forcing a few of the inmates into offering sexual favors in exchange for certain perks. In sleep, she got a firsthand experience of the sensations that go through a man's body when on the receiving end of a blow job in a bathroom stall. But that wasn't what disturbed her. The disturbing part was that her supposition that God would take her dreams away if she used them to help those in need was completely wrong. Whatever debt she had with the Almighty, it seemed there was plenty more to pay.

Sometimes, she retraced their journey from the prison to the farm. After he had taken it upon himself to get her off the grid, Father Patrick took her on a winding road trip, driving at odd hours through both Dakotas and into the mountains of Montana and Idaho before doubling back into Wyoming and leaving her with his friends. They ditched the black flip phone that she had been given as her link to the FBI some three days after the priest had informed her that they had shaken off their tail. Maureen had only been casually aware of the black sedan, but after ditching the phone, the sightings stopped. After that, it had still been another week and a half before she was left in the care of Natalie and the others. If she were honest with herself, she would admit she still felt angry at the old man for not staying with her. There were times she even missed his long, professorial musings on the nature of God and man and each of their places in the universe. But he assured her that his friends could be trusted, that she would be all right without him, and that he'd never truly "leave" her.

"Old bastard was right on that count," she mumbled at the rocks and stones. And it was true. Despite her disdain for religion and its moral platitudes, since meeting him, whenever she felt the urge to do anything questionable, she always asked herself what the old priest would want her to do. The answer was always the same: sit still and be patient.

Maureen decided to continue farther into the heights rather than sit for too long and stew over things she had already spent enough time thinking about. She'd hiked that way more than once. There was no worn path up there, but it was easy enough to pick her way through the rocks. The land began to green ever so slightly as she went, and in a few places wildflowers sprang out from the ground, soaking up the last drops of moisture from the cool air before the currents pulled them down to the farm.

At last, Maureen let out a puff and stopped climbing. She hadn't paid much attention to how fast she was going or how far she had hiked, but the rush of energy that drove her had finally given out, and she became aware of a gnawing pain in her side. She turned around. The sun had changed positions and was now toward her right, telling her that morning had given way to afternoon. Far below, the land spread before her, far beyond the farm. Far off in the distance lay the horizon, its hazy blue line melting so completely into the greens and browns below it that it was nearly impossible to discern where exactly the sky ended and the earth began.

Maureen sighed to herself and looked back over her shoulder. The mountains were still miles away.

"One day I'll pick up everything and just get lost up there," she asserted. But for now, as her stitch faded, she faced back to her prison and began to descend.

The slope of the land now worked in her favor, and it only took half the time to return to the barn. As sweaty and hungry as her hike had left her, she felt a pull toward the outbuilding and decided to enter. She pushed a side door open and went inside.

The interior was empty. The only movement was the dust floating in the shafts of sun stabbing through the window and illuminating patches of the dirt floor. The old farm equipment and ATVs sat in the shadows of the opposite end of the barn. In front of her, the dim light folded itself around the area of the building used as the training area for Avery and his buddies. They were nowhere to be found, and Maureen realized that it was Sunday. She'd be alone.

She stripped her cap from her head, threw it into the corner, and tightened her ponytail. She shook out her limbs and began to bounce on her toes, as she had become accustomed to doing during her training sessions. After a few moments, she began to feel her heart rate increase, and she stepped closer to the makeshift gym. A heavy bag hung to one side with enough room to move around it in a complete circle. There was a well-used weight rack with rusted dumbbells on it lined up in no particular order, as well as several hooks drilled into the barn wall with training bands and jump ropes hanging on them. A perfectly usable space.

Maureen selected a jump rope and began to skip, building speed until she was ferociously spinning it over her head as fast as she could. She continued until her lungs were on fire. Finally, she stopped and threw the rope to one side. After a brief breather, she went to the weight rack and selected a pair of smaller dumbbells and began to work in a circuit that Avery had taught her, going through a routine of working each of the muscle groups in her arms.

At last, she was feeling weary, but the prospect of sitting in the house until nightfall and reading one of the seventeen books that she'd already read twice each forced her to continue. She went to the wall near the punching bag to find the gym bag filled with the boys' spare gloves and hand wraps. Maureen wrapped each of her hands and selected a light pair of heavy bag gloves and began to work around the bag. She circled, pumping two left jabs with a right cross following behind, the basic combination she had been taught. She built speed and added hooks and then knees and elbows. After a while, she lost track of whether she was performing the movements correctly and simply tried to hit the bag as hard and as fast as she could. The faces of each of the priests and nuns from St. Dymphna's superimposed themselves onto the worn leather as she pounded away. Then came the faces of her mother and father, followed by Agent Layton's smug stare, followed by every cheapskate boss and every leering drunk. She even envisioned hitting Manny once or twice. There was still plenty inside her that she needed therapy for.

Finally, Maureen wrapped her arms around the bag to stop its swinging and rested her forehead on it, leaving a round stain of sweat behind. The dirt floor around her was soaked as well. She pushed herself back and stripped off her gloves and wraps, placing them back in the bag before finding her cap and opening the barn door. The sun had begun to sink farther into the west, but it was still high enough in the sky to indicate that it couldn't have been much later than five.

Maureen crossed the yard and headed back into the house. She went straight to the kitchen and turned on the kitchen sink to fill a water glass. Before coming here, she had never had well water. It had a funny taste that she hadn't quite gotten used to. It lacked the certain chlorinated flavor that told her city brain that it had been cleaned. She swallowed the water down in large gulps before deciding to put something else past her lips that she knew was safe.

One thing she had to admit about Natalie: the woman knew her whiskey and kept Maureen well supplied. Not that she drank as hard as she did prior to her incarceration. Thankfully, aside from crawling around inside the head of that asshole guard at the prison for six months and some blurry images of a not-too-close-by drunk who beat his wife occasionally, no one in her vicinity was doing much in the way of evil these days, and her sleep had been relatively peaceful. Still, Maureen poured herself a glass. Old habits die hard.

After her drink, she headed up to the bathroom off her bedroom and washed off the dirt and grime from the day. The water at her feet turned deep brown as it circled down the drain. The shower pressure was superb. The last time she'd had a shower like the ones she experienced here was at Manny's house in Sycamore Hills. Sometimes she worried it was making her soft, but after all she'd seen, maybe she could be afforded a little luxury.

Maureen toweled off and tossed her dirty clothes into the hamper by the bedroom door. Natalie would do her laundry when she came the next day. She never asked her to do it, but she didn't stop her either. If the woman wanted to act like her maid, who was she to argue? She put on a pair of sweatpants and a new sports bra and headed back downstairs. She didn't bother with another shirt. On Sunday nights no one was ever around, and she could have walked around naked if she felt so inclined.

There were plenty of TV dinners in the freezer for her to heat up. Maureen showed no aptitude when Natalie had tried to teach her how to prepare her own meals; her life on the road meant that she had never developed any kitchen skills. So rather than waste time trying to teach a deficient student, Natalie made sure she had them if she wasn't going to be around to cook. Maureen grabbed a turkey and mashed potato meal and threw it in the oven, setting the timer for the fifty minutes recommended on the box.

It was still light outside when she finished her meal, but she settled into the big chair in the living room with another drink. In her other life, it would be just about the time when whatever bar she was working at was just starting to get lively.

She once asked Natalie about getting a job but was told that it wouldn't be practical at that point since they were so far out of town and the establishments that she'd have the skills to work at only ever hired family members or close friends. And so her companions each night were the crickets. Still, it could have been worse.

The alternative was to be beholden to the FBI as their performing monkey. Her release after her six-month incarceration hinged upon a three-year indentured servitude, allowing the government to use her as a glorified Magic 8-Ball. Agent Layton had termed it "consulting profiling," but all they really wanted was for her to solve their cases for them when they were stuck. She had no real experience in criminal investigation. Manny had really been the one who solved the "shepherd murders"—as the media called them—so she didn't know what they expected. But not having the phone and Father Patrick's care in bringing her to Wyoming gave her some comfort.

Maureen began to consider getting one more drink when she heard what she thought was a loud wind outside. It lasted only for a few seconds before the silence returned. She shrugged and got up to go to the kitchen for one more pour. She had gone only a few steps when she saw a silhouette cross in front of the window out of the corner of her eye. A moment later, there came a loud knock at the front door. Maureen froze.

She held her breath, hoping that her ears and eyes were just playing tricks on her. An unnerving moment passed before another knock came. She let out a heavy sigh and bowed her head. The gnawing feeling growing in the pit of her stomach told her that not answering the door wasn't an option—and there was no back door to escape out of—so she slowly loped to the door and ripped it open. Two men in black suits stood on the porch.

"Ms. Allerton," the shorter, clean-shaven one said, pulling out a wallet and flipping it open to reveal an FBI badge. "I'm Special Agent Owen Samuelson, this is Special Agent Steven Turnberry. We're going to need you to come with us, please."

The man continued talking, but Maureen was well beyond hearing. She pushed past them and walked around the side of the house. The setting sun left the western sky awash in a sea of purple, red, and gold. The air was getting pleasantly cool. But she paid no attention to it. Some hundred-or-so yards down the gravel driveway, near the road, a black helicopter sat, silently waiting to reel her back into the world.

"Ah, shit," she mumbled to herself.

FOUR

Maureen stared out the window of the helicopter. The white-capped peaks of the Rocky Mountains loomed up on her right as they crossed the border between Wyoming and Colorado. The sound of the blades spinning filled the cabin with a dull murmur. Out of the side of her eye, she saw the agents speaking closely together. They weren't looking at her directly, but she still assumed the conversation was about her. Or the case. There was nothing else that they could be discussing. She decided within a moment that she needed to insert herself into the proceedings, if for no other reason than to keep her from pulling her hair out in frustration.

"How did you find me?" Maureen said over the din. The question had been pressing on her brain for almost an hour, and if she was going to be stuck with these men for the foreseeable future, she might as well get the small talk out of the way and find out who she was dealing with.

"That priest friend of yours was pretty good," the shorter one said. "But we're better."

"It's Samuelson, right?" Maureen asked.

"That's right," he said with a bored look on his face. He didn't seem very interested in talking to her.

"So have you guys known where I was this whole time?" It was a fair question in her mind. She'd had a taste of what the FBI was capable of back in Missouri when Layton demonstrated how easily he'd ascertained Father Patrick's true identity. It seemed to her that if they were as good as they claimed to be, figuring out where she was shouldn't have been a challenge. But if that was the case, surly they would have paid her a visit before now.

The agents exchanged glances. Samuelson tilted his head, and the other agent shrugged his shoulders.

"We lost track of you for a few weeks," he said, leaning in closer to her, "but it wasn't hard to figure out where you were after we started tracking the good father's mail. He sent several letters to a PO box in Laramie. We suspected he would write to you, and given where the tail lost you, we liked the location. The box was registered under a fake name, but they have a security camera on-site that we were able to tap into. Didn't take us long to identify Natalie Archer as the person who would pick up the mail. We figured out she keeps her properties in her son's name, and we sent out a surveillance drone and caught you on video soon after."

"I don't remember seeing a drone," Maureen said.

"It would defeat the purpose if you did."

"So why wait till now to come get me? Is this some kind of game you guys are playing with me?"

"Let's get something straight, Ms. Allerton," the agent said, looking intently at her. "The FBI isn't in the business of unnecessarily interfering with the lives of free citizens. But you're not *really* free, are you? The only reason you're not in prison is because one of our guys in the bureau seems to think that you have something of value to offer if you're allowed to be part of our investigations."

Maureen looked deep into Agent Samuelson's eyes. "You don't want me here," she said stoically, refusing to blink first. For some reason, this idea almost amused her. Almost.

A short, wheezing laugh escaped Samuelson's nose as a sneer curled his lips. He leaned back in his seat and crossed his arms, nodding his head slightly as if he were having an internal conversation about her.

"I don't buy into the whole psychic thing," he said after a few moments. "And if you want me to be honest, no, I don't really see the point of you. I've read your file: felony possession, bail jumping, medical fraud, and criminal trespassing, just to name a few of your crimes. I think you belong back at Waseca, not consulting on federal investigations."

"If that's the case," she replied, "why don't you just take me back to the farm and leave me alone? I don't want to be here any more than you want me here."

"Neither of us have a choice," he said flatly. "So I'll do my job, and you'll do yours."

The rest of the flight was silent. Samuelson's last words had only served to intensify the vibe radiating from him. She wasn't sure whether to describe it as tension, irritability, or just plain indifference, but Maureen resisted the urge to poke the bear. She'd save that for when he inevitably annoyed her to the point where retaliation was necessary to keep him in his place. Instead, she turned her eyes back over to the mountains and watched the world sink into darkness.

The sun had been fully set for a good while when the helicopter finally landed on a small airstrip in the middle of the mountains. There were only a few floodlights and the lights of the chopper to illuminate their descent, and Maureen found herself wondering how the pilot managed not to crash and what the landscape around them would look like in the light of day—anything to keep her mind off why she was actually there.

There was a black sedan waiting for them, though if its headlights hadn't been on, she would have never known it was there. Samuelson and the other agent, Turnberry, led her over. The driver, a younger man dressed in the same black suit and tie as the other two agents, nodded at them. Turnberry got into the front passenger seat and Samuelson got in the back seat with Maureen, which did not thrill her.

"Why can't your partner sit back here?" she asked.

"I lost the coin toss," the agent dryly replied.

"Sucks for me," she chided back. "He's better looking."

Samuelson turned away from her and looked out the window. Maureen smiled, satisfied that she had gotten the mental upper hand on him. It would keep her sane for the time being, knowing that she found the pressure point she could press to keep him in check. Every man had one.

After driving for some forty-five minutes, the dim lights indicating the approach of a small mountain town became visible over a rise in the road. Maureen was completely turned around, though knowing where she was or the name of the town wouldn't have made a difference. The less she knew about what was going on, the better. If she were going to get through this and maintain her sanity, she'd have to make sure she didn't make the mistake of getting emotionally invested. Not like last time.

The car pulled into the lot of a small motel just off the highway with a blue-and-red neon sign reading "Bed Head Inn – Vacancy."

What a shitty name for a motel.

The driver shut off the car and handed an envelope to each of the other agents. Samuelson opened his and pulled out two keys, each with a white plastic circle attached. On each circle was a red number. He handed her the one that had 9 on it and kept the one that had 8. Maureen frowned as she got the key from him and stared at it. The feds were certainly prepared.

"I'm guessing Agent Turnberry is in number ten," she said.

"He is," Turnberry piped up from the front seat.

"He speaks!" Maureen remarked with mock enthusiasm before turning toward the other agent. "So you guys are going to have me surrounded so I can't run, is that it? You don't trust me?"

"I don't know you," said Samuelson. "But considering that your file says you have a tendency to go rogue, then no, I guess I don't."

"Well, as long as Uncle Sam is footing the bill and there's pay-per-view and a decent minibar, I'll be glad for this little vacation. So don't you worry about me."

The agent didn't answer. Instead, he pushed his door open and stood outside the car. Maureen did the same, hoisting her duffel bag over her shoulder. She stood for a moment, waiting for her marching orders, but when none came, she circled around the car and stalked across the parking lot. She found room nine, the second-to-last one on the ground floor and indeed flanked by the agents' rooms. She looked back. The agents had just finished their conversation, and two were beginning to cross the lot. She noted that the driver of the sedan had gone to take his place in the passenger seat instead of the driver's. Maureen snickered. He was to be the lookout in case she tried anything.

Maureen turned the key in the lock and pushed open the door. She flipped on the light switch, and a dim orange glow illuminated a room that contained a circular table, two double beds with ugly yellow and brown comforters, and an old box television on a dresser with a mini fridge next to it. She dropped her bag next to the bed closest to the door and went to see if the fridge was stocked. To her chagrin, while there were drinks inside, it only contained four bottles of water, six of soda, and a six-pack of seven-ounce beers. That wouldn't be enough to even get her buzzed, let alone keep the nightmares at bay for one more night.

She grabbed a beer, twisted off the top, and drank it down in one gulp before grabbing the rest of the pack and setting it next to her as she sprawled on the bed. She stared up at the popcorn-textured ceiling while nursing her drinks. She began to consider what it meant to be going back into the dreams, to link minds with evil, to wear another person like a mask and feel what they feel. And then there were the consequences on her own body: the vomiting, the migraines. She wondered if the feds would be good enough to get her a steady supply of whiskey or, even better, a bottle of Darvocet to help her medicate.

The empty bottles clinked together as she shifted her weight and turned on her side, facing away from the door. She only had one full beer left, and that would soon be gone. She would have to force herself to sleep soon, though. With the feds holding her leash, she had a suspicion that she'd be waking up far earlier than she was used to. People like Samuelson and Turnberry—men who seemed married to their jobs and who were staunch adherents to regulation—were just the type to get up at the crack of dawn like clockwork.

Her thoughts were interrupted by a loud knock at the door. Maureen's head spun toward the sound. She knew that it couldn't be anyone else but that agent Samuelson, so she decided to make him knock again before she let him in. A few silent moments passed before another knock came, but this time the dull thudding of the heel of a balled-up fist replaced the sharp rap of knuckles. In spite of the childishness she knew she was displaying, Maureen allowed herself a grin before smoothing her face and crossing the room to open the door.

"I trust I'm not disturbing you," Agent Samuelson said in his businesslike tone as he pushed past her into the room.

"By all means, come in," she retorted, closing the door and leaning her back on it. She took a tiny sip of her beer to keep any more words from coming out.

Samuelson, hands in his pockets, ambled over to stand between the beds and stared down at the empty bottles. His mouth twitched, almost like he was holding back a smirk. He shook his head and then continued to stare, as if he were looking through the bed to figure out his next words.

"You and I aren't going to have any trouble, are we?" he asked after what felt like an hour to Maureen.

She wasn't quite sure how to respond. The part of her that felt like he was intruding in her life certainly wanted to give him a bit of hell, if only to show the FBI that they didn't own her. She decided to maintain some level of discretion, though. "If you just let me do things my way, we'll be fine," she managed to say.

"And just what is 'your way'?" he asked.

Maureen shrugged. She didn't know how to explain something that just seemed to happen to her with no logical reason. How should you tell someone who seemed to like to be in control that they weren't going to have any?

Samuelson let out a grunt and ran his hands over his face. "Okay, maybe you could tell me if your little premonitions, or whatever you call them, are going to kick off tonight?"

"I can't guarantee anything," Maureen replied. She knew the answer wasn't going to be good enough for him.

"And why is that?" he persisted. His jaw began to clench. He was clearly trying to be nice to her, but she was certain she was annoying him. "How exactly does this whole thing work?"

Maureen shrugged again. "You think I wouldn't tell you if I knew?"

"I honestly don't know, Ms. Allerton."

"Well, if you ask a friend of mine, the dreams are a gift from God that I'm supposed to use to make the world a better place."

"You're talking about the priest who killed Preston Lane last year." It wasn't a question.

"So *that* you know, but me telling you there's no good explanation for what happens to me when I sleep is a surprise!" She wanted to throw up her hands but kept mastery of herself. "Look, man, you came to me. I didn't ask for any of this, and I never guaranteed you guys anything when I made that deal last year. It's your bosses who decided I was worth it. If something happens while I'm here, it happens, and hopefully you and your boys are smart enough to use whatever I give you."

"Well, you better give us something, or it's going to be all our asses. And you're not doing anything right now to change my mind about you."

"But enough about me, Agent Samuelson, tell me a little more about you," she chided back, seeking to rile him a bit and get the focus off her. "Wife? Kids? Got a little dog waiting for you back home? You a baseball guy? Or are sports not your thing?"

His eyes twitched briefly. It had worked; she was really getting under his skin now. It felt good but not quite as satisfying as she'd hoped.

"Good night, Ms. Allerton," he said flatly, crossing the floor in four quick paces.

He stood over her for a moment before reaching around her and turning the doorknob. Maureen took a step forward to avoid getting hit by the edge of the door as he opened it, and he stepped into the night.

"Asshole," she mumbled under her breath as she returned to sit on the bed.

This agent was not going to make this little foray a pleasant one. It seemed to her that beneath that stony exterior, there was a roiling well of emotions. His eyes reminded her of another agent she'd met, the very man who had bound her in her deal with the FBI, Agent Layton. She recalled first meeting him, nearly a year ago now, in that tiny interrogation room in the Sycamore Hills Police Department. She thought then that his eyes were those of a man who had seen a lifetime's worth of horrors, reflecting a lifetime of service in their gray pools.

Samuelson was younger; his eyes didn't have the lines around them that Layton's had but seemed just as old. While there was still a glint of peace in Layton's stern gaze, the younger agent seemed stripped of everything but a focused ambition driven by some deep disturbance.

Thinking of lawmen inevitably led her mind to Manny. She looked down at her bag at the foot of the bed. When she was packing it some hours ago, she resisted the urge to put his Cardinals shirt in with her own assortment of jeans, T-shirts, and her flannel shirt. Now, though, she felt a pang of loss fill her chest. Even if she had brought it but didn't actually pull it out, it would have been a comfort for her to know that a little piece of him was close by.

Maureen pushed the sentimental thoughts away; they wouldn't help her at the moment. She lay down on her side and tipped the last of her beer into the side of her mouth. She felt a thin trickle of liquid escape and drip down her cheek and onto the comforter. She let the empty bottle fall from her hand. It hit with a thud, and she heard it roll under the bed.

She let out a deep sigh and pushed her head deep into the thin pillow. She closed her eyes and began to count back from one thousand. As she counted, Maureen became keenly aware of the low hum of the room's fluorescent lights. She didn't bother to get up and turn them off. It didn't matter. Light or dark, sleep wasn't going to come easily tonight.

FIVE

"So, what do we think of her?" Turnberry asked as Owen closed the door to Maureen's room. Turnberry had been waiting outside for him.

"I don't know," Owen replied, shaking his head. "If I had to make a call right this second, I would say that she's full of bull and that she pulled one over on the boys down in Missouri last year. But who knows? Stranger things have happened."

"Can't say I'm surprised," the other agent responded. "From what I got to read in the case file, it didn't sound like they had the best people to work with. That police department down there sounds like a total shit show. Not to mention they sent *Layton* down? He's an organized crime guy, not homicide." He paused, shooting Owen a rueful look. "No offense."

Owen shrugged and looked out into the night. "You see enough bodies either way," he mumbled. He hadn't meant the words to be spoken aloud.

Turnberry shifted at his side. "What about the new kid?"

He meant Rick Navarro, the young agent who'd been assigned to be the third member of the team.

Owen couldn't help but let his mouth upturn ever so slightly at Turnberry's attempt to change the subject. He decided to play along. "You think I'm hazing him by having him sit up in the car."

Turnberry shrugged. "Rick's two years out of the academy now. Maybe he feels like he could do a little more?" He cleared his throat. "And maybe he could have his own room?"

"Budget cuts. Nothing I can do about it."

"And yet you've got your own—"

"Watch it," Owen cut him off. Privately, he was glad Steve Turnberry was trying to help him relax. Lord knew the days ahead were going to be filled with enough to make any man stress. "I need my space to organize and interpret all the info *you're* going to bring me. As for the kid, I need to see how he works. He's number three on this investigation, and he better get used to it. But you're right. It's not fair to keep him in the car this whole investigation. You can go ahead and grab him at around one and bring him in. And tomorrow, after we finish up our business at the coroner's office, you can take him across the mountains to give you a hand with the follow-ups with the families, friends, and local authorities. I don't want anything to slip through."

"Understood." Turnberry sighed with a smirk.

Owen knew he didn't need to impress upon the other agent how he wanted the job done, as their rapport had been well established over the years, and both men were comfortable with the semantics.

"And her?" Turnberry said, nodding in the direction of Maureen's room.

Owen turned and looked at her window. The dull light that made its way through the curtains puzzled him. He decided that she was trying to stay awake. Whether it was out of stubbornness or some sinister motivation to sabotage the investigation, he didn't know. It didn't matter anyway. "The plan goes forward as briefed," he said.

Turnberry nodded. Nothing more needed to be said.

Owen turned and walked to his room. The fatigue that began to press on him was surprising. It wasn't the late hour, and it wasn't the mission ahead. It was that slight, honey blonde-haired woman he imagined sitting in the room next door—in that old flannel shirt, propped on the bed, sipping beer, and thumbing her nose at everything the FBI stood for. The woman had no respect, no idea of how seriously his bosses took her as a resource.

Owen took off his jacket and undid his tie. Sleep was an hour or two away. He had a few things to review before the morning. He sat down at the table and began to sort through the case files. Focusing on those would put Maureen Allerton out of his mind for a while.

"We go forward as planned," he murmured to himself as he opened one of the manila folders, a smirk briefly crossing his lips. He knew he shouldn't find satisfaction in what was coming, but he couldn't help it.

Maureen wasn't going to like the plan, but that didn't matter. Tomorrow, Owen was going to take back control. And tomorrow, Maureen Allerton was going to learn some respect.

SIX

Agent Navarro pulled up to the coroner's office and shifted the car into park. From his place in the back seat, Owen stared out of the tinted windows at the small crowd of local reporters who had gathered outside the building. Despite his hopes, the news of the second body's discovery had apparently gotten out. He sighed heavily. Small-town reporters were the worst types of parasites to deal with, always trying to sensationalize whatever was going on to make a bigger name for themselves. And now he had a self-professed psychic shackled to him to boot.

"Navarro," he said to the driver, "I'll need both you and Turnberry to play some defense against the press while I get Ms. Allerton into the building. Once we're in, Steve, you can come and join us inside while Navarro stays outside by the doors. Don't let anyone past you, Rick."

Navarro and Turnberry both nodded and got out of the car.

Owen looked over at Maureen. She'd taken her sweet time this morning getting herself ready. He'd stood outside her door, pounding until his fist was red before giving up and using his own key to enter. There she was, fully dressed and ready, giving him a snide remark as she strutted past. She hadn't said a word since she entered the car. Instead, she sat in the back seat with an air of mocking reverence as though the idea that the FBI had come to her for assistance on this case amused her to no end. She was testing him, that much was certain, but even so, he could tell she'd rather be anywhere in the world except for here.

I'd love to make her wish come true.

Owen pushed his door open and circled around to the opposite side of the car. He opened the door to let Maureen out. She stared at him for a moment and then, making no effort to hide the rolling of her eyes, kicked her feet out onto the concrete and exited the vehicle. Owen held her at the elbow lightly so as not to draw too much attention and guided her past the gaggle of reporters. Their overlapping shouts echoed in his ears as he stared straight ahead, keeping his vision and his mind on his objective: the doors.

"Agent, agent, one moment, please," a short, bald man with glasses cried out, waving his handheld recorder in the air.

"Is it true this could be the work of a serial killer?" a blonde woman in a red pantsuit called out, holding out a microphone.

"When will the FBI be making a statement on this latest killing?"

"Do you have any suspects?"

"Have you informed the family?"

The questions continued, dancing around and over each other. Owen kept his jaw set, determined to keep his composure. The last thing the FBI needed was one of its agents losing their temper and assaulting a reporter.

Owen was almost through the crowd when the path to the front door to the building was suddenly blocked by the frame of a bold reporter. The short man was holding a small notebook and wearing a Broncos cap, sunglasses, a tweed jacket, and mismatched slacks. Owen tried to gently move around him, but the man's movements mimicked his own. Owen sighed and stopped, but he resisted his instinct to pull either his badge or gun.

"Can I help you?" the agent asked as patiently as he could.

"I believe so, Agent," the man said as politely as possible. "I have just a few questions about the body that was discovered."

Owen didn't respond. Instead, he leaned in to look more closely at the man. The reporter flinched slightly at his movements. After a moment, Owen reached out and slowly removed the man's sunglasses and cap, revealing a balding head and familiar face. Having removed his paltry disguise, Owen knew him instantly as Gabriel Lowdon, a columnist for the *Boulder Daily Post*. That was his day job. Lowdon's true passion was government conspiracy theories and unfounded sensationalism. He'd run into the man several times over the course of his career and had personally killed one of his more inflammatory stories before it made it to print. There was no love lost between the two.

"Should have known it was you, Gabriel," Owen said as he pushed the cap and glasses into the man's chest.

"Nice to see you again, Samuelson," Lowdon replied. "Now that I have your attention, what do you have to say in response to the rumors that this body was found like Shelly Lindstrom, without many of its internal organs?"

"I don't have any comment at this time, and even if I did, I wouldn't be giving it to you."

Owen stepped around the smaller man and pushed Maureen in front of him toward the door. He turned back to

Turnberry and nodded in the direction of Lowdon. The other agent stepped forward to escort the man away, but Lowdon, a veteran of many a run-in with the FBI, ducked under his outstretched arm and darted closer to Owen.

"I've heard the victim was connected to Lindstrom," he said softly, obviously wanting to keep certain information away from the rest of his competitors. "That they belonged to the same National Guard platoon."

"That information can be found by anyone who looks hard enough for it. If you're trying to impress me, why don't you tell me something that no one knows." Owen turned and walked to the door, opening it and guiding Maureen through.

"I have a source inside the bureau," Lowdon said, speaking up, but only loudly enough for Owen to hear him.

A flash of anger at the man's assertion hit Owen and forced him to round back and stalk up to the reporter, making full use of his height as he stood inches away and glared down at him. Gabriel shrank back at first, but he then raised himself back up to his own full height and looked up at Owen with a grin that said he knew he wasn't in any physical danger from the agent.

"Rumor is," Lowdon whispered, "that you fellows are bringing in some sort of psychic detective on this one."

"And just who told you that?" Owen snarled.

"I would never reveal my sources, Agent," the reporter sneered before nodding his head toward Maureen, who was standing by the front door. "Is that her?"

"You don't know as much as you think, Lowdon," he replied, making sure he engaged in the man's speculation as little as possible.

"Then why don't you set me straight?"

"Not a chance."

"The people deserve to know what their government agencies are up to. You might not value transparency, but *I* do."

Owen felt his lip twitch and his nose crinkle in response to his body's desire to punch the smug little reporter square in the nose. His brain held on to the control of his muscles, however. Lucky for Lowdon.

"I'm going to write the story regardless," Lowdon continued, clearly still trying to provoke something. "It's your choice whether it's mine or yours."

"Try it," Owen said, lowering his voice to covey to the man that he was in even more peril. "You have no idea how miserable I could make your life if I wanted to." Satisfied that he had gotten the last word, Owen turned back toward the building and marched through the door.

"What was that all about?" Maureen asked when he joined her in the entry alcove.

"Don't worry about it," he mumbled.

They walked a few yards farther into the building before they were met by two men in white lab coats, one a gray-haired man who was in his fifties and a taller, sandy-haired man who looked to be a few years younger than Owen himself. The older man, Dr. Edward Heim, was known to him, though it had been a few years since they last met. He didn't know the other.

"Welcome, Agent," Dr. Heim said, offering his hand to Owen. "I don't believe you've had the pleasure of working with our deputy ME before. This is Dr. Eldon Frank."

Owen shook hands with both men as Turnberry came up

to join them. "I'm Special Agent Samuelson. This is Special Agent Turnberry."

"And is this the woman your office called about?" Dr. Heim asked.

"Yes," Owen said, grudgingly. "This is Maureen Allerton, our . . . 'consulting profiler.'"

"I understand," said the doctor, nodding to Maureen before addressing the crowd again. "Well, let's head on back to the lab and have ourselves a discussion."

Dr. Heim and Dr. Frank led the three of them straight back through the beige-colored hallways toward the rear of the building. They turned left and headed down another long hallway before stopping in front of a set of glass doors. On a bench along the wall sat a sun-worn man with a light brown beard, flecked with gray and white, that matched his neatly combed head of hair. Though out of uniform, Owen could see that he wore a park ranger badge on his belt, and though he may have looked every bit the part of a lower-totem federal employee out of his depth, the man carried himself as anything but. The agent could sense immediately the man had military service in his background.

"Agents," said Dr. Heim, "this is Ranger Alec Tyce. He's the gentleman who found the body. I thought it best that he be here to give his statement directly to you while we go over our examination. He can also lend you some of his expertise on the terrain and location of the scene."

"Sir," Ranger Tyce said formally, nodding and shaking hands with both agents.

"Nice to meet you, Ranger," replied Owen in kind. "I'm Special Agent Samuelson, and this is Special Agent Turnberry.

Thank you for taking the time to come down here this morning."

"No trouble at all," the ranger said with a brief smile. "It's a quick drive from home for me."

Ranger Tyce turned to Maureen, who continued to stand silently next to Owen. The ranger stuck out his hand to her as well. "I don't believe we've been introduced, ma'am."

"Maureen," she said, eyeing the man's hand before taking it.

"She's what we call a 'consulting profiler,'" Owen explained to the ranger. "She's going to climb inside the head of the person who did this and point us where we need to go."

It was the agreed-upon explanation for the woman's presence, and it was enough of the truth that it should satisfy most inquiring minds. Of course, the doctors knew who she really was, but that was a matter for later.

The group headed into the coroner's lab. The body of Christopher Niemann was laid out on a steel table, his naked skin a sickening bluish color from the refrigeration process. Owen took a position at the head of the body with Turnberry next to him. The two medical examiners stood by the torso on either side of the slab, and Maureen and the ranger stood away from the table and near the drawers that likely contained dozens of other cadavers.

"All right, Doctors," Owen said, "the floor is yours."

Dr. Heim and Dr. Frank looked at each other and nodded.

"Christopher Niemann," Dr. Heim began, consulting his notes on the clipboard he carried, "twenty-six years old. Cause of death is believed to be a ketamine overdose. Clean incision down the torso, beginning at the base of the sternum and ending just above the pelvic bone. Internal organs missing. We also believe that the victim was dead before entering the water. The body bears many key similarities to the body of Shelly Lindstrom, allowing us to theorize that the deaths may be related."

"How can you confirm that the body was dead before entering the water and that the organs weren't simply eaten by scavengers?" Owen asked. He didn't really doubt the examiners' observations, but he would need to understand the science involved with coming to these conclusions in the event he found himself testifying on the stand.

"The body had reached rigor mortis before being placed in the water," Dr. Frank answered. "The victim's jaw was frozen as you see it now, in a closed position, and no evidence of water was found in the esophagus. This tells us that the victim was not breathing when he went in."

"Also," Ranger Tyce added, stepping forward, "over the years I've seen the bodies of a few unfortunate people who got lost in the park, ended up deceased, and were preyed on by scavengers. In this case, I would make my guess that the body of this man had washed up on the shore only a few hours at most before I saw it. I was on the overlook when the first vultures started to circle, and it took me a little less than an hour to get my horse down to the body. I didn't note any other recent animal tracks around the body. And sure, vultures peck and tear at a carcass, but they won't open it up in one big rip like this. And even if they did open the body up, I don't think they'd have the time to eat the cavity clean out. When I found them, they had eaten out this guy's eyeballs and were working on the skin around the arms and face." The ranger pointed his finger at the patches of skin missing from Niemann's body. "These are where the vultures were feeding."

"I'd have to agree with the ranger," Dr. Heim said. "The incision made in the body doesn't bear resemblance to a raptor's beak. It looks closer to a surgical tool."

"Like you have here," Owen said. "Are you saying that our killer has some kind of medical training?"

"It's very possible," Dr. Frank chimed in. "The way that Shelly Lindstrom's skull was cut could indicate the use of a surgeon's craniectomy tool. Although a handheld reciprocating saw or circular saw might also be possible. We really can't say for sure unless you bring us the suspected instrument to compare it to the cuts on the bones."

"What about the bruising on the body?" asked Owen. The body was covered with purple splotches all over the sides, legs, and arms; they were made even more apparent by the chilling and subsequent paling of the corpse.

"I'd put my money on it getting battered around in the river," Ranger Tyce interjected. "The body looks like it was in the water for a while, and the river flows from the north, through the lakes, and then through the valley where I found it. I know that section pretty well. There're a few areas where the river runs pretty fast and the riverbed is rocky."

"Doctors?"

Both Dr. Heim and Dr. Frank nodded.

"Skin saturation would suggest that the body was in the water between twenty-four and forty-eight hours," Dr. Heim said. "And the bruising is very clearly postmortem."

Owen nodded his head. Nothing that was said ran in contradiction to what he had already thought after reading the file. He turned toward Turnberry. "Steve, what do we know about this guy's personal life?"

"We're going to be getting more from family and friends over the next few days, but he's got enough of a public profile that we have a good bit to start with. Born in Pueblo to Carl and Evelyn Niemann, chemical engineer and attorney respectively. Upper-middle-class upbringing and received a swimming scholarship to Saint Christine's Academy. Scholar/Athlete. Graduated with a 3.59 GPA and holds state records for the two-hundred-meter freestyle, four-hundred-meter freestyle, and the one-hundred-meter individual medley. Scholarship to Cal-Berkley and led the swim team to two conference titles and third place at the NCAAs in his senior year. He was an alternate for this year's Olympic team as well."

"Impressive guy," Dr. Frank said.

"And of course, most importantly, a member of the same National Guard platoon as Shelly Lindstrom," Owen reminded them. "All right, gentlemen, I think we're all on the same page now. Agent Turnberry will be heading out with Navarro tomorrow to talk to Niemann's relatives and friends on the other side of the mountains. We'll have two war rooms, one here in this building and one at our motel in town. I'll be bouncing between the two. Ranger Tyce, I thank you for your time today. If I need anything, I'll be sure to let you know."

"Agent Samuelson, sir," the ranger said, "the parks department was hoping I could act as a liaison to the investigation. One government agency to another, so to speak. So I'll be around in a support capacity. With your permission, of course."

"I don't know what we'd possibly need from you that we haven't already gotten, but as you like. For now you can head out, and I suppose we'll discuss how to make use of you tomorrow."

The ranger nodded and left the room. Once he was gone, Owen turned back to the rest of the group.

"All right, gentlemen," he said, "let's head off to our next objective."

This part of the day had been planned for with deep thought. He believed that there was a very real chance that Maureen Allerton would not cooperate with them unless properly motivated. Or forced. In either case, he had exactly what he felt he needed in another room of the building. Dr. Heim showed them to a staircase that led to the lower level.

At the bottom of the stairs, the party turned left and headed down the dim hallway back toward the middle of the building. It was silent except for the echoes of their footsteps ricocheting off the walls. He looked back at Maureen as they went along. She didn't seem to be taking in any of her surroundings, just walking along with a disinterested look on her face that he was beginning to believe was her factory setting. It was just the state of mind that he was counting on.

Within moments, they halted in front of a set of double doors on the right side of the hallway set between two other single doors. Owen nodded to Dr. Frank, and the younger man stepped forward and unlocked them. Turnberry subtly placed himself behind the young woman as the doctors began to open the doors. As they herded Maureen toward the opening, he sensed her starting to tense up.

"What's going on?" she asked, her voice showing the beginnings of suspicion.

"It's very simple, Ms. Allerton," Owen said, placing a hand on the small of her back and guiding her into the room. "This is going to be your office for the duration of the investigation."

SEVEN

Maureen felt her stomach sour and her lower intestines tighten as she scanned the blinding white room. In front of her was a hospital bed surrounded by machines with blinking lights. There were windows in each of the walls, and behind each, she could see a number of nurses and other doctors, some moving around and some sitting and staring at computer monitors. To her horror, she realized what was about to happen, and her flight instincts took over.

She turned to run, but Samuelson and Turnberry each caught her under an arm and held her fast. She struggled against them but could not break their grip.

"Get off me!" she desperately shouted into the empty hall outside the open door. "I'm not doing this! Get off!"

The agents pulled her several feet inside the room as the doctors came up behind and shut the doors. They shoved her back and let go of her arms, leaving her to face all four of them. Maureen could feel her breath coming in gasps, and she felt like a caged animal. She knew from the tenseness of her body and the panic in her eyes that she looked every bit of one as well. She glared hard at them for what felt like an eternity.

"Look," Agent Samuelson said, finally breaking the silence. "This is the deal you made. We're on a tight schedule, and I don't have time to babysit you. So this is what's happening: you're going to stay here until you make your little psychic connection or whatever it is you do."

"Agent, I don't think taking that tone is the best remedy for our situation," the tall, younger doctor said, stepping forward and placing his hand on the agent's shoulder. "May I?"

Samuelson glared at her for one additional moment before straightening himself and nodding at the doctor. *Frank*, she reminded herself, *Dr. Frank. Easy name.*

Dr. Frank edged past the other men and stood next to Maureen, placing a hand on her shoulder and gently staring down at her.

"Ms. Allerton," he said, "it's okay. We've all heard about you here, and we've developed what we think will be the most effective way for you to help us."

He turned her to face the bed and walked her over to it. Dr. Frank then began to explain the procedure, picking up wires with little suctions attached and gesturing to each window as he did so.

"What we're going to do is attach these electrodes to your head and then give you a blend of sleep medications—doxepin mostly with just a little zolpidem—to speed up your process. Once you're asleep, we have people in place to monitor your three separate brain functions: electroencephalography, electromyography, and electrooculography. In other words, we'll be monitoring your brain waves and muscular functions during your dreams. With luck, not only will you help these agents catch the person responsible for these crimes, but you'll also be helping science document psychic brain functions. And you'll be one hundred percent safe."

The medical jargon went in one ear and out the other, but Maureen understood the message clearly enough. She still didn't want to comply, but she was outnumbered and saw only worse things happening to her if she chose to continue fighting.

"What's with all of them?" she asked, pointing to each room.

Dr. Frank followed her finger. "Them? They're from the local sleep institute, here to help us monitor you."

"I thought I wasn't supposed to be exposed," she grunted. "Doesn't seem the feds are as into secrecy as they made themselves out to be."

"Don't worry," the doctor said, lowering his voice, "they don't know the details. In order to keep up appearances, they've been told that you're a volunteer testing a new recovery drug. As far as they know, you've had a serious head injury, and your postsurgical therapy medications have been badly interrupting your sleep patterns. The drugs we are giving you are 'newly developed convalescent medications that are supposed to limit the insomnia side effects.' Because it's supposed to be so experimental, they think they're here to monitor your brain functions while you're asleep to make sure there're no dangerous side effects, when really the FBI just wants to know more about how your purported psychic abilities work. Clever, huh?"

"Yeah, clever," Maureen mumbled. She almost felt insulted. Did she really look like a person with brain damage? "One question. What happens when they want to take all that data they're collecting on me and write a paper to get published, or whatever they think they're going to do with it?"

The young doctor balked at the question. It was obvious he hadn't thought about that. "Uh, I suppose the FBI will just seize everything when they're done?" He shrugged, apparently trying to look unconcerned. "They'll probably make them agree to some kind of confidentiality and nondisclosure agreement. You know, scare them with jail time if they blab. The government can do that sort of thing, right?"

"Great," she spat through gritted teeth, glaring at Agent Samuelson in particular. Nothing about this felt right. "Well then, let's all gather around and watch your little monkey dance."

Maureen lay down on the bed as the two doctors attached three sets of electrodes to her head. She felt ridiculous and was glad she didn't have a mirror.

They should really be paying me for this.

Dr. Frank carefully inserted an IV into her arm, and soon she began to feel a wave of relaxation wash over her. For a moment, she began to think that the feeling was almost worth the deal she had made with the FBI. She could get used to feeling this numb. But she knew what was waiting for her once she slipped under, and that thought kept the full effect of the drugs from taking hold for a few moments longer.

It must have been hours later when she awoke. The first thing she was aware of was the sound of one of the machines behind her, steadily beeping in time with her own heartbeat. As her eyes cleared, the harsh white light of the room poured into them, causing a blinding pain to shoot through her skull. She raised her hand to shade herself from the beams knifing down from overhead. It didn't make much difference.

Around her, the chatter of voices began to ring clearly in her ears. She pushed herself up to a seated position and looked around the room. Agent Samuelson was having what looked like a heated discussion with the older doctor she had met upon her arrival. *Dr. Heim*, she reminded herself.

"Define unusual," the agent said, not appearing to notice that she had woken up.

"Agent, I'm not an expert in sleep science," the doctor replied, "but what I do know is that it's not normal for a person to fall from stage one to stage four and remain there for the period of time that she did without entering either two or three—or REM for that matter. It just doesn't make sense."

"So she's a freak," Maureen called to them, eliciting a violent turn of the head from each man. She felt the corners of her mouth turn up, though with no real mirth. "Bet you wish you could have just left me out of this, don't you, Agent?"

"That depends," he replied, straightening his tie and stepping over to her bed. "Do you have anything useful for me?"

Maureen thought as hard as she could, but it was no use. All that there was between the moment she felt her eyes close and reopen was an inky void. The only indication that any time had passed at all was the stale taste of unbrushed teeth in her dried-out mouth.

"No, I didn't dream anything," she said firmly. She wasn't going to let him talk down to her.

"Well, that's just perfect!" Samuelson groaned, clasping his hands behind his head and turning toward Dr. Heim. "That's seven hours wasted on this experiment! Doctor, get me some results. Change the medication, I don't care! Just get me some results! I'm heading back to the motel to do my real work. I'll be back tomorrow to check." With that, he waved his hand as though ridding himself of them and turned to leave.

"Hey! Don't I get a say in this?" Maureen protested, taking offense to the agent's blatant disregard for her.

"No!" he called over his shoulder.

"It's just that, I might know why it didn't work," she called after him.

The agent spun around and crossed his arms. "Oh, really? Enlighten me." He made no attempt to hide his sarcasm.

"Your guys here dosed me full of drugs to make me black out. That's what I used to do to keep the nightmares away. Booze, painkillers, whatever it took to make sure I couldn't remember anything when I woke up."

Agent Samuelson cleared his throat and took a deep breath. "And why," he said with a thin whisper, "are you just telling us this now?"

Maureen knew the real answer—it all happened so fast that she was out before she really understood what was happening—but the temptation to poke the agent was too enticing. "I don't know." She shrugged. "I just thought you guys would have known if you had done your homework. And I like the feeling of getting a little high on the stuff. I guess I missed it."

The agent shook his head. "I don't believe this." His words were barely audible. "How much longer do I have to deal with this crap?" He looked up and raised his voice.

"Fine, whatever. I couldn't care less how you get it done, but get it done. Light some candles, contact the astral plane, do a voodoo dance around a dead chicken. Have a blast down here. And get comfortable because you're not going anywhere until you show me that you're worth my time!"

"What about my stuff? I need a change of clothes. I mean, damn! I'm not opposed to wearing the same underwear a couple days in a row, but I'd at least like some deodorant or something if I'm not going to get a shower."

"You'll get your stuff when you give me a suspect!" he growled.

Maureen crossed her arms and raised an eyebrow.

"Fine," the agent relented, his lip still curled in a snarl. "I'll find someone to bring your bag." At that, Agent Samuelson stalked past Dr. Heim and kicked open the door before disappearing into the hallway.

Maureen watched the door, wondering if he was going to barge back in and try and get one more word in. She almost felt disappointed when the door remained shut, though she did feel proud of herself for not allowing him to railroad her, even if she was stuck in a room that might as well be a prison cell.

"What time is it, anyway?" she asked the doctor after a moment.

"It's about a quarter past seven," he replied after looking down at his watch. "You must be hungry."

"Starving," she found herself saying without a thought. "I don't suppose I could get something to eat? And maybe a whiskey and soda to go with it?"

"Food, yes," the doctor said, chuckling slightly. "But alcohol? Obviously not."

"Guess I'll just take a double cheeseburger and some fries, then."

"I'll have someone run out and get your order as soon as I can—there's a great little stand just up the road. What do you like on your burger?"

"The works. But no tomatoes."

Dr. Heim nodded and left the room.

Maureen lay back on the pillow and stared up at the ceiling. The heavy silence in the room was broken only by the continuing beeping of her heart rate monitor. Deep within her, a sense of relief was rising. The dreams were still with her, she knew that much even in isolation, but maybe they were beginning to fade. Maybe this time she wouldn't be an asset to the murder investigation, and she could go back to the farm and just live for a little while. Maybe. As hopeful as she was, there were still far too many maybes.

A short time later, Dr. Heim returned carrying a white paper bag and a plastic cup with a straw stuck through its lid. The smell wafting from the bag made her mouth begin to water. The doctor pulled a rolling tray-top table over to the side of the bed and set the paper-wrapped burger and pouch of steaming french fries on it.

"Fresh off the grill." He smiled. "I know you wanted a more adult beverage, but as your caregiver, I'm going to have to limit you to a *root* beer."

The older doctor's bedside manner and attempts at humor reminded her a little of Father Patrick. She couldn't help but wonder what it was that made certain older men like them act this way around women who were young enough to be their daughters. Most would simply be ogling her right now. Maureen shrugged the thought off for the moment and grabbed a fry from the pile, popping it into her mouth. It was warm and crisp, and she smiled as she reached for more and stuffed them into her mouth. There was no reason to stand on ceremony with her manners; doctors should be used to seeing people's less-than-graceful behaviors.

The doctor busied himself around the room, checking monitors and writing down whatever information they were telling him. Maureen was halfway through her burger when a question that had been weighing on her mind spilled out of her mouth.

"You work with dead people, so why are the feds having you and that Dr. Frank handle this whole experiment? Why not have one of those other specialists do it?"

"Probably because it would cost the government more money." He chuckled. "But seriously, your situation is very unique, and this whole affair is about as abnormal as it gets. I believe that the government simply wanted as few parties involved as possible to try and prevent the leak of any information that they didn't want getting out. And Dr. Frank and I both had experience in general practice before we became medical examiners, so we know what to do. As far as how to keep your vitals solid, anyway. As for the whole psychic thing, we're flying pretty blind."

"Clearly." She snorted before taking another bite of food. "It sounds like you don't have a clue about how to read those scans you're getting from me."

"I don't think anyone could make sense of what we're seeing," he said defensively. "But we'll try to put you under again to see if what we just saw was an aberration or the norm."

"And if it's the norm?"

"I honestly don't know."

Maureen stuffed another fry in her mouth to prevent a sigh from escaping. She was already tired of the whole affair but decided she'd do her best to endure. At the very least she might get a couple of days with some good greasy meals while she was here. Instant dinners and Natalie's home cooking were fine, but she found she missed the griddle-charred beef and chicken on a toasted bun that epitomized the short-order restaurants and pubs that had been part of her existence for so long.

"I suppose you're going to hook me up to the drugs now," she said to Dr. Heim as soon as she finished her meal.

The doctor was crushing her garbage down into the can in the corner of the room. He looked back at her and smiled somberly. "Maybe not." He dusted his hands on his lab coat and came over to her bedside.

"But Agent Samuelson said—"

"Agent Samuelson doesn't run this place. So relax for a little bit. I have to meet Dr. Frank to see about reformulating the medication. We may not even be able to come up with something different tonight. So who knows? You might get to have a more normal evening than we thought. I still wouldn't try to get up, though. The drugs we gave you took a lot out of you. Best to stay in bed." Dr. Heim then got up and exited the room.

Maureen stared after him for a long time, wondering what a fifty-year-old doctor was even still doing in the building at that hour. Surely, he must have had a life outside the coroner's office to get home to. And for that matter, what about the other doctor? He was still young and was relatively good looking. Wouldn't he prefer to go out to a pub or dive bar—or wherever people gathered around here—or at least look for a hookup? It must have been the pressure the FBI was putting on them that made them put their own lives on hold. Things would get back to normal for them when she left, she was sure.

Whatever normal is for two guys who look at dead bodies for a living.

Maureen settled back and stared up at the ceiling, pondering the boredom that lay ahead before she would inevitably be forced into sleep again and wondering why she had to be stuck down in the depths of what was otherwise a simple medical office building. After all, even if Samuelson and his cronies wanted to keep their doings a secret, what was the harm in setting her up in a more comfortable room? The majority of the people in the building were dead anyhow; they couldn't tell anyone. And even if a different room were impossible, there was more than enough room in this one for a TV. Even a magazine would be welcome at this point. Anything to distract her from her thoughts.

Instead, the slideshow of her life for the past year, which was always wont to play before her mind's eye in the silent times she had to herself, flashed on. She pushed past the memory of Manny's lips pressed to her own and the feeling of his body on top of hers, refusing to allow herself to fall back into the fantasy. Instead, she dove into the rest of her trail from a broken-down car in a Missouri town to finding a black chopper waiting for her outside the farmhouse. She thought of the little things, like the sound her shoes made while running down Main Street in Sycamore Hills, the smell of the incense inside St. Mary's, and the creak of the wooden floorboards in her little studio apartment. These thoughts came mixed with the impactful, life-changing things, like staring down the barrel of the gun being pointed at her by that demented bastard Father Preston, staring into the empty eyes of a young boy's burned corpse, and the feeling of the Naismith boy's arms wrapping around her neck after he was rescued from a fire. Every detail was so vibrant—burned not just into her mind but into her very bones—that before she knew it, nearly two hours had passed, and the footsteps of a returning Dr. Heim called her back to the present. He was carrying a syringe and a small vial of liquid.

"Yes, another shot," he said, seeming to read the perturbed expression on her face. "Dr. Frank and I thought it best to try a very mild sleep aid tonight to make sure you get a full night's rest and reset your clock for tomorrow. Out of curiosity, how much do you usually knock back to 'keep the nightmares away,' as you put it?"

Maureen hadn't given that question much thought for a while. "I don't know if I can put a medical number on it. Enough to black out. Say, a half bottle of whiskey if I was just drinking?"

"In how long?"

"Oh, jeez, I don't know. An hour maybe? It would take a lot more if I was sipping. If I mix it with a painkiller, I only need to chase it with three or four doubles before I pass out. Does that answer anything?"

"A bit," Dr. Heim said, nodding. "That being the case, I think you'll find this akin to falling asleep after a few beers.

This drug may as well be over-the-counter strength. So it's entirely possible that this won't block anything out tonight."

Maureen nodded in understanding.

"Settle in now, Ms. Allerton," he said softly, sticking the syringe into the vial and drawing the liquid. "We'll see what the morning brings, hmm?" With that, he pushed the needle into her IV tap.

It took a while, but the drowsiness eventually came on—and much more gently than her first experience. Whatever was running through her veins now was a major improvement. At least she could find one thing pleasant about the experience.

Hang on to that thought, girl, she thought as the darkness began to pool at the edges of her eyes. *You know better than to believe it's going to get better.*

EIGHT

Chirurg looked down at his watch. It was a few minutes to eight. Across the street, the lights of The Parisian were just becoming visible in the gathering twilight. He looked impatiently up and down the road. She was nearly half an hour late, and he was beginning to worry that his best-laid plans had somehow come undone. He'd told her not to make contact again until they met at the small French restaurant, which he'd chosen specifically for the atmosphere. There was little else in the area that would serve his purpose. Or make this believable. If she decided last minute to disregard her instructions, things would get very interesting. Fortunately, there was little to trace anything back to him.

He was just beginning to consider the evening a lost cause when a black sedan slowly pulled up. A well-dressed woman got out from the back and stepped over to the front passenger-side door, leaning toward the window. After a moment, the car drove away, leaving her alone on the sidewalk. Her clothes alone marked her as the woman he was waiting for, but even if she had dressed like the rest of the locals and had driven herself to the restaurant, the look on her face would have marked her. She was confused, wary, and unsure of why she was there. She was perfect.

Chirurg waited for a few minutes after she went inside before getting out of his own car, a sedan very similar to the one she just arrived in, and crossing the street. He pushed his way into the restaurant, stopping for a moment in the entryway to examine himself in the mirror. The sandy wig on his head, the matching goatee carefully glued to his face, and the thick-rimmed glasses he decided to wear almost made him laugh, but they did the job in obscuring his identity. His work was beginning to gain attention, so he had to embrace what needed to be done in order to continue to walk invisibly among the people. He didn't want to move on just yet.

He found the woman seated at a table near the back, just like he had instructed. A glass of wine sat untouched in front of her. She seemed in her own little world, staring down as if she were trying to deflect any attention. She shouldn't have worried. It was very unlikely that anyone in the establishment knew who she was.

"Lynn?" he asked innocently as he reached her table.

She looked up, startled. Clearly she had not marked his approach. "Uh, yes?"

"I'm sorry to startle you," he said, taking the seat opposite her and waving away the waiter—who had begun to cross the room—so they could speak privately. "I need to speak with you."

"I'm don't mean to be rude—"

"*He* sent me," he said, lowering his voice and leaning forward.

Lynn opened her mouth as if to either protest or feign

ignorance, but he held her eye with a level stare and raised an eyebrow. It worked. She bent over to listen.

"He got held up and didn't want you thinking he was standing you up. I'm to take you to his place for a private evening."

"Why you?" she asked, a hint of suspicion in her voice. "He knows I have my own driver."

"True, but he has a bit of a surprise set up in my car. A tiny gesture to show you how he feels and to whet your appetite for the evening."

"I don't know. Maybe I should call him, just to be sure."

"You can try, but he won't be reachable for another hour. I understand this is all a little unusual, but then so is you being here in the first place. He told me that this is the first time you've come out here. He's just trying to make things special."

"Well, when you put it like that," she said with a smile, "how can I say no?"

Chirurg smiled as they made their way to the front of the restaurant. No matter how intelligent a woman was, she would always be betrayed by her emotions.

"One more thing," he said as they approached the hostess stand.

"What might that be?"

"Do you have a special to-go order?" he asked the young lady behind the stand. "My friend would have put it under the name Chirurg."

The woman lifted a large bag from out of sight and checked the receipt stapled to it. "Cassoulet, duck confit with foie gras, and dacquoise?"

He nodded and took the bag, giving Lynn a wink.

"Well, Mr. Chirurg," she said as they crossed the street toward his car. "I had my doubts, but it seems as though he really has gone to a lot of trouble. It's actually rather exciting. This is the first time I've done anything like this."

"I told you he wanted to make it special."

"And to think, he ordered my favorite dessert. Most men wouldn't remember something like dacquoise. They'd just assume chocolate cake was the same thing."

"Well, you know him. He listens and knows more than you think."

They reached the car, and he opened the door to the back seat for her. She slid in, and he took his place behind the wheel. He started the car and—as subtly as he could—checked to make sure the child locks were engaged before he pulled away.

"I took the liberty of decanting a good bottle of scotch," he said over his shoulder. "He tells me that you like to have one before dinner."

"I do, but I can wait until we get to his place. Besides, I'd hate to have you pulled over with an open container."

"It's a small town, madam." He smiled. "And he'll be a while. Help yourself and relax. We'll be there soon enough, and you'll still have a bit of a wait ahead of you. He'll never know."

Chirurg heard the clinking of glass followed a moment later by the sound of liquid being poured. All according to plan. It amused him sometimes how easily he could manipulate people's feelings. It was a beneficial complement to his scientific mind. In the beginning, he didn't see the need to use psychology, but the longer he practiced, the more thankful he was. It made things so much easier, and he didn't have to resort to outright physicality when carrying out his work, which lessened the chance of him leaving behind any trace evidence when he was finished.

Their drive took them in circles through the town before turning north toward the mountains. If Lynn suspected anything, she didn't say anything. He felt safe enough. She didn't know the town and had no clue where they were supposed to be going anyway. After another few minutes, the sound that he was waiting for came from the back seat. She let out a soft groan, which was followed by the thud of a scotch glass on the carpeted floor of the car. He looked into the rear-view mirror. Her head was sagging, and her eyes were rolling. Her hand futilely groped for the door handle.

"It's no use, my dear," he said softly. "Best not to fight it. Just close your eyes and relax."

Her body obeyed his words. She slumped down and stopped moving, her breath coming in shallow gasps. Chirurg grinned. She was all his, another fine specimen to add to his collection. He turned on the car's radio and selected a CD to play. The brilliant works of Wagner blared from the car's speakers. The music did nothing to rouse its passenger, but it spurred him on his way.

In the night, the car sped along, mirroring Chirurg's own excitement and eagerness to reach his laboratory.

nine

Maureen opened her eyes and sat up in her hospital bed, drawing her bare feet in and tucking her knees under her chin. The room was dim and quiet as she looked at one of the windows that looked in on her room. She didn't need any light to know that there would be no one on the other side. The people from the sleep institute left the day before.

She only knew that two days had passed since she was shut up in her little prison because that was how many times she'd seen Agent Samuelson since he left her there. Each day, around dinner, he would stop by to meet with her and Dr. Heim or Dr. Frank for a report on the day's activities. And each day, he would leave unsatisfied, quietly seething because of what they had to tell him. There were no dreams, no premonitions, nothing from her for him to go on.

Unfortunately, those meetings with the agent were the only things that broke the monotony of the rest of the day. Though she called her room a prison, in reality, the whole county building was the real detention facility. She had the run of the complex—she had access to the cafeteria for meals and the staff locker room for showers and was even allowed outside occasionally—but she always found herself accompanied by one of the doctors or, more often, a chatty nurse named Aidy. She was at least a decade older than Maureen and was an obvious mother hen. If they went outside, she would tsk-tsk Maureen about not wearing sunscreen or that the top she was wearing wasn't leaving enough to the imagination. Maureen, for her part, bore it as best she could, comforted to an extent that nothing the nurse ever brought up seemed to indicate that she knew anything about who Maureen really was or what she was doing at the facility. So, at least to some extent, the FBI's cover story was working.

Still, that afternoon, listening to Aidy's constant prattling about what she could do to better attract a man to settle down with had left her mentally exhausted enough to nap. Maybe, she thought, a midday nap would trigger something. The realization that she actually wanted to dream had surprised her, but she resolved that it was simply because she would do anything, even crawl inside the mind of the psycho who was hollowing people out, if it meant being let out of that room. No such luck. All there was was the yawning void between closing and opening her eyes, and she contemplated how unhappy Samuelson would be when she saw him later. Maybe this would be the time that blood vessels in his head would finally burst with frustration. She could almost smile at the thought of what the look on his face would be if it weren't for the tiny voice in the back of her head telling her that she was failing those who needed her. She tried to bury it under a pile of self-preservative justifications: she wasn't a performing seal, she didn't want to be here anyway, and who knew if her dreams would even be helpful this time. It only helped a little.

Must be Father Patrick getting into my head.

Maureen got to her feet and went over to the chair where she had tossed her shoes and socks before lying down. She slipped them back on mindlessly. She didn't have any real idea of what she was going to do. The clock on the wall said it was just after five, too early for dinner normally, but she hadn't had breakfast or lunch that day, opting instead to spend the morning in isolation in her room. She'd slept until late in the morning, having decided to keep herself up until the wee hours of the morning in order to replicate her usual sleep patterns from the prior years. She then tried out some breathing techniques she'd read about, and she did some shadow boxing as though she were training with the boys in the barn. She even tried—as Samuelson had sarcastically suggested—to reach out with her mind and consciously attempt to find the person they were searching for. She felt foolish and had no notion of how to perform such a task or why she would even try. It was then that she went for her walk with the nurse, which led to her failed attempt at dreaming during her nap. With nothing else to do, Maureen pushed through the door and headed into the empty hall.

Maureen wandered around the lower level of the building for a while. It was quiet. At other times when she'd walked this exact path through the dimly lit taupe corridors, she'd at least run into a doctor or two, coming or going from other doors that were set at odd intervals along the walls. Normally she'd welcome the stillness, but for some reason, it unnerved her; it was as though she was walking through the calm before a storm, and a thunderclap was waiting for her just around the next corner. It wasn't, though. Just more emptiness.

Beginning to feel so annoyed that she would actually welcome some more human interaction—as long as it wasn't with Aidy—she found her way to one of the stairwells and jogged up to the main floor. She emerged into a carpeted hall with darkened offices. She knew then that she was on the other side of the building in the administration area. She had been through here once before—she was running the stairs for a little exercise and got curious as to what was on the other side of the doors she'd been passing—and had been met with several confused looks from the workers. Obviously, those who worked in these offices kept bank hours, so with no one to question what she was doing there, she decided that instead of turning around and going back through the same door, she would simply continue through to the main hallway and follow the signs to the cafeteria.

Minutes later, Maureen entered the cafeteria and looked around. Here and there, seated at the few tables that dotted the room, were various second-shift workers who were eating their "lunch." Only a few of them seemed to be doctors. Most wore uniforms that signaled them as maintenance or janitorial staff. Her kind of people. Though she'd never interacted with any of them, she did recognize a face or two that she'd passed before. Her presence didn't disturb any of them. That was fine. She didn't want to actually talk to anyone, just soak in a little human energy.

She walked over to the food line. The county office provided a daily free meal for anyone who had building credentials, which Maureen had been given on her first morning. Usually it was luck of the draw for what was offered. Mornings were a selection of cold cereals or hot oatmeal and fruit, afternoons were cold cuts and bread, and both evenings she'd ventured in, she was greeted with some kind of pasta casserole. There was always salad and cold vegetables too, and coffee and water were always on the house. A visitor could choose to purchase something from the grill, but Maureen didn't have any money with her, so she had been stuck eating the much less appetizing fare from the free cart.

She walked over to see what it held today. After showing her laminated card to the spectacled line worker, she stared down into a pan of dry-looking chicken bits and wilted peppers and onions. She shook her head at the woman and grabbed a handful of cold carrot sticks and an apple from the next tray. She stalked over to the grill to see what was on their menu and cursed that she lacked the six bucks she'd need to indulge in a basket of chicken tenders and fries.

While she was standing there, mindlessly chewing on a carrot, a voice came from behind her.

"On a diet or something?"

She felt a flash of indignation and rounded to find the assistant medical examiner, Dr. Frank, standing two paces behind her, slurping a can of soda. He wore a subtle smirk on his face, apparently pleased with his little jab. It reminded her of the way Manny would poke at her when they first met. She wanted to slap the doctor as much now as she had wanted to slap the detective then.

"Ever stop to think I'm just not that hungry, dick?" she snapped.

"Call me Eldon," he said. "Dick's my father."

Maureen crinkled her nose.

Dr. Frank chuckled. "Just kidding. Small joke."

"Hilarious." She snorted dryly. *What is it with guys and teasing as a way of flirting? This guy, any drunk at the bar, Manny.* Maureen started to maneuver her way around the doctor. He was good looking, probably better looking than Manny, objectively, and taller, but standing there with him only made her aware of what she had left behind, and at that moment, she would have rather felt any other feeling in the world.

Dr. Frank blocked her path. "Why don't you let me buy you something from the grill. No one should suffer through the free stuff they offer around here."

"I couldn't accept."

"I insist," he said with a grin.

"Fine. Only because I actually am hungry. I'll do one of those chicken-finger baskets."

"Coming right up."

He gave her a little bow of his head before walking up to the grill cart and returning with her food and a basket of his own. He handed hers to her and began to walk over to a nearby table. Maureen stood, hesitating. Dr. Frank turned back. He must have read her mind.

"You don't want company?"

Maureen's voice caught for a moment. He was just being nice. Maybe she could return the favor. "It's just . . ." She needed the right words. "I don't really feel like sitting." It didn't sound convincing, even to her.

The doctor took it in stride. "Let's take a walk, then. I've been sitting at a desk for hours and could use a leg stretch."

Maureen simply nodded.

So the two walked through the building, eating their food as they went. They passed the same doors she had passed a dozen times before, only this time Dr. Frank would tell her what was behind them. This was especially useful on the upper floors, which were not dedicated to the county morgue's and coroner's offices. Here was the office of the county executive, behind this door was the department of public works, parks and recreation was down the hall, and so on. Maureen found herself wondering how, with all these other people congregated in the same building, the FBI managed to keep their presence relatively unnoticed.

"I wouldn't say you've been unnoticed." Dr. Frank laughed as they entered a stairwell on the top floor. "The community definitely knows that you're here. Fortunately, the town and the county in general don't have a very big population, and for the most part, the folks around here are pretty traditional in the way they view law enforcement. They just kind of get out of the way and leave them to themselves. I think that's especially true this time. The feds don't come out here that often. Most people are pretty intimidated by them, so I imagine they'll stay really out of their way—our way."

"Well thank fuck for that." Maureen snorted.

"I haven't heard any talk about you, if that's what you're worried about." His sense of her was uncanny, especially since this was the first time they'd been alone together.

"I wonder what will happen when I get booted out of here."

"What makes you say that?"

"I don't think Samuelson is a fan of mine. Especially since I can't seem to make any kind of connection to this killer. Maybe he's moved on or something."

"It could be," Dr. Frank agreed.

"Anyway, I'm not sure what they expected. I don't know what I expected, to be honest. I only helped the cops one time, but it was way different than this. Sitting down in that room day after day, not being able to see any of the information on the investigation, is enough to make you go batty. They might have suspects for all I know and are just keeping me captive to prove that I'm useless. And if they solve the case without my help, will I be free to go back to the farm? Will my probation be taken away, and I'll go back to prison?"

Maureen stopped speaking and looked around. They were at the bottom of the stairs in the stairwell. Dr. Frank was leaning against the door to the hall, staring at her with a puzzled look on his face. She felt her eyes widen as she realized what had been coming out of her mouth.

"I'm sorry," she said, flustered. "Since you're working with them, I assumed you knew and . . . jeez, why didn't you stop me?"

"You sounded like you needed to get it off your chest." He shrugged. "I don't need to know what you're talking about to listen. And don't worry, I'm not going to pry." He gave her a quick smile and raised his eyebrows before opening the door with his hip and ushering her back into the fluorescent light of the basement hallway.

They walked in silence for half the length of the hall before the doctor cleared his throat. "It's kind of a shame, though," he said thoughtfully. "It would be really interesting to verify if you really are psychic."

"You don't think I'm telling the truth?" Maureen wasn't entirely sure whether she cared one way or the other, but something about the word *verify* made her feel a little defensive.

"Oh, you don't strike me as someone who's lying to get attention or anything like that," he said smoothly. "It's just that science demands repeatable experiments with observable results. Since you haven't had any of your dreams—or whatever happens to you—we can't really test it, if you see what I mean. I just think it would be interesting to see what physically happens in the brain of someone who is having psychic visions."

"I see," Maureen mumbled.

They rounded the last corner and came to her room. She reached to turn the doorknob and then stopped.

"What's the matter?" Dr. Frank asked.

"I just have a feeling that Agent Samuelson is on the other side of the door," she replied, feeling her jaw clench. "Probably waiting to rip me a new asshole when I don't give him what he wants."

"Hey!" he said in an exaggerated tone. "Your first psychic flash! Quick, let's get you inside and hooked up to the EEG!"

"Oh, you're just full of jokes today," Maureen sniped back.

Dr. Frank gave her a look of satisfied amusement. She crinkled her face at him in return. The tension was lessened a bit, but she still hesitated to open the door.

"Well," the doctor said after a moment, taking a look down at his watch, "as much as I *love* talking with Samuelson, I think you're going to have to handle him on your own."

"And where will you be?" she asked, frustrated that he meant to hang her out to dry.

"Me? I've got an appointment with another patient."

"There're other patients here? I thought this wasn't actually a hospital."

"Well," he said with a cocked head, "she's not technically alive."

"Another murder?"

"No, no, nothing like that." The doctor laughed. "At least, let's hope not. Just a forensic pathology case from the hospital that needs a second opinion. More like a confirmation really. Older woman. The lawyers want to settle the estate, but there's some legal red tape that requires the autopsy to be verified. I don't know, just doing what I'm asked."

"I imagine it's a little mundane compared to the last few days."

Dr. Frank shrugged. "A body's a body when it really comes down to it. We're all meat and bones. The only thing that makes each of us truly different is how we die. Anyway, I'll be on my way. Good luck in there."

Maureen watched him disappear around the corner before pressing her ear to the door. There was a sound of muted voices coming from the other side. She bit her lip and slowly, as quietly as she could, turned the knob and inched through the door. In the opposite corner, Samuelson and Dr. Heim were talking in hushed tones. The doctor was holding another one of his charts and showing Samuelson something, pointing his finger to it as he spoke. Samuelson turned his head to the older doctor and asked him something. Dr. Heim looked flustered and shrugged. It was then that they noticed her watching and stopped talking among themselves.

"Do you have something for me this evening, Ms. Allerton?" Samuelson said as he stalked over to her side and stared intensely at her. "Something better than yesterday?"

His mannerism and the way he spoke to her woke her

defiance. The man's idea that he could force something that she had never been able to control chaffed her to no end.

"No," she said, making no effort to hide her disdain for him. "I've got nothing for you."

The agent's eyes twitched momentarily, but in a flash he mastered his face, putting on an expression of ambivalence.

"Why am I not surprised," he hissed. "You've been nothing but a waste of my time since the moment I picked you up from that shack you're calling home. But I swear, if you're keeping information from me purely out of spite, then I have news for you: I will use whatever means necessary to pry it out of you, and then you'll be brought up on obstruction charges."

Maureen maintained eye contact with the agent, consciously preventing herself from blinking. She would show him that she was not intimidated. "Look, *Agent*," she said as steadily as she could, making sure to bite down hard on the last consonant for emphasis, "I might not be the best person in the world, I may not want to be here, and I might even detest you with every fiber of my being for tossing me down here alone, drugging me up, and letting these guys"—she gestured to Dr. Heim—"try to go cave diving in my head, but I'd like to think that I've grown beyond withholding information when people are dying."

"Then what the hell is the matter with you?" Samuelson shouted at her.

"I don't fucking know! Listen to me very carefully, Agent. I. Can't. Control it! It just happens. There's no rhyme or reason behind when the dreams hit me. So you have to be patient and let it happen on its own. Or else send me on my way and leave me the hell alone!"

Samuelson opened his mouth to say something but resisted the urge. It was clear to her that he was self-aware enough to know that he was on the verge of really losing control of himself. And that put him in dangerous territory. He straightened his tie and looked over his shoulder to the doctor, who hadn't moved a muscle.

"Dr. Heim," he said quietly, "I think it would be best if Ms. Allerton and I were alone for a few minutes."

Dr. Heim made no reply, simply making a quick nod and shuffling out of the room. Agent Samuelson ran a finger through his hair and began to pace the tile floor.

"You know," he said after a moment, not bothering to look at her, "as much as I didn't really believe in all of this *dream* nonsense, I found myself hoping—just a little—over the past couple of days that this might work. Maybe, I said to myself, just maybe she'll surprise you. It's clear to me now, though, that the only ability you have is the ability to piss me off."

Maureen held firm, determined not to give him any reaction. He was going to give her the opening she needed, she was positive of that. All she had to do was wait.

"I don't know how you duped those idiots down in Missouri," he continued, "but as far as I can tell, you're just a charlatan who gamed the system. You were only able to help them because you had so much access to information from the investigation that had no business being shared with a civilian."

"If that's the case, and I was able to help them there, then why don't you follow their lead and do the same thing here?"

"Oh, no!" He wagged his finger at her with a patronizing shake of his head. "That will never happen. This was the only way to ensure that you really were what you said you were; we needed to keep you separate and see what you came up with on your own. Since you couldn't sneak any looks at any of our notes and use them to make us think you were psychic, you showed me I was right about you. There's nothing you can do to help us."

Maureen nodded along with him, a trick she had picked up over the course of her life: make a man think you're agreeing with him and then hit him over the head. "So, clearly the investigation is going well, then. You probably have a nice little list of suspects already if you can find time to come down here and poke a stick through the bars at the bureau's little captive pet."

"For your information," he said, his voice beginning to rise against his control, "Navarro and Turnberry have nearly finished up their canvass with the local authorities on the other side of the mountains. And thanks to the techs back at the office, I have a full analysis of both victims' financials and background checks. So far, nothing in their lives connects them outside the National Guard unit. So, unless you've had some new insights in the last thirty seconds, by tomorrow we'll be ripping apart the lives of the other members of their unit looking for skeletons." He paused for a moment and stared at her as if expecting her to suddenly affirm or contradict his assertion with some kind of mystical prophecy. She stared back, keeping her face blank. "Yeah, that's what I thought. Look at you. A waste. Why don't you just get out of here!"

And there it was. Maureen inclined her head with the barest of nods and, with an embellished grace, strode over to her duffel bag that lay at the foot of her bed. Without a word, she pulled out her old flannel shirt and threw it on over her T-shirt before securing her hair in its ponytail. Then she hoisted her bag over her shoulder and moved toward the door.

"What the hell do you think you're doing?" he said as she passed him. She made no reply, just raised her chin and continued on her way. She'd reached the door by the time Samuelson processed what was happening and closed the distance between them, barring her way with his arm. "You're actually going to leave?"

"You said you didn't want me here," Maureen replied with a mocking sweetness. After everything he'd put her through over the last two days, after basically telling her to leave, he had the audacity to be insulted that she was taking him up on his offer. Not wanting to waste any more time trying to talk to him, she ducked under his arm, ripped the door open, and made her way into the hallway.

"You know very well I can't let you just walk out." He chased her down and slid himself back into her path. "The bureau has put a lot of resources into you, and letting you loose without an escort is the worst thing that could be done." His face was stern, and his breathing was starting to speed up.

Maureen wondered if these were his words or the words of his superiors regurgitated against his own wishes. In either case, the mere act of speaking them seemed to be causing him some form of inner conflict.

"Try and stop me," she said as firmly as she could muster without raising her voice to match his. She stepped toe to toe with him and raised a finger to poke him in the chest but kept enough sense in her head to stop just short of actually touching the agent. There was no sense in risking being tossed back in prison for assaulting a federal agent. She had no doubt that such a charge was in no way beneath Samuelson. Instead, she rose up on her toes and whispered in the agent's ear, "I dare you. You can't chain me to the bed or throw me in jail or anything like that. People will start asking questions. And we wouldn't want the FBI's use of a psychic to find its way into the papers, now would we?"

She felt guilty for acting so childishly, but she didn't see any other option. Maureen knew that Samuelson valued the integrity of his crime solving over anything else. A threat to it was her only chance of getting by him and to freedom. He glared at her for a moment before stepping to the side.

"Good luck finding anyone to take you back," he called to her as she walked by.

Subtlety had apparently gone out of the window. Still, she wasn't going to let him have the last word. "You don't think there's someone out there who would take pity on poor little me?" She made no effort to hide her sarcasm. She reached into her pocket and pulled out her motel room key. After weighing it in her hand for a moment, she looked up and threw it past him. The echo of metal clinking on the tile floor hung in the air. "Call that a wager that I won't be back!"

Maureen turned back to the doors and continued on her way out. She couldn't help but smirk to herself. In spite of the undignified way she was leaving, she felt a strange sense of satisfaction. She would be free soon enough with only the faintest gnawing of guilt that she was leaving with the job unfinished. She told herself she could live with that, that she had done her best. It was more than she would have done in the past, anyway, and that was progress. Father Patrick couldn't be disappointed in her if she was simply unable to do what was asked. And Manny would never have treated her like Samuelson had. Leaving was justified. She reached the door to the stairwell and allowed herself to sneak a look back. Samuelson had turned and was back down the hallway, stooping down to pick up her key.

Yeah, you better walk away, asshole, she thought.

The sun was setting behind the mountains as she exited the front doors. The air was beginning to cool as evening in the mountains approached, but it felt pleasant regardless. Maybe it was the burden of meeting the bureau's expectations being lifted from her, but there was almost a sweetness in the breeze. She stopped for a moment, closed her eyes, and breathed deeply. She stood in the calm of the moment until she remembered that she still had the task of finding a way back to Wyoming on her own. She left the building in such a hurry that she hadn't been able to form a real plan. It seemed to her that her teasing comment to the agent about someone picking her up on the side of the road was, in fact, her only real option. That or go back and tell Samuelson she was sorry and would stay and do as she was told.

No chance in hell.

Maureen crossed the parking lot and gravel to the highway. She then began to slowly plod along the shoulder, looking up and down for approaching cars. After a few hundred yards, she saw a truck rounding a bend in the road, its headlights dim in the gloom. Maureen was just beginning to raise her thumb—and desperately hoping she could convince the driver to pick her up when she didn't have any money and without having to resort to measures she *really* didn't want to take—when she heard the sound of footsteps rushing toward her. Maureen looked back, expecting to see Samuelson or maybe a local cop hurrying to stop her from hitching a ride. To her surprise, it was neither. Rather, it was a shorter man wearing a baseball cap.

"Excuse me," he began calling as he came nearer. As his face came into focus, she was able to recognize him as the reporter who her federal handler had a brief run-in with the other morning. Gabriel was his name, if she was correctly remembering what Samuelson had called him. Whether it was a first or last name, she had no clue.

"Miss? Miss? Do you have a moment?" the man puffed as came to a stop a few steps from her. He looked sleepy, his clothes were wrinkled, and he wore a patchy stubble on his chin.

Maureen surmised that he must have been sleeping in his car, waiting for the chance to speak with someone involved in the case. She wasn't sure she wanted to be that someone. "Not really," she said, trying to brush him off. The truck sped by. "And thanks a lot for costing me a ride!"

"You need a lift somewhere? Hang out here for a minute, I'll grab my car. I think we could have a really nice conversation."

"No thanks."

"I just have a few questions about the investigation."

"Then I suggest you go into that building"—she pointed back down the road toward the coroner's office—"and speak to the agent. Or find the MEs and get them to spill."

"I want the story from the psychic," he said bluntly.

Maureen's breath caught in her throat. She smoothed her face and turned back to the reporter. "I don't know what you're talking about."

"Please don't be like that. The people deserve to hear your side."

"Back off before I do something I'll regret."

"Look, Ms. Allerton."

Maureen started at the sound of her own name coming from his lips. The reporter seemed to notice because his mouth broke into the ugliest grin and his eyes lit up.

"Yeah, I know your name," he said proudly. "So you see, I'm a very good reporter, and I could write the best story about you. The true story of this investigation. Imagine what that will do for you. The money that the big networks will pay to get the interviews with you. The fame. What more could you ask for?"

"How about to be left alone," she spat. "You think you're smart? That you're 'in the know'? You don't know shit. So beat it!" She turned and began to walk down the road again.

He ran after her. "Playing hard to get, I see. That's okay. I like a woman who makes me earn it. But you'll find I'm not so easy to get rid of."

He reached out and grabbed her elbow. Maureen felt a rush of disgust run through her veins the moment he touched her. Her fist clenched around the strap of her bag. Just as she began to ready herself to swing the duffel into his face and follow up with a kick between the legs, a large truck passed and screeched to a halt. The driver threw it into reverse and sped back to level with them on the other side of the highway. The truck cab's window rolled down to reveal the face of the ranger who had been in the examination room when she was first taken to see the body that had washed up along the Colorado. *Tyce*, she reminded herself.

"Gabe!" the ranger shouted across the road. "What in the blue hell do you think you're doing!"

"Al!" the reporter crowed, letting go of her arm like a kid with his hand caught in a cookie jar. "The young lady was looking for a ride home. I was just trying to help her out."

"Yeah, I'll bet," Tyce grumbled as he got out of his truck and stalked across the road. Dressed in the same brown ranger shirt and Stetson hat that she had seen him in when they first met, the ranger towered over both Maureen and the reporter, though to her eyes, Gabriel seemed to shrink even more the nearer Tyce got. "Is it true? Did something happen? And where's Agent Samuelson?"

Maureen glanced over at the reporter before answering. "It would seem I find myself finished here," she said as pragmatically as possible. "It wasn't a good fit. You could say I've been fired."

"Ha!" the reporter chirped. "So you admit it! I knew you'd give yourself up eventually."

"Hey, asshole," she said, "everyone and their mother knows that I'm a profiler. It's you who's fixated on this whole 'psychic' thing." She hoped her bluff was convincing enough and that she wasn't digging herself in deeper. To avoid saying any more, she began to backpedal up the road once more, holding her thumb out at waist level. She saw the reporter make a move to continue after her, but the ranger stopped him with a firm hand on the shoulder, then pushed past him and approached her himself.

"So," he said gently as he came up to stand next to her. "Where's home?"

Maureen flushed, embarrassed to tell him. "It's a farm in

the middle of nowhere in Wyoming. I'm not much good with directions."

"Then how was Gabe, or anyone else for that matter, going to get you there?"

"Well, I'm pretty sure I can get you there from the little town nearby. I think it's called East Pass."

"Uh-huh," he smirked, clearly satisfied that he was getting her to see all the flaws in her plan.

"Hey, give me a break. I've only been there for a few months. And I didn't exactly drive myself there."

"Well, is there anything you can tell me about the place? The name of the road this farm of yours is on, for instance?"

Maureen closed her eyes and thought for a minute. The name of the road was written on the mailbox at the end of the dirt drive that led to the barn. "Stone Table Road!" she said triumphantly. "And I remember now that the lady who owns the place told me once that we weren't too far from an Indian reservation."

"All right, then," Ranger Tyce said, "that's plenty to start on."

"I don't understand."

"I keep maps of all the surrounding states in my truck," he said matter-of-factly. "Those GPS things that people put in their cars nowadays aren't much good out here. I don't think anyone else you'd run into around here could get you home like I can."

"And you're willing to go all the way to Wyoming at this time of day?" she asked, furrowing her brow skeptically.

"If you'll take the ride."

She considered it for a moment.

"I mean, consider the alternative." He thumbed over his shoulder at the reporter.

"Good point." She leaned around him to take one last glance at the reporter. "Let's go."

They crossed the highway together. Maureen quickly walked to the passenger-side door and reached for the handle. She had a feeling the ranger was the chivalrous type who would want to open it for her. She may have been accepting his ride, but she still felt uncomfortable with men who insisted on such acts. It made her believe they thought she was fragile and helpless, when she was anything but—the need for a ride notwithstanding. Ranger Tyce crossed in front of the truck and was coming toward her, but in an instant she could see that it had nothing to do with helping her in. Gabriel had followed them across the road, still determined to get a last word in.

"So you'll go with him but not me, huh?" He had a mockingly wounded tone. "And as for you," he said to the ranger. "You never change. Can't resist helping a pretty girl in a tough spot. Are you honestly that noble that you're just going to 'drive her home'?"

"That's about the way of it," Tyce replied, showing no signs that the reporter's barbs were getting to him. "Not that it's any business of yours."

"And where's home for her, may I ask?" the reporter continued as Maureen climbed into her seat.

"Middle of nowhere in Wyoming," she answered for Tyce.

"Sounds fishy," Gabriel said to the ranger, seeming to pretend as if she couldn't hear him. "You sure it's not some kind of secret government facility? Maybe they have more like her there."

Maureen twitched in her seat and balled up her fist. Tyce seemed to sense her desire to punch the man in the face and gently closed her door.

"We're leaving now, Gabe," he said calmly. "Don't stand too close to the truck, or I might clip you on the way by."

Without another word, the ranger walked back around the front of the truck and took his place in the driver's seat. Maureen turned and looked out the window. Gabriel was backing up two steps but was making no further effort. He simply continued to stare up at the truck. She held his gaze through the tinted windows, wondering what was going through his mind. Something about him unsettled her.

Tyce turned the key in the ignition and pulled forward a few feet before swinging the truck back in the opposite direction and accelerating down the road. Maureen kept her eyes on the reporter as he stood like a statue, disappearing into the growing dusk.

TEN

"So how do you know that guy?" Maureen asked from the passenger seat as the truck followed the main road north through the town.

"Who?" Tyce had been lost in his own thoughts, mostly wondering where his offer to drive the young woman all the way back to some farm in the middle of Wyoming came from. It was most likely a knee-jerk reaction to seeing a younger woman in distress. The chivalrous actions of an older generation.

"That reporter guy you rescued me from," she elaborated. "It seemed like you knew him, that's all."

"Gabe and I go back a ways. In fact, he was in my wedding party."

"So you're friends."

Tyce smiled in spite of himself. "You could say that." He chuckled. "I married his sister."

"That crackpot's your brother-in-law?" she said, sounding surprised.

"Was." Tyce allowed himself to snicker despite the brief pang of sadness at the memory of a broken marriage. "We divorced about nine years ago."

"Sorry," the young woman mumbled.

"It's fine."

A silence hung in the cab of the truck for several agonizing minutes. He was out of practice when it came to talking to women, even if he didn't have any romantic interest in them. She seemed to be just as uncomfortable. In the brief time he'd been around her, he hadn't heard her speak much. She struck him as the type who didn't willingly share a lot about themself and deflected by asking a lot of questions to whomever they were speaking. He decided to offer up the information to make things easier on her.

"Gabe's not a bad guy," Tyce finally said. "He's a great uncle to my girl. He's a good writer too, but his college political science professor was into every conspiracy known to man. We're talking men in black, Roswell, government experiments, the whole nine. Gabe picked up on a lot of his theories, maybe to his own detriment. Being so into that sort of thing is probably what's kept him in Boulder all these years instead of getting his chance to write for one of the papers in Denver where his readership would be national instead of local. Still, every now and then, he stumbles onto something that's interesting."

"Like what?"

"You." He let the word linger before continuing. "I overheard some talk about you. Whispers from Dr. Frank and Dr. Heim the day you arrived. Just between the two of them, mind you. I don't think they're discussing these things with anyone else, but I have a keen ear, and they weren't being quite as discrete as they thought."

Tyce cast an eye over to the young lady in the seat next to him. She was staring out the window, watching the buildings of the town slowly begin to give way to the spread-out homes and cabins that fronted the river.

"Is Gabe right? Is 'consulting profiler' FBI speak for psychic?"

There was only silence from her side of the cab.

"All right," Tyce said, "you don't have to talk about it if you don't want to."

"What's there to talk about?" she finally replied. "Would you really want to know the truth?"

Tyce nodded and waited patiently for her to give him more.

"Fine," she said after a few beats, "but don't expect the whole story. It's not my favorite thing to talk about, and I'm not sure you could handle it all."

"That's fair."

"I guess you could say I helped out on a case for the FBI about a year ago," she said with some reluctance. "The less said about it, the better. Suffice to say, I was apparently useful enough for them to bring me in on this one."

"But, obviously, something's gone wrong. Forgive me for saying so, but you wouldn't be sitting here in my truck if you were doing what you were supposed to be. Are you actually psychic?"

"Depends on who you ask." She adjusted herself in her seat, turning slightly toward him. "All I'll say is this: yes, it's true that I see things in my dreams that, it's becoming increasingly clear, no one can find a good explanation for."

"You've been tested?"

"Well, I certainly wasn't down in the lab communing with the body for the last few days. The feds got it into their heads that it would be a great idea to keep me down in the basement and monitor my sleep. That, and they decided it would be a fun idea to try different methods of sleep induction to see if they could force me to dream. They tried a combination of anesthetics, sleep deprivation, going au naturel. Regardless, I wasn't giving them the results they were looking for, and since Samuelson didn't want me there anyway, we had a nice little blowup and I took off." She shook her head sullenly. "I shouldn't have let them talk me into it. Or, at the very least, I shouldn't have let them talk me into taking any drugs. That was never going to work."

"How do you know?"

"Because it's the sort of thing I do to *block out* the dreams. Only I prefer blacking out with pain killers and booze instead of hospital anesthetics."

"That doesn't sound very healthy."

"It beats the alternative. Doesn't matter, though. Sooner or later, they always bubble back up. It's been that way my whole life. Just a part of who I am."

The way she said those last words struck Tyce's ear. It was clear that she was trying to seem as matter-of-fact as possible about her plight, but there was a subtle undercurrent in her voice that betrayed her. To most, she would have had the appearance of a tough-as-nails, take-no-prisoners type of woman who could handle anything thrown in her path. That facade covered what lay beneath the surface, though. Whatever was going on in her head, she hadn't truly made peace with it, and whether she admitted it or not, it tore at her. He could empathize.

"Why did you decide to give me a lift?" she asked suddenly.

Though he'd asked himself that, Tyce was surprised to hear the question from her. He still wasn't quite sure how to answer. "I guess I'm just old-fashioned," he said after thinking for another moment. "I see a young lady in need of help, I offer to help."

It didn't sound like the truth out loud, but it was, and he would stand by his words. Most in his position would jump at the opportunity to be alone on the open road with a young and attractive woman like Maureen, but for far less honorable reasons. They would fill themselves up with fantasies that their kindness would be rewarded with some sort of physical favor, and the idea that even decent men could behave that way made him sick. So in the end, perhaps he had volunteered for this trip not as a simple chivalrous act but out of a more paternal sentiment to keep a woman safe.

"Well, I'm not your typical damsel in distress." Maureen smiled at him. "But I appreciate it all the same. I can give you some money for your time when we get to Wyoming, if you want."

"We can talk about all that when we get there." In all honesty, Tyce hadn't thought about the cost of driving so far. His truck was hardly a gas sipper, and now that he thought about it, he'd need at least two, if not three, fill-ups for the round trip. Still, the idea of taking money from someone he was helping was uncomfortable.

Only if she really insists, he decided.

Silence was the answer he got from the passenger seat, so Tyce decided to stay quiet himself for the time being. The trip was long enough that they'd run out of things to talk about eventually, so it was better to not come to that point too soon. The twilight was fading fast as he turned his truck onto the main highway and continued north. The Colorado River was disappearing into the growing dark to his right and soon would be obstructed from view by the riverside cabins and homes that lined the road heading into the foothills. The homes varied in size from the original two-bedroom wood homes, which had been built into the riverbank when the town was first founded, to the newer estates built for those with more discerning tastes. The people who owned them were as different as the homes themselves, from the folks who passed down their homes through the generations to the weekenders from Denver who didn't want to rough it too much. Despite those latter types beginning to own more property in the area, gentrification was still miles off, and for that Tyce was exceedingly thankful.His mind wasn't on any of that at present, however. He was focused on Maureen's revelation that she was indeed an honest-to-goodness psychic.

In regard to most things, he was a man who believed in what he saw and what could be proven. It was for that reason that whenever Gabe went on one of his tangents, he would simply smile and play along without getting sucked into the nonsense. Still, he couldn't be wrong about everything. Even though Tyce had worked for the government of the United States for the majority of his adult life, he was well aware that he didn't know more than a tiny fraction of what went on behind closed doors. And there were plenty of other things in the world he believed in that couldn't be explained rationally either, like God, love, and other mysteries of that sort. Tyce shifted his weight in his seat. Almost unconsciously, his hand ran over his thigh as he recalled at least one miracle he'd witnessed. Would it be so farfetched for a real psychic to exist?

Tyce looked over at Maureen again. Her head was leaning on the window, and her eyes were closed. She would have almost looked peaceful, but her brow was furrowed, and her eyelids were twitching. Tyce tried to keep his own eyes on the road, but he couldn't help glancing back at her. After a few moments, her head began rolling from side to side. A low whimper escaped her slightly parted lips, and her face became more distressed by the second. Tyce heard her begin to whisper, unintelligible at first, but he thought he caught at least one word before she fell silent.

She was still for several moments, and Tyce settled back, thinking it no more than a passing nightmare. The road ahead began to climb and soon would be surrounded by walls of rock. The mundane nature of the highway from then on would test his endurance. He was just beginning to reflect on how he'd make it through the night when Maureen sat bolt upright with a deafening gasp. The surprise nearly forced Tyce to career into the oncoming lane. He looked back over at her. Her eyes were wide, and her breathing came in gasps. He was worried she might hyperventilate.

"Pull over," she said, breathlessly clawing at the door handle. "Pull over right now!"

She looked like she was going to be sick. Tyce pulled off to the side of the road, and Maureen opened the truck door and leaned out. He couldn't see what was happening over her hunched shoulders, but her convulsions were apparent. After a few heaves, he heard a thin stream of liquid hitting the ground followed by a hacking noise and the sound of the young woman spitting.

Maureen pulled herself back inside the cab and squeezed her eyes shut, slamming her head back against the seat several times. The light from a passing car's headlights illuminated her face for one brief moment, and Tyce could see the tears beading under her eyelashes. She began to slowly shake her head, and her lips moved as if physically manifesting an internal argument with herself. After a moment, she ran her hands up her cheeks and to her head, rubbing her palms into her scalp, and looked over at him. A weak, regretful smile crossed her lips.

"Turn around," she sighed quietly. "Take me back."

ELEVEN

"All right thanks, Steve," said Owen. "We'll talk again tomorrow."

Owen hung up his cell phone and tossed it on the table, then he flopped down into the hard motel chair and grabbed the carton of shrimp subgum sitting next to the open case file. He poked absentmindedly at the food, which had gone cold from over an hour of sitting out half eaten. Truth be told, he didn't have much of an appetite after the scene at the coroner's office. Or what happened after it.

Agent Auger had given him quite the earful when he called in to report that he, as he put it, had taken it upon himself to dismiss Maureen from the case. He knew he was taking a risk, so he massaged the truth of why she departed while being completely honest about letting her go off without any kind of debrief or supervision. If his boss found any holes in his explanation, he didn't express them. In the end, it was his exemplary service record that allowed Auger to overlook his faux pas, provided that Owen found a way to get Maureen Allerton back under FBI control. He was fairly certain she would have found a way to get a ride out of town, and since she wasn't actually stupid enough to try and go on the run again, he could be confident she would head back to the farm. He had already coordinated with the Colorado State Police to set up a traffic stop on the highway between Walden and Cowdrey, and he had agents ready to mobilize in Wyoming if their drones spotted her back on the farm. It wouldn't be long before she would be brought back to them. He almost regretted having to take it that far, wishing he could have just let her go like she wanted to, but his own wishes were not going to be paramount in this case.

Owen pushed away from the table and paced in front of the dresser holding the television and briefly considered turning on the local news to see what the coverage of the murder was like. Mostly just to make sure the bureau was being represented well, he told himself. There had been a lot of cameras around during his confrontation with Gabriel Lowdon, and the last thing he needed was some kind of local spin on what had occurred to get back to his boss. He felt he dealt with the situation fairly well considering the antagonism that he was facing from the reporter. But these local media types were one big club, and he wouldn't put it past some biased mouthpiece to suggest that the big bad federal agent was seen bullying one of their own.

Owen resisted the urge to grab the remote sitting next to the TV and went into the bathroom to splash some cold water on his face. The rush of it brought clarity back to his mind. He toweled off and prepared to return to his files when he locked eyes with his own reflection. Owen leaned in toward the glass and peered. Each case closed, each killer brought to justice left their marks on his face. To himself, he hardly ever looked like anything other than the vigorous rookie he had once been, except when he took the time to remember all the sacrifices he'd made in the name of justice. It was in those moments when he marked the extra gray hairs streaking his temples, the wrinkles at the corners of his eyes, and the frown lines that had sprung up around his mouth. They served as a reminder of how far he was prepared to go, how many sleepless nights he'd endure if it meant that he never again had to—

A sharp knock at the door caused his head to snap around. With Turnberry and Navarro on the other side of the mountains, he didn't expect anyone at his door, especially at this time of night. Tearing himself away from his own introspection, Owen left the bathroom and walked over to the nightstand next to his bed. He took out his sidearm before slowly making his way to the door. He looked through the peephole and was greeted by the last sight he expected. Maureen Allerton was standing outside, shifting her weight and glancing in either direction, looking haggard. Owen sighed, slipped his gun into the back of his pants, and opened the door.

"You're back," he said stiffly. "May I ask how?" It was too soon for any of his own people to have gotten her.

Maureen turned around and gave a wave. A truck sitting out in the parking lot flashed its brights before turning around and making its way back onto the road. The dim light of the motel sign washed over its back end, revealing a government license plate and a state park decal.

"Ah," Owen said under his breath.

"Frohman," Maureen said, barging through the door and beginning to pace around the room.

"I'm sorry?" He decided against mentioning that he hadn't actually invited her in.

"He's killed more people than just the two you've found."
She ran her hands through her hair as though she were trying
to massage information out of her head. "One of them was
named Frohman, and I think he was killed before these other
two."

"And what makes you think that?" he asked suspiciously.

She stared at him, and there was a strange look in her eyes.
Beneath the obvious veneer of indignity, she looked almost
haunted. "How do you think?"

"You're saying you've finally made a connection with the
killer?"

Maureen nodded.

Owen ran his hand over his mouth before sitting down
at the end of the bed and putting his fingers to his temples.
"And?" He sighed.

"Christ, I'm wasting my time. I can tell you're not going to
believe anything I have to say. I'll just go tell one of the local
guys. Maybe they'll actually help."

She made for the door, but he jumped up and stopped her
from opening it. He could see that his suspicions and mistrust
of her were getting in the way of making any kind of progress.
As much as it pained him, he knew that he needed to keep an
open mind.

"Please, sit down and tell me everything," he said as gently
as he could muster.

Maureen squinted at him for the briefest of moments and
slid over to his mini fridge and opened it. He craned his neck
to look over her shoulder and see what she was up to. He
felt foolish when she turned back around holding the six-
pack of short beers that were stocked in the fridge. If he had

been thinking about everything he read in her file, he would have known that she'd be looking for something to drink. He said nothing. She sat down on the floor and crossed her legs, twisting open one of the bottles and taking a big sip.

"I told you that it happens when you're not looking," she said, casting an eye to the side and letting out a morose chuckle. "I was driving out of town with that ranger, and I must have drifted off. All those drugs you had them pump into me really took it out of me. That's when the dream hit me. I was in a sort of bunker somewhere. I can't say for sure, but I remember concrete walls and dim lighting. I was leafing through some sort of bound notebook or folder. I don't remember everything that was written on the pages, but they looked like some kind of scientific reports or something. I remember, though, that the top of each page had a name on it. First was Frohman, then the two that I heard you mention in the morgue."

"Lindstrom and Niemann," Owen said.

"Yeah, them." She finished the beer in her hand and opened another. "And on the last page was another name I haven't heard yet. Sand something. Sanders, maybe? Things get blurry sometimes. Then the guy said something. I don't remember what, but the voice was definitely deep, so I'm saying it was a guy. After that, I closed the notebook and heard a muffled scream coming from another room. I walked down a short hall and opened a steel door. Inside the room was a woman strapped down to a chair . . ." Her voice trailed off, and she stared at the carpet as if whatever she was going to say next deeply disturbed her. She shook her head and took another drink, avoiding eye contact with him.

"Go on," he said, trying to sound encouraging.

"Her eyes," Maureen whispered. "They were so wide. And piercing blue. And afraid. So afraid. It was at this point when the hands grabbed a needle from the table next to her and slowly began to inch closer to her. That's when I woke up."

"So who is this guy?"

"Layton didn't explain how this works, obviously." She shot him a look that he didn't particularly like.

Owen didn't understand. All he could do was raise an eyebrow.

Maureen rolled her eyes and grumbled a curse to herself before finishing her second beer. "Jesus, I hate having to explain this all the time." She sighed, rubbing her eyes and taking a breath as if she were gathering herself for something that was going to tax her resolve. "Have you ever heard of a little thing called Demon Sight, Agent?"

Owen shook his head.

"Don't worry, it's not a real medical term, just something my dear mother used to say. I see through the eyes of evil. When the dreams find me, it's not like watching a movie, it's like I'm wearing the person who's doing these things like a mask. I see and feel what they see and feel. And unless they step in front of a mirror, I don't know who's doing it. And before you ask, no, I can't predict the future. I see things as they happen. It sucks." At that, Maureen popped her third beer, tossed the cap across the room, and drank down half of the seven-ounce bottle.

Owen shook his head. This couldn't be real. "Okay, let's just say I believe you. What would you suggest our next move be?"

"I don't have a next move. You're the pro investigator here. I gave you a lead. Now go investigate."

"You gave me some superstitious talk about dreams. I can't do much with that. I need more."

"I don't know what to tell you." She stood up and began to pace again. "Maybe when you find the body of that Sand person, you'll get some answers."

"Ms. Allerton—Maureen—you can't be that callous."

"No. And I'm not. But I can play the part."

Owen watched as she made her way over to the table by the window and began to shuffle through the papers that he had laid out. He winced as he imagined the disarray she was bringing to his carefully ordered piles. "Are you looking for something?"

"My room key," she said as casually as if she were making a fast-food order. "I'm guessing you've still got it."

Her words caught Owen off guard. It seemed she intended to stay. He did indeed have her key. It was in the nightstand next to his bed, lying on top of the tattered NIV Bible.

Slowly, Owen walked over and opened the drawer. He kept his eyes fixed on Maureen the entire time and felt around inside until his finger touched the plastic disc attached to the key. He pulled it out and crossed the room to where the younger woman was standing, handing it to her without a word.

"So what are you going to do now?" he asked.

"I'm stuck here until this is all over, I suppose."

"And you're going to do your job for us?"

"Agent, I don't see this as 'my job.' But I'm chained to this guy now, and as long as I'm around, I'm going to get deeper into his head. I may not be able to tell you who he is, but soon enough, I'll be able to tell you what he's feeling and, with luck, his motivation for killing. It's going to be up to you to piece it all together and track him down." She turned to leave and was halfway through the door when she turned back. "Agent, getting hit by these dreams leaves me with some pretty bad migraines. I used to treat them with a prescription. I'm going to need something to keep functional. Even if it's just extra-strength over-the-counters and whiskey. I didn't bring much cash with me."

"If you had bothered to ask before," Owen replied, "you'd have known that I arranged the standard forty-five-dollar per diem for you. I was saving it for when you'd actually done something to earn it. There's three days' worth in your room right now. You'll have to make that work. You're not getting any more until tomorrow. Liquor stores are open till midnight."

Maureen seemed to take his words as some sort of hint and held out the carrier with the remaining three beers for him to take back. Amused, Owen shook his head and waved his hand toward her. She shrugged before disappearing with the rest of his beer behind the closing door.

Owen stood there for a long moment before pulling his gun out of the back of his pants and setting it on the table. He took a seat back in front of his notes but didn't bother to look at them. He'd read through them enough times to know what they said, and Maureen, whether she realized it or not, had given him plenty to think about.

The agent leaned over to the window and pushed aside the curtain, staring out into the night. If Maureen was right, somewhere out there an innocent woman was being held hostage, and soon, if the bastard responsible followed his pattern, she would be drugged to the point of overdose, mutilated, and her corpse would be dumped into the river. It was anybody's guess as to when or if they would find her. He needed to find a connection between the victims. And, as much as he hated to admit it, if Maureen Allerton were truly psychic, he might need her in order to find it before it was too late.

The weight of another victim's impending death pressed down on his shoulders and kept him at the window into the early morning hours.

TWELVE

Maureen sat in the corner of the room that the coroner's office had set aside for the FBI's use—the war room, as Samuelson called it. It seemed like an odd location to be meeting at, considering she knew they had another office set aside at the sheriff's department down the road. But she wasn't about to question his methods. Clearly, the man had a plan and was going to follow through on it, no matter what she thought. She'd learned that lesson already.

The agent sat at the head of the long table. On either side of him were the two medical examiners, Dr. Heim and Dr. Frank, looking as somber as she'd seen them in the last couple of days. There were three local uniforms seated as well. Samuelson had introduced them to her as they filed in, but she didn't retain any of their names. Last of all, seated at the end of the table and closest to her, was Ranger Tyce. He turned toward her and offered a brief half smile. She raised her eyebrows and offered a slight nod in return.

"Thank you all for coming in this morning," Samuelson said. "We've got some things to go over, so let's get started." The agent shuffled the stack of papers in front of him to one side and opened a laptop. "First off, we've got some early reports from Agents Navarro and Turnberry. They've spoken to Christopher Niemann's next of kin and a few close friends. We don't have any indications as of yet of any people in his life who would wish him harm. As an Olympic alternate, he doesn't have sponsorship money coming in and actually has a part-time job to pay his rent. His parents and friends have also verified that he does not have a significant other or even a casual romantic relationship to speak of. The elimination of money or love as a motive further ties his death to Shelly Lindstrom's in support of our primary theory that we are dealing with a budding serial killer. Suspicion obviously falls on someone from their National Guard unit, but as of yet, we have no firm suspects within that group.

"It seems that Mr. Niemann came into town four days before he was found in the river. According to his parents, he intended to do some cross-training in the mountains to change up his training, since it didn't look as though he would be getting a call to join the swim team in Beijing. We have credit card receipts from a gas station and at the Rocky Mountain National Park entrance on Thursday and Friday. Ranger Tyce, your thoughts?"

"Unfortunately, no one can positively say that they saw him," Tyce replied. "We get over ten thousand people per day, and the faces of the people driving in blend together. I can say that the place where I found his body is surrounded by only one hiking trail, and it has an expert rating, so there are generally very few people around. Most of our day hikers and campers stick to the northern trails with the gentler slopes."

"It would make sense as a place to commit the murder," Samuelson said. "Only—"

"Only we found no particulates in the abdominal incision that would indicate he was cut open in that location," Dr. Frank said, cutting him off. "The evidence would point toward him being dissected indoors, in a relatively clean environment."

"You're forgetting about the postmortem bruising," Dr. Heim said to him.

"Well, yeah, obviously," said the younger doctor, beginning to blush.

"Thank you, doctors," Samuelson said, visibly annoyed at the interruption. "And while I appreciate the forensic explanation, I think we could have assumed the murder happened elsewhere just by the fact that it would have left the killer exposed for too long, increasing the likelihood of him being seen."

The officers at the table stifled their laughter at the agent putting the doctor in his place. Even Tyce hid his mouth behind his hand.

"Button up, boys," Agent Samuelson said, shooting them a glare. "Let's move on. Some other recent developments have led us to believe there may be other victims of this killer out there. Doctor Heim, did you find any recent unsolved murders in the area relating to a person by the name of Frohman?"

"Well, Agent," he said slowly, appearing unsure of what he was about to say. "We didn't find anyone by the name of Frohman. The closest name in our files is a man by the name of Bronson Freeman. Though I'm not exactly sure that Mr. Freeman is even a murder victim. I performed the autopsy myself and did not determine it to be a homicide."

"Well, let's run through it just the same. Maybe something will shake out."

"If you say so." Dr. Heim looked doubtful. "Bronson Freeman, sixty-two, was found in the Colorado River early last April. He'd been missing since the middle of December. His wife informed us he wanted to get in one last kayaking trip down the river when we had that quick burst of unseasonably warm temperatures. He left their home outside Winter Park on the thirteenth and never returned. His body was eventually dredged up by some fishermen in the section of the river just north of the lakes. It was pretty well preserved by the cold water, but it was almost entirely stripped of flesh. Dental records were used to identify him, and there was no evidence of perimortem trauma."

"Was his kayak ever found?" asked Samuelson.

"No," said Dr. Frank as he and Dr. Heim shared a look before he turned back to the agent. "At least, I don't think so."

"I don't remember any of the local authorities mentioning the kayak at the time either," said the other doctor, looking down the table at the three officers. "What about you boys?"

"I don't think any of us worked the case," one said, looking at the other two men, who were shaking their heads. "And there was no talk around the station of any kayak."

"Does anybody know anything else about Freeman?" Samuelson asked the room.

"I know a little about him, sir," Tyce said, holding up his hand. "I believe he was a professor of some sort at CU. I've had quite a few conversations with him over the years. He was a regular at the park. Loved his kayaking. Knew the Colorado between its source and Sulfur Springs better than any private citizen I've ever met. I'd see him in the summers, both before and after he retired, on the water almost every weekend. The man was a beast on the river. I would bet he could have rowed circles around boys half his age."

"So how does a guy, even at sixty-two, who was that good in a boat find himself dead in the river he knows so well?" mused the agent. "Ranger Tyce, did he ever show any signs of disregarding safety?"

"Never that I saw. Always had a life vest on, and his kayak was always in top condition."

"Okay, thanks. I have a gut feeling that we need to look further into any connections between Professor Freeman's death and Shelly Lindstrom's and Christopher Niemann's. Boys, do me a favor and ask around the station about that kayak and report back to me with some more particulars about his life."

The three local officers nodded.

Maureen looked at the men from face to face to see if they truly understood what was being asked of them. Agent Samuelson had called his reasoning a "gut feeling." Clearly, he didn't want word getting out that he was using her as a source for leads.

"Great," the agent continued, still addressing the three officers. "You guys can head on out now. Please remember to keep us apprised of any new missing person reports that come in. Thank you for coming in."

The locals got to their feet and shuffled out of the room. A silence hung in the air for a moment after the door closed. Samuelson sighed quietly, clearly trying to not make it obvious. He looked tired. Maureen found herself wondering how much sleep he had gotten. He was enough on edge without being exhausted as well. And it wouldn't help his already gruff personality.

"Now that we're alone," he began again, "we can discuss other matters of a more confidential nature. As you know"— he turned toward the doctors—"it is the FBI's *belief* that Maureen here has an ability to see into the mind of killers in her dreams." His edge on the word *belief* made her stiffen. "Apparently, our attempts to induce this state over the last few days were counterproductive to the process. She now says she's made that connection, and the questions regarding Freeman have their source there. That, along with some other information she has gleaned, I ask her to relay to you all at this time."

A lump lodged in Maureen's throat as they all turned toward her corner. No one spoke a word as she looked from face to face. Dr. Frank coughed, Dr. Heim fidgeted with the pen he was holding, and Ranger Tyce held her with an empathetic look. Her eyes turned to Samuelson. He stood, arms crossed, with a stern look on his face, yet the corner of his lip was ever so slightly turned up.

You son of a bitch, she thought, narrowing her eyes at him.

"Ms. Allerton," the agent said, taking his seat at the table, "the floor is yours."

Maureen rose from her chair and slowly made her way to stand in front of the rest of them. She swallowed hard. She had never been asked to speak like this in front of people before, and her nerves were getting the better of her. She didn't know why Samuelson was forcing her to recount her dreams to the others. He could have just as easily done it himself, though on the way in that morning, he had hinted that he may ask her to speak to the group. She took it as no more than an idle, passing threat to keep her in line. Surely the man who showed such disdain for her inclusion in the investigation wouldn't taint it by having her get this involved. She was wrong. Clearly this was some small measure of revenge he was exacting for her leaving. She took a deep breath.

"Well," she said timidly, "you boys already know that I'm here to hopefully make a connection with the killer and try to give you a sense of his or her motives. Last night, I did. I can tell you this much: this person keeps a notebook of his victims. I saw the names Frohman, Lindstrom, and Niemann on separate pages. Then, on the final page, I saw another name. The full name was blurry, but I definitely remember it begins with *Sand*."

"Forgive me, Ms. Allerton," Dr. Heim said, "but how can you be sure about what you saw? We've double checked, and there are no disappearances in the area involving a person named Frohman. There's only Mr. Freeman, who we just discussed."

"I just know what I saw," she replied, trying to hide her annoyance at being questioned. "Words and numbers are usually the clearest things I remember, especially when it's the first time I've connected with a person. I don't remember everything, and sometimes not in the right order, but that's how it goes. Maybe I thought I saw the name Frohman and what I really saw was Freeman, but I really don't think so. The longer I'm connected, the more I'll see and remember. But for now, I can tell you that this person has likely already killed this Sand woman. I pulled out of the dream just before she was injected with a big needle. The place where she was being held felt like it was underground. There was lots of concrete.

It could be anywhere, but it's probably somewhere north of town—that's where I was when the dream hit, and they're always more clear when I'm closer to the person."

"There's an awful lot of homes and cabins along that route," Tyce said almost to himself. The other men looked at him expectantly. Tyce looked around the room, cleared his throat, and continued. "But, it does make sense. If you take a look at where the bodies were discovered, they're progressing farther and farther down the river. The tides could account for that."

"Or he could be dumping the bodies farther from his home," Samuelson added. Tyce nodded, and the agent tented his fingers under his chin. "It's a good theory, worth looking into. But we can't just go knocking door to door at every home along the river without cause. I think we'll let the locals keep on the whole Frohman/Freeman business for the time being. The same goes for you, doctors. Go back over your report and see if there's anything in your notes that you might have missed. When Agent Turnberry and Navarro come back this evening, we'll focus on this other woman who might be out there. Maureen, do you have anything to add? A description of the woman perhaps?"

The thought of trying to remember her dream in vivid detail again made her stomach turn. She had felt the woman's terror, and it wasn't something she was keen to relive. Maureen was also wondering in that moment why Agent Samuelson seemed to be coaxing her to share more. Especially since he wasn't shy about his skepticism of her.

"Well, she was a white female," Maureen began slowly after clearing her throat. "Darker hair with some gray in it.

Tied back but maybe medium length. I don't know how old she was, but she seemed older than me—and probably you too, Agent. Maybe closer to Dr. Heim's age? And her eyes were as blue as I've ever seen. That's about all I can think of. I don't know how much that helps."

Maureen decided she wouldn't wait to be dismissed and retreated to her seat, drawing her feet up onto the chair so she could lean forward and rest her chin on her knees. She hoped that they were satisfied with her for the moment and would ignore her for the rest of the meeting.

"Fine," said Samuelson before turning his attention to the ranger. "Tyce, if the park is still offering to let you off your day job, you can lend a little manpower by going through the local missing person reports and seeing if you can find a woman who matches the description Ms. Allerton provided us. I've made arrangements with the sheriff's department to utilize their database. Just head over and ask for Janet in the resources office. She'll have everything arranged. Meanwhile, I'm going to set to work on attacking this Frohman character from another angle. If the deceased professor isn't the person we're looking for, then it's possible the real victim wasn't killed locally or even in Colorado. Preliminary reports don't show any at-large serial killers with this MO around the country, but maybe we missed something."

At this, the agent stood up and began to gather his laptop and files from the table. The other men followed suit. Maureen stayed seated, not sure what she was supposed to do next.

"All right, gentlemen," Samuelson said to them, apparently forgetting, unintentionally or not, that a lady was also present. "Thank you for your time this morning. I'll be busy with the field office for a while, but I'll be in touch with each of you as needed. If you discover something, don't hesitate to call my cell phone."

With that, Agent Samuelson nodded to them and exited the room. The rest of the men followed suit, leaving Maureen alone. She gradually rose from her chair and began to circle around the table, running her fingers over the laminated wood, unsure about what to do with herself and wondering why everyone except her had been given an assignment by the agent. The thought actually came as a shock to her, as normally she would have been glad to be left out of the grunt work. At the moment, however, she felt less than enthusiastic at the prospect of being left to herself in an unfamiliar town. She had no idea what she'd do with herself.

Ranger Tyce's head appeared in the doorway. His sudden appearance shook her briefly. The ranger smiled warmly to reassure her that he didn't mean to startle her.

"I was just checking to see if you were okay," he said. "Everyone rushed out on you so quickly I don't think anyone stopped to think about how this is all affecting you."

His concern was heartwarming, though her ingrained distrust of people's motives forced her to take a moment to answer. "I'm fine," she finally managed.

The two of them left the conference room and walked together in silence as they navigated the labyrinth of halls. As they rounded a corner, Samuelson emerged from another room, flipping through papers inside one of his folders.

"Ranger Tyce," he said without looking up, "perhaps you should take Ms. Allerton here with you on your assignment. She could be of more use to you than to me right now."

"And just what is that supposed to mean?" Maureen retorted. She wasn't sure why, but something about the way he said it sounded like an insult.

"Seeing as you say you saw our latest victim's face, then clearly you should be with the ranger going through the missing person reports with him. It'll go that much faster since I'm sure you'll be able to recognize her instantly if you see her again. Assuming your recall is good enough." He pushed past the two of them and made his way down the hall before calling over his shoulder, "Also, I can't spare any of my people to keep an eye on you."

"I guess that makes sense," Tyce said as Samuelson disappeared through another door that led to one of the building's stairwells. "Though I could have done without that last little bit. What does he mean 'keep an eye on you'? It's not like you're a child or something."

"No," she replied, trying to hide her bitterness at the agent's insinuation. "Just a freak who needs to be kept on a leash. Otherwise, she'll take a giant dump on the investigation. Congratulations, Ranger. You're on shit duty."

"Thanks," he said awkwardly. "So you're okay to come with me then?"

Maureen shrugged. There was nothing better she could be doing anyway. "Lead the way."

The ranger nodded, and Maureen followed him down the hall. The two of them continued without another word through the rest of the building and out the front door.

THIRTEEN

Tyce drummed on the top of the front counter at the sheriff's department with his fingertips. The elderly secretary seated at her desk looked up at him. Her look wasn't what he might call one of annoyance, but the sound clearly caught her attention. Tyce mouthed an apology to her and turned back to find Maureen. She was pacing in the front lobby, staring at the various plaques and pictures on the wall. He could tell she wasn't staying at any one long enough to actually read what was written on them, just passing the time, trying to look involved enough so that somebody wouldn't try and make conversation with her.

A middle-aged woman with dark hair tied up in a bun rounded the corner and headed toward him. "Ranger Tyce, I presume?"

"You can call me Alec if you want. And that's Maureen over there. I'm guessing you're Janet?"

"That's me. Why don't you two come with me, and we'll head into the room we have prepared for you."

Tyce turned and waved over to Maureen. She put her head down and crossed her arms as she strode across the lobby to join him. Though she had agreed to assist, for whatever reason, she didn't seem comfortable. She hadn't said a word since they left the coroner's office and spent the short drive over staring out the window of his truck.

They followed Janet around a corner and toward the back of the building. She showed them into a dim room with several computers. She woke one up and pulled a page up on the screen.

"This is the search engine for the missing persons database," she explained as she sat down in front of the computer. "I can search by age, sex, height, weight, date, whatever you like."

"Middle-aged woman, abducted in the last week," said Maureen quickly.

"Hang on," Tyce said. "That's too narrow. Make it all missing persons in the last six months. Search area within, let's say, a thousand square miles of here?"

Maureen pulled him aside. "What are you doing? You know what we're looking for!"

"It's not that I don't believe you, but dreams can be hazy, and you yourself said things get clearer the longer you're connected. So, it's possible that you saw a more feminine-looking male with longer hair."

She rocked from side to side uncomfortably. "I just don't what to be here all day," she whispered.

Tyce smiled. "I'll try to make sure it's not too painful for you. But we wouldn't be doing anything to help unless we cast a wide net and make sure nothing slips out. Let's just sit down, hmm?"

Maureen did nothing to hide the rolling of her eyes but did as he asked. Janet had finished pulling up the information they were looking for and moved aside to let Maureen take her place.

"Let me know if you need anything," she said as she left them to their work.

Tyce sat down next to Maureen, grabbed the mouse, and began clicking through the slides of the missing people. With each click, he looked over at Maureen, who would simply stare at the screen for a moment and shake her head. After a few minutes, the silence in the room became unnerving.

"So, Ms. Allerton," he said, hoping he was making the right decision in opening up a door she might not want opened. "How long has this thing with you been going on?"

"I don't like to talk about it," she said curtly, not taking her eyes off the screen. "Would you just show me the next one, please?"

Tyce clicked the mouse. The face of a middle-aged woman with dark hair filled the screen. "Kimberly Feist, age forty-seven. Last seen on March 8 outside Jensen, Utah. That could be her," he said.

"It's not," said Maureen flatly.

"You sure?"

Maureen gave him a sour look.

"Okay. You're sure."

He clicked to the next slide. It was a young, black teenager. Tyce didn't even wait for her answer before moving on. And on. The number of faces that flashed before his eyes started to make him feel uncomfortable. All these people were missing with loved ones out there who had no closure. In only the last two years. And this wasn't even every missing person in the country.

"Listen, uh, Ms. Allerton," Tyce said unsteadily. "I can see this whole thing is taking its toll on you. Like a big cross on your back. And I don't just mean what's been done to you in the last few days."

"Yeah? And you think if I open up some more about it, I'll magically feel better? Don't hold your breath. You already know more than I'd like. And I'm not looking for any new friends here. Or anything else, for that matter."

"That's not it at all. And frankly, it hurts that you'd say something like that."

Maureen turned to him. "I'm sorry." Her voice was sincere, if not a little sad. "I just don't think you'd understand, and I'd really rather not talk about it. I'll say this, though: you're right. It's been a long life of dealing with this, and having to do this work with the FBI hasn't made things any easier."

"Well, you might be surprised at how much I can understand."

"No offense, but talk to me when you can see through the eyes of a psycho slicing the throat of a ten-year-old and have it feel like it's your own arm jerking the knife."

Tyce knew nothing about what she was referring to but gleaned enough to figure she must be making a reference to the case that got her tangled up with the feds. He didn't see the need to push, but he knew enough to know that there was one thing he could say to make her understand. It didn't hurt that he knew deep down it was something he needed to talk about, and Maureen Allerton was as good a person as any to have that conversation with.

"I don't need to imagine what that's like," he said quietly.

"You mean you . . ."

Tyce nodded. "I was on the ground during Desert Storm. It's the only actual combat I've ever seen, and as those things go, it was a pretty easy operation. Some of the fighting at the front was intense, though. Even steamrollering the Iraqis like we did, we took some casualties."

"So you saw a lot of people die?"

"One or two really close friends, yeah. And I killed my share, too."

"You don't have to talk about it if you don't want to. Lord knows I know what it's like to get bombarded with questions."

"You didn't ask me anything. I started telling you. And it's okay. I don't talk about these things as much as the psychologist I saw after my discharge said I should."

"Wouldn't have taken you for the therapy type."

"Not in over a decade and a half, but at the time it helped me deal with the fact that I was no longer going to be in the service."

"You're going to tell me why, aren't you?"

Tyce laughed to himself. She could be a hard one, this girl. But still, she seemed genuinely interested. Or maybe concerned? He wasn't exactly sure. Reading women wasn't one of his strong suits. "I was with the 3-41 Straight and Stalwart."

Maureen's eyes blinked and her lips twisted in confusion.

"Sorry. Military jargon. It's what we called the division of the army regiment I was a part of. The forty-first infantry regiment, third division. We were the head of the spear of the 2d Armored Division when we went in alongside the marines to finish up ground operations at the Kuwait Airport at the end of the war. It was a mostly lopsided victory, all told. But, as with all things in war, it wasn't without causality. We were working to push through the Iraqi mine fields. They were sloppily set up except for a small cluster that just happened to be in our line of advance. One of the mines went off as a tank we were supporting passed over it. I was maybe twenty feet from the blast and got spammed with shrapnel. A five-inch piece buried itself in my leg." Tyce realized his right hand was tracing its way down his thigh.

"I'm sorry to hear that," Maureen said quietly. "That must have been terrible, but I don't see how it's like my situation."

"I didn't say it was. I just said I understand how it can feel. See, the thing is, I was in a group of four that day. I was the only one who made it out alive. All of us were the same distance from the blast, but the other three were riddled with metal, and I found out later that the force of the blast compressed their chests to the point that it caused massive internal bleeding. I don't know how, but the single piece in my leg was all I got hit with. It wedged itself right between the femoral and popliteal. An inch either way, and I would have bled out in a matter of minutes.

"What that lump of metal did do, though, was cause a significant amount of nerve damage and forced me to be discharged on disability. That didn't sit well with me. I had a new wife and a child on the way, and I felt like I wasn't going to be able to do my job in providing for them. My shrink called it 'survivor's guilt,' and looking back, she was right. All I could think about was why I deserved to live while three other men had to die. To this day, I still have the occasional nightmare about that day, and for months after, I could barely get off the couch. I didn't really appreciate being alive until my daughter was born. The first time I held her, I realized why I was left in this world."

Maureen shook her head, a cynical grin on her lips. "Soldiers and their regrets," she said, almost to herself.

"What's that supposed to mean?" It was an odd comment.

"Nothing," she dismissed. "You just remind me of someone. So"—she turned full on toward him—"you're a war hero, and I suppose you're a top-notch dad on top of it too, aren't you?"

"I do my best for Aly, yeah."

"How old?"

"Turned sixteen a couple of months ago, God help us all."

"Driving yet?"

"Just passed her exam."

"College plans?"

"Out of state, sadly. Luckily, I've managed a little bit of a nest egg to help her out. I don't want money to stand in the way of her going where she wants to go. Even if it means she'll be rooting against the Buffaloes."

"That's some sports thing, isn't it?"

"College sports. A very serious thing, you know."

"And a sports freak to boot." She snickered, rolling her eyes. "Apparently, I attract a certain type. Good thing I'm not into older guys."

"Good thing I'm not into younger women," he played back.

"I don't believe that for a second. All guys want to be seen with the youngest, hottest piece they can get, don't they?"

"Not me." And he meant it. "I'm at the point in my life where I'm looking for someone who's closer to where I'm at in my journey."

"In other words, better adjusted than I am." It wasn't a question.

"I didn't say that." He smirked. "But yes." Sometimes it was best to be brutally honest.

"I thought this little talk was supposed to reassure me that you understand what I go through. So far, I haven't heard anything that makes me believe that."

"Then you haven't been listening carefully. Everyone has demons in their life, in their past. And we all carry them with us every day. Some people's are heavier and scarier than others'. I don't know the trauma that your situation carries, but I know trauma. I guess what I'm trying to get through to you is, you can have those demons and still live a life. And I mean a *real* life."

"I'll keep it in mind." She turned back to the screen.

Tyce held back a chuckle at her hardheadedness and continued to click through the images of the missing people on the computer. The routine continued in silence. Tyce clicked the mouse, and Maureen shook her head once a new face popped up on the screen. Within a half hour, they had gone through every missing person on the list.

"So much for that," Maureen said, sliding her chair away from the computer.

Tyce sighed and rubbed his eyes. "Yeah, I guess so. Suppose we should find Agent Samuelson and give him our report."

Maureen said nothing in reply. She simply got up without even looking at him and began to slowly make her way to the door. Tyce paused for a moment before heading out behind her. They walked through the halls until they came to the front desk again.

"We're all done in there," he told the desk attendant. "You can tell Janet that she can shut down the computer."

The attendant nodded and went back to her work.

Nice woman, Tyce thought, giving her a pleasant smile that she would never see.

Maureen was waiting at the door for him, arms crossed, staring outside. He came up behind her and stood for a moment. She looked as if she wanted to say something but her mouth wouldn't allow it. He waited for a moment before he opened the door and indicated that she should head out ahead of him. It had the effect he was looking for.

"Did you mean what you said?" she mumbled as they walked out into the parking lot. "About being able to live a normal life, even with all that shit in my past?"

"Everybody's got shit of some kind. Only difference is the smell."

"Helpful," she scoffed.

Tyce smiled. Folksy platitudes wouldn't work on her. He sighed and stuck his hands in his pockets and looked down at the pavement. "I don't know much about you, Ms. Allerton. You seem like you have a tough exterior that you want people to think goes all the way down to the inside. But deep down, you seem to want a peaceful life. Even real friends. Maybe a family. But it seems like you use this thing you have in your head as justification for why you can't have those things. I guess I just think that if you focused more on the one than the other, you could really find something."

He turned and found she was no longer walking next to him. He turned back. She had stopped about five paces behind and was staring toward something off to her left. There was a disgusted look on her face. He followed her gaze and groaned when his eyes fell upon what she was looking at.

Making a beeline for them, with a smug smirk on his face, was Gabriel Lowdon.

FOURTEEN

"You can't honestly believe what you're saying." Ranger Tyce snorted from his seat in the dirty-yellow-colored booth before taking a swallow of cola.

The reporter sat opposite them, stuffing french fries in his mouth. "Why not?" he shot back, unapologetically firing off a spray of potato crumbs from his mouth. "It's as good an explanation as any."

The two men had been going on like this for what seemed to Maureen like forever. She and the ranger had reluctantly accepted Lowdon's invitation to lunch. As they followed him to the small diner on the north end of town, Tyce had considered turning back and trying to lose him. In the end, however, they agreed that if they did that, the reporter would simply keep intruding on the investigation until he got her alone. It was better to play along for now and do their best to convince him there was nothing about her that warranted his attention.

She frowned and took a bite of her own lunch. She hadn't ordered it—Lowdon had smugly taken the liberty for her, insisting that this place had some of the best meatloaf in the state—but she was hungry enough and didn't want to invite any more debate than was already occurring. Truth be told, she couldn't have said whether the meatloaf was good or bad. Like the mound of mashed potatoes on the side, it was covered with the thickest layer of goopy, brown gravy she had ever seen, and she couldn't taste anything beyond that. It was probably the reason the reporter liked the place so much. He seemed like a man who would think everything was better with more gravy on it.

"Government experiments?" Tyce spat in annoyance. "And just what kind of experiments would they be doing now?"

"Could be anything," Lowdon said, now with a pocket of burger in his cheek. "But if I had to guess, I'd say they might be trying to create some kind of super-soldier."

Tyce turned toward her and raised an eyebrow. Maureen just rolled her eyes in return and said nothing. She began to almost want the reporter to continue. Firstly, so she wouldn't have to talk, and secondly, to show what a moron he really was. Her look was all it took.

"Russia," he said adamantly. She and Tyce stared at him, prompting him to continue his explanation, not without a certain sense of self-important satisfaction. "During the Cold War, many rumors came out of the Soviet Union. One of them was a secret program of Stalin's centered in secret Siberian bases where his scientists were believed to have been experimenting with human-ape hybrids in order to create super soldiers who would be unmatched in strength, stamina, and ruthless killing capacity."

"Uh-huh," said the ranger, seemingly unimpressed.

Lowdon took no notice and continued. "There were reports of human females being inseminated with chimpanzee samples, and that, in rare cases, the embryos took and came to term. Most concurred that the resulting offspring wouldn't likely have survived long, but the point remains that governments have been interested in scientifically manipulating humans to create the perfect soldier for generations."

"And how does that prove that the United States is up to that sort of thing too?" Tyce challenged. It was clear to Maureen that his pride as a soldier was being challenged, and he was growing irritated.

"She's proof, for one thing." Lowdon pointed at her.

Maureen felt herself go stiff. She knew that he suspected her role in the investigation ever since he first accosted Samuelson outside the medical examiner's office, but his certainty made her feel uneasy. She did her best to maintain a mask of composure and leaned forward. "Please, enlighten us," she said in her best sarcastic tone.

The reporter grinned at being granted the opportunity for another soliloquy and began. "In the seventies, the CIA began funding research into remote viewing, which was conducted at the Stanford Institute. The research gained the attention of the defense department, and they were soon sending representatives to look in on the experiments. Hundreds of people who purported to have psychic abilities were tested, including Uri Geller, and many experiments led to successful results, including one where a girl by the name of Rosemary Smith was able to give them the location of a lost Soviet spy plane. After that, army intelligence moved operations to buildings at Fort Meade and continued their research on the military applications of those with ESP. Dozens of psychics and mediums were employed to use their abilities in espionage against other countries and in pursuit of agents and criminals inside the US. The project was leaked in the mid-eighties to unfavorable reviews, and as of '95, the official word is that it was closed down. But, there're still reports of soldiers today overseas who have a certain precognition for danger and are used as a sort of sniffer dog for trouble during their missions."

"And Russia has what to do with all of this?" Tyce sounded tired by the reporter's rhetoric.

"Simply this." Lowdon smiled. "The Stargate Project wouldn't have gotten its start if not for the intelligence out of Russia in 1970 that their government was spending millions on their own research into parapsychology. Now let's tie it all together. If the US government got its ideas for Stargate from the Soviet Union, it clearly shows that we had the ability to infiltrate foreign governments on a scale far greater than the public was aware of. It stands to reason that the CIA would have known all about the super-soldier project of the early Cold War days as well. And if the defense department took the ideas to do psychic research—and given the arms-race climate of the times—wouldn't it stand to reason that somewhere in the bowels of some top-secret military facility they were doing their own human experiments?"

"I don't buy it for a second," said Tyce.

"Open your eyes, man!" Lowdon banged the table.

Maureen looked around the restaurant. Many of the customers and some of the waitstaff had stopped their own conversations and were staring in their direction.

The reporter noticed too, so he leaned in and lowered his voice. "Think about it: the government was clearly studying bioweapons at Lab 257, and I'd bet that no matter what they say, there's still work going on there and that it goes well beyond what we already know. There's perhaps the largest concentration of federal laboratories in Colorado, and you can't tell me they're all studying the weather. So do you really think it's a coincidence that, with a new administration coming into the White House, we start seeing hollowed-out National Guardsmen washing up around here?"

"That's all pretty thin," said Tyce. "And why would it be National Guardsmen they're experimenting on when they don't fight except in extreme circumstances?"

"Why do companies test on animals? To make sure that what they're developing will work before taking it to the true consumer. Same thing here. You start working on a branch of the military that possesses enough malleable people—people with a sense of patriotism and who are expendable to a certain extent—and try out your stuff on them before you move forward with the fighting soldiers. If they die, you chuck 'em and move on."

"So why are there even bodies? If what you say is true, why not just burn all the evidence or something?"

"People ask too many questions if someone just disappears without a trace. Wouldn't the best way to hide their experimenting be to cut out all the organs affected by whatever it is they're doing and leave the bodies out for other authorities to find? If it does nothing else, it keeps eyes away from them."

"How *do* you know about the missing organs?" Maureen blurted before she could stop herself. His inner knowledge of the state of the bodies took her off guard and loosened her tongue. Fortunately, Lowdon was too wrapped up in himself and his intellectual prowess to hear her, and his next words coming so closely on the heels of her own seemed to confirm this.

"I have a source inside the FBI." He grinned. "I know more than Samuelson and Turnberry think."

"And who's this source of yours?" Tyce didn't sound convinced.

"Oh, no." Lowdon laughed, wagging his finger. "I'm not going to give you a name that you can take to your new masters."

Tyce bristled at the sound of the word *master* but quickly settled back. Maureen was impressed by his restraint. The reporter was sitting there, taking shots at everything that meant something to him, and he hadn't responded. She would have hit him by now.

"That being said," he continued, turning toward her, "I could always use another source, Ms. Allerton. I trust I've opened your eyes a little further on how they're simply using you. Together, we could put them in their place."

Maureen snorted. He sounded like a used-car salesman. And not even a good one. She leaned back in the booth, crossed her arms, and stared at him. The fact that she was being used by the FBI was not the brilliant revelation he thought it was. Agent Layton made no secret of that eleven months ago when he coaxed her into signing on the dotted line. And, while she wouldn't dismiss it entirely, the idea of her being part of some revitalized shadow government project fell on her ears as nothing more than the ramblings of a sad little man angry at the world for not recognizing his genius.

"What do I have to do to convince you I'm on your side?"

Lowdon asked, clutching a hand to his chest with a mock wounded look.

"More than lunch, that much is certain," she replied, trying to dismiss him.

"How about some dessert, then? You look like a woman who hasn't had something delicious inside her in a while."

Maureen gritted her teeth and leaned forward. "The next time you say something like that to me, I will rip your tongue out of your mouth."

"Sweet on someone else, huh?" He grinned. "A certain federal agent, maybe? You know, he's not the good guy he makes himself out to be."

Maureen almost choked on her own breath at his conclusion. True, there was an FBI agent out there who she held close to her heart, but the fact that anyone could think that agent was Owen Samuelson was laughable. Whatever source he had inside the investigation didn't seem to be giving him all the facts. Of course, he'd proven himself more than capable of taking half-truths and questionable information and turning them into his personal gospel.

"Samuelson's a dick," she spat out. "I have no delusions otherwise. But I at least have to give it to him, he'll do whatever it takes to catch this guy. And, no, before you let another one of your perverted thoughts spill out of your piehole, I'm not about to spread my legs for him."

"You have no idea how far he'll go. That man is dangerous."

"Aw, Jesus, you're not going to start this shit again, are you?" groaned Tyce. He turned to Maureen. "Don't listen to—"

Before he could finish, Lowdon began to talk over him, and before Maureen knew what was happening, the two men were badgering her from both sides with their own version of a story they clearly had contradictory viewpoints on. It sounded like it involved a standoff between a murder suspect and Agent Samuelson, but she could only pick out one man's words at a time, depending on who was talking louder.

"There's clear body cam footage," Lowdon pontificated. "Hickson dropped his weapon and was giving himself up!"

"He had another piece on him—"

"Easily planted it on him. They never proved it belonged to—"

"Just going to forget about the fourteen-year-old in his trunk? Sometimes I think you're intentionally—"

"Not forgetting anything, but we pay our officers to enforce the law, not take it into their—"

"Gonna cry for that piece of crap—"

"And then goes and gets my story pulled from—"

"I would have done worse to you than pull a story. You know you were just trying to—"

"Both of you shut up!" Maureen slammed her fist on the table. Both men stopped their argument and looked at her. She took a deep breath and tried to recapture a measured tone. "I think I'm going to leave before you two get us kicked out of here." She reached into her pocket and pulled out her cash, tossing a ten at Lowdon. "A decent person who invited us to lunch would offer to pay, but you don't strike me as the type. Don't know how much of the bill that's gonna cover, but I'll leave you two to figure out the rest." Before either could say another word, Maureen turned and stalked out of the restaurant and into the afternoon sun.

FIFTEEN

Tyce didn't immediately follow Maureen out of the diner. She didn't seem overly angry as she left, just annoyed with the whole affair. The problem was, he wasn't sure if annoyed was more dangerous than angry where she was concerned. He never had the best judgment in that area. Better to be on the safe side of a woman's wrath.

He got to his feet slowly and pulled out his wallet, looking expectantly at Gabe. The reporter stared back for a moment, biting his lip. After a moment, he shrugged and waved Tyce off. That was certainly unexpected. Gabe usually was good enough to pay for himself, but he couldn't remember the last time he treated him to a meal. Maureen's ten-dollar bill on the table was probably a factor. Maybe he should grab it for her, if for no other reason than to give Gabe a little of his own medicine. Tyce decided to leave it alone, grabbed his hat, and headed for the door.

He stepped outside and scanned the parking lot for Maureen. He didn't think she could have gotten too far, but she was nowhere in sight. A brief panic set in. Even though she could obviously take care of herself, he felt a certain responsibility to keep an eye on her. The diner was far enough from the main drag of the town that a number of things could happen on the way back. With a killer lurking around the area, there was no reason for her to go walking the streets alone.

Tyce jumped into his truck and took off toward town, believing that it was the only logical direction Maureen would go. It was mere moments before he saw her ahead, her ponytail bobbing behind her as she walked, but he was still surprised by how far she had gotten in the few minutes since she left the diner. She wasn't running, but her pace was quick. Tyce passed her and pulled in front of her some fifty yards.

Maureen looked up from the ground as she approached the truck. Her face was even, with no visible trace of surprise at him showing up. Almost as though she expected it. He opened his door but stayed in the cab. She slowed her approach and stopped a few paces away, crossing her arms.

"Just couldn't stand being in the same room as that guy for another second," she said before he could ask.

Tyce smiled. "Well, I can certainly understand that. It was all wearing pretty thin on me too."

"I shouldn't have let you talk me into it."

"Well, I'll apologize if you like, but at least we got what we were looking for."

"Yeah? What's that?"

"Well, we know that he knows a little something about you thanks to his 'source,' but as usual, he's taking it way too far."

"I don't see how that's a good thing."

Tyce stepped down from the truck's cab. He took a moment to measure his response. The situation was far from ideal, but he hoped he could reassure her that there wasn't as much to worry about as she might think. "Most of the time when Gabe gets on the scent of one of these conspiracies, he forgets about the actual story. The way I see it, the wilder his ideas, the less dangerous he can be to the investigation. And that's really what we need to focus on now."

"I'll do my part." Maureen shrugged. "But if it comes down to being Ms. Team Player or becoming the subject for one of the jackhole's stories, I'm sorry, I'm looking after myself and finding door number three."

"Fair enough, but why worry about an article three hundred people are going to read?" Tyce laughed.

"That's three hundred more people who'll know I exist. And that's about three hundred and six more than I'd like."

"Am I one?"

Maureen cocked her head to the side and gave a little shrug. "Okay then," she said, curling the corner of her mouth into a smile. "Three hundred and *seven*."

"Get in the goddamn truck," Tyce said dryly. Maureen didn't protest and silently got into the passenger seat.

They were among the buildings of the town when Maureen looked around and said, "I don't want to go back to the motel right now."

"What would you suggest?" replied Tyce, somewhat taken aback by her assertion.

"I don't know," she said, shaking her head. "I just can't sit around and watch TV right now. Isn't there someplace where I can just walk for a while and not be bothered by anyone?"

"I think I know just the place." He turned his truck back northward.

Tyce drove along the highway for nearly half an hour before arriving at his destination. He turned off the road and onto a lane lined with pine trees. After some four hundred yards, a small hut appeared. He stopped in front of it and rolled down his window. A red-haired woman stuck out her head.

"Hart," Tyce greeted her. "How's things?"

"Al," she replied with a wry grin. "We were beginning to think you'd left us all behind and we'd never see you again! You gonna fill us in on all the excitement?"

"When I'm allowed to. Gotta keep things tight for now."

"Understandable." The other ranger leaned forward and gestured to Maureen. "New girlfriend or something?"

"Ward," Tyce replied with a dry grin. "This is Maureen Allerton. Maureen, Sheila Hart."

"Pleasure," said Hart.

Maureen nodded stiffly.

"We got the afternoon free and were thinking about getting some fresh air," Tyce continued. "We'll be up on the bluff trail. See you when we get back."

Hart tipped her hat to him and waved them through. Tyce pulled past the public parking lot and into an empty employee space behind the welcome center. As he and Maureen got out of the truck, he looked down the service road. The desire to hike down it to the stables and take Digger out for a ride came over him, but he resisted. Maureen didn't seem like the horse-riding type. When this was all over, though, he'd run the old boy like he hadn't been run in years.

"Well," he said to Maureen, "here we are. Fresh air, plenty of room to hike. Just like you wanted."

Maureen looked around. "Good as any place. Lead the way."

Tyce led her to the trailhead. "This is the bluff trail. It's got some great views. You don't mind an uphill climb, right?"

Maureen threw him a look and took off up the path at a pace that shouldn't have surprised him the way it did. He jogged up next to her, and the two of them continued up the stony trail. The afternoon was hot, and after a while, Tyce found himself beginning to sweat. He looked over at Maureen. She had barely a glow about her. His jest seemed foolish now. Maureen seemed to sense it and slowed down. It was appreciated, but he couldn't let her know it.

"You think he was onto something?" Maureen asked suddenly.

"What, you mean Gabe?"

"Yeah, that whole 'Star Wars' thing, or whatever he called it."

Tyce shook his head. "I have no doubt that the *Stargate* Project existed. But you'd be the one who'd know if you're part of some secret CIA program."

"Would I? You don't think, like, maybe I could be patient zero in this thing?"

"You don't really believe that, do you?"

"I guess not, just wanted to see what you thought." She laughed for a second, but her face dropped almost immediately. "But, it wouldn't shock me. I'll never be surprised by what people would choose to do just because they can. Especially people with power."

"I take it you're talking about those experiments the boys were running on you?"

"It's not just that. I've been dealing with authority abusing me my whole life."

"It can't be as bad as all that."

Maureen stopped and rounded on him, her eyes flashing. He sensed he'd said the wrong thing, but instead of unleashing on him, she took a breath and calmed her body. She then continued down the trail. "My brother was kidnapped and murdered when I was eight," she confessed after a moment. Her tone was sullen, detached, but he could tell beneath all that was a sense of relief. Even if she seemed to be talking to the trees that lined their path, it was clear she wanted him to know, however much of an effort it was for her. "The first of the dreams I remember was him being buried in some leaves. I could see the mile marker of the freeway, and I called the police. Instead of getting thanked for what I had done, an FBI psychologist suggested I be committed to an institution, and after being there for a while, I wasn't welcome back home. My mother decided I had a demon inside me and I needed to be turned over to a special boarding school. For nine years it was all whippings, exorcisms, and abuse from the other girls and the priests and nuns who ran it. Prison was easier.

"So, I broke out. And, yeah, I had to break the law along the way—you know, to get a credit card, some pills to help with the migraines, maybe an apartment or car. I did what I had to in order to survive and stay ahead of the dreams. Then I got sucked into the murders in Sycamore Hills last year. I could see through the eyes of the psycho killing those kids. I went to one of the crime scenes to see if I was seeing what I thought I was and got pinched by the cops, crammed up in cell, and judged guilty until the fucker killed another one while I was on the inside. And then what did I do? Instead of getting out of there like I should have, I let a priest of all people convince me that I should help out. I even ended up working with that same detective who figured me for a murderer in the first place.

"And in the end, we got the guy and saved another kid along the way. And what was my reward? The damn feds found out what I can do and used my past to blackmail me into doing this—being their 'consulting profiler.' In return for three years of servitude, I'd get my criminal record expunged. But wait, I had to do six months in a federal prison for the DA to okay the deal! So there you go. I've had nearly thirty years of getting screwed over by those in charge. And now you've got the story you've been looking for, and we've shown each other our scars. I've got some physical ones, too, but I'm not in the mood to take off my shirt or shoes."

They had emerged from the woods and came to the crest of one of the bluffs overlooking the foothills rising to meet the peaks in the distance. From where they stood, the path would eventually wind its way to the southeast, descending and rising in and out of the tree line. He stopped to let the vista views calm Maureen but also to give him a moment to process everything she had confided in him and to measure an appropriate response.

"I guess that pretty much makes us even," Tyce said warily, offering her a smile. He hoped it would downplay the gravity of the situation.

Maureen shrugged. "Well, don't think for a second I've told you everything. But since you insisted on telling me more about yourself than I wanted to know, I figured I'd see what you could handle about me."

"Does that make you feel better?"

"No. But then, keeping it all in doesn't either, so whatever." She crossed her arms and stared across the landscape for a few minutes. A breath of wind swirled out of the valley and hit their faces. It felt good to have it blow on the sweat beads still clinging to his face. Maureen must have liked it too. She closed her eyes and inhaled. "Must be nice getting to work out here every day."

"Moments like this when you can take in nature without the noise of other people around are definitely a major perk."

"I'll bet," she said with a sarcastic sneer. "Why don't you go away for a minute so I can enjoy it in peace."

"Not a chance."

"Afraid I'm going to run off into the wild and disappear?"

Tyce snorted. "You wouldn't last two days."

Maureen cocked her head. "Maybe not. Out back behind the farm there're hills and mountains like these. Well, not exactly like these. Those mountains are rocky and brown, not green like here. But there's nothing but wilderness for miles past the barn, and there's an old footpath that I walk most days. I can't tell you the number of times I've thought about just running away into those mountains. Only the idea of dying cold and starving prevented me from going through with it."

"Exposure is the worst way to go. Give me something quick and painless."

"I'd imagine people get lost out here all the time."

"Sometimes. I've been in my share of rescue parties. It doesn't always end well."

"It's hard to imagine horrible things like that happening in a place that's so beautiful."

Tyce shifted his weight. The morbid turn the conversation had taken was uncomfortable. He wished they could shift back to more pleasant things. He'd brought Maureen here to get her mind off death and gloom, but it seemed like it followed her no matter where she went. It stuck to her, refused to break its grip. He could remember what that was like. It was about at her age when he was finally able to force enough separation between him and the things he'd seen to be able to live a normal life. Aly was the real difference and was something Maureen didn't have. Maybe he could help her along, but it was becoming clear that he was going to have to find someone else to pay forward in full what others had given to him. For now, the macabre and morbid might have to be their milieu.

"Down there is where I found Chris Niemann's body," he told her, pointing into the distance toward the river valley. "You can't really see it, but if you follow the cut of the valley down from those two taller mountains, that's about where it was."

"It's always worse in person," she said. Tyce turned to her and raised a questioning eyebrow. Maureen continued, though seemingly with great reluctance. "When they're in my dreams, I can at least try and pretend they're not real. Like I'm watching a movie. On my last case, while I was still a suspect, I had a dream in my jail cell where the bastard was cutting out a dead boy's innards. Only, unlike this case, after he did that, he set the remains on fire as a sort of twisted sacrifice."

"Jesus. Why would he do that?"

Maureen shrugged, but made no effort to hide her disdain. "The radical actions of a fervent believer."

He stared at her, dumbfounded, but wishing for clarification.

She brushed his look aside. "The less you know, the happier you'll be. Trust me. Anyway, the cops took me to the crime scene and that asshole fed, Layton, made me look at the boy's body. Have you ever stared into the burned-out eye sockets of a charred corpse?"

Tyce winced at the question. "Yes," he said quietly, trying his best to push away an unpleasant memory of his own.

Maureen's eyes widened and she sucked through her teeth, seeming to connect the dots. "Oh yeah, sorry."

"Don't worry about it," he said, hoping that he sounded reassuring. He didn't want to make her self-conscious about asking him things now that they were finally beginning to establish a sort of quid pro quo. He could handle talking about things he'd rather not if it meant he could get her to do the same. It would do her good to keep doing so.

Maureen let out an audible sigh at his side. He could tell there was more churning below the surface, but as the minutes passed, it became obvious to him that she wasn't going to be letting out any more today. It was well into the afternoon anyway, and he still wanted to call Agent Samuelson, even if it was to tell him that they hadn't come up with anything from the missing person reports.

"Ready to go?" he asked, knowing the answer.

Maureen nodded, and Tyce led the way back down the trail. They met a few other hikers on the way down, trading pleasantries or just a simple nod as they passed each other. Aside from that, their footsteps crunching on the path, and the chirping of birds, it was a quiet return to the truck.

The drive out of the park was equally silent. Tyce kept his eyes on the road, only occasionally glancing over at Maureen.

She kept her eyes cast out across the landscape as if deep in thought. They passed back through the gate and headed down the highway back toward town. After a few miles, he began to whistle. There was no particular melody, just something he made up as he went to break the tension.

"You don't have to do that." Maureen's voice rose over his tune.

"Sorry, is it bothering you?"

"No, nothing like that. I just meant you don't have to pretend to be all cheery after I brought up those bad memories of yours. The whistling isn't necessary, especially if you're just doing it 'cause you're upset with me for making you think about something you'd rather keep buried. I know *I* sure get annoyed when people get me to talk and think about things I'd rather not."

Tyce took a moment to ponder what she'd just said. He wanted to be sure his response was correct. "I think," he began slowly, "you misinterpreted the situation a bit. Yeah, I don't like remembering certain things about my time over there, but I wasn't mad at you. I was trying not to make you feel bad about bringing it up. Guess I should have just said something, huh?"

Maureen looked at her feet and laughed through her nose. "I guess I'm not as good at reading people as I should be, either. Definitely not used to people who will forgive me for my mistakes so easily."

"Don't trouble yourself over something as small as this. I'm sure there're a lot of big, unforgivable things you've done that you can dwell on."

"Dick," she said before offering him a quick grin. "Thanks."

"Don't mention it." He decided to lighten the mood and change the subject. "You want me to drop you at the motel?"

"Eh." She shrugged. "How about somewhere close to it where I can get something to eat?"

"Hungry already?" he teased.

"Hey, I got the dough in my pocket from the feds, don't I? I've spent enough of my life going to bed hungry. Might as well make the most of it when I can."

A few minutes later, Tyce pulled over onto the side of the road. Across from them was a collection of storefronts and eateries. He slammed the car into park and began pointing at each of them.

"Pretty much anything you could want," he said. "Sandwiches there, that one's a pub and grill, that's a grocery. Take your pick. You gonna be able to find your way back to the motel from here?"

Maureen looked around. "Yeah. I'm starting to get my bearings around here. It's about a twenty-minute walk down that way, right?"

Tyce nodded. "Well, Ms. Allerton, I'll wish you a good night and pleasant dreams."

Maureen looked back at him and made a face as she opened the door. "Really?"

Tyce reciprocated with a smirk. "See? My turn to make it awkward."

"Mm-hmm," she said, rolling her eyes and jumping out of the truck.

He watched her cross the road before shifting into drive and heading for home. He rubbed his eyes as he drove, beginning to realize how much the day had worn on him. Even a twelve-hour day on horseback at the park didn't take it out of him like these events had. And what made him even more tired was the idea that there was no telling what the morning would bring. Another body? A suspect? Nothing at all? Whatever came, he knew full well that he'd have no control over it. The idea was unnerving. At all other times in his life when he was left to the whims of others, or fate, it hadn't turned out too well for him. He had a bad feeling that this time would be no different. Sighing, Tyce turned on the radio and drummed the steering wheel in time with the music.

Best to put those thoughts out of his head for now, or Maureen wouldn't be the only one having nightmares.

SIXTEEN

Chirurg dried his hands on the course paper towel, scrubbing to make sure every speck of blood had been removed. The body hadn't yielded much—her heart had long stopped beating before he began his dissection—and it didn't pay to be sloppy. As much as he was enjoying working so close to an FBI investigation, one minor slipup and it would be over. All of his work would be for nothing.

He looked over at the woman sitting reclined in his lab chair. It was a shame that he didn't have more time with the body. He had originally planned for her to be the centerpiece of his work, being who she was, but after what he had learned in the last twenty-four hours, he had a new prize to chase. When he first decided to shift his focus, he considered sinking this body in the river like he had the professor's, but science demanded otherwise.

Chirurg crossed the room and stood over her. Through the slit he'd cut in her torso, he could see into the body's cavity. It was almost strange to see the liver, intestines, and lungs still in their proper places. He cast an eye over to the shelves that held his work. Her heart was suspended in a proprietary formaldehyde mixture of his own creation. The heart would preserve in the jar quite well, and he could come back to it later. Chirurg smiled to himself, wondering how long it would take the feds to figure out why he only took the one organ this time.

He shook himself out of his thoughts and reminded himself that avarice wouldn't further his goals. Chirurg took one more look over the body. The sterile smell of the disinfectants he'd used to wipe it down were slowly dissipating. Her once piercing, blue eyes were beginning to show the first signs of clouding. Rigor mortis wouldn't be far behind, but he didn't have to rush. It wasn't quite the right time to venture out. The cover of darkness was to be his ally.

Chirurg stepped into the adjoining room and began to run down his checklist in his mind. Body sterilized. Tarp laid out in his back seat. Check and check. He'll burn the bloody towels in his fireplace when he returns, and there is no need to waste sterilizer on the cement floor and walls in the laboratory itself at the moment. If he needed to move on after this was over, he'd take care of it then. Though really, if that eventuality happened, better to just burn down the whole house. It wasn't in his name anyway, and by the time the authorities could untie all the red tape leading back to him, he'd be long gone.

One more thing remained for tonight, though. Chirurg went to shelf that held his notes and folders filled with other important collections of his work. He opened one of these and pulled out a small, sealed plastic bag. Inside was the last thing he needed to execute his experiment. He slipped the packet into his pocket and cast an eye over to the hook where his sanitary suit was hanging. No traces, no evidence, nothing to forensically tie him to the body.

Chirurg sighed contentedly. He was ready for the next step in his work. He didn't think he'd ever get the chance to take it into this type of uncharted territory. But, as a scientist, he needed more proof before he decided to take the final step. He'd know what he was going to do by the next day. Chirurg grabbed another notebook and flipped to the first blank page. He picked up a pen, and in the upper-left corner, he wrote the words that excited him so:

Allerton, Maureen.

SEVENTEEN

Maureen pushed through the door of the deli with a brown bag filled with a turkey club and some kettle chips in one hand and a fountain drink in the other. She decided to eat light after the lunch she and Tyce had had with the reporter. If she saved her per diem, she could afford a bottle of the good whiskey at the corner liquor mart in another day or two. Tonight, she'd make do with the half bottle of four-dollar white wine in her motel room fridge.

The sun was sinking low in the western sky as she walked toward the motel. Thanks to her little trip with Ranger Tyce, she decided it was of some benefit to her mind to really look around and allow herself a few moments to get lost in her surroundings. Mountain towns were interesting. In her years on the road, she'd driven through only a few, usually preferring to stick to the flatter areas of the country. Something about the heights made her feel slightly uneasy.

The views were beautiful, she could admit that much. The mountains in the distance were majestic, especially against the deep reds, oranges, and purples of the sunset. And if it weren't for the bodies floating in them lately coupled with her fear of hypothermia, she could see herself taking a swim in the rivers and lakes. The buildings on the main drag were spread out and looked like they hadn't had a face-lift since the midcentury, aside from one with a fresh coat of paint here and there. The small businesses that occupied them seemed settled, as if they hadn't changed in decades. Here and there people made their way along the sidewalk, taking their time, much like the cars along the road. Things just moved slower. Even slower than they had in Sycamore Hills. Maureen had once let herself wonder how it might be to settle down there. In the year since, she realized more than ever that wouldn't be her fate. At least not for a long while.

By the time she arrived at the motel, her soda was already gone. She dumped the empty cup in the trash can outside the office and continued to her room. She passed Samuelson's window. Through the half-closed curtains, she could see him sitting at the table inside. He was doing what she'd expect him to: poring over the case files. The man could stand to watch a little TV once in a while.

That sounded like a fine idea. Maureen pushed her way into her room and turned on the set. She clicked through the channels until she found a movie that would entertain her for a while and tossed the remote on the bed. She fished the bottle of wine out of the refrigerator before flopping down and propping herself up against the headboard. She spread her sandwich and chips on the paper bag and began to nibble her food, washing it down with tiny sips from the bottle.

The night had deepened outside her window by the time she finished her food. There were still a few sips of wine left, though. She had been nursing it to make sure it lasted. Maureen stood up and switched off the television. She began to pace the room. The active part of her brain was seeking some kind of stimulation to keep awake. She toyed with the idea of heading out to a bar and finding some sucker to pay for a few drinks. To do that, however, would require getting made up and flirting. She didn't have any makeup, and the thought of putting on a show for a couple of loser townies made her sick. In the end, her body surrendered to fatigue, and she dropped onto the bed. She stared up at the ceiling until the darkness closed in.

She could feel the dead weight in her arms as the night air brushed past her face. The crunch of gravel under her feet echoed in the mask that covered her face. She felt little exertion in the legs of the body her mind inhabited, the arms were strong, and breath came with no more effort than if she were taking a Sunday stroll. The eyes looked down at the load she was carrying. The moonlight revealed the face of a woman, older than middle aged, with gray flecks in her hair. The woman's eyes were open, unblinking and seeing nothing. She could still detect their piercing, blue color under the milky glaze that was beginning to cover them. The part of her mind that she still had mastery of recognized her immediately. It was the same woman she had seen tied in the basement the last time she'd worn the mask. Instinctively, Maureen tried to pull herself out of the horror of the dream. A translucent curtain began to fall, and the familiar blackness began to consume the edges of her vision.

No, a voice inside said. *Stay.*

Maureen let go of her consciousness and allowed the presence in the mask to regain control. She watched as the arms stopped and carefully placed the body down on the rocky ground. Out of the corner of her eyes, she could discern water. As their gaze rose, a river came into view. Its flow was slow, breaking the reflected moon into ribbons. The view from the mask swung to the left, and she could see, far off in the distance, what looked like a concrete wall with water streaming over the edge. Beyond, the mountains changed the color of the sky ever so slightly; there was a bare hint of where they lay. There was little else to be seen. Wherever they were, there was enough ambient light to see the body clearly, but little more.

The eyes looked back down at the body, examining it from head to toe. The woman was naked, and a large red gash was evident running down the middle of her torso. An arm, covered in a bulky white sleeve, reached out. The black-gloved hand—thumb and forefinger pressed together—hovered over the woman's chest. Maureen felt the fingers as they gently pulled apart, and the hand drew back. A deep voice rumbled out of her throat.

"Let's see what they think about that."

The eyes rose up and turned away from the body. The crunching of feet on gravel again hit her ears as they walked away. She could feel the ground gently begin to rise under her feet as she continued on, and soon the darkness parted to reveal a car. The hands reached out again and opened the back door to reveal the back seat covered in plastic. The barest amount of blood was pooled in the middle. She felt the arms reach back and then heard the sound of a zipper being pulled down. The hands threw, what seemed to her eyes, a white jumpsuit on top of the plastic and shut the door. The car began to blur as she walked around to the other side. Darkness covered her vision.

Maureen sat straight upright. She took in a few deep breaths and waited for her heart rate to return to normal. The motel room came into view with the annoying neon light from the sign in the parking lot giving her just enough illumination to see. She felt a familiar sensation begin to roil up in her stomach. She spun her feet onto the floor and reached for the wastebasket under the nightstand. Bringing it up to her knees, she hunched over as a convulsion erupted from her diaphragm. Very little came out. She heaved once more, spat twice, and the queasy feeling passed. Maureen let out a deep breath, returned the basket to its place, and stood up.

"Guess I'm getting deeper into the bastard's head," she muttered to herself as she went to the bathroom. She splashed some water on her face and took a swallow to clear out her mouth before returning to the bedroom and finding a pair of shorts in her bag. She slid them on, pulled her hair back into a ponytail, and—almost mechanically—went out the door.

She made her way to Agent Samuelson's room and knocked. It took a minute for the agent, rubbing the sleep out of his eyes, to answer the door. He seemed taken aback for a moment before he stood to the side and silently beckoned her in. She stepped into the room and took a seat at the table next to the window. Samuelson took a seat on the edge of the bed opposite her and rubbed his temples.

"I assume you're not here on a social visit," he said.

Maureen shook her head.

"You better let me have it, then."

"She's dead. He dumped the body."

Samuelson pushed himself to his feet—letting out a sigh—and paced in front of her for a moment, rubbing his temples. He stopped in front of the window and looked out into the night. "Where?"

"I'm not sure," Maureen replied. "All I know is that he put her next to the river somewhere, but he didn't actually put her in the water."

"That doesn't fit."

"But that's what happened. I stayed with the dream all the way back to his car."

"It's just, why change the MO? He's submerged every other body. Could he have been interrupted or something? Maybe there's someone out there who saw him?"

Maureen shook her head again. "I got the feeling that he did it on purpose, that he wants her to be found."

"Bastard's getting off on this," the agent growled, rubbing the knuckles of his right hand as if he were preparing to punch something.

"Seems that way. I can't be certain, but I think he left something on the body this time. And before you ask, I don't know exactly what it was. There wasn't enough light to see. All I can say is that it'll be small and near her chest."

"Then we'd better find the body fast before the evidence disappears. What else can you remember about where you were?"

"There was a lot of gravel or small rocks near the water. The water itself was flowing, that much I'm sure of. Not fast, but even in the dark I could tell it was moving. There was some kind of concrete wall in the distance. I get the feeling that the water was flowing over it. Does that mean anything to you?"

Samuelson didn't answer. Instead, he reached under the table and past her feet to pull out a bag. He shuffled through it for a moment before pulling out a folded map. He spread the map on the table and stared at it for a long, unwavering moment.

"We're down here," he said to her, tapping on the paper. "The Colorado runs pretty fast as it continues to our southwest, so I'm thinking we can eliminate that. Where you surrounded by the mountains?"

"No, the mountains were in the distance, on the other side of the concrete wall."

"Hmm." The agent rubbed his chin before tracing his finger along the map. "If I'm reading this right, there's an abandoned access road behind this old campground. There's a dam on the south side of the lake here, and the Colorado flows over it. It's not as wide there. I'd venture that it would be flowing at the speed you described. It's also out of the way, so it's very unlikely anyone would have seen him come or go in the middle of the night. It all fits. We'll start our initial search around there."

He didn't seem to be looking for her agreement, but Maureen nodded anyway. He said "we," and she found herself wondering if that meant her as well. She got her answer soon enough.

"I'm going to get dressed and get Turnberry and Navarro up. You can head back to your room if you want."

Maureen took a deep breath. He was giving her a way out if she wanted to take it, but somehow, deep inside, she knew the answer.

"I'm here to do a job." She cringed even as she said the words. "So I'm coming."

Samuelson looked at her for a moment before shrugging. Maureen took it as a dismissal and backed her way out the door.

"Be ready in twenty," the agent's voice called to her as she reached her own door.

Bastard just has to get the last word, she said to herself as she pushed into her room.

EIGHTEEN

Owen sat with his fingers tented under his chin as the car bumped along the packed-dirt road behind the old campgrounds. Sunrise was still over an hour away, but even now the sky was beginning to turn from black to deep purple. Even so, it was going to be necessary to use flashlights to search along the river. The shadows were still deep enough that they might mistake a body for a large rock if they didn't.

Maureen sat in her usual position next to him. Predictably, she had been silent the whole ride from the motel. It wasn't her usual defiant stoicism that lay on her face, though. Even if she were trying to hide it from him, he could sense a change taking place beneath the surface. It was in her eyes. She'd deny it, but the bubbling hatred that lay in them—and that had been directed at him—was being projected in a new direction.

If what he was sensing were indeed the truth, he was unsure how he'd handle it going forward. He had become accustomed to her only saying what she needed to say and no more—that or getting in the odd jab to make her feel like she was in control. He'd made peace enough with that and decided to give her the space that she was looking for. A determined Maureen Allerton was something he was not prepared for.

The headlights of the sedan shined across a county van at the end of the road. Dr. Heim and Dr. Frank stood talking to another man who Owen assumed was the crime scene tech he insisted they needed to bring when he called them. He was a little surprised to see that they had beaten him to the agreed rendezvous spot, but it didn't matter now. Navarro parked the car, and they all got out.

Owen blew his breath as he shut the car door behind him. Even though the doctors were clued in to Maureen's secret, he still felt uneasy about the odd protocol he was asking everyone to follow. If the young tech talked, gossip would soon spread about the FBI secretly removing a body from a crime scene without bringing in the county personnel. Though both doctors held the proper licenses to be at a crime scene, Dr. Heim and Dr. Frank's usual practice was to wait in the lab for the bodies they were to examine. He'd have to take steps to make sure the third man didn't ask too many questions.

"Gentlemen," Owen greeted them gravely as he walked up, "thank you for coming so quickly. The tip we received had indicated that the body of a woman has been left somewhere along the river here. You three are going to head south from this point with Agent Navarro. Agent Turnberry, Ms. Allerton, and I will head in the opposite direction. Whoever finds the body, signal the other party immediately."

The men nodded, and the doctors turned to head down the hill toward the riverbank. The third man hesitated to follow and turned back to Owen.

"Sir, I have to ask. Is this body we're looking for another victim of the person who killed the two National Guardsmen?"

"It's possible," Owen replied flatly.

"Then why are we out here with just me?"

Owen straightened himself to play his authoritative role. "My reasons are quite simple, Mister . . ."

"Glover. Mark Glover."

"My reasons are quite simple, Mr. Glover. First, because this anonymous tip we received cannot be easily verified, and therefore, I don't wish to waste manpower on an endeavor that might prove fruitless. Secondly, and more to the point, because I say so."

The other man let his gaze wander past his shoulder to where he knew Maureen stood. Glover opened his mouth as if to say something, but Owen caught his eye, tilted his head, and raised an eyebrow, daring him to ask another question. Glover got the message, closed his mouth, and turned to follow Navarro and the doctors.

Owen turned himself toward Turnberry and Maureen. "Steve, why don't you start heading down toward the dam, but stay up here along the top of the ridge."

"Footprints and tire tracks?"

Owen nodded. "Precisely. Go slow so you don't miss anything. You know the drill. Maureen and I will take the water's edge and try and find the body."

They parted ways, and he and Maureen headed down the bank. Owen scanned the river at a distance with his flashlight before continuing forward. The ground beneath the gravel deposit was firm, so he didn't hold out much hope of stumbling across any footprints. Still, he held off his body's desire to dash in the direction of the dam. He had a gut feeling the body lay that way, which was why he had chosen it for the direction he and Maureen would search.

They continued on with only the sound of their footsteps breaking the silence. Owen found Maureen in his periphery. She was staring straight ahead, arms folded around herself, barely even seeming to breathe. Owen swung his flashlight side to side, searching for a clear path down the bank. He found a spot of beaten-down grass resembling a track. The slope was gentle enough and seemed free of any impediments. As lightly as they could, he and Maureen made their way onto the gravel-covered shore. Ahead, he could just make out the river, quietly gurgling over the rocks. He placed himself within a few yards of the water and turned to walk northward.

It was only a few short moments before the beam of his flashlight splashed across a large object lying some fifty yards ahead. He put out his arm to stop Maureen. Instinct crept up from inside his stomach, and Owen knew he was about to come face to face with the body they were searching for. Maureen obeyed his silent command, and he stalked forward slowly, examining the ground closely. As he neared the body, he came upon a row of rounded divots leading from the bank on his left down toward the river. There was no visible tread within the imprint, but he hadn't expected there would be. Still, he took them for footprints and made an effort not to step on them. It was possible that they could get at least an idea of the shoe size of the perpetrator. It was a small thing, but it may help narrow down the suspect pool.

Owen made his way to the body. The woman was lying on her back, head cocked to the side as if she were staring out over the river. Her eyes, however, were dull and clouding over, but as the light from his flashlight washed over them, he could still detect the blue color that Maureen had described from her dream. He could make out a thin line running from her navel up her torso and ending between her breasts. He knew it to be the line of a razor cut and was sure once the autopsy was done, they would find the cavity to be empty just like the others.

As he squatted down next to the body, Owen heard the trepidatious footsteps of Maureen crunching on the gravel behind him. He turned to look up at her. She stopped a few feet behind him and was staring past him at the body. Her face was steady, but her body seemed tense and uneasy. He knew from his file on her that she'd seen a dead body before, but it was clear to him that it still disturbed her. He inserted himself into her line of sight and tilted his head to invite her to come closer. If the FBI were going to keep using her, she'd better toughen up.

Maureen came forward another step and knelt on the ground next to him. Owen felt himself about to wince, but he smoothed his face and caught himself. A quick glance around confirmed her knees hadn't disturbed any of the imprints around the body. They continued to stare at the body as the first rays of the morning sun began to break over the mountains. The purple glow of dawn made his flashlight obsolete, yet he continued to point it at the body until its beam had completely disappeared. Finally, he clicked it off and turned to Maureen.

"Is this her?" he asked.

Maureen nodded but said nothing.

Owen nodded back. Privately, he hoped she'd gotten it wrong—if only so that he didn't have to continue to believe in all this psychic nonsense—but deep down he knew his hope was in vain. She was who everyone said she was, and he knew he'd better become okay with that. If nothing else, she'd gotten him to this body ahead of the press. With any luck, they'd be able to remove it and keep this murder from the news cycle for a few extra days. No need to panic a public that was already on edge.

Rising from the ground, Owen pulled his phone out of his pocket and hit the speed dial.

"Steve," he said once Agent Turnberry answered on the other end, "we got the body. Where are you?"

"About five hundred yards from the dam, still on top of the bank."

"Find anything?"

"I might have a tire track, but I'm not sure. Ground's pretty bare, so there's not much to put an imprint in. I marked it with a flag just in case."

"All right, we'll have a look at it after we evacuate the corpse. Why don't you head back toward us. We're only a little more than half a klick south of you. Call in the doctors on your way."

"Be there in a few."

Owen hung up the phone and put it back in his pocket. He looked out again at the river, now beginning to show the first signs of glinting in the gathering gloom. He could make out the ragged clouds that wrapped themselves around the setting moon in the western sky. The world was quiet. The world was always quiet when he was standing over a body. The urge to break the silence with some sort of small talk with Maureen came over him, but he pushed it away almost as quickly. There was nothing to be gained from useless banter. Instead, he pulled out his personal camera from his jacket's inner pocket and snapped a few pictures of the dead woman's face. Hopefully they'd be clear enough to get a jump on identifying her without having to wait for the crime scene photos to be developed.

The sound of footsteps from his left signaled Turnberry's arrival. Owen turned and nodded at the other agent as he approached the body. Turnberry shined his flashlight down on the body but shut it off when it became apparent that it was invisible in the growing light. He moved carefully to stand by Owen.

"No sign of submersion," Turnberry said quietly. "We sure this is our guy?"

"It's him," came Maureen's voice from behind them.

Both men turned to look at her. She was staring down at the corpse as if lost in her own thoughts. After a moment, she looked up at them, and the look in her eyes seemed to be one of a person who hadn't expected to be heard.

"You're sure?" Agent Turnberry asked, taking a step toward her. "With all due respect, Ms. Allerton, I don't know how this whole hocus pocus you do is supposed to work. You've said yourself you can't control it. It could be that you've connected with someone else, and we have two killers running around now. The original and a copycat."

Owen said nothing but continued to stare at the woman. Maureen's mouth twisted ever so slightly, and he saw her hands start to clench. She didn't like being questioned.

"It's him," she said firmly.

"Okay, fine." Turnberry threw his hands up. "It's just a departure from his MO is all I'm saying."

"He did it on purpose. To mess with us. You're also going to find something on her chest."

"And what might that be?" Owen chimed in.

"I don't know. Something small, almost invisible. But I have a feeling it'll be important."

Before Owen could ask anything else, his eyes were drawn to the approach of Dr. Heim, Dr. Frank, and Glover. He waved them over and indicated to Turnberry and Maureen that they should give the three men some room. "All right, boys, let's do the quick standard sweep and get this body back to the slab for the autopsy."

Glover looked at him. "Sir, shouldn't we—"

"No," interrupted Owen. "Sweep the body for any trace evidence and see if we can get anything from these prints."

Glover squinted down at the depressions around the body. "I don't know what I can get out of these. There's no tread mark and no discernible shape."

"Just get me a general measurement, then." Owen sighed. He was growing tired of the young man's contradictions. "If nothing else, it'll at least narrow it down to a couple possible sizes. I can work with that."

The younger man's head dropped, and he loped toward the body. Owen watched as he squatted down and began to look it over. Glover pulled forceps out of his bag and began to open the flap of skin between the woman's breasts to get a look inside the cavity. Owen turned quickly toward Maureen. Her eyes flashed, and she quickly jerked her head in the other man's direction.

"Hang on a second, son," Owen called. "Before you go opening up the body, why don't you do a quick once-over on her skin. Focus on the torso."

"Anything in particular I should be looking for?" Glover was not doing a great job at hiding his feeling that he was being talked down to. Owen tried to pay it little notice.

"It'll be small, but you'll probably know it when you see it. You might find a black light helpful—if you have one in your pack."

Glover reached into his bag and pulled out a small black light. He slowly began sweeping it over the body. A moment later, he let out a knowing hum.

"You find something?" Owen asked.

"Seems so." Glover carefully closed his forceps on something and held it up.

Owen squinted closely and could just make out a thin hair. "Bag it and make sure it's labeled as critical." He turned his eyes back up to Maureen. She stared back, her eyes filled with intensity.

"Critical?" came Glover's skeptical voice.

"Just do it," he replied, walking back toward Maureen and Turnberry and signaling to the doctors to join them.

"Glover is bagging a hair found on the body," Owen said once they were in a semicircle. "I want you guys to pay special attention and analyze it quickly. I got a feeling it might be important."

Dr. Frank and Dr. Heim glanced at each other. It was clear to Owen that they had been watching his interactions with Maureen and Glover.

Dr. Frank turned to Maureen. "You knew it was there, didn't you?"

"I knew *something* was there," she said quietly, staring at her feet uncomfortably. "I didn't know what exactly."

"We don't need to talk about it anymore right now," Owen said quickly. "Get the body back to the office as soon as you can. We'll come by later this afternoon to discuss your findings. Hopefully by then we'll know who she is and if she has any connection to the others. We're going to head out. See if Glover can get anything from the tire tracks to the north up top. Turnberry left a flag for him to find."

The doctors said nothing, simply nodding and turning to join Glover at the body.

Owen led the others back up the bank toward their car. He pulled his camera out of his pocket again as they walked and handed it over to Turnberry. "Let's see if we can get the boys in tech to do facial recognition on these. Download them and run them against missing person reports."

"Nationwide sweep just to be safe?" Turnberry asked.

Owen nodded. "MO would indicate that our killer knew her and she was local, but nothing about the scene fits the MO, so we might as well cast a wider net."

As the group approached the car, Owen was met with the last sight he wanted to see. Standing next to the sedan and jawing away at Navarro—who didn't seem as annoyed as he himself would have been—was Gabriel Lowdon. Owen bristled at the sight of the reporter. How on earth could he have known they were out here? If he ever found this source inside the bureau feeding the man information, he'd strangle him. If such a person even existed. Owen was still not completely convinced.

"Good morning, Agent," the reporter greeted him with mock sincerity. "Out for a little sunrise body discovery, I take it?"

"Lowdon, I don't have time to wage our little war of words," Owen grumbled as he pushed past the other man and reached for the door handle. He could feel the reporter's mocking grin burning the back of his head.

"Never mind about all that," he heard Lowdon say. "I'm not really here to talk to you anyway. I'm more interested in continuing my conversation with your *psychic* profiler here."

The sound of the word *psychic* made Owen's head snap around. Lowdon was already stepping up next to Maureen, who had been hanging back herself, arms still folded across her chest.

"What d'you say, Ms. Allerton?" Lowdon said to her. "I could tell there were things you wanted to tell me at our lunch meeting."

Maureen said nothing. She simply stared at the reporter, then turned her eyes to look at Owen. Owen tilted his head at her, irked by the notion that she'd been speaking to Lowdon without his knowledge. Her brow furrowed as she pulled from his gaze.

"Nothing to say?" Lowdon continued, unabashed. "Maybe my charm and good looks have got you tongue tied. It's all right, I can untie it—if you catch my drift."

Lowdon reached out and twirled a strand of Maureen's hair in his fingers. Maureen's hand flew up and knocked his hand away. Undeterred, he tried to move close to her again. She responded with a hard slap across his face. Lowdon's head snapped to the side with the force of her blow. The outline of her hand burned red on his cheek. The look of shock and indignation made Owen want to laugh.

"You might just earn yourself a lawsuit there, babe." Lowdon rubbed his face.

"I think not," Owen interjected.

"Think you can stop me, Agent?"

"Actually, I can. Try it, and I'll make your life a living hell. And believe me, I would love for you to test me. Besides, the way I saw it, you molested Maureen first. I'm sure Turnberry and Navarro will agree."

Lowdon held Owen's gaze for a moment and then turned his back on him. He glanced back at Maureen before tucking his tail and walking up the road toward his car. Owen opened the door to the sedan and motioned for Maureen to get in. She obliged, however grudgingly.

"Why didn't you tell me you had lunch with Gabriel Lowdon?" Owen huffed once they were settled into their seats and driving back toward town.

"Didn't seem important," Maureen indignantly replied.

"He's a parasite, and I don't want any information leaking out to the press about what's going on."

"I'm not stupid," she snapped. "He just ambushed me and Ranger Tyce yesterday morning. Tyce used to be married to his sister. I guess that made him think he could get in good with us."

"You saying I'm going to have to bar Tyce from continuing to help with this case?"

"No," she sneered. "I think all of Lowdon's conspiracy talk bores him. Neither of us said anything. We mostly just sat there as he talked about something called *Stargate*. Claimed that you guys at the bureau were starting it up again and that I must be the focal point of it. Is that true?"

"I don't know of any psychic we use outside of you," Owen mumbled, looking out the window. He sat staring for a few minutes, wondering if he should even bother asking the next question on his mind. "You know anything else about that hair they found?"

"Like what?"

"Like where it's from or what the significance is? I don't appreciate you holding out on me when people are dying."

"I've told you everything I've seen," she snapped. "It's not my fault if you still don't believe me."

Her point was a fair one, Owen had to concede. He had been looking for any misstep in her viewings, but so far there had been none, unless one counted the name mix-up with the earlier victim. It might go easier for him if he just went along with it.

"Fine," he replied. "I'll agree to believe what you tell me if you just promise me that you're telling me everything."

She said nothing but shrugged her shoulders and nodded her head before turning away from him to look out the car window and into the growing morning light.

NINETEEN

Owen leafed through the contents of the folder he was carrying as he walked through the lower hallways of the medical examiner's building. He did it mindlessly. He'd read through the information four or five times since Turnberry handed it to him just after lunch and had it all but memorized.

He looked ahead toward the door to the examination room. Maureen, Ranger Tyce, and Turnberry were waiting for him. Now that he saw the group, he began to have second thoughts about having all of them in the room—and by all, he really meant the ranger. With the information that has been seeping through the cracks in the investigation thus far, it may be a better idea to have fewer people in the room with the doctors. After all, Tyce *was* well acquainted with Lowdon. He could easily be feeding his former brother-in-law information, despite what Maureen said. And Maureen herself, harboring the animosity that she did, could also easily be the source of the leak.

Can't be thinking like that. The reporter seemed to know about Maureen even before the ranger truly became inserted into the investigation. And Maureen seemed to hate Lowdon even more than she hated him. Best to have them in on this.

If any of the information disseminated in the next hour or so ended up in the public record, he'd know more.

Owen nodded to the group as he approached and pushed through the double doors. The pale, fluorescent light illuminated the body, which was modestly covered by a light-blue cloth. Both Dr. Heim and Dr. Frank were standing a pace or two from the victim, waiting for him. Her eyes had been closed by one of the doctors. He stepped up to the side of the table on which she lay, looked at her face, and sighed. Her name was written on a piece of paper in his file.

"Thank you all for coming," he said to the assembled party as he stepped to the front of the room. He was pleased to see that the whiteboard and magnets he requested were set up. He reached into his folder and pulled out the picture on top of the rest of the papers, fixing it to the board. "Our victim is Lynn Sandburg, fifty-six years old. Originally from Eugene, Oregon, she was last seen leaving one of her homes in Henderson, Nevada, five days ago and was reported missing by friends in the area approximately thirty hours later."

"One of her homes?" Ranger Tyce asked.

"Ms. Sandburg is quite a wealthy woman," Owen explained. "She owns property in Nevada, San Francisco, Oregon, and Washington."

"How's that work?" Dr. Frank piped up.

"Steve?" Owen said, nodding to the other agent.

"Ms. Sandburg's parents developed a proprietary artificial heart valve that is currently used in nearly half of the aortic valve replacements in the country. Ms. Sandburg herself has a PhD in biomedical engineering and has used her trust money to fund research in numerous areas, but all of them focus on improving surgical technology to make it not only more cost effective for the medical professionals and, therefore, the consumer, but also to decrease the frequency of tissue rejection among patients. Outside of her three residential properties, the remainder of her extensive real estate portfolio consists of commercial buildings, which both house her research facilities and provide her with extra income through the renting out of the remaining space."

"That's some woman," Ranger Tyce blurted out.

"Indeed she is," Owen said. "And now she's lying on that slab, and we need to figure out why. Thank you, Agent Turnberry. Doctors, if you want to take the floor and present your findings?"

Dr. Frank and Dr. Heim stepped forward. The older man nodded to the younger.

"Close-spectrum analysis of the cuts on the torso indicate that the same style of blade was used to open up the cavity and remove the inner organs," Dr. Frank began. "As with the other victims, preliminary toxicology indicates that death was the result of a ketamine overdose. Based on blood coagulation in the wounds, we estimate that death occurred between four and ten hours before the perpetrator began their dissections. Unlike the other victims, only the heart was removed in this case."

"So you have a clearer time of death?" Owen asked.

"Absolutely," Dr. Heim chimed in. "Liver temperature puts time of death a little more than twenty-four hours before we found her."

"And what about the hair that was found on the body?"

"Dr. Frank?" Dr. Heim said, nodding to the other doctor.

Dr. Frank cleared his throat. The young man looked pleased with himself. "The hair was not a DNA match to any sample in the FBI database. But on a hunch, I decided to compare its morphology with the hair samples of the other victims. It turns out that the hair is a match to Christopher Niemann."

Owen nodded his head. He wasn't quite sure how to feel about this bit of information. On the one hand, it tied this body—which otherwise had no connection—to the other victims. On the other hand, he had hoped that the hair belonged to the killer, and even if they found no match now, they might be able to match it to a suspect later. Maureen was right, though. This bastard was enjoying what he was doing and was so confident that he was beginning to taunt them. *Let him,* Owen thought. Overconfident criminals trip up sooner or later. Sooner, if he had any say. "Any other trace evidence?" Owen asked, eager to move the conversation on.

"No other foreign DNA and no particulates in the skin outside of those matching the dump site," Dr. Heim replied. "We were able to discern the residue of an acidic cleanser on the body, however."

"Anything unusual about the chemical makeup?"

Dr. Heim shook his head. "It's a fairly common chemical compound. It's found in most industrial cleaners as well as in the sanitation solutions used in any hospital, laboratory, or high school chemistry lab."

"So the killer was smart enough to scrub the body using common enough chemicals that would make tracing them impossible."

Dr. Heim nodded.

"And we didn't find any trace of this stuff on the other victims?"

"Those other bodies were submerged in water," Dr. Frank said. "The chemicals are easily washed away in water."

Owen drummed a knuckle on the table. "What did Glover have to say about the footprints?"

"He was able to narrow down the potential shoe size to between a men's size nine and twelve," Dr. Frank said.

"Well that's something," Owen grumbled.

"What about the tire tracks that I marked?" asked Turnberry.

Owen shook his head. "The tires treads are those of the most popular size and brand in the United States. They don't even narrow it down to a domestic or foreign vehicle, only that it wouldn't be larger than your standard sporting SUV and it doesn't have four-wheel drive. So that gives us just under forty-five hundred vehicles registered within thirty square miles that we'd need to check out."

The other men cast their eyes downward, acknowledging the fruitless effort that would be.

"All right," Owen sighed, rubbing his eyes, "I think the key is going to lie in connecting these people to each other. There has to be a place where all their lives intersect."

"Are you thinking they might all be into something shady?" asked Dr. Frank.

"I suppose it's possible, but I find it unlikely. From everything we can tell, these folks all have perfectly clean backgrounds."

"Not all of Ms. Sandburg's financials have come back yet," Turnberry offered. "Maybe there's a skeleton hiding in what we haven't seen."

"I just don't see it." Owen said. "I mean, obviously and by all means, keep digging, but my gut tells me we're not going to find a connection between a respected university professor, a scrupulously ethical money manager, and an Olympic-caliber swimmer in the financial history of a second-generation patron of the medical research community."

"Forgive me for interrupting," Ranger Tyce broke in, "but maybe that's the key to finding the connection between these folks."

"How do you mean?" Turnberry asked.

"Well, it's just that we keep talking about how great these people are. They've all done really special things in their lives. And there's something that I remember Ms. Allerton saying in my car a few nights ago."

"What did she say?" Owen broke in before Maureen could speak.

Tyce looked apologetically at the young woman. "Well," he began slowly, turning back toward Owen, "when I was driving her north, intending to take her home after your spat, I guess she had one of those dreams that you all keep talking about. As she was coming out of it, I heard her very clearly say the word '*impressive*.' I didn't think much of it until now."

"Do you remember this?" Owen asked, rounding on Maureen. He hoped their agreement for transparency hadn't fallen on deaf ears.

"No," she said firmly. "I mean, I *have* remembered what I said in dreams before, but it's usually only after I hear it again while I'm awake. Or when I've been connected to the person for a while. But that was the first connection I made, so I usually only remember words I see or symbols that stick out."

"Sounds very convenient," retorted Owen. He shouldn't have said that, but he didn't much like the idea that she, a supposed psychic, couldn't see everything she should and that so much had to be left to chance that she'd see something useful and then remember it after. However, she had been on the mark as far as the name of the latest victim was concerned and about the hair they found on the body. The only other person who could have known at the time she told him was the killer himself.

"I respect your idea, Ranger Tyce," he continued after a few moments, "and I'll keep it in mind, but I think we need to focus on where else these folks' lives could have intersected. We find a common thread or a person they all have in common, and we find our killer."

Owen looked around the room. Tyce nodded his head. Maureen folded her arms and stared to the side, like she always did. Dr. Frank was scribbling notes on his clipboard. Then his eyes fell on Dr. Heim. The doctor was staring down at the body with a blank look on his face.

"Dr. Heim?" Owen said.

"Huh?" the doctor said, shaking his head and looking up.

"You seem distracted. Is everything all right?"

"Of course. It's just that, no matter how often I see a body like this, it still affects me."

There was an odd tone in the doctor's voice; Owen had never heard him speak like this before. In all of his dealings with Dr. Heim, he always came across as a man who could separate his personal feelings from the professional necessities of the job. Facts were always paramount. There was something different about this case. He'd have to keep an eye on the doctor and make sure whatever it was didn't stop him from doing his job.

"Okay," he said to the group, "we got a lot of work to do, so let's get to it. Maureen and Ranger Tyce, I don't think we need anything more from you today, so you can head wherever you'd like for tonight. We'll reconvene tomorrow. Steve, we'll head back to the motel and see if Navarro has gotten any more back from HQ."

As they all left the doctors to finish dealing with the body, Owen allowed the ranger and Maureen to get a little ways ahead of him before grabbing Turnberry by the arm and slowing their pace.

"Need a word, Steve," he said, lowering his voice.

"Shoot, boss."

Owen looked back over his shoulder before continuing. "I think we need to keep a close eye on the doctors."

"I was going to bring that up. The MO for these murders has to indicate some kind of medical training, yes?"

"Not only that. I'm getting a funny feeling from Heim. That line he just gave in there—I've never heard him talk like that. There's something different about him with this body, I think. But let's keep it quiet until we figure out what it is. It might turn out to be nothing."

"I'll have the boys at the office get to work as soon as I can."

"Good. And have them dig into Frank and all the other doctors and surgeons practicing in the area as well. We'll want all our bases covered."

They walked the rest of the hall before Turnberry broke the silence. "What do you really think of her?"

"Maureen?"

"Yeah. I know she's only here because the bosses made us bring her. And I know that's gotta piss you off because you think they're telling you that you can't get this one done on your own."

"That's not necessarily true." It wasn't exactly false, either.

"Well, if it makes you feel any better, I certainly feel that way sometimes. But that's not the point. I just mean, Ms. Allerton's as stubborn a person as I've ever seen. She seems almost angry when she does the right thing. Sometimes I wonder if she'd rather let this guy get away with murder than do something to help."

"I could have told you that just from her file."

"Well, all I can say is this: it's enough work trying to catch this sick bastard without having to decode her dreams on top of it. I'll do what I'm asked and I won't complain, but she'd better pay off in a big way soon outside of just leading us to the bodies."

"You call this not complaining?" Owen scoffed.

Turnberry shrugged and nodded as they began to climb the stairs to the street level. They had almost reached the door to exit the stairwell when Turnberry decided to speak again. "She is easy on the eyes, though." He was trying too hard to sound nonchalant.

"When's Katie due again?" Owen replied stiffly—not that he had to remind his partner of his pregnant wife, or his six-year-old daughter for that matter. He simply knew where this conversation was headed, and he would do anything to prevent it from reaching its destination.

"I wasn't talking about for me," Turnberry persisted, undeterred. "It's okay to admit it, even if you don't like her. It's been long enough, boss."

They had reached the hallway, and Owen picked up his step just a little to avoid backhanding the other agent. Now he turned and stared hard at his partner. Why did Steve always have to take it one step too far?

"You know better than anyone not to go there," he said in a low voice.

Turnberry stood still but didn't break eye contact with him. "It wasn't your fault."

His fortitude surprised Owen. Steve had the habit of trying to get him to open up about this topic, but usually, when he said he didn't want to talk about it, Steve would back down without another word. Maybe his glare wasn't as intimidating after eight years. Owen turned without saying another word and kept a pace ahead of Turnberry for the remainder of their walk.

They rounded the last corner before entering the main lobby of the building. Pushing through the glass doors at the front, the agents exited into the bright afternoon sun and began to make their way to the car. Owen could see Navarro's head through the driver's-side door. The younger agent was drumming on the steering wheel, probably listening to some of that God-awful music he liked. His suspicions were confirmed when, as they drew nearer, Navarro noticed the approach of the two senior agents and leaned to the side to turn off the radio. The car was silent when Turnberry opened the passenger door.

"I'm going to walk for a bit," Owen said. He was looking at Navarro, but Turnberry must have realized he was clearly talking to him.

"Come on, boss," he said apologetically. "Forget what we were talking about. Just get in."

"Rick, come on back here in an hour to pick me up. We'll grab something on the way back, and we'll have a working dinner at the motel before we turn in for the night." He leaned in to Turnberry. "I just need some time to organize my thoughts on the case and decide what we should focus on next."

The other agent didn't seem to believe it any more than he did, but Turnberry—despite a twisting of his mouth—nodded and closed the door. Owen watched the car drive away before turning and ambling in the opposite direction. There was nothing much to look at, as the coroner's building was on the state highway outside the main town with only the other municipal buildings nearby, but he wouldn't be looking at the sights anyway. He kept his head down. He was still on the section of the highway that—while there were no sidewalks—provided a wide berth between a pedestrian and traffic. He was in no danger of veering into the road, even if he wasn't watching where he was going.

Deep inside he detested the necessity of these moments when he was in need of solitude. It felt like weakness, even though the suggestion to do so was about the only useful thing the shrink had given him. He had always believed that a man should be able to handle anything without falling to pieces, but as the years rolled along and age began to pile up on his mind as well as his body, he began to realize the necessity of being alone and stilling one's mind. Owen stopped his feet and raised his face to the west, heaving a loud sigh he was grateful no one would hear. He was a man whose life was counted in bodies, and if he tried hard enough, he might even be able to remember the names of all of them.

But one name would define him until the end of his days.

†WEN†Y

Maureen turned off the faucet and stepped out of the shower. She lost track of how long she had stood under the water, trying to wash off the filth of the day. The sight of the dead woman, Lynn Sandburg, lying in front of her on the slab painted the insides of her eyelids every time she closed them. Adding that to the memory of seeing her both bound and gagged and laid motionless on the riverbank in her dreams, she decided that she was better off trying to stay awake until the killer slept.

She dried herself and dressed quickly, not bothering to look in the mirror. She knew that if she caught her reflection in the glass, she'd be a prisoner in the bathroom for an eternity. Although it might go a long way toward her goal of making it at least until a few hours before sunrise, the inevitable self-assessment would force her to seek the bottle.

Maureen left the towel on the floor and shuffled into the bedroom. The twilight was leaking in between the half-open window curtains as she searched around for a distraction. She grabbed the remote to the television and propped herself on the bed, probing through the channel guide to find an exciting show or action movie to keep her alert. She found one that sounded like a fit and turned up the volume to make sure her eyes stayed open.

Thank goodness for cable, she thought.

The deep of night surrounded her as she stared through the mask. She heard the breathing rasping in her ears as she slowly sneaked through the parking lot. The eyes looked up to see the neon sign spelling out "Bed Head Inn." The light of the sign lit up the air around it to reveal the rain pouring down from the night sky. She became aware of the sensation of water dripping down her face as the eyes turned back toward the row of motel room doors.

The sound of the rain and the thud of footsteps splashing across the wet pavement replaced the sound of the breath in her ears. The eyes bobbed up and down in time with each stride taken, and within moments the doors came up to meet her. The eyes inside the mask darted back and forth, searching. The numbers on the doors came into focus, and slowly the eyes crept forward along the sidewalk in front of them until they stood looking at the number nine.

The eyes looked down at the doorknob, and a hand reached out to grab hold. At that moment, she became aware of a dull noise to her left. The eyes, seemingly startled, snapped ninety degrees, and she was aware of a blue glow pouring out through the window. Slowly, she felt the body press its back to the brick wall and begin to slide toward the window. The muffled sound of the television gently rose as the eyes found themselves staring into the motel room. The ghostly outline of a head stared back from the glass, but the drawn-up hood of a jacket concealed the face within.

The inside of the motel room was awash in the same blue glow that leaked through the window. The television, playing a different movie than the one she last remembered watching, was casting its light onto a figure sprawled out on the bed. As the eyes stared, the part of her mind that wasn't hers began to tingle with what she could only describe as a perverse sense of anticipation. She continued to watch and quickly became aware that she was looking upon her own body through the window. Her eyes were squeezed shut, and her chest rose and fell with shallow, rapid breaths. Every now and then, her head snapped to one side or the other.

Maureen reached out with her own consciousness and began to feel her own sense of danger and dread. She tugged as hard as she could, trying desperately to break the connection. He was here, right outside. She needed to escape.

Maureen felt her eyes fly open, and she sat bolt upright on the bed. Her eyes darted around the room, and she felt her heart pounding against her sternum. She shook her head and rubbed her temples as she tried to calm herself. The sound of the gunfire on the television hammered into her skull—forcing her to confront the notion that a searing migraine was in her future—so she groped with one hand to find the remote and turned it off. The room plunged into darkness, and she sat for a moment before the realization of what she had just witnessed slowly crept back into her mind.

Maureen went stiff. Was he still out there, lurking in the dark? Was he still watching her? She inched her eyes toward the window, silently hoping that she wouldn't see the ghoulish face of a killer filling the pane. There was nothing there, and she worked up the courage to leave the bed and tiptoe across the room to look out into the parking lot. The rain continued to pour, but she could see little else. She began to feel as if she could stop holding her breath.

Her exhale was cut short as a huge shadow darted across the window and sped off to her right. Maureen felt herself fly back a step before she regained her footing. Without a second thought, she yanked the door open and ran out. She had just enough composure left to bang on the door of room number eight before wheeling around and sprinting in the direction that she had seen the shadow go. She pounded a fist on Turnberry's door on the way past and shouted at the top of her lungs, "He's here!"

Between the raindrops ahead, she saw the figure disappear around the corner of the building. Her legs wouldn't allow her to slow and wait for the agents, despite the shock of the concrete stinging her bare feet. She ran hard after the Peeping Tom, but by the time she found herself in the alley behind the motel, the sound of his footsteps had been swallowed up by the night. Maureen gritted her teeth and stalked forward a few more steps. Nothing moved except the wind-driven rain. Still, something about the abandoned alley troubled her to the point where she decided she couldn't go any farther. She retreated but only turned her back after she was safely in the open.

As she rounded the corner and stepped back into the dim light of the parking lot, she was met by the sight of both Turnberry and Samuelson running toward her, T-shirts and shorts sticking to their bodies, with guns drawn.

"What happened?" shouted Samuelson over the rain, droplets of water spouting from his lips.

"He was here," Maureen gasped, realizing that she had been holding her breath. "He was watching me while I slept. I saw it. He ran around the back of the building and disappeared. I couldn't keep up."

"Did you see his face?"

Maureen shook her head. "He was wearing a hood."

"Steve," he said to the other agent, "why don't you head around back, and I'll head in the other direction. If he's hiding somewhere back there, we'll surround him."

Turnberry nodded in agreement and jogged back around the building. Samuelson began to head in the opposite direction, past the line of motel room doors, and toward the other end of the parking lot. Suddenly he stopped and turned back to her.

"Don't follow me," he said. "Go back to your room and wait with Agent Navarro."

"Don't tell me what to do," Maureen scoffed, offended that he didn't think she could handle herself. She followed him.

They loped along, Samuelson moving his pistol from side to side and Maureen giving him three or four paces of space. The rain began to fall even harder as they went along, and she became aware of how soaked through she was. She now regretted her choice of a white T-shirt, and she crossed her arms in front of her chest. The agents hadn't appeared to take notice, or else they didn't care, but if they caught the guy, she'd be damned if she was going to give him something else to ogle.

A crash of metal in the alley shook her out of her thoughts, and she looked up to see Samuelson running ahead of her toward the corner of the building. Maureen trotted behind but hung back to keep watch. As the agent slowed to approach the corner, a dark figure sprinted past him and took off toward the road. Samuelson immediately took off after him and joined Turnberry, who was a few steps behind, in pursuit. Samuelson caught up to the fugitive within seconds and managed to cut him off. The suspect stopped in his tracks, and the sound of the agents' orders were muffled by the rain. They must have told him to get on his knees, though, because the third man raised his hands in the air and knelt down. Maureen could just make out the sight of Turnberry slowing and holding his gun on the suspect as he helped his partner yank the kneeling figure to his feet.

"I thought I told you not to follow me," Samuelson grumbled. "You're not trained, and you're a civilian. You could have gotten hurt."

"I'm not as helpless as all that. Besides, it's my life and it was me he was creeping on, so it's personal. If I want to go and get myself killed, that's my business. Think of it like this: if that happens, you and the rest of the feds won't have to worry about me anymore." The agent glared at her and ground his teeth. "At least let me see who the fucker is."

Samuelson let out an exasperated sigh. "Fine. I don't have time to argue with you. Just stay behind me."

The two agents led the man, hood still drawn against the rain, back toward the motel and shoved him against the brick wall. Maureen cautiously came over to get a look at the monster who had decided to hunt her now. Secretly, she hoped the agents would let her get a punch or two in on him before they led him away.

Turnberry had just ripped the hood off the man's head and spun him around to face them when she came up. Her feet stopped short as the parking lot's lights lit up his face. She recognized him instantly. So did Samuelson.

"Well, well, well," he said, pressing his gun into the man's chest.

†wen†y-one

Owen couldn't help but allow himself the smallest of grins as he stared through the tinted window into the interrogation room where Gabriel Lowdon sat handcuffed to the table, squirming in his chair. He made sure the reporter had been afforded every discomfort in the holding cell. He knew it was vindictive, but it also had a purpose. All he had on the man was that he was found in the alley behind the motel after a psychic insisted that she saw him staring through her window in a dream. He couldn't use that as his reasoning for holding him, so he needed a confession. And that meant he needed his suspect to be as tired, confused, and uncomfortable as possible—to give him an edge.

What complicated matters even more was that Lowdon had given Turnberry alibis for the last two murders. Turnberry was running them down now. Owen prayed they weren't good, but he knew better than to pin his hopes on that. He needed to maintain his focus on the task at hand: breaking the man. He let out a big sigh and opened the door.

"I gotta say, Lowdon," he said as he entered the room, "I'd be lying if I said I was surprised that I found you stalking Ms. Allerton."

"Are those her words?" Lowdon asked. "Is that what she calls being kind enough to take her and my dear ex-brother-in-law out for a nice lunch?"

"No. I'd call that a veteran move from a professional weasel trying to pump some information out of my people."

"And her unprovoked slap at the crime scene yesterday? Despite your protection of her, I'd still be perfectly within my rights to file assault charges."

"Please. Don't pretend like she hit you that hard. Besides, you had it coming. No, Lowdon, we move into stalking when you get caught peeping through her window at two in the morning."

"Agent, this is all a big misunderstanding."

"Well then, please, enlighten me."

"Obviously, yes, I was keeping an eye on the motel once I found out where you guys were staying. But you have to understand: I've got a loyal readership that expects me to go to depths that other journalists won't to expose the truth." Owen couldn't help but snort at his bravado, but Lowdon continued as if he hadn't heard. "They deserve to know that the FBI dabbles in the paranormal to help solve their crimes. I've been saying it for years: it's not simply grunt police work that gets the job done as you like to profess. Our government hides too much from the people, and they need to be held accountable. I'm not some crackpot spouting out tinfoil theories, Agent. I've told you flat out that my information comes from people in the know. I'm not hiding anything.

"But that's beside the point. This isn't about our personal battle. This is about last night. I know what it looks like, but it's not. I was in my car in the parking lot over by the door to the office. It was almost 1:30, and I'd just woken up from a snooze when I saw someone walking through the rain toward the side of the motel that I knew you three were staying in. It struck me as odd that someone would be out in that weather first of all, but it struck me more so that whoever it was acted like they didn't want to be seen. Moving real slow. Sneaking almost. I got a strange feeling in my stomach, but I didn't want to go out in the storm, so I waited and watched.

"It was hard to see, but it looked like they were reaching for the knob of one of the doors but got distracted by something. Next thing they did was crouch down by the window and just stared inside the room. It was at that point that I just said screw it, threw up my hood, and got out of my car. Something spooked the peeper, and they took off around the back of the building. I guess maybe they heard me or saw me? Don't ask me why, but I decided to follow and sprinted after them. But they had too big a lead, and I never caught up to them. I found a hole in the fence behind the alley that led into a thick grassy area. I figured the peeper went that way, but I didn't want to go barreling after them in the dark and rain.

"That's when I heard a yell behind me and saw Agent Turnberry running toward me. I didn't know it was him at first, I just saw a gun. So I ran. Obviously, I just figured that whoever was messing around the motel had armed backup, and I didn't feel like my investigation was worth getting shot over. It wasn't until you got in front of me that I realized what was going on."

"Turnberry insists that he announced himself," Owen broke in. "I can file charges for evading a federal agent if I see fit."

"Water and wind in my ears. I can't be expected to understand what he's saying. I'm sure you'd agree it's a pretty thin charge to hold me on."

Owen slowly got out of his chair and made his way behind the reporter. He stared intently at the back of the other man's head, trying to pick up anything. Lowdon was confident, almost cocky. If he was lying, he was committed to the act. He gripped the back of the reporter's chair and leaned in to talk in his ear.

"You know, I've read some of your stuff over the years. You're a very good writer. I mean that. You have a rare gift of injecting just enough truth into your stories that the exaggerations—or let's be fair, lies—are so easy to swallow. Or you report only the ugly side of a story and conveniently leave out an important fact that would have otherwise moved the sensational into the mundane. In either case, you would have been a much better author of popular fiction than you are a journalist. You've missed your calling. Truly.

"Here's the thing, though." Owen began to pace around his prey, readying himself to strike. "This obsession of yours with the macabre, it's not enough to just think about. It's not enough to just report the news. I think that you've been perched on the sidelines for so long that you took it upon yourself to start making the news. That way, you could sneak those little nuggets of truth—those little details that your devoted readers credit to your gusto for research—into your stories, and you could kill and hide in plain sight.

"Because it's not about the truth with you, really, is it? It's about proving you're smarter than the authorities. It's about proving you're smarter than everybody. What better way to go on a killing spree and be able to maintain plausible deniability than professing that you're just doing your job and chasing leads? It must be thrilling for you, this idea that your big, national story would also be the confession that no one picked up on."

"You're one to talk about writing fiction, Agent." Lowdon turned his head toward Owen and stared deep into his eyes. "You might want to give a publisher a call and pitch that idea of yours. I won't deny that I'm always on the lookout for the next big story that will get me out of Boulder. But I'm not about to kill to further my career. Unlike some."

Owen bristled at the reporter's words. They both knew he was talking about Frank Hickson. Fighting to keep a measured tone, he leaned on the table. "Don't you dare presume to bring that up. We both know even though he threw down that Glock, he was reaching for the backup .38 in his belt. I didn't have a choice."

"You had on Kevlar, and you were less than twenty-five yards away. A man with your training and composure surely could have hit him with one in the shoulder instead of four to the chest. But no, you took justice into your own hands. Then you were rewarded for it, and my story got pulled. What does that say about our government?"

"Your story got pulled because it was a smear piece meant to whip up the ultra-libs into a frenzy and paint me as a monster. Your words turned a dead man who killed half a dozen teenage girls into a martyr. What does that say about you?"

"I stand by my work with every bit of pride that you stand by yours, Agent. But I don't have any blood on my hands, metaphorically or otherwise."

Owen stared hard at Lowdon as he spoke, trying to probe the riddle of his words. Despite the lack of any substantial evidence against him, he was sure the reporter was involved somehow. Or was he simply allowing his personal dislike for the man to cloud his investigatory sensibilities? If he weren't careful, the worm would wiggle off the hook.

A loud knock shook the mirror.

Owen gave Lowdon one last look before turning toward the door. "I have to say," he said before opening it. "It was bold of you not to ask for a lawyer."

"Why give you another reason to think I'm guilty? You don't need a lawyer if you're innocent."

Bastard always needs to have the last word. Just let him win this one. Owen shook his head and left the room.

Turnberry was waiting for him in the hallway. Owen checked to make sure the door to the interrogation room was fully closed before speaking.

"What have you got for me, Steve?"

"Not the news we're looking for." The other agent handed him a manila folder. "His alibis for the Sandburg and Niemann murders are confirmed."

Owen frowned as he leafed through the pages in the folder. "Are you sure?"

"He doesn't fit in with our timeline for Lynn's murder. We've got coworkers at a restaurant in Boulder confirming he arrived just after 5:30 yesterday for their boss's birthday party. They also say he left around quarter to midnight."

"That doesn't clear him."

"We've got security footage of him leaving his motel before 4 p.m. and coming back a little before two in the morning.

Based on how long it would take to drive to Boulder and back, he would have had to drive straight through. No detours. He didn't leave again until a little after 4:30 when we were already on our way to the crime scene."

"So he didn't dump the body. Doesn't mean he didn't kill her."

Turnberry put his hand on Owen's shoulder. "Look, boss. I know you got a history with this guy, but we've got nothing on him. And besides, if we're going to be using Maureen Allerton in this investigation, we have to build a case strong enough that doesn't bring her involvement to light while still following the leads she gives us. If we believe her and accept that the person who killed Lynn Sandburg is the same person who dumped her body, then we have to rule Lowdon out for now."

Owen nodded his head. Turnberry was right, of course. "I have a feeling there's more that exonerates him, isn't there?"

"We have statements from his coworkers and family in Boulder verifying that he didn't leave the city during our kill window for the Niemann murder either."

Owen felt his head drop. He desperately wanted Turnberry to be wrong, but he knew the other agent's dedication to details was almost unparalleled. He was going to have to let Gabriel Lowdon go. Out of the corner of his eye, he saw Maureen edge her way into the hallway. She couldn't have heard the conversation they just had, but she would find out eventually. He nodded to her to come over.

"What's the story?" she asked as she approached.

There was no point in sugarcoating it for her sake. "Doesn't look like he's our guy. His alibis for the last two murders are solid, and I'm sure he'll have solid ones for the other two as well."

Maureen nodded her head. The stoic expression on her face remained unchanged. It was almost as if she had expected this.

"Are you sure of what you saw in your dream?"

"That whoever I'm linked to was staring into my window watching me sleep? Yes. But I already told you I couldn't see his face. It wouldn't shock me if Lowdon isn't our guy. He doesn't strike me as a killer, even if he is a bit of a dick."

"At least we agree on that point."

"So what are we going to do now?"

"*I'm* going to go back into the interrogation room and chat with him a little more and then I'm going to have to let him go. *You're* going to leave before he exits the building. He's trying to expose what we're doing here, and even if he's on to the truth, he'll find a way to blow it so far out of proportion in his garbage newspaper that the FBI will have a major PR nightmare on their hands. I don't need you and him occupying the same space."

He waited for a moment, expecting Maureen to challenge his instructions with one of her usual obstinate comebacks. To his surprise, she said nothing. She simply shrugged her shoulders and disappeared back around the corner and down the hallway that led to the front doors. Owen waited for a moment longer to make sure she was really gone, then turned to head back in. Out of the corner of his eye, he caught the amused look on Turnberry's face.

"You gonna run down the rest of Lowdon's alibi, there, Steve?"

"Yes, sir." Turnberry resumed his business demeanor and headed down the hall in the opposite direction.

Owen fixed his best glower on his face as he opened the door. Without a word, he crossed the small room to Lowdon's chair and unfastened the handcuffs from around his wrists. The reporter looked up in amazement before a grin broke out on his face and he began to rise. Owen put a hand firmly on his shoulder and kept him in his seat.

"If you mean to let me go," Lowdon said, subtly shrugging off Owen's grasp, "I don't think I have to answer any more of your questions."

Owen took his seat opposite the other man and stared hard, folding his hands on the table. "Your friends in Boulder have alibied you out for the time being. I'd say don't leave town, but I don't think there's any danger of you doing that, is there?"

Lowdon scoffed.

"I didn't think so. But before you walk out of here, you *are* going to explain a couple of things. First off, how did you come to find out what motel we were staying at?"

Instead of answering, Lowdon cocked his head to the side.

"Of course. Your anonymous source inside the bureau. Fine, forget about all that. I'll deal with it later. Let's move on to last night. Let's say I believe your story that you were chasing down the person who was stalking Ms. Allerton. Can you describe him at all?"

"It was dark."

"You gotta do better than that."

Lowdon blew out a puff of air and leaned back. "He seemed pretty athletic. I mean, I like to think I'm in decent shape, and he outran me with no problems."

It was everything Owen could do not to burst out laughing. As if Lowdon's budding paunch weren't enough proof that the man spent far more time curling donuts than dumbbells, there was also the fact that the reporter had had a running start on him and yet Owen managed to overtake him in mere seconds without increasing his own heart rate. In the rain. Barefoot. It wouldn't take an Olympian to give Lowdon the slip in a dark alley.

"How about anything physical. Height? Build?"

"He was taller than me, maybe Turnberry's height or an inch or two more. He was wearing a jacket, so I couldn't guess body type."

"But you're sure it was a *him*, right?"

"Don't know of many women who would be spying like that on another woman."

Owen had to give him that, but he could see he wasn't going to get much more out of Lowdon. He rose to his feet without a word and strode to the door, yanking it open and staring back at the reporter. It took the other man a moment to take the hint. Lowdon finally jumped to his feet and began to make his way out of the room. Owen placed his arm across the door just before Lowdon crossed the threshold and leaned in.

"Listen, Gabe. It's no secret that I don't care for your reporting and that you and I are never going to be friends. But if you see something out there, how about coming to me or Turnberry before you go and print it for the world to read? You go and do that, and it could blow this whole investigation. I'm asking you out of professional courtesy here; think of the victims' families."

"Agent, I'll take your words into serious consideration."

"You'd better."

With that, Owen lifted his arm and allowed Lowdon to pass. He followed the reporter through the hall to make sure that he exited the building. As they rounded the last corner, he was greeted by two unwelcome sights. Outside the glass double doors at the front of the building, a crowd of reporters had gathered, and at the sight of one of their own, the throng pressed forward. Their overlapping voices were muffled by the glass. That sight only marginally registered for Owen, however, as he was focused on the other unwelcome sight, that of Maureen standing against the wall in the corner of the lobby. Before he could stop it, Lowdon caught sight of her and escaped to meet her. Owen followed closely.

"Look at them all," the reporter said to her as he approached, gesturing to the doors. "Every media personality from here to Denver is out there, and they're all going to want to talk to me. I could bring you out there, too? Let you tell your story to the world? It'll get you out from under this one's yoke." The reporter nodded his head toward Owen.

Owen wanted to reach out and choke the words out of the man's throat. Lowdon just couldn't resist the urge to undermine him.

Maureen stood with her arms folded across her chest. After a moment, she looked at him and nodded toward the reporter. "Can I clock him again?"

Owen managed to stifle his laugh. "You only get one pass with me, and you've used it. Unfortunately."

Maureen shrugged her shoulders and continued to stare at Lowdon. When it became clear he wasn't going to get anything out of her, the reporter took a few steps back before turning and heading toward the front door.

"I thought I told you to leave," Owen said to Maureen as they watched him go.

"Would you really want me walking out into that piranha tank out there?"

Touché. "Why haven't you taken him up on his offer?" Owen asked aloud as they continued to watch the reporter. For some reason, the question had been gnawing at him since the morning.

"Who says I still won't?" She turned toward him, arms still folded. Her eyes, though, had just the barest glint of whimsy in them, and the upturn of the corner of her mouth was less of a sneer than he was used to seeing. The look vanished quickly as she apparently mastered herself and nodded back at Lowdon. "There're some people out there worse than cops. I don't have time for conspiracy-nut reporters, and I damn sure don't want the attention that would come with being in one of his little stories. Besides, I *hate it* when men think they know what's best for me."

He took her meaning and decided to keep silent for the time being. Across the lobby, Gabriel Lowdon opened the doors with a flourish and was swallowed up by the sea of humanity waiting to welcome their conquering hero.

Twenty-Two

The roar of the crowd around him washed over Gabriel like a tidal wave. He tried to keep a smile on his face as he waded through his peers and colleagues. Ordinarily, a chance to be hailed as a hero would have given him more satisfaction, but at the moment, he just wanted to get to his car and head back to his base of operations.

"Mr. Lowdon," a black-haired woman said, putting a handheld recorder to his face, "would you care to make a statement following your release from police custody?"

"There's little to be said, Terry," he said as professionally as he could, recognizing her as Theresa McHenry, one of the field reporters from a network in Denver. He'd run into her a few times, but she always seemed above him somehow. "It was a simple misunderstanding, which has been corrected."

"Do you have an alibi for the time of the murders?" asked a shorter woman, heavily made-up with a double-thick layer of foundation and blush. Shannon Astrid. She was a big deal in the nineties on local television before the cameras switched to HD. Her career involved less and less TV time as the years went by, and lately, even her columns were becoming sparser. Another poor victim of the superficial world they lived in.

"Yes, I do," he replied. He didn't feel the need to elaborate.

Those close inside the circle began to fire questions on top of each other.

"Where were you?"

"Who is attesting to your whereabouts?"

"Do you think your arrest stemmed from the animosity between you and the lead agent?" a brown-haired man in a blue jacket asked, waiting for a lull in the din. Lowdon didn't know his name, but they were near each other in the media scrum the morning the feds brought in Maureen Allerton.

"Agent Samuelson and I aren't friends," he replied. "That's not a secret. But he thought he was justified in bringing me in."

"That seems to be a pretty judicious answer," the other man replied.

"So?"

"I just mean that you're not exactly known for political correctness, Mr. Lowdon."

Lowdon stopped walking and turned to face him. "I know what you're trying to do, pal. I wrote the book on riling up a target to get them to say something they want to keep private. So you can dispense with your charade. What's your real question?"

"There're rumors you were apprehended at the location where the agents and their consultant were staying. Any truth to that?"

Gabriel sucked at his teeth.

"What were you doing there?" the man continued, apparently taking his silence for an affirmation.

Gabriel stood blinking but kept his jaw set. He was trying to decide whether to listen to or ignore his instincts about what to do in the moment. It didn't take long. "Okay, everyone." He beckoned the crowd closer. "Gather around, and I'll give you a short statement. Yes, it is true that I was apprehended by the FBI last night outside their motel rooms. I observed an unidentified person snooping around the site, and when I attempted to confront him, he ran. I followed him but lost sight. It was at that time when the agents spotted me and mistook me for the offender."

"And how did you know where they're staying? That's not public knowledge."

"I guess I just work harder than the rest of you."

"And what were you doing there so late at night in the rain?"

"Like I said, working harder than you."

"And so now that you're free, do you have any idea if the feds have any other suspects?"

"I have no idea," Gabriel said, looking directly into one of the news cameras. "But if my arrest is any indication of the status of the investigation, I'd judge that they're nowhere near solving these heinous crimes. And if I were them, I'd button up the investigation. Seems to me there're some leaks."

The crowd exploded into a chorus of voices demanding he clarify his statement, but Gabriel backed away from the crowd and headed toward his car. A few of the more persistent media members followed behind for a while, but he outpaced them and jumped into the old Saturn. The door squeaked as he slammed it shut, and the motor screamed as he pulled away from the throng. He smirked as he skimmed through the channels on the radio, looking for a good song. The jab he took at Samuelson and the feds felt like a victory after what they put him through. His comments would hit the news cycle within two hours, and—if it worked the way he expected—the top dogs at the Denver office would be breathing down boys' necks soon after.

Still, he felt a little bad for Steve Turnberry and Rick Navarro. He never had a problem with the former, and the latter was a good kid. Malleable, maybe, though that wasn't a bad thing for Lowdon. But when you take orders without question from a tool of the military industrial complex like Owen Samuelson, you're going to be hit by the blowback aimed at another. It didn't have to be that way. Regardless of what some would say, Gabriel really felt like he respected law enforcement officials—local ones who did their jobs right and still respected his civil rights, anyway. It was these assholes at the top who hid all of their doings from the American people and trod all over the Constitution. Especially when it came to the First Amendment.

All of that didn't deter him, though. Eventually, he'd expose what was going on around here and get the respect he'd worked his whole career trying to earn. And now there was a second angle to work. His dig at the feds put the idea in his head. It would take a lot of vigilance and legwork, but it was almost crazy enough to work—as long as he kept his profile low from here on out.

Gabriel pulled up to the motel he was staying at. It was a pay-by-the-hour/weekly rate place located on the far outskirts of town. It made the spot the feds and Maureen Allerton were staying at look like the Ritz, but it was all he could afford on the expense account he was given. He had a lump sum to work with, whether he was on the job for a day or a week, and he intended to remain in town until he found his story. Besides, here, no one bothered him or asked stupid questions—so long as he didn't stare too long at any weekenders heading into one of the rooms with their side pieces or paid companions.

Today, there was no human activity in the crumbled, asphalt parking lot. Gabriel parked his car and headed into what passed for the front office of the establishment. The door jingled as he entered, and he expected the disheveled manager to look up from his miniature television. Instead, to his delight, Gabriel found that the tattooed girl with a nose ring was behind the counter instead. He found something alluring about her in spite of the stereotypical detachment and ironic sense that went with her fashion choices. If he was honest with himself, it was purely physical. Even with black fingernails and over-eye-shadowed eyes, she was hot with a body that said she was a regular gym rat despite the fact that she would probably call exercise facilities fascist if asked. A dragon head was centered above her cleavage, and its body disappeared under her tank top. He could just imagine the tail of the beast curling itself around her ample breasts, still untouched by age. He envied the man who got to see the whole thing.

He cleared his throat and stepped in close to the counter, hoping the subtle bulge that was developing in his pants was hidden and would go away as he tried to push those thoughts out of his head.

"I'll be adding another week to my stay," he said, offering his best smile.

"Room?" she asked disinterestedly.

Gabriel glanced over her shoulder at the row of a dozen pegs that held the room keys. The management's system for keeping track of occupied rooms was nothing more than a whiteboard, above the pegs, upon which the checkout date was written in marker. There was only one other room that was occupied for an extended stay and two others that were rented for the day. He clearly had not made enough of an impression for her to remember which one he was in. *Ouch.* "Lucky seven. And I won't need service, just a couple more towels."

"Two forty-five," she said absently, barely bothering to look up from the piece of paper she'd worked out his fee on.

Gabe shook his head and pulled out his wallet. Cash businesses always insisted on their money up front. He counted out the bills and laid them on the table. "There you go." He smiled. "Exact change."

She said nothing in return, just grabbed the cash, turned around, erased his old checkout date, and wrote the new one. She then bent over and grabbed a stack of three white towels and put them on the counter. Gabriel tucked them under his arm and pushed through the door. He took a quick glance over his shoulder to see if she was watching him, but she had already sat down in the chair behind the counter and was reading a thick book she had picked up from the back shelf.

Gabriel tightened his grip on his load and headed along the row of doors toward his room. He fit his key in the lock and turned. The old bolt creaked and gave a quarter turn but didn't open. It wasn't the first time. He hunched over, balanced the towel stack between his elbow and knee, and jiggled the knob and the key in the lock simultaneously. After a moment, the lock gave way, and Gabriel was able to push his way into his room.

The specks of dust kicked up by the door's vibrations drifted in and out of the rays of sun that managed to make their way through the window. Gabriel tossed the towels to the side. They fell at the feet of the wobbly armchair that stood in the corner. He didn't bother to pick them up. Truth be told, there was no shortage of clean towels in the bathroom. He just wanted a reason to keep talking to the desk girl.

With a sigh, Gabriel flopped onto the unmade bed and reached under it to pull out his briefcase. It was stuffed to the brim with paper, which to any other person would look like a disorganized jumble of notes. But he had them all perfectly organized in his brain. He'd meticulously documented everything he'd seen and heard since arriving in town.

There were two directions he could take his investigation in. The first was the one he'd spoken about with Tyce and Maureen at the diner, and he'd love nothing more than to prove his theory true—that Stargate had never actually been disbanded and Maureen Allerton was just one of many psychics in the employ of the government. Worse, her involvement would indicate that they were no longer using these people solely as counterespionage agents against the countries they thought of as enemies, they were using them to spy on their own citizens. There was a problem with this line, though, which was apparent now that he had some time to sit and think about it. If the National Guardsmen turning up as eviscerated corpses were the result of a government scrub as the current administration was on its way out, why would the FBI be actively investigating, and why would they risk having one of their psychics out in the open?

"Could be that the FBI isn't aware, and this is a CIA thing," he mused aloud. "But that doesn't seem too likely."

There was another problem that he was beginning to see as well. The name of the latest victim hadn't been released to the public yet, but his source had given it to him. Lynn Sandburg, as impressive a woman as she was, seemed to have no actual ties to the government. Based on his quick research, her grants seemed to almost exclusively go to public universities for their research. It was possible she was working on projects for the government in secret, but he could waste weeks going in circles trying to find enough evidence to make for a credible story.

The other direction he could take his story in was the hunt for a serial killer. His source had told him that was the focus of the FBI's investigation, and, while still justifiably suspicious of anything coming from a government employee, he didn't have any reason to think he was being lied to outright. The kid was dissatisfied with his position in the bureau and frustrated with the level of responsibility he was being given–the exact type of person you wanted on your side. You wouldn't get political answers from them, and they genuinely believed they were telling you the truth.

"There's a third option," he said aloud again. "Maybe my theory about the guardsmen is right, or close, and Sandburg was done by a copycat."

He thought on that for a brief moment before dismissing the notion. From what he knew about serial killers and copycats, there would need to be more bodies spread over a larger area to elicit the urge in others to try and duplicate their methods. These slayings, while bizarre, weren't on that scale. Yet. The possibility of them becoming sensationalized was there if more victims were claimed.

So, serial killer it was. He'd have to attack this story less like a journalist and more like a detective. He almost became amused at the idea of being able to write a multipart piece for his readers, detailing his own findings as his digging ran parallel to the FBI's investigation. If he were able to find a piece of case-breaking evidence, the look on Samuelson's face would be priceless. *Oh, that's good!* Gabriel flipped his notebook to a fresh page near the back and began to scribble notes on his new objective. He became so wrapped up in his work that he didn't notice the silhouette that filled the open door.

"You look pleased with yourself," a gruff voice said.

Gabriel started and looked up. The bright sun peeking over the man's shoulder meant that he couldn't make out the face of the speaker. He didn't need to, though. The man's head was topped with a Stetson that he'd recognize anywhere.

"Come in, Al," he said cheerfully, though his ex-brother-in-law was the last person he'd expected to find on his doorstep. "Make yourself comfortable."

"I'm not here for a social visit," Tyce said, taking his place at the foot of the bed and removing his hat. "I heard about all the excitement from last night and this morning and just came to look in on you."

"Well, as you can see, I'm just fine and dandy. How'd you know where to find me, anyway?"

The ranger's mouth twitched into a sneer. "If there's one thing I know about you, my friend, it's that you like to pocket as much of your expense funds as possible. Since you never bothered to call me and ask to stay at my place, this is the only place around here you could be. I drove by a few times this morning until I saw your car in the lot."

"Well, thanks, I guess, but if there's nothing else, I've got a lot of work to do."

"That's the other thing I'd like to talk to you about. You've really been pushing the boundaries around here. If you were thinking about writing one of your gaslighting pieces on this one, I'd reconsider it. Things are bad enough without you trying to whip people up into a frenzy."

"The public—"

"Has a right to know," Tyce finished for him.

Gabriel frowned at him. He didn't like Al patronizing him—almost as much as he didn't like being so predictable that Al could finish his sentences. Still, he couldn't let it go completely unanswered. "So it looks like I got a catchphrase, huh? Doesn't change anything. And who are you to tell me what I can and can't write about, the muscle of the investigation sent here to scare me into backing off?"

"You know better. I'm not a man to do something like that. I'm only here to warn you about this one. There's a dangerous feel about this whole thing. I don't want to see you get hurt."

Gabriel cocked his head at Tyce's words. He sounded like a concerned older brother. Maybe he still felt like one. Or maybe . . .

"Does this have anything to do with Maureen Allerton? You seem to have taken on the role of her personal bodyguard. You sure there's not more to it? You certainly didn't seem to like me working my charms on her."

The ranger's face twisted with a look of amusement that actually struck Gabriel as genuine. No, it wasn't about attraction. Tyce straightened his face and put on his serious tone. "That girl has been through enough without you causing trouble for her. I'm warning you. Leave her be. She doesn't want or need the spotlight you want to put her under."

"And if I don't leave her be?" Gabriel asked defiantly. He needed to see how serious the ranger was.

"You know I know how to straighten you out," Tyce said.

Gabriel took his eyes off his former brother-in-law's face and looked down. The ranger's right hand had begun to clench into a ball. Message received, but something about this conversation made him want to push just a little further.

"I hope that's not how you try to scare the boys who come around to take Aly out," he mocked. "It's not very intimidating."

Tyce flinched ever so slightly at the mention of his daughter's name. He nodded grimly and stood to leave. "Just think about what I said, huh?"

Gabriel felt bad about bringing up his daughter, but he was also feeling wounded by Al coming here and playing this game of postures, even if his intentions were pure. Maybe it was more than that. He tried his hardest not to harbor any ill feelings toward Al. It wasn't his fault that his marriage to his sister ended. She wasn't easy to live with. She always needed to have things just so. He was sure that she liked the idea of marrying a soldier but wasn't ready for what that actually meant. And when Al got injured and needed to come home, well, a wounded vet and a high-maintenance woman were an explosion waiting to happen. It was a shame, too, because he really liked his brother-in-law. They used to fish and barbecue, and up until two years ago, they had their annual Rockies game. Sharon never really approved of that one. She took it as a personal attack that he'd continue to see her ex. But in recent years, he and Al had grown apart. Sometimes it stung.

It started when Sharon finally moved in with her longtime boyfriend, Austin. Nearly a decade younger than her, he was a real piece of work. He came from money, and Gabriel had absolutely no idea what he did for a living. He claimed to be a club promoter, but what clubs were there in Denver that needed his supposed services? In any case, he gave her the type of life and attention that she had craved for the past four years, and the fancy suburban home and carat-and-a-half diamond that he put on her finger some nine months ago sealed the deal for her.

But as well as he treated his sister—and Gabriel had to admit that Austin seemed very much in love and devoted to her in spite of his douchey personality and entitled behavior—the man had no interest in being a stepfather to Aly. Fortunately, his niece would only be at home for two more years and had made no bones about the fact that she wanted to go to school far away from Colorado. He noticed that she had also begun to engage in more after-school activities than she ever had before. She maintained it was to build her resume for college, but Gabriel sensed it was more so that she wouldn't have to spend as much time in the house.

Al, of course, was aware of all this. He wouldn't let it show, but Gabriel knew how much it affected him. The ranger didn't hold his ex-wife's fiancé in very high regard either. The one time they met, Austin, aided by one too many martinis, was dismissive of Alec's military service, mocked his age, and openly chided him for his outdoor vocation and lifestyle. Tyce kept his cool that uncomfortable evening, but it was after that when Gabriel noted that Al would stop making trips to the other side of the mountains and Aly's trips in the other direction to see her father had grown further between as well. He himself had also withdrawn from his sister and niece since the engagement. He hadn't even been invited to Aly's sixteenth birthday party. The family was broken, and they all carried the baggage.

"She misses you," Gabriel called to Al before he crossed the threshold. Tyce turned back and leaned on the door frame, the barest hint of a sad smile on his lips. "I caught up with her at her summer job a few weeks ago to give her a check for her birthday. She talked about how sometimes she wishes she could come live with you."

"I'd love nothing more," Al replied, looking down at the floor. "But that decision was made a long time ago."

It was true. Sharon had won custody pretty easily. She wouldn't give up the alimony easily. Sometimes Gabriel wondered if that was the reason she and Austin kept saying they weren't in any rush to actually tie the knot, to preserve the money that Al paid her until her daughter's eighteenth birthday. He didn't want to think like that about his sister, but with that fiancé of hers in her ear, anything was possible.

"Well, I just thought you should know," he said aloud to Al before adding, "and I appreciate your concern for my well-being, but you don't need to worry about me. I know what I'm doing. But if it makes you feel better, I'll be sure to toe the line. For you."

Al didn't make a reply, just nodded and left the room, closing the door behind him. Gabriel got up and went to the window to watch him walk slowly across the parking lot. His bowlegged gait had become more pronounced in recent years, the product of all his time on horseback. The ranger got into his truck and drove off, leaving a cloud of fine dust floating in the air in his wake. Gabriel stayed at the window for a few more moments, just to make sure Tyce wasn't going to turn around, before making his way back to his notes on the bed.

"Toe the line," he whispered to himself. "Sorry, brother, I don't know if I can do that."

Gabriel wasn't sure where things were going to take him. It was entirely possible that nothing he could get into would put him in any harm. But if he did get close to something salacious crawling around in the background of these events, he could fully expect some serious trouble. But first things first, he needed to find his in, and he could only see one. The web of occurrences in the last weeks all converged at one focal point, and no matter what promises he had made, he needed to find his way into it. He needed to do whatever it took to talk to Maureen Allerton. And what was more, it needed to be in a situation where she could speak candidly. So, come hell or high water, he needed to get her alone.

ꝉWEN꜀Y-꜀HREE

The room around her was dim, and yet in front of her eyes was a sharp, clinical glow. A small lamp stood on a dark table in front of her. In its light, on a metal tray, sat an oblong gelatinous blob. It shined a brilliant red, and she could make out several small tubes protruding from what must have been the top. She wasn't sure exactly how, but she knew it to be a heart. A human heart.

A pair of gloved hands appeared and picked up the organ, turning it over and over, inspecting every inch of it. She could feel the tissue give under the pressing fingers, and a sour, fetid odor wafted into her nostrils. The smell made the part of her mind she controlled sick, but she felt little from the other part, only a cold sense of wonder and curiosity.

A scalpel appeared in the right hand. Its blade glinted in the light as it pierced the heart and slowly worked its way around it, bisecting. The hands pulled apart the heart to reveal its four inner chambers. They then set down the scalpel and picked up another metal instrument. A caliper. It took extensive measurements of each of the chambers and the thickness of the walls—lengths and widths. Once finished, the left hand pulled the glove off the right, which in turn picked up a pen nearby and began to write the numbers in a notebook. She strained her own consciousness to read what was on the page, but she couldn't will the eyes to obey.

The urge to leave the scene behind and wake crept into her mind, but she pushed it aside. Instead, she gave herself over to the consciousness of the vessel she inhabited, sitting back in quiet observation and hoping to see and retain clearer clues to its identity. The eyes moved to the other end of the table and rested on a jar filled with a tinted liquid. It looked like water that had come from a rusty faucet, but it was apparent almost immediately that it was anything but. When the lid was removed by the hands, another foul smell gripped at the back of her throat. The part of her mind that wasn't hers had little reaction. The heart was deposited into the jar, and the lid was screwed back on. This time, a piece of tape on the lid came into view. The word written on it in black permanent marker read *Sandburg*.

The hands carried the jar away from the table and through a door into a darkened room. The ambient light from the room they had just left only allowed for her to see a dark shape, maybe four feet high, in front of her. The eyes moved to the side of the object and continued on their way toward the back wall. In the gloom, she could discern several other small shapes in a row, just above eye level. The jar in the hands filled a space between two of them as the hands set it in its place before the eyes turned and left the same way they came in.

She kept her own mind silent and continued her ride behind the mask, and after a few steps, she found herself at a metal sink. She felt the warm water running over the hands as they rubbed together. The smell of rubbing alcohol mixed with soap rose from them as they dried themselves with a coarse paper towel. The hands threw the towel in a nearby trash can as the eyes crossed the room. The sound of footsteps on wood echoed in her ears, and she felt herself climbing. *Staircase,* she thought as her right hand flicked a light switch.

The next sound was a door creaking closed behind her. She was at the top of the staircase in a wood-paneled hallway. The eyes began to move forward, but their vision blurred as she felt her own consciousness separating. Normally she would be glad about that; not having to strain to separate herself was a relieving experience. But now, as the familiar black curtain fell over her vision, she strained with her mind, pushing hard to find her way back. At last, after what felt like hours of swimming against the dark current, she found herself staring through the mask once again.

She became aware of the room around her. It was small—a den, she guessed, judging from the wall of books she was sitting next to. Before the eyes was a book sitting on a lap. She felt the weight of it as if it were on her own lap. The words on the page were in a language she didn't recognize and were accompanied by black-and-white pictures of beautiful women, many with young children. As the pages turned, they revealed other exhibits and drawings—sketches of different faces transected in various places by dashed lines and sketches of naked people with the same—all annotated in the same unreadable language the rest of the book was written in.

After looking at more pages than she could count, the eyes rose, and the hands carried the book to the shelf and put it back in its place among the other books. These, too, were old and leather-covered with words in the same foreign language on the spines. One of the hands ran, almost tenderly, across a few of these. The gaze never stayed on any one for too long, but she tried her best to memorize the names of the books, hoping she'd recall them when she woke up. As if triggered by the thought of waking, the black curtain began to seep in from the corners of her vision. She was floating back into nothingness, and this time, she let it take her.

Maureen opened her eyes. The motel room was dark, and she was lying, still dressed, on top of the covers of the bed, on her side, and facing away from the front door, toward the bathroom. She noticed that she had left the light on. Out of instinct, she pivoted her feet to the floor and tried to rise. But as soon as she lost the support of the bed, she found her legs had no strength in them, and she toppled forward, only just catching herself on her elbows before she hit her face on the ground. Her head swam, and the room seemed to spin in circles before her eyes. Maureen felt a familiar surge in her stomach and groped wildly for the garbage can. Before her hands could find it, the convulsions in her throat seized her, and she fell to her side, rocking to-and-fro with her entire body.

It was several minutes before she steadied herself again and pushed up into a seated position. Her first thought was a grumbling sense that she was going to have to clean up a huge puddle of vomit from the carpet. When she looked down at the spot where it should have been, however, there was nothing to be seen. Confused, Maureen put her hands to her mouth. She found only a small patch of saliva under her bottom lip. It was all too strange. She had been inside the sicko's head several times already; she never reacted like this after having been connected for so long. Then again, she had never forced her way back in after a dream faded to black. She didn't even know she was capable of such a thing. Maybe it was the strain from this forcing that caused her reaction.

The piercing flash of pain behind her eyes reminded her that some things never changed regarding the aftermath of one of her psychic experiences. She reached over to the nightstand and opened the drawer, pulling out the bottle of aspirin inside and dry swallowing three of them. She struggled up to her feet, the strength in her legs returning to its normal state with only a slight bit of shakiness left. Her new thought was to jump in a hot shower to try and relax herself when another image took to her brain.

A word from one of the book spines she'd seen in her dream consumed every corner of her mind. Before she knew what she was doing, she rushed over to the table and grabbed one of the motel pens. She scribbled the word directly on the tabletop and dropped the pen back down. Shaking herself as if to wake up once more, she stared down at the black ink on the wood. It read *Lebensborn*.

Maureen had no idea what that meant or if it were even a real word. But then, it wasn't the first time she'd scrawled a foreign word on something for what seemed to her absolutely no reason. She may not know what it meant, but it was obviously important.

An underground laboratory. A killer who cut out his victim's organs and then, apparently, dissected and measured them. Books filled with medical diagrams in another language and now this word. It all painted a picture of who this person was. If only she had a clue what it all meant. Well, it wasn't her job to figure that out. That honor belonged to Samuelson and Turnberry.

You're forgetting something important.

Maureen looked up and stared at the window. He had been spying on her just the night before. Why? The reporter, Lowdon, had made mention of a potential leak in the investigation. It could be true. How else would he know so much about her? And if he had ways of learning about her, maybe someone else did too. The thought sent a chill up her spine.

But what could I possibly have in common with the victims?

Even so, she was suddenly uncomfortable. Maureen slowly opened the door and stepped outside. She hugged her arms around her and scanned the night. For what, she didn't know. The killer was in a house somewhere, and there were no houses close enough to the motel, so he couldn't get here so quickly. And the victims were said to have a large dose of drugs in them. She couldn't believe he would try to drug someone standing alert. Almost amused by her own paranoia, she shook her head and turned back to go inside and have that shower.

The sight of the pen-marked table stopped her one step into the room, reminding her that she was going to have to report what she had seen in her dream. The clock on the nightstand read a few minutes before one, but still something told her she shouldn't wait. Maureen gave one last longing look toward the bathroom and, almost ruefully feeling the satisfaction of hot water running down her shoulders, turned back. She walked next door and stood for a moment in front of Samuelson's room before slumping her shoulders and knocking. She had barely drawn her hand back before the door opened to reveal the agent, without his jacket and tie but also still dressed in the clothes he had worn that day.

"We need to talk," she said. Samuelson said nothing but opened the door further and stood to one side. Maureen shook her head. "My room."

TWENTY-FOUR

Owen stared at the door of the war room. He needed an extra moment this morning before heading in. Inside, Dr. Heim, Dr. Frank, Ranger Tyce, Maureen, and Turnberry were waiting for him. Not very patiently. Through the door he could hear the muffled sounds of conversation. He didn't have to use much imagination to take a guess at what they were discussing. They had all been given access to the research into the word from Maureen's latest dream. It wasn't pretty. He sighed, suddenly feeling the inevitable mental fatigue that the next few hours were going to bring him, and pushed open the door.

The room went quiet as Owen entered. Five sets of eyes were fixed on him. Normally, that wouldn't have given him any pause, but today was different. The implications of what this man was doing to his victims made him sick and furious at the same time. Owen straightened his tie and cleared his throat as he took his place at the head of the table.

"All right, everyone," he said, sitting down and opening his laptop to pull up the research files. "Let's dig into this. Agent Turnberry, run it down."

"Lebensborn," Turnberry began. "German state-sponsored program with the goal of raising the birth rates of Aryan

238

children. Beginning in 1935, it was initiated by the SS under Heinrich Himmler, and the facilities eventually spread to Nazi-occupied countries throughout World War II until they ultimately numbered twenty-eight in total. Though it began as a welfare program for SS wives needing assistance during pregnancy, it eventually evolved into having facilities where many unmarried, 'racially valuable' women could give birth in privacy and avoid stigmatization. After the outbreak of the war, officials began to kidnap children in occupied countries, especially in Norway, who they believed possessed Nordic and Aryan blood, with the goal of bolstering the German population. Several tests were administered to the children, and those deemed acceptable or desirable were either placed as foster children with parents enrolled in the program or sent to German boarding schools. Those who were unacceptable were sent to concentration camps."

"Wasn't there forced breeding involved too?" asked Ranger Tyce. "I thought I learned something about that in school."

"Forced breeding, no," said Turnberry. "That was an exaggeration by the Allied media at the time. But relations between SS members and Nordic women were encouraged. Evidence and postwar testimony does seem to confirm that many soldiers did in fact sire children in the program. Additionally, the Nuremberg Laws made it compulsory for engaged couples to be tested for hereditary diseases before getting married. That, coupled with the fact that rulings from the Hereditary Health Court resulted in the forced sterilization of nearly half a million people, probably led to that confusion."

"Nevertheless," said Owen, "it at least gives us some insight into this killer's beliefs and motivations."

"How do you mean?" asked Dr. Heim.

"He obviously has some sort of fascination with the Third Reich," explained Owen, "and especially the idea of eugenics. After all, why else would he be taking the victims' organs?"

"You think he's studying them for some reason?" asked Dr. Frank.

"We know he is," Owen replied, glancing at Maureen. No one reacted. By now, they all seemed to understand what he meant by statements like that. "I would surmise that it's a part of the same neurosis that is causing him to kill. Maybe he fancies himself some kind of scientist."

"Maybe it's a Dahmer-type situation," offered Dr. Frank.

"How do you mean?" Owen asked, confused by the doctor.

"Well, wasn't Dahmer, like, experimenting on his victims? I thought I saw something on TV where they said he was cutting into their heads and was trying to create zombie slaves."

"Only one of our victims had their head cut open. Shelly Lindstrom."

"I don't know. Maybe he's trying to flip-flop their organs? You know, play God? Frankenstein was German, right? I'm just spitballing."

"Why don't you let us come up with theories to suit our evidence, Doctor."

Dr. Frank shrank back into his chair. Owen felt a pang of guilt at snapping at him, but they couldn't afford to be distracted by his nonsense. The man was a good pathologist and useful in that vein, but his constant attempts to make himself appear the detective were beginning to get old.

"One thing isn't adding up," said Dr. Heim, looking up from the book of notes on the table. "It says here that it was the people the Reich considered inferior who were killed or castrated. None of our victims had any type of medical issues or deformities that you would think someone would view as physically inferior."

"But at the same time," Turnberry said, "none of them would be considered Aryan by 1930s Reich standards. Ms. Sandburg and Chris Niemann were brunettes, Shelly Lindstrom's father is black, and, if Professor Freeman was a victim, well, he was Jewish. Those last two certainly sound like people who would be targeted by someone with Nazi beliefs."

"Come on, people," Owen groaned, growing tired of the idle speculation and lack of focus. "Every serial killer chooses victims based on a unifying fact. There's a scientific underpinning to all of this. What fundamentally ties each of these people to the ideals of Nazi racial purity and eugenics?"

The room went quiet as Owen stood still, staring down at the desk in thought. After a moment, he raised his head and looked around the room. No one was making eye contact now. No one except the ranger. Tyce, looking straight back at him, shifted in his chair and cleared his throat. A sullen laugh passed from Owen's lips as he shook his head.

"Ranger Tyce," he said, "I think I owe you an apology. At our last meeting, you said something that I shouldn't have dismissed so readily. Remind us."

"Uh, well, I said that all these people are really impressive people."

"Yes, but you also pointed out that Maureen, just before she woke up from that first dream of hers, said that very word," Owen reminded him. "Impressive. We have to assume that this killer has a specific goal that is motivating him to do these things. The targets are people who are examples of physical, mental, and moral prowess. We know he's studying the Nazi's Lebensborn program, but he also has a collection of other books, which we should assume contain more information on the subject of eugenics with a focus on the dealings of the Reich during the period we've discussed. He's harvesting organs, and we know that he, at the very least, has a sort of scientific notebook with a separate page for each victim. And there just might be more than the ones we've found recently. We have no idea how far back this goes, but it's become clear that he's practiced his methods. And he's confident. I wouldn't be surprised if he were keeping all these notes and information for more than just his own personal pleasure."

"I'm still a little lost," said Dr. Heim. "This is *one guy* doing all of this, not a team of people with financial backing and such. Don't you think we're giving him a little too much credit?"

"Joseph Lister was just one person," said Dr. Frank, "and we still use his fundamental principles of sanitation in our own lab. You shouldn't underestimate the capabilities of a single person to change the world."

"Let's not go that far," Owen said, "but I get your meaning, Dr. Frank. He's not going to stop of his own volition. If we can't figure out who he is soon, he *will* kill again." Owen paused to let his words make their impact on the assembled party. Truth was, he knew there was very little most of them could do to prevent another killing, but he needed everyone to consider themselves integral to the investigation in order to keep them motivated.

"Well, I guess we'll go and review the autopsy reports and see if there's anything else to learn," said Dr. Heim, edging up out of his chair and nodding to Dr. Frank to join him.

"I'll head back to the sheriff's department and join the boys relooking at the Freeman case," said Ranger Tyce, grabbing his hat and leaving quickly from the room.

"I'm going to find something to drink," Maureen mumbled as she rose and sauntered past him. Owen watched her slumped form disappear before turning back, flopping back into his own chair, and driving his knuckles into his eyes. Turnberry closed the door and took his place next to him.

"This has to be one of the most twisted cases I've ever worked," he mused, clearly trying to sound upbeat in the face of all the horror. "I'm thinking I'm going to take some of my vacation time after this."

"You should." Owen leaned his head back to look up at the dimpled ceiling.

"What about you?"

"I'm not thinking about vacation right now."

"No, I mean, how are you doing with this new turn?"

"It's just one more thing. Doesn't change anything."

"But—"

"Don't," said Owen firmly, keeping his eyes upward. "I'm not going to think about that right now."

"So what do you want to talk about?"

"I want to talk about you getting on the line with the boys back in Denver and digging some more into Ranger Tyce."

"What's he got to do with anything?"

"He was alone when he found Niemann's body. And he came up with the explanation of how the victims were connected out of nowhere."

"But he was in the car with Maureen when she supposedly made the connection with the killer."

"Yeah, but I have to entertain the possibility that our killer isn't working alone. I'm beginning to have a hard time believing that he can act so brazenly and get away with all this right under our noses without some kind of help."

"Does this have anything to do with that bastard reporter? You know, since he went on TV yesterday and gaslighted the media with all that talk about a leak in the investigation?"

"I'm just being thorough."

"Thorough or paranoid?"

"It's not being paranoid if everyone is out to get you." Owen snorted.

They were both silent for a moment before Turnberry spoke again. "I guess it's a possibility." Owen didn't say anything. Turnberry continued. "Why else would he have been at our motel that night unless he had some inside knowledge into the investigation?"

"See? I'm not so crazy after all. Even so, it's all pure speculation. We have no solid evidence."

"And even what we do have isn't exactly admissible," Turnberry pointed out. "We can't ever let it get out that Allerton—and her dreams—is our source for information."

"Obviously. We can't get warrants based on psychic phenomena."

Turnberry opened his mouth to say something, but Owen was already ahead of him and shot him a look to shut down the notion. They both knew his feelings about using Maureen. Turnberry shifted focus. "And there's the hair that we found on Sandburg."

"Like I said," Owen said, looking back at the table and lightly drumming his fingers on it, "he's starting to enjoy this. If we find another body, I wouldn't be surprised to find something of Sandburg's on it."

"Can't think like that, boss. We'll get this guy."

"Yeah," Owen said softly. *But how?*

Turnberry shifted in his seat. Owen could tell there was more he wanted to say. He arched his eyebrows to encourage the other agent to speak. Turnberry caught his hint. "You didn't mention the other thing that's been on your mind since we brought in Lowdon."

He was right. It wasn't just the notion that there was a leak in the investigation that was weighing on him. The man they were chasing was always ahead of them; he had to be tapped in to their doings. Maybe it was the same leak that Lowdon claimed to be exploiting. Maybe it was someone at the coroner's office. Whatever was going on, though, he now had a sneaking suspicion that the killer's next victim had already been chosen.

"There's no reason to scare her until we're sure," Owen said softly. "If she starts thinking she's a target, she's likely to try and take off again. We've got a more important whale to chase without having to start a second manhunt for our own consultant."

"Still, why don't we bring in a couple more guys. Just to make sure this guy can't get anywhere near her."

Owen shook his head. "I called Auger this morning before the meeting. The department won't approve any more bodies out here. And besides, we're walking a fine line as it is. More agents in town, working in close proximity to Maureen, will only further raise suspicion in the press and the public. The bureau is not willing to risk exposure. We're on our own."

"I don't know how I'm supposed to feel about that," the other agent grunted.

"Neither do I," Owen whispered.

"I won't say I told you so to the bureau, but you have to admit we were right from the start. She's more trouble than she's worth."

Owen said nothing. He didn't wholly disagree with Turnberry's assessment, but at the moment, he was filled more with concern for Maureen's well-being than with frustration at her complicating everything. After all, she didn't ask for whatever was slamming around inside her head, and she sure as hell didn't ask for that very thing to make her the target of a killer. It was just as much of a burden on her as it was on them.

"Okay," said Turnberry sliding back from the table and pulling himself to his feet. "I'm going to leave you alone for a while and go find Navarro. We'll see you at the motel for the nightly debrief?"

Owen nodded but continued to stare ahead. He needed to be alone and didn't want to encourage Turnberry to say more. The other agent seemed to get the hint and left without another word, his footsteps ringing in Owen's ears until they were swallowed up by the closing of the door.

He lost all track of time sitting there, ruminating on all aspects of the case, taking Maureen out of the equation for the time being. There were any number of people in the area who had the technical abilities to commit the murders, and two prime candidates were working right under his nose. The problem was that neither of them seemed to fit the psychological profile. And so far, none of their lives intersected with any of the victims. He felt as if the whole affair were going around in circles, and he hated having his hands tied while waiting for the boys back at the office to do their diligence in digging into these people's lives. He didn't know what he'd do if something didn't break soon.

For Owen, there were already too many bodies stacked against him on this one to be able to make a dent in his own karmic debt to the universe.

TWENTY-FIVE

Maureen paced around her motel room. She'd only taken a couple swallows out of the bottle of whiskey in her hand since she returned from the liquor store. The fact that it cost her nearly all her daily allowance was her reasoning behind the nursing. Also, she didn't have her usual desire to pass out into the sweet oblivion of a drunken blackout. There was something more to learn about the killer, and at the moment, she was toying with the idea of just going to bed and seeing if she would dive back into his head that night. Still, the stress of the week had opened the door to old habits and put the bottle in her hand to take the edge off. She'd have to be mindful and moderate.

The slamming of a door close by and a flash of motion outside caught her attention. The curtain on the window was drawn back halfway, and Maureen could see into the parking lot. She walked over and stared out into the night. The figure of Agent Samuelson, still in his suit, was walking in circles around the lot as if lost. He wasn't on the phone and he didn't seem to be talking to himself like he was wont to do, but his posture was angry, feral even. She'd noticed his edge sharpening even more throughout the day, and now it seemed on the verge of exploding.

After a few minutes, the agent let out a big sigh and stared up at the night sky. He then slumped as he stood and made his way to the other side of the lot, throwing himself onto the wooden bench that sat in the middle of the patch of grass that lay between the road and the building. He leaned forward, put his head in his hands, and sat like a statue.

Maureen watched for a moment longer, wondering whether he needed company or to be left alone. She decided that no one should be alone in the dark like that, no matter how much of a jackass they could be, and grabbed her flannel shirt, pulling it over her T-shirt. She grabbed the whiskey bottle and quietly slipped out into the darkness. Despite the heat of the day, the elevation ensured a chill in the air after the sun went down. Maureen buttoned her shirt with one hand as she tiptoed across the parking lot.

The shuffle of her feet caught the agent's attention, and he raised his eyes to her as she approached. They were full of a pain that she hadn't seen in them before. She stopped in front of him and shifted from foot to foot uncomfortably. She had acted on instinct and couldn't come up with anything to say to him as she was walking up. Maureen decided to do what she knew best and raised the hand that held the bottle, offering him a drink. Samuelson's mouth twitched with a brief smile, and he obliged, taking a large swallow before handing the bottle back. She slowly lowered herself onto the bench next to him and placed the whiskey between them. They sat in silence for what seemed like half the night before the agent, perhaps sensing either her discomfort or her silent earnestness for him to open up, decided to speak.

"This whole new wrinkle to this guy hit me kind of hard," he said quietly. "This whole Lebensborn and Nazi garbage."

"Why's that? I'd have thought you'd be happy to have a deeper insight into his psyche. It gives you another avenue for finding him."

"It's not that. It's the fact that thinking like this still exists. It's the idea that not only is he sadistically depriving these people of their futures, it looks like he's doing it in the name of one of the most evil ideals in human history."

"People will always surprise you by how evil they can be." She took a drink from the bottle to try and push down the memories of her own past that threatened to bubble up.

"I'm Jewish on my mom's side," he said as though he were confessing some great secret. "Not that I really practice. I never even had a bar mitzvah. But this Nazi bullshit has still been a part of my heritage. I guess I just never thought I'd be facing something like this in my lifetime."

"I never thought I'd face down a psycho priest pointing a gun in my face. I mean, I knew priests were assholes—well, most of them anyway—but I always thought the worst thing they did to kids was manipulate them sexually. Now I know that at least one of them guts and burns kids in some perverse sacrifice to their God that's supposed to purify their parents for the coming apocalypse. And now I know better, so there you go."

"I didn't get all that from the report that I read," Samuelson said, almost laughing.

"Pretty fucked up, isn't it? I guess that's why some new-wave Nazi doctor running around hacking up people doesn't seem to faze me."

"Not at all?"

"Well, of course it does some. Just not like I expect it would for your average person."

"Well, if nothing else, you've proven yourself to be anything but average."

"I'll take that as a compliment."

"Wasn't meant as one."

His dry attempt at levity, she was sure, masked the deep tides of the emotions that were swirling underneath his skin. She offered him a short laugh through her nose in appreciation for his willingness to continue their battle of wits. She'd have begun to worry about him if he had let an opportunity to take her down a peg slip by, regardless of his state of mind.

"I try not to let it get to me," Samuelson continued. She surmised that he must have thought he found a sympathetic ear. "It usually doesn't. There's just something about serial killers that I hate."

"Besides the killing part?"

The agent's face dropped, and he turned his head to give her a sidelong look. "It's the *number* of killings that have to happen before you get the guy." He picked up the bottle and took another sip. "And inevitably, you have to get lucky to get him. It's always something random: a parking ticket, a traffic stop, someone getting away. I feel helpless sitting around and waiting for that kind of break. Every person who dies while I'm on the case is like a knife in my heart."

"How often does that happen?"

"Too often. But for me specifically? This is my fourth official serial killer in my career."

"Did you get the other ones?"

"Eventually. They all made a mistake, and only one of them wasn't who I thought it was from the get-go. But this one? I don't even have a viable suspect. All we got is what's in your head. I can make guesses about the guy. He has access to medical equipment. Has a knowledge of anatomy. And he's a Nazi. Shouldn't be too hard to find, right?"

"You think it might be a local doctor? Like even Heim or Frank?"

"I'm not ruling anything out. I've got an eye on them, of course, but I haven't found any concrete evidence so far. Turnberry and Navarro are still digging. The problem is, he's now amping up his killings. This happens with a lot of serial killers; they start off slow, and eventually, as they continue to get away with it, their kills get closer and closer together timewise until they're killing out of compulsion. If Professor Freeman was his victim, and assuming that this guy might have started even before him, you can see how exponentially his pace has quickened. For all we know, he's already holding his next victim." Samuelson turned to look at Maureen. Expectantly, she thought, as if he were hoping she had something else to give him.

"I haven't seen anything that would suggest that," she said, trying to reassure him.

The agent sighed, leaned back against the back of the bench, and looked up. Above them, a blanket of stars had come out. Maureen couldn't remember the last time she looked at the stars, if she ever even had. It was a moment of peace in any case, an escape from the chaos on the earth below.

"Why do you do it?" she asked after a few moments.

"Work the bodies?"

"Yeah. The FBI does other things, right? So why murder? No offense, Agent, but it's clearly taking its toll on you. You look older than you probably are."

"I look older than forty-four?"

"Kinda. You just told me as much, that it stresses you out. That you take it all so personally. Why do it?"

"Jackie Everly."

"Who's that?"

"She was my fiancé. And I killed her."

"You did what!"

"I might as well have. It was over fifteen years ago. She and I had been together for years, through my time in the air force and on the police force in Denver. A few months after we got engaged, I decided to apply to the FBI Academy, and I got accepted. Being away from each other was hard enough as I trained on the east coast, but it became even harder after I began the job. I was in criminal enterprise when I started, and even though I was based in Denver, the job took me all around the country. It wasn't long before the trouble started. First, I noticed she'd buy an extra bottle or two of wine to keep in the fridge. Then it was four bottles of hard stuff. She said that the cocktails took the edge off while she was at home worrying about me. Soon, she needed three or four drinks just to begin to unwind for the night. Then it was Percocets. I tried to get her to seek help, but she said she could stop whenever she wanted. I was still low on the totem pole in the bureau, so I couldn't take any leave to help her deal with it. And, I admit, at the time, I wanted to be an agent more than anything else in the world. It strained us to the point that we broke off our engagement, and she left Colorado. Not four months later, I get a call from the authorities in California telling me that she was shot and killed outside a nightclub on the Sunset Strip during a drive-by."

"That's not your fault. You didn't kill her."

"It didn't matter. Her mother told me at the funeral that Jackie fell even deeper into drugs after our breakup. She blamed me for her daughter being outside that club when the shots went off. Some of the witnesses say she was so high that she didn't even duck when the shots started. She took three bullets, one in the shoulder, one in the stomach, and one in the chest, before she went down. She bled out on the sidewalk and never even knew what was going on. If I hadn't been so focused on my career, if I had been a better fiancé, she wouldn't have even been out there. What's worse is that since it was a random drive-by, no one was ever caught."

"So that's when you decided to concentrate on murderers?"

"I put in for a transfer to homicide three days after the funeral, yeah. Sounds silly, I know, but every killer I put away feels like I'm sponging away a little more of her blood from my hands. I don't know what it will take to get it all. Most likely, I never will."

"Forgive me for saying so, but I would think that burying yourself in your work is the opposite of honoring your fiancé. Maybe you'd be less of an asshole if you took some time for yourself. Maybe found someone?"

"There was only ever one woman for me," the agent said sadly. "Besides, I've been this way for so long I don't even know if I can be anything else."

"You can try. Take a vacation—or get laid at least. Do something."

"Maybe after this is over." He took a drink out of the bottle between them.

"Liar."

"You see right through me. But I see you, too, Ms. Allerton. You fought me every step of the way as we came down from Wyoming. You were combative and disrespectful, and all the while you insisted you didn't care about justice, you didn't care about helping. Yet when you had the dream out on the road, you chose to come back without any prompting. Once you came back, you had the option of disappearing into the background and discreetly giving over information to me. But you've attended meetings, you didn't really talk back when I sent you off with Ranger Tyce, and even when you didn't need to be there—and really should have stayed at the motel—you came to the crime scene. And you stick your chin out at that bastard Lowdon at every turn. Nice swat the other day, by the way. He earned that one." He chuckled. "It's a far cry from how you first wanted to be perceived by me or anyone else."

"You want to know why I'm suddenly so helpful?"

The agent raised his eyebrows and tilted his head.

Maureen wasn't sure she wanted to talk about it, but he'd been more than honest with her. It was only fair that she return the favor. She took a sip out of the bottle for courage. "I know you guys know most of the ins and outs of the Sycamore Hills case. You know I was pulled in after first being a suspect in those boys' murders. The detective, now one of your agents, felt I could be useful with my abilities. Apparently, as I found out later, your Agent Layton thought the same thing. You probably know that Father Patrick saved my life when Father Preston had me at gunpoint. Your files will say that he did it because he was a mentor to me, that we had a special relationship, and that's what prompted him to kill another man and then try and hide me after I left prison.

"What you may not know is that before Father Patrick's counseling prompted me to help, I was looking for any opportunity to go on the run again. Just like always. The dreams had only represented suffering in my life. They cost me a home, a childhood, my innocence of the ugliness and cruelty of the world. But Father Patrick made me believe that if I used my abilities to help bring justice, I would be doing God's will and therefore would be using the dreams for the purpose that He gave them to me for. I actually thought that He'd take the dreams away and set me free once I'd caught that psycho priest and saved the Naismith boy." Maureen sighed and took another drink. The memories of her talks with the priest and Manny's face now at the front of her mind lay heavily on her.

"Doesn't work that way is all," she continued. "The dreams didn't leave, obviously. That much I figured out in prison. And that deal that Layton had me sign did nothing but piss me off. That's why I tried to hide after my release. And as boring as life on the farm could be, I found a little peace for a while. I knew deep down that it could never last, but for a sliver of time, I almost let myself hope. And then you and your boys showed up, and it was like the dam broke, and a flood of anger came pouring out. Anger at God, or whoever controls our lives, for not taking away the dreams and leaving me in peace. Anger at the FBI for forcing me into performing for them on their terms. The only way I know how to react when I feel backed into a corner is to fight back. I hated you for tossing me down into that basement and just leaving me like I was nothing. I hated you for how you talked to me, how you looked at me. You made me feel like I was beneath you. And even when I had the first dream, I seriously considered not coming back. I didn't want to help you. I wanted you to fail because of what you had done to me. But then this fucker would keep on killing, and I couldn't let that stand either. So here I am, doing what needs to be done, detesting every second of it, but doing it nonetheless. You can feel free to give me a medal when all this is over."

"You don't really hate what we're doing, do you?"

"I don't love it. Hate, though, might be a little strong of a word. But I will say this: I didn't think I'd miss the farm as much as I do right now."

"You're going to go back there after this is all over, then?"

"I can't think of any place that's better. Now that you all know where I am, maybe I'll be allowed a little more freedom. Maybe I'll even get a job in town. I won't be chasing down murderers for you guys forever."

"So, here we are, then." The agent sighed, taking another sip of whiskey and handing the bottle back to her. "Two people bound only in the common purpose of getting another killer off the streets. What are we going to do about catching this punk?"

"I don't suppose waiting for that break is an option?"

"It wouldn't be my first choice, no."

Maureen got to her feet and paced in front of the agent. An idea had begun to form in her mind, but she wasn't too keen on trying it out. But her mind was blank as to a better solution, so she took one more sip from the bottle and turned back to Samuelson. "I think you're going to need to make some calls."

TWENTY-SIX

Maureen pushed the motel room door shut and stood with her back against it. Her right hand felt strangely light with the absence of the whiskey bottle, which she handed off to Samuelson for safekeeping. It was just as well. With the plan that she had just set in motion, booze was the last thing that she needed. She sighed and went to the mini fridge; she remembered there were some sodas in there, miniature sized like the beers she had that first night. She grabbed all of them, went over to the bed, and stared down at the sheets. For whatever reason, the lumpy mattress looked incredibly inviting. But she resisted the urge to dive in and shut the world out. There wasn't going to be any sleep for her tonight. Her plan depended on it.

She turned back to the table and pulled the chair to the middle of the room, away from anything she could lean on. Then she turned on the television and surfed the channels, looking for something that would keep her attention until the morning. Most of what was on were crummy infomercials and all-night news programs, but once she cycled through a second time, she found a thriller on the movie channel. Maureen popped open a soda and drank it down. She was counting on the caffeine jolt and whatever adrenaline the movie could provide to be enough to counteract any effects of the whiskey she had already consumed.

She watched the movie through to its end, not recalling a single detail of it, and finished the last of the sodas. It was a relief to be done. Her stomach was beginning to feel sick with all the sugar. Maureen got to her feet and shuffled into the bathroom where she turned on the sink faucet. She stuck her face under the running water, both to allow the cold to keep the fatigue away and to take in several gulps. She felt a little better as she reemerged.

The television was still going, beginning to play another movie she'd never heard of, but she barely paid it any attention as she walked to the window. The parking lot was still. She looked in the direction of the motel office, searching for Gabriel Lowdon's piece-of-junk car. She could see two trucks and their black sedan lit up by the glow of the motel sign. If there were any other vehicles in the lot, she couldn't see them. That gave her some relief. Even if Lowdon wasn't the one going around killing these people, having him stalking in her shadow was creepy.

As she turned her gaze upward, the moon shined three-quarters full and high in the sky, signaling that she still had several hours before dawn. Maureen found herself wondering who else was staring up at the moon that night. Was Manny still awake in his new home, walking the backyard that his new job status paid for? Father Patrick was probably up late, reading one of his dusty books. She even thought of her mother, as unpleasant as that was. Or maybe the moon was still visible in the morning sky over in Germany, where she last heard her father was. Maybe the killer's next victim was out there tonight, staring up at the night sky and not realizing he or she was about to meet an ugly fate.

A chill ran down her spine at that thought. She hadn't told the agents, but a suspicion began to grow in her mind ever since she saw herself asleep through the killer's eyes. Somehow, he must have known what she was. Why else would he be creeping around outside her motel room in the middle of the night? She hated the idea of having to look over her shoulder and for the past couple of days had secretly been thankful for all the cops surrounding her. The irony would be enough to make her laugh if she had the capacity to do so at the moment. But the gravity of what she was going to undertake in the morning dried up all the levity inside her.

Her plan was far from perfect. It hinged on the fact that their killer wasn't completely nocturnal. His worst acts were committed under the cover of darkness, for sure, but being inside his head during those times hasn't helped Samuelson catch him. Just like how it didn't help Layton and Manny catch Father Preston back in Sycamore Hills. It was the memory of a dream—nearly a year old now—that revealed a killer's seemingly inconsequential, mundane actions that gave her the idea to take the gamble. She wasn't sure it would really work, but it was the best idea she had. She had to help, and Samuelson needed to find this man soon, for both their sakes.

Maureen heaved another heavy sigh and leaned her hands on the windowsill, bowing her head. She didn't want the responsibility, but she couldn't deny it any longer; it was all up to her.

†WEN†Y-SEVEN

Chirurg paced back and forth in the moonlight. Its pale glow shimmered on the ripples of the Colorado as the river drifted lazily past the narrow gangway between his house and the bank. He should have been sleeping, but a mounting frustration kept his eyes open. He couldn't believe how difficult it was proving to get Maureen Allerton into his chair.

Earlier that night, he decided to stake out her motel room again. Learning from his ill-fated attempt to get close to the building, he had taken up his position in the shadows across the road and observed through a pair of binoculars, searching for any chink in the defenses. As eager and bold as he had become, he knew full well he couldn't spirit her away from the motel unless he could get her far enough away from the agents for them to be unable to hear any struggle that might ensue.

Then, a curious thing happened: Agent Samuelson came out into the parking lot, looking like a man driven insane by an unseen tormentor. Chirurg almost laughed aloud at the effect he was having on the buttoned-up agent. It was a nice side benefit of his work. His mirth died moments later when Maureen Allerton herself came out and sat with him on a bench under one of the parking lot lights. He continued to watch the two talk back and forth, waiting for the inevitable moment when one said something out of line to the other, and the conversation imploded. It never came. They sat, they spoke, and they passed what looked like a bottle of alcohol back and forth. No arguing, no antagonism. It wasn't what he had come to expect from his other covert observances of the pair.

Eventually they both headed inside, and the parking lot was left still again. Chirurg decided to stay for a while longer, if only to see whether an opportunity presented itself. Unfortunately for him, the lights in both of their rooms kept their vigil, and he didn't dare leave the safety of the shadows. It was past midnight when he decided to head for home, doubling back through the town a few times and making sure to not look at his address when he arrived, just in case Allerton had found her way into his head.

And now here he was; the perfect victim was dangling in front of him, and he was unable to reach out and grab her. Chirurg reached down, picked up a stone, and flung it into the darkness. The sound of it hitting the water far out of sight struck the night air. He wanted to scream but mastered himself and turned back toward the house. *Patience,* he reminded himself. *She'll be yours before this is over.*

He mounted the wooden steps that led up to the back door of the house, taking them two at a time, before flinging the door open and stepping into his darkened kitchen. Chirurg stood still for a moment, taking a deep breath to further calm himself and slow his heart back to its normal rhythm, and reminded himself that he could ill afford to get worked up. He cast his gaze around the room and caught a tiny flash of light coming from the counter. He groped over to it and found it was coming from his phone. His work phone no less. He opened it and saw he had a voice mail.

Curious, Chirurg called up his mailbox and listened to the message through to its completion. Then, to make sure he'd heard right, he listened to it a second time before deleting it and slipping the phone back into his pocket. A broad grin burst across his face. He could hardly believe his luck, and a plan began to form in his mind. The universe had heard his prayer, and if he played it all just so, he would get another shot at examining a psychic.

Suddenly Chirurg felt like he was going to sleep very well.

ᵀWENTY-EIGHT

"You're sure you want to go through with this?" Owen asked Maureen as she sat on the bed in the cold, white room. It was just a few short days ago that he'd confined her to this place and tried to force her to do what she was volunteering to do now. He couldn't help but admire her for her perseverance in this case and feel a little remorseful, if not entirely foolish, for how their relationship had begun. He'd have to properly apologize for that one day, especially if her experiment worked.

"I think I've only got a couple more minutes before my eyes close by themselves as it is," she said, rubbing a hand across her eyes. "Too late to turn back now. Let's just do it."

Owen nodded and backed off a few paces to sit in the corner next to Navarro and Turnberry. The lights were dimmed at his signal. He watched as Maureen settled herself onto the bed, and within a few minutes, her eyes squeezed shut and her breathing became regular. They settled back and waited, and Owen wondered how long it would take before knowing if they had anything.

The plan was fairly simple. After their discussion on the bench the previous night, Maureen suggested that they take her back to the examiner's office and monitor her as she slept.

With luck, she'd be able to jump into the head of the killer and identify where he was. They'd have a squad from the local PD on standby, ready to go at a moment's notice, to bring the bastard in.

Owen looked around at the windows that looked in from the three adjoining rooms. Each one had the same people—the staff members from both this facility and the sleep institute—inside, and they were running what they were told were the same sleep experiments they had a few days prior. The absence of the use of drugs was explained as the need for control readings. It made good scientific sense, and if any of the staff were suspicious, they didn't voice their concerns.

"You think this'll actually work?" Turnberry's voice roused Owen out of his thoughts.

"I don't know," Owen sighed, rubbing his eyes and stifling a yawn. "She says she can't control when these things happen. I guess we'll just have to see."

"I know, but don't you think we've gone with this whole 'psychic' thing long enough? I mean, I'll admit she's done *some* good work. I'd even go so far as to say I'm willing to believe she might have some kind of sixth sense after she led us to Lynn Sandburg's body. It was great that we were able to get the body out of there quietly, ahead of the press. Except for that Lowdon bastard, anyway. And if her profile is right about this guy, well, you can't hide the kind of neo-Nazi shit or whatever this guy's into forever. One of those names that the boys at the field office are running down will be our guy. I really believe we're a lot closer to getting him than taking a gamble on this experiment would suggest. Why risk our credibility on a stunt?"

This question had crossed Owen's mind more than once. He never made it a secret that he hadn't thought much of having to bring Maureen into the case, much to the detriment of his relationship with her. But an answer had also formed alongside it that was too logical to ignore.

"Let's put it in military terms," he explained. "Let's say there's this murdering dictator, or military general, or someone like that who's been taking out our boys over there in the sandbox. And let's say I'm given the order to go and take him out. Well, I can go about it two ways. I can drop in with the SEALs, burst into his home—where he, his wife, his family, and close friends are—and unload my clip into the crowd. I'm a pretty good shot, so it's possible, even probable, that I hit him. Maybe in the leg or maybe in the torso, but eventually he bleeds out and dies. But maybe a couple other people are hit in the process as well. Or, I can set up outside a window with a high-powered sniper rifle, put the crosshairs on his head, and take him out with one bullet the moment he's standing by himself. You get what I'm saying?"

Turnberry cocked his head and stared back skeptically.

"I choose to try the sniper rifle first." Owen pointed at Maureen, asleep across the room. "As much as it pains me to have a civilian psychic be at least partially responsible for closing this case, if we use the tool correctly, we're going to have to use one bullet."

Turnberry opened his mouth as if to protest but closed it just as quickly and nodded his head. The other agent might not have liked it, but Owen was in charge. Turnberry knew when it was time to follow orders.

I just hope I'm right. If Maureen makes me look like a fool after coming so far . . .

He didn't have time to finish the thought. The hospital bed creaked under Maureen as she shifted her weight and groaned. Her head began to roll back and forth on the pillow, and her breathing became rapid. Navarro jumped to his feet but remained rooted in his place, seemingly unsure about what to do next. Turnberry sat straight up in his chair. Owen felt himself lean forward. The feeling that crept up his spine mirrored what the other two men must be feeling: anticipation mixed with a certain dread.

The minutes seemed like hours while Maureen was in the throes of whatever vision afflicted her in sleep. She continued to thrash about, sometimes wavering on the edge of the bed, but never falling off. Every now and then a soft moan would escape from her lips. Her brow remained furled and creased with worry. Owen found himself wondering if she would ever wake up.

Then, without warning, Maureen heaved a loud gasp, and her eyes flew open. She sat bolt upright on the bed and gazed around wildly. Owen rushed forward to her side, followed closely by Turnberry. Navarro came behind as well. Maureen winced and began to rub her head as the men came up to her.

"Do you have my medication?" she asked, speaking into her hands.

Owen nodded to Navarro, who was holding the bag he had insisted—much to the confusion of the young agent—be brought. He reached inside and pulled out the half-full whiskey bottle that she had left with him the night before. She had told him then that she needed to sober up and keep awake until the experiment to have the best chance of bringing him something useful. Now, though, she snatched the bottle out of his outstretched hand and took several swallows before shaking her head as if trying to clear out the cobwebs.

"He was watching," she said quietly, subtly nodding her head to the left toward one of the windows. "From over there, in that direction."

Owen swallowed hard. Maureen didn't know who was in each room, but he did. The eyes of each room were upon him. He straightened up and, as subtly as he could, made sure his pistol was loose in its holster. He nodded to each of the other two agents and turned to apprehend their man. Maureen's words stopped them before they'd taken three steps.

"He's not in there," she said. Owen turned back to stare at her. She'd risen from the bed and stood, feet apart, intensity coursing through her body. Her eyes were narrow slits, and her breasts rose and fell with each gasping breath. Before he could say anything, she pushed past him and the other agents and stalked out the door.

Her pace quickened as she turned down the long hallway. Owen could hear her whispering to herself. She clearly had a purpose and seemed to be repeating it to herself. He jogged the two paces needed to come even with her and stared at the side of her face until she acknowledged his presence.

"I stayed with the dream as long as I could to get everything possible out of it," she finally explained, not slowing down to talk. "He was watching me from the room. Obviously, he's involved in the investigation, and that's how he's been able to stay ahead of us. Taunt us. The fringes of the dream were too blurry to see anything useful, and I couldn't hear anything except breathing in my ears, but after a few minutes of him watching me sleep through the window, the eyes left the room and came down this hallway."

"Maureen," said Owen, "I appreciate your candor, but come to the point. Are we going to get this guy, or what?"

"Fine," Maureen grunted back at him. "He ended up in the morgue. It was creepy. He opened the drawer that has Lynn Sandburg's body. He just stared at it for a long time. Then I saw his hands. They looked like they wanted to touch her face. They just hovered for a while. That's when I came out of it and woke up." She fell silent.

Owen reached his arm out to stop her. He didn't really need to hear any more of her explanation, but the mention of the word *morgue* made up his mind that his suspicions were well founded and were about to be proved true, one way or another.

"All right," he said. "Assuming he's still in there, I think it would be best if you stayed back. If he's cornered, there's no knowing what he might do. I don't need your blood on my hands."

Maureen cocked an eyebrow and stared at him as if trying to compel him to change his mind. Owen said nothing but kept his gaze firm in return. After a moment, she pulled her eyes away and stepped back, leaning against the wall with her arms crossed. Owen nodded to Turnberry and Navarro, and the three men continued on.

Within moments they arrived at the doors to the morgue. Owen put an ear to the door but heard nothing on the other side. He pulled his pistol out of its holster, turned the knob as quietly as he could, and nudged the door open with his shoulder.

They were greeted by the sight of an empty room. The metal table where the doctors examined their bodies shined coldly in the glow of the fluorescent light hanging above. The dull hum coming from the light was the only sound. Owen looked back at the other agents. Both Turnberry and Navarro stood in the doorway with their weapons drawn, confused looks on their faces.

He felt the tension in his body begin to release, but it was replaced by a flash of annoyance. Maureen was either wrong, or they were too late. Either case did not sit well. He was about to direct the other men out of the room when another idea flashed through his mind. First, if the room were really empty, there would be no reason for the light to be on. But there was something else.

He'd been in this room several times, but one thing never occurred to him before now. He turned back and scanned the room. Where were the drawers for the corpses? Maureen said the killer opened a drawer, and in most medical exam rooms he'd been in throughout his career, there was a wall of refrigerated drawers for the bodies. Not in this room; the room was too small.

Owen's eyes fell on another door in the back of the room. It had no signage on it, but to his mind, there was little doubt that the room beyond stored the hospital's dead. Reinvigorated, he hurried forward and pushed the door open, raising his pistol.

The sight of a gray-haired man in a doctor's lab coat met his eyes. He was standing over the body of Lynn Sandburg, pulled out from the wall, just as Maureen had described. The sound of Owen entering the room made him raise his head from his examination of the body. Owen scanned the other man for any sign of a weapon, but there was none. His hands lay lightly on the table, and nothing was in them. Nevertheless, Owen tightened his grip on his pistol and inched carefully forward.

"Step away from the body," he said steadily. "You're coming with us, Dr. Heim. I've got some questions for you."

Dr. Heim's eyebrows furrowed, but he said nothing, raised his hands, and took two steps back, patiently waiting for Agent Turnberry to take hold of him.

†ШЄΝ†Џ-ΝIΝЄ

"His lawyer has arrived," Navarro said as he stuck his head into the break room of the sheriff's station. Owen was sitting at one of the tables, stirring his coffee absentmindedly.

It had been nearly three full days since they had taken Dr. Heim into custody. They'd been stretching their rights to hold him to the limit, knowing that the DA would want more than the dreams of Maureen Allerton and the doctor's presence in his own morgue to bring charges. Fortunately, he'd been able to cite exigent circumstances to forgo a search warrant for the doctor's home, and that plus a heated and focused background check into Heim's life had uncovered a good amount of evidence, almost enough to get a conviction. The folder containing all the information lay under his right hand. Owen traced his finger on the folder's cover and took a deep breath. Evidence was all well and good, but a confession was better. That way, there would be no trial, no appeal, and justice would be done. Lawyer or no lawyer, he was going to get Heim to give himself up.

Owen pushed himself to his feet and left the break room. The interrogation room was only a few dozen yards down the hallway to his left, but he turned right instead and made his way out into the lobby area. He was going to take his time getting to the interrogation room. Owen pushed through the front doors to the outside.

The summer sun wasn't at its apex, yet it was still hot, especially for the elevation. While he was standing, trying to allow the sight of the distant mountains to bring him to balance, Agent Turnberry approached. He was holding a cup of coffee in each hand.

"I noticed you left yours in the break room," he said, handing one to Owen. Owen nodded his thanks to the other agent and took the cup. It was then that he noticed that the cup was only a little more than half full, and he could see the faint outline of his own lips on the brim.

"You couldn't be bothered to bring me a fresh cup?" He smiled.

"I'm your partner, not your secretary," Turnberry shot back with a mocking tone. "Sue me. I figured if you went to the trouble of making yourself a cup just how you like, you'd at least wanna finish it."

One thing Owen appreciated about Steve Turnberry: the man knew how to keep him grounded. The one thing that annoyed him about Steve Turnberry: the man had an unfortunate habit of questioning every little detail of an investigation if he felt a case they built was anything but a clear slam dunk. Not that Turnberry wanted murderers to go free, he simply didn't want them to even have the *chance* to go free. It chaffed Owen to no end sometimes, but he had to admit that the inevitable back-and-forths with his partner had kept him sharp and had made him a better agent in the long run. At this moment, though, knowing there was only one reason Turnberry would be coming over to him before an interrogation, and he wasn't looking forward to whatever was about to come out of the other agent's mouth.

"You think we got enough on him?" Turnberry asked.

"We got plenty," Owen replied, trying to speed the conversation to its end. The last thing he needed before facing his suspect was for doubt to creep into his mind.

"It's just the fact that we didn't find his little murder room—it's really bugging me. If what Allerton says is true, there should be a lab in his basement, some of those Nazi books, and some research notebooks or something."

Those missing items had made things murky until they found the other evidence that was now contained in the folder he was holding. "We're the only ones who know about that other stuff, and we don't need a psychological profile to put him away. He could have easily gotten rid of the books. Maybe he buried them. The forensic team is still tearing apart the backyard, right down to the waterfront," Owen reassured him. They both could acknowledge that the doctor's home on the river provided him with the perfect means to dump the bodies in the way they had been.

"We don't have any of the organs that he took from the victims, either."

Owen was starting to get perturbed by his negativity. "I've got enough to break him. We'll find out where all that other stuff is once I do."

"If you're sure." Turnberry took a sip of his coffee and stared ahead.

"What, you think he's innocent?"

"Oh, hell no. I'm just saying it's gonna be tricky. Especially with a lawyer present."

"Don't worry about the lawyer. I can work around that."

He patted Turnberry on the shoulder, turned back, and went inside. He quickened his pace, wanting to get to the interrogation room while his confidence was still running high. Even if it was curbed a little by Turnberry's warnings, he wouldn't allow the doctor or his attorney to see. He found the door he was looking for, took one last deep breath, and pushed it open.

Dr. Heim was sitting at the table next to his attorney. Owen grumbled to himself when he saw the doctor had called in the services of Tony Crocker. The attorney had earned quite the reputation over the last twenty years in his defense practice. He'd lost just as many high-profile cases as he'd won in that time, and there wasn't a defendant terrible enough for him to turn down. The fact that Heim had chosen him spoke volumes. Crocker had a smug, self-serving look on his face that made Owen want to puke. Or punch him.

The doctor's face, on the other hand, was devoid of any describable emotion. Whether he was simply worn out from trying to hide the demon inside him or the conditions of incarceration didn't agree with him, Owen couldn't tell. It didn't matter. If the doctor were compromised in any way, so much the better.

"All right, Doctor," he said, sitting down opposite the other two men and slapping the folder down on the table. "Your attorney has given you his legal counsel, and you've agreed to this interrogation before we submit our case to the DA and the state brings its charges against you."

"We're only doing this as a courtesy to you, Agent," Crocker said. "So that you don't waste your time trying to get these thin charges to stick once we explain a few things to you."

"You'll have your chance, Counselor," Owen shot back. "But if you don't mind, since you've agreed to play in my arena, I'm going to take control of this little talk."

Owen opened the folder and pulled out the top sheet of paper. He knew what it said backward and forward, but he pretended to read it for a moment. Just for effect. He just needed to decide how he was going to start, delicate or with force.

"You've led a pretty interesting life," he began, sliding the paper across the table. "I've known you for a few years now, but I never really put it all together. You were quite the prodigy: your intelligence tests were off the charts as a child, top of your med-school class, very well-regarded trauma surgeon at Denver General. You had the world. But there're some anomalies: never married, no close family, and then about six years ago, you leave your career to be a small-town medical examiner on the other side of the mountains. You've said it was burnout, but I don't see it. The way I've seen you go after this job doesn't say to me that you're burned out on medicine. It says that you're smarter than everyone and you know it, and that you're fascinated by death."

Dr. Heim blinked at him but said nothing. He didn't even look down at the paper.

Crocker reached over and slid the page in front of him. "My client appreciates your compliments, but as for your implications about his psyche, well that's all very thin."

"This isn't," Owen said as he pushed another page across the table. "This is a financial history of donations from Lynn

Sandburg's organization to your alma mater, Doctor. Funding for their medical research department, it appears. She had been quite generous over the years. And then, about ten months ago, the donations stop."

"What's your point, Agent?" Crocker scoffed.

"You mean your client hasn't informed you of his prior relationship to the victim?" Owen pulled out a stack of papers bound with a paper clip and slapped it in front of the doctor. Dr. Heim flinched in his seat but remained quiet. Owen decided to lean on him a little more. "I could read the contents of those e-mails for you if it would help jog your memory, Doctor. There're some very intimate things. I had no idea you could be such a poet."

At that, the doctor raised his head. A lump slid down his throat. "That won't be necessary, Agent Samuelson." Crocker opened his mouth to interrupt, but Dr. Heim raised his hand before he could speak. "I'll handle this, Tony. You are correct, Agent. Lynn and I did have a relationship."

"And why did you fail to disclose this little fact when we first found her?"

"A mistake on my part." The doctor straightened in his chair and placed his hands atop the stack of e-mails, closing his eyes and taking in a deep breath. He looked as though he were feeling his words through his fingertips. After a brief moment, his eyes opened and he continued. "I was afraid public knowledge of our relationship would cause issues with the investigation."

"Like, say, you becoming a suspect?"

The doctor allowed himself a morose laugh. "I suppose there is a certain irony here, isn't there?"

"Why don't you just lay it all out there. There's nothing left to hide from us."

"Lynn and I met at a medical research convention some five years ago where she had given the keynote address. I had tangential knowledge of her, of course, so I was thrilled when I was able to bend her ear for a few moments afterward. We had an immediate connection. It so happened that I had a friend at the university with an interest in the development of a better surgical coagulant that would eliminate the kidney issues that can sometimes occur with the use of these drugs, and I used that to continue talking to her throughout the night. We had dinner together the next day and exchanged e-mail addresses."

"Did you sleep with her?"

"Agent, that doesn't have anything to do with this case!" interjected Crocker.

"I'll decide what has bearing on the case," said Owen evenly, not bothering to look at the lawyer.

"It's fine, Tony. Not that night, Agent. You see, her husband had just passed unexpectedly a few months prior, so, while we were both tempted, we decided not to give in. Out of respect, you see. But if it matters, yes, in the years after. I won't hide the fact that our relationship became intimate."

"How often?"

"We'd only see each other at medical conventions. We'd make arrangements to attend the same ones a few times a year and steal an evening together out of the limelight whenever we could."

His story fit the recovered e-mails perfectly, so far. None of the information was new to Owen. He simply wanted the man to begin to get accustomed to talking about it. He'd bring it all home when the time was right to spring his trap.

"So it would be safe to say that your relationship with Lynn Sandburg was a major factor in your friends at the university getting their funding, correct?"

"I would take great offense to that," the doctor coolly replied. "Lynn funded things that she believed in. Simple as that."

"And yet, she pulled her funding." Owen waited for a reply. The doctor fell silent, so he pressed further. "It must have made you angry. Perhaps it made for a great excuse to select her for one of your little experiments?"

"I wasn't personally involved in that research, Agent. And, if you must know, the reason for Lynn pulling her funding was that she had funded another research project pursuing the same ends. The other project yielded much better results much sooner than the one here did. The university was planning to move the research in a different direction anyway when Lynn pulled the grant. There were no hard feelings between any of us."

"I'll bet." Owen snorted. *Patience. Work the angle. You're going to get him.* "Let me ask you something. How many times did Lynn Sandburg come visit you here? And for that matter, how many times did you visit her at one of her homes?"

"Never in either case."

"Interesting." Owen reached across the table and flipped through the stack of papers in front of the doctor until he came to the last few pages. "Why don't you read those last few e-mails."

Owen sat back with a satisfaction that almost made him ashamed. He pictured the words on those pages in his mind:

It's been too long since I have touched your lips. I don't care what the consequences might be. We deserve to be happy. There were several e-mails saying much the same, imploring Lynn Sandburg to come out to Colorado for a clandestine rendezvous. And then, less than a week ago, a reply: *I'm on the next flight out.*

The doctor's eyes moved back and forth in their sockets as they read the words he'd written. The stoic mask that he had put on began to slip, his face twisting with pain. Finally, he turned over the last piece of paper and looked up. "I didn't write those," he said firmly.

"Forgive me if I don't believe you. Those were pulled from your personal computer, and the IP addresses match."

Crocker looked over to Dr. Heim. "Don't say another w—"

"I didn't write those!" Dr. Heim shouted, cutting off and ignoring his attorney.

"It's funny, Doctor," Owen said, rising from his chair, ready to deliver his long-prepared coup de grâce. "These murders have all the hallmarks of a detached sociopath callously dissecting his victims in some twisted homage to Third Reich experiments, and yet blind passion provides him with his last victim and proves his downfall. Was it some final, sick act of devotion to her that made you only take her heart and leave the rest? Very symbolic, wouldn't you agree? Why else would you dump Lynn Sandburg's body along the riverside rather than submerge it like the others? You'd killed someone you had personal feelings for, and you couldn't hide your sentimentality! That was a huge mistake."

"You can't possibly believe—"

"Ed, stop talking!" Crocker urged.

"Heim," Owen continued. He had his suspect on the ropes. He was emotional. It was imperative that he press his advantage. "That's a solid German name, isn't it?"

"Austrian," Dr. Heim said before he could catch himself.

"We did some studying for history class. There was a Nazi doctor by the name of Heim. He was called lots of other things too: 'Doctor Death,' 'the Butcher of Mauthausen.' He was known for conducting horrific experiments on the inmates of the concentration camp he presided over. After the war, the word is he escaped to Egypt and was named one of the most wanted men in the world for years. But no one knows what ever really happened to him. Maybe he had family?"

"My family has been in this country for over 150 years!" The doctor's lips began to quiver.

"Then you must feel some sort of kinship with the man based on your family name. It's not a hard leap to think that some kind of psychosis would tell you to continue the man's work if you admired him as much as you do."

"This is based on what? Your precious little psychic's visions?"

"I don't need Maureen to bring you down, pal." Owen pulled a photo out of his folder and threw it in front of the other two men. The image was that of a white hazmat suit. "Found in your home. Our people found traces of blood on it. It's a match to Lynn Sandburg's."

The doctor and his lawyer stared at the picture. It was clear to Owen that neither had anticipated this. He wondered why. It wasn't like he made much of an effort to hide the suit in his home. Perhaps he wanted to get caught.

"Doctor," he said, lowering his voice. "I have you on murder one for Lynn Sandburg, and I can tie you Niemann and Lindstrom. You were the physician on record for both of their physicals when they joined the Guard. I'll find plenty more if I keep digging. But I'd rather save Uncle Sam some time and money. If you cooperate and are prepared to make a full confession, I have it on good authority that the DA will not pursue the death penalty. And most likely, you won't even have to serve out your life sentence at Florence. I've got a feeling that you'd be a prime candidate for the institution over in Pueblo. It'll be daily analysis sessions instead of playtime in the yard with the boys. It's the best you can hope for."

Dr. Heim was silent for a moment before he looked up at Owen. "And Professor Freeman? Our working theory is that he was another victim of this killer. Do you really think you can prove I killed him as well?"

"Give me time," said Owen sternly.

Dr. Heim nodded his head. "All the same, Agent." His voice was solemn. "I don't think I'll be taking that deal."

"You want to be a fool and trust this asshole to get you acquitted?" Owen sneered, pointing at Crocker.

"Yes," said Dr. Heim calmly, "because I'm innocent. I believe Mr. Crocker has enough savvy to effectively defend an innocent man. In any case, I'm finished talking to you."

"You're what?"

"You heard my client, Agent." Crocker shot him a spiteful look. "We're done here. Please leave me and Dr. Heim alone to speak privately."

Owen could hardly believe what he was hearing. He *had* the man dead to rights, and he was going to try his luck in court *and* with the possibility of having to face down the needle? Owen shook his head as he collected his papers and left the two men alone in the room.

The man must have a death wish, he said to himself as he slammed the door behind him. It didn't matter. Dr. Edward Heim wasn't his problem anymore. Justice would be served.

"What did you get from him?" asked Turnberry, who waiting for him at the end of the hall.

"The usual defense," Owen replied without stopping.

"The e-mails?"

"Said he didn't write them, of course."

"The white hazmat suit?"

Owen allowed himself a little smile. "Not even Crocker could come up with anything to say about that one."

"But no confession."

"I'd be smiling a lot wider if he gave one," Owen allowed.

"I'm sorry, boss, but I'm just gonna say it. I'm still a little worried. They gotta know that we bent the rules to get that evidence. The defense might try to get it all thrown out. You're positive the DA will risk taking on Crocker and his team with what we're giving them?"

Owen stopped. They had come back to the front of the building. Across the lobby, Maureen was standing with Ranger Tyce. The two were speaking softly together in a corner. Upon the arrival of him and Turnberry, she broke off her conversation and looked over at them. Her face asked a silent question. He nodded to her, and she returned it in kind. It wasn't the end either of them was hoping for, but it was an ending.

Owen put his hand on Turnberry's shoulder. "Let's just take the win. The lawyers will handle it from here."

✝HIR✝Y

Maureen sat, elbows on the bar, cradling her drink in both hands, as the evening crowd started to filter in. The hum of the crowd began to rise, and soon it would be too loud to hear herself think. The irony that she once welcomed such a bustle—and the money that went with it—when she was on the other side of the bar was not lost on her. Tonight, however, she was drained from the investigation and, now that it was over, just wanted to numb up and sleep in peaceful blackness.

Tyce sat on the stool next to her, eyes fixed on the baseball game on the television behind the bar. They'd come in together, but as soon as their appetizers were finished, they had both fallen silent. The revelation that someone inside the investigation was the person they had been searching for seemed to hit him hard. She could understand. She felt the same.

It made her sad in a way. Dr. Heim had been so nice and comforting to her during her own ordeal at the hospital. It was similar to the ease that Father Patrick could put her in and yet, at the same time, wholly different. Where the priest's voice held a certain authority that seemed to quash anxieties held deep in her consciousness, almost without her even noticing, it was the apparent compassion in the doctor's eyes that made her believe what he said. She thought back to the emotionally dead yet frenzied stare of Father Preston. She expected the person responsible for these killings to have the same look.

Shows what I know, she thought to herself bitterly as she took a sip of her drink. *I guess finding and nabbing two serial killers doesn't make me an expert.*

She cocked her head to the side to look at the ranger sitting next to her. He was gazing ahead at the television, yet out of the side of his eyes, he seemed to sense her. He turned slightly and offered her a slight upturn of the corners of his mouth. She returned it in kind. Nothing was said, but there was an understanding between them. Deep down, she felt bad for the man. He'd been so open with her about himself and expected nothing from her in return. She reassured herself that he was lucky, though. He shared in a secret about her that few knew, and he didn't have to be burdened by all of her own baggage that came with that secret. So there they sat, two people broken in their own ways, comforted, at least a little, in the knowledge that they'd interrupted their own struggles for long enough to make a small difference in the world.

The game came to an end, and Tyce slammed down the rest of his beer. He wiped his mouth, tossed some money on the bar, and got to his feet.

"Well, Maureen Allerton," he said, extending his hand, "it was a pleasure to have worked with you. You certainly are one of a kind."

"I'll take that as a compliment," she said, taking his hand and shaking it.

"It is. Seriously, though, I hope you get a break after all this. You deserve it."

"Thanks. I hope you're right. Are you sure you don't wanna stay? Have another drink?"

"Wish I could, but I have to head back to my day job tomorrow, which means I'll need to be up by five."

"Can I give you a few bucks for the drinks at least?"

Tyce smiled and shook his head. "I'll make you a deal. I know you're not one for attachment and all, but what do you say to finding your way back through town one day and taking me out for a beer then?"

"That's a deal," she replied, returning a smile.

Tyce picked up his hat from the bar top and placed it on his head, touching the brim with two fingers and nodding his goodbye. Without another word, he turned and made his way to the front doors. Maureen turned to watch him leave, feeling almost sorry to see him go. He was a nice guy, and she found herself hoping that whatever he needed in his own life to become whole again, he would find it soon.

"Is this stool taken?" a familiar voice said behind her.

Maureen turned back around to come face to face with Dr. Frank. It was a jarring sight, seeing him outside the coroner's office in jeans and a short-sleeved golf shirt instead of his familiar scrubs and lab coat. For a moment, she found herself speechless.

"No, go ahead," she said once she found her voice.

"I saw you over here with the ranger," he said as he sat down, grabbed a coaster, and set his beer down. "But I didn't want to interrupt in case . . ."

"It's not like that," she said with a short laugh.

"Oh, God, I'm sorry," he said, putting his hand to his heart. "I just assumed. Being as good looking as you are, any man would be an idiot not to be interested."

"Well, not him. Tyce likes his women older and without clairvoyance."

"His loss could be my gain," said the doctor with a coy smile.

Maureen winced at the sound of his pickup line. She couldn't deny that the idea of a roll with a handsome doctor she was never going to see again held a certain appeal, but the image of Manny's face flashed in her brain. For some reason, she couldn't push past it.

"That was too forward," Dr. Frank said, clearly picking up on her reaction. "You have someone, don't you?"

"Sort of. I'm flattered, though. Really."

"Well, would you mind if I hung out with you for a while anyway? I'm not really in a headspace where I feel like being alone."

"Yeah, that's fine." She took a sip of her drink. "You want another beer? I'll get the first round."

"Yeah, sure." He finished his bottle. "Only if I get the second."

"Beer and another whiskey and soda," Maureen called to the bartender, putting a twenty-dollar bill on the bar. The bartender nodded and quickly produced another bottle for the doctor and mixed her drink.

"What should we drink to?" Maureen said to the doctor, raising her glass.

"Let's drink to justice," Dr. Frank replied, gently clinking his bottle to her glass. "May it comfort all those who have been wronged."

"That's a pretty deep toast," she said, taking a sip of her drink.

"You think?" he said, his smile betraying the modesty he was clearly trying to portray. "I just made it up."

"So, how are you doing?" Secretly, Maureen hoped he wouldn't want to delve too deep into his feelings, but she felt obligated to at least ask. Nothing else was appropriate to say at the moment anyway, and she had enough cash and a bartender in front of her to handle it if an uncomfortable level of emotions were thrown at her.

"I honestly don't know how to feel right now," he said, leaning an elbow on the bar. "I mean, Dr. Heim was a mentor and even a friend. I can't believe he'd do something so sick. And for as long as he did? Right under my nose? I don't know, I guess I wonder how I didn't see it."

"Most of the time you don't know," she said as sympathetically as she could. "Samuelson says with serial killers, it's usually them messing up that gets them caught. If he hadn't gotten cocky or killed someone intimately connected to him, where would we have been right now?"

She shouldn't have said those details aloud, since her debriefing wasn't scheduled until the next day, but Dr. Frank was involved in the case already, so she didn't really see the harm. Chances were he knew even more details about it than she did.

"You were the real X factor here. I don't think the feds would have stopped him without you."

"I don't know about that," she scoffed. The idea that the success of any investigation hinged on her was an uncomfortable thought.

"Your abilities? They were the real catalyst that put this one away. You should feel proud of yourself."

"You'd think that, wouldn't you? Fact is, I know this thing in my head can help people, and I do my best with it. But pride? No, I don't feel anything like that. Truth be told, I'd give almost anything to be rid of it."

The doctor rubbed his chin in thought, nodding. "I wonder if whatever allows you to do what you do is something that can be gotten rid of."

"I've never given it much thought." She stirred her finger in her drink. "If you ask a friend of mine, it's some sort of divine gift that I need to use in order to be rid of it. I don't know, though, maybe you could take me back to the hospital and cut it out."

He smirked and sipped his beer. "You know," he said cheerily, "surgery is a pretty intimate step. I thought you made it clear you weren't looking for anyone to get inside you tonight, but maybe I'm wearing you down. That almost sounded like a proposition."

"Nice try, buddy. I'm not that easy of a conquest."

"You can't blame me for trying."

"Well, quit trying, Doc. If I decide you're worth taking my pants off for, I'll let you know. But don't hold your breath."

"I'm turning you off with the forwardness, aren't I?"

"Only a lot."

She felt bad about being so hard on him. He was having a hard time, but he was starting to annoy her with his simpering efforts to screw her. If she drew a firm line, she would have no issues hanging out with him for a while.

"Okay," he said, apparently getting the message as he shifted back on his stool a few inches. He cast his face downward with the look of a teenager who had been rejected in the back of a limo on prom night. "You're right. I shouldn't be acting this way. I'm just so mixed up right now. I don't know what to do."

"I understand," Maureen replied and, trying to show him there was no ill will, added, "I know I'm a hot piece."

"So, who is he?"

"Who?"

"This guy who you've spurned the advances of a stud like me for." He shot her another grin as he spoke.

Maureen hesitated, unsure about how much would come spilling out if she talked about Manny. It would be better if that stuff remained hidden deep where it belonged.

The doctor picked up on her discomfort. "You don't want to talk about him."

"It's not that." She took a big drink. "It's just he's in another state and focused on his career and . . . you know what? No." She finished her drink and slammed the glass on the bar. "I'll be right back. I've gotta use the ladies' room."

Without giving him a chance to reply, she pushed herself to her feet and strode to the back of the restaurant. Not too fast. She was already feeling embarrassed about letting her emotions get the better of her and didn't need to go looking like a crazy person running through the maze of tables and chairs.

Once she got inside the bathroom, she quickly looked around to make sure there was no one else there. Fortunately, she was alone. She let out a frustrated groan. "You have to stop thinking about him!" she cursed at her reflection in the mirror.

She and Manny could never be. She knew that. He had his career with the bureau now. If he had really wanted to, he could have found her by now. He could have reached out when she was in prison, and since her location after her release was apparently common knowledge to the feds, there was nothing stopping him from seeing her there either. The fact that he hadn't reached out proved that his feelings for her had changed.

"So why can't I have a little fun?" she whispered to herself before splashing some cold water on her face. She gripped the sink counter hard and, as if giving her reflection permission to take over for a while, declared, "I'm allowed something."

When Maureen came back from the bathroom, she saw that the doctor had taken the liberty of ordering her another drink. She slid back onto her stool and took a sip. It was stronger than her last couple, and it definitely tasted like the bartender had used a different brand. Something from higher up on the shelf, she decided. Doctors could afford the better stuff, after all.

"Thanks," she said to Dr. Frank.

Maureen did her level best to quiet the voice inside her head telling her not to play her charade and slid her stool closer to the doctor. It already felt hollow, but she assured herself that there was nothing wrong with filling a need. It wasn't about intimacy.

But it is. Just not with the guy in front of you, the voice whispered. *You still feel something, and you're afraid. Taking this one to bed isn't about a physical need, it's about trying to kill what's already there. You're trying to feel nothing again.*

You're wrong, she whispered back. And to prove it to herself, she reached out with her foot and slid it up and down the doctor's calf as he spoke. He had begun to talk, unprompted, as she sat down, but she wasn't paying attention what he was saying. She did notice the reaction to her gesture.

His eyes flitted down for a moment before he composed himself and straightened up as he continued with his story, trying to show a sort of callous cool. He of course made no attempt to stop her, despite her assertion just minutes before that she was not available. He was a man; he didn't care.

You're going to regret this. The voice continued to block the doctor's words from registering.

So what? One more thing in my life that I regret. Big deal. A few more drinks, and I'll barely remember it. She finished the remainder of the drink in her glass and nodded at the bartender to fill it again.

"And I guess I should have known, once I realized who we had on the slab," the doctor was saying as she silenced her internal conversation and began to pay attention to him again. "I just never thought he'd hurt Lynn."

"Wait a second," Maureen interjected. "You're saying you knew about the two of them?"

The doctor dropped his head. "I'm sorry," he said meekly. "Dr. Heim forgot to close his browser one day a while back, and I couldn't help but see one of his e-mails to her. I didn't mean to peek, but what he was writing was just so unlike him. I was fascinated. I should have told Agent Samuelson, but I was afraid that if I did, Dr. Heim would know it was me. He may have been a monster, but I still didn't want him to feel like I'd betrayed him. In spite of everything, he was always a good friend to me. More like a father, really."

"Well, I guess I can understand that." Who was she to judge, considering the way she'd tried to help Father Patrick? "But you still should have told someone."

"I know," he admitted, taking a sip of his beer. "And I'd

like to think I would have if you and the boys hadn't caught up with him as quickly as you did."

Maureen could see his inaction had caused him enough pain, so she decided she could give him just a little bit of her own, personal experience. She polished off her drink to help the words come out, waving the bartender over and indicating she fill it up again. Another sip and she was prepared. "I know what it's like to protect a father figure," she told him. "I don't really know my own father. He left my mother when I was about eight, and I haven't seen him since. I hadn't even known what a father was supposed to look like until I met my friend Father Patrick on a case last year. He saved my life, but he had to kill someone else to do it. I'm only working with the FBI as part of a deal to keep them from bringing charges against him."

"I could see that you didn't want to be here when you first showed up, but I had no idea it was like that."

"Well, believe it. But if I had known what the deal was going to include, I'd have picked up and hiked into the wilderness the first day I arrived on the farm and let myself die of starvation." She didn't really mean that, but it proved her point.

"Samuelson can be a hard ass, can't he?" The doctor laughed.

"Eh, we came to an understanding. It's taken me years to admit it, and I still struggle, but accepting people is a lot easier when you allow yourself to get inside their heads."

"Sometimes I wish I had the ability to do what you do. It might make all this easier."

"It doesn't."

"Well, I'm not so sure. Maybe if I had been able to know what other people were thinking, I would have gotten along better with my own father. And mother for that matter. But it's too late now."

"So they're . . ."

"Gone," he finished for her.

"I'm sorry. How long?"

"Several years now. Since well before I started at the ME's office. Before I met Dr. Heim, even."

"And you don't have anyone else?"

"Not really. I had a grandmother, but she's been gone longer than my parents. I actually miss her most of all. No, I'm pretty much alone now. I really don't go out, and it's kinda hard to find someone when everyone you meet isn't breathing." Dr. Frank gave her a sad smile and took a sip of his beer. "Sorry, I'll bet you'd rather talk about almost anything else."

Maureen was about to tell the doctor that he could go on for as long as he pleased when she began to feel the room turn under her. She looked around in astonishment. Her empty drink glass duplicated itself before her eyes. She didn't even remember finishing it. None of the walls were clear, and Dr. Frank's face was blurry in her sight. On pure instinct, she tried to stand, but her legs had no strength in them, and she felt herself stumble back onto the barstool. She felt her head start to sag, but she worked to keep enough focus. Clutching her head in her hands, she tried to shake loose from the sound of pumping blood in her ears, but her mind remained in a fog. She tried to count her drinks.

Four? No, five? Six? In how long? Her mind refused to cooperate. *Something's wrong.*

Maureen felt a firm hand on her cheek turn her head. She heard Dr. Frank, speaking as though he were underwater.

"Easy there," he said. "Are you okay? How much have you had?"

"She looks like she's going to be sick," the distorted image of the bartender said to him.

"Don't worry, I'm a doctor." He placed both hands on the sides of her head and held it up. His face was nothing but a skin-colored blob. "Yeah, she went at those last couple drinks pretty hard. She'll be fine after a good night's sleep. I know where she lives. I'll see that she makes it there in one piece."

Maureen felt a few garbled words fall out of her mouth before she realized that they were moving toward the door. Even though it was night outside, the single streetlight shining through the glass felt brighter than the sun to her eyes. She began to panic, to feel the danger she was in, but she was powerless to fight back. The noise of the bar died away as the door shut behind them, and she could feel every one of the laborious steps that took her farther from the eyes of anyone who could help. She collapsed but, at the same moment, felt her feet leave the ground. She was floating, floating away into the night.

A moment later, all movement stopped, and she tried once more to raise her head. It only worked for a moment, and then she slumped back into the doctor's chest.

"What did you do?" she managed to whisper, though her voice sounded almost alien to her own ears.

"You're a fascinating woman, Ms. Allerton," he said in a low tone, almost shaking with anticipation. "You are truly one of a kind. I can't wait to examine you."

A metallic pop broke the night air, and she knew instantly what it was: the sound of a car trunk opening.

THIRTY-ONE

Gabriel sat in his car with the window down just far enough to allow the night air in. It had been a long day of getting shut out by the sheriff's department, and he was tired. At least his FBI contact came through with the scoop that Dr. Edward Heim was in custody for the murders. The authorities had been very tight-lipped about that. In the two days of him watching local and national news, he hadn't heard any anchor or field reporter even report that anyone had been arrested. It was the type of story that could seriously bolster his career, but there was one thing missing that would *make* it. Gabriel looked across the street at the neon lights that lit up *The Lookout*, the name of a popular sports-themed bar on the south side of town. It had been a good while since his brother-in-law had gone in with Maureen Allerton.

Al had come knocking at her motel room door as he was sitting in the parking lot, getting ready to head over and try once more to conduct his interview. Her testimony would be the last piece of his greatest story, and he was determined to get it. Or at least take one more slap to the face for his efforts before he broke the news. Once he saw Al leaving with her, though, he decided to tail them in the hopes that a better chance to speak with Maureen alone would still present itself. He didn't really feel like talking to his former brother-in-law at the moment.

It wasn't that he was nursing any grudge over his little visit to his motel room, he was simply in the way, just like he had been since this little adventure started. The way he jealously protected her whenever he was around really struck him as something beyond a casual friendship. He'd hardly allowed her to say a word at their lunch, and he'd nearly ran him over earlier in week when he tried to talk to her. It was almost as if she were like a little sister. Or a daughter. He laughed to himself at the realization, amused that he'd ever considered anything romantic going on between them. He could almost see Alec in the bar right now, seated with a comfortable few feet between him and Maureen, quietly drinking a beer with his eyes fixed on the ball game. No ladies' man was he.

It wasn't long before he saw Al emerge from the bar and head over to his truck. Alone. He couldn't say he was surprised. The man had a day job and an almost irritable sense of responsibility. He was headed home to bed, and Gabriel knew from the information he'd received on Maureen that the woman liked her drinks. Some added quality time with the bartender would surely make her more pliable to his advances. He could be patient, but the real challenge would be staying awake.

The minutes crawled by at a snail's pace. There was no sign of Maureen Allerton. With her ride gone, he expected her to eventually emerge and walk the three miles back to the motel. He'd begun to wonder if there was a back exit to the bar when a couple came stumbling out. As he looked, Gabriel noticed that the woman seemed barely able to keep on her feet. She leaned hard into the man at her side. Soon it became apparent that she was going to faint.

"Too much to drink, lady?" he smirked out loud.

His laugh was cut off before it could pass his lips when the couple passed under the light of a streetlamp. Gabriel couldn't see their faces, but the light shined on the woman's honey-blonde hair tied back in a ponytail. As she was lifted into the man's arms, the flannel shirt tied around her waist draped down and hung, swaying as he carried her into the night. He recognized the shirt instantly.

I'll be damned.

As quietly as he could, Gabriel opened his car door and crept down the street, trying not to follow too closely. He crossed to the other side of the street to make sure he stayed hidden from their view, sneaking around the streetlights as best as he could. The man carried Maureen to a car parked in the shadows between two dark buildings. He watched as the man opened the trunk and then strode around to the driver's side of the vehicle, arms empty, and opened the door. As soon as Gabriel saw the man disappear again and heard the door slam shut, he double-timed it back to his own car.

He made sure to keep his headlights off as he followed the black car through town. They were heading north, toward the mountains. He kept his distance but still tried to get a license plate as they bumped along. One of the bulbs that lit it up was out, so he had a hard time making out the three numbers at the beginning, but he eventually was able to memorize the letters at the end.

The other car turned onto the northern highway that led

into the mountains. The lights of the town dimmed as Gabriel followed, and it was almost impossible to see anything but the taillights in front of him. He was forced to move closer to keep his own car on the road. It wasn't that difficult; the man didn't seem to be in too much of a hurry, nor did he seem to have picked up on Gabriel's tailing. He wondered where the other man was taking Maureen. They were fast running out of side roads to turn off on before they faced the twists and turns of the mountains.

As Gabriel was going over his thoughts, the other car made a sudden shift to the left and hit its brakes. Before he could react, he felt the sudden impact on his door. Gabriel lost control of the steering wheel and found himself spinning off the side of the road. There was a loud popping sound, and he hit one more bump before finally coming to a stop. The other car sped off into the night. Gabriel floored the accelerator, but the engine only revved; his car didn't move.

Cursing, he got out of the car. Even in the ambient light, he could see that the pop he heard was his back passenger-side tire blowing out. There was no way he was following the kidnapper now. He looked down the road back toward town. There were no cars coming, and it was going to be a long way to walk back to town to find some help. If only he'd been able to use his connections to get Agent Samuelson's phone number. The idea of calling the agent irked him, but it was better to talk to him than the locals. At the very least he could prove his value to the top end of law enforcement and get the respect he deserved.

He pulled out his phone to dial up the number for the agent's motel in the hopes of tracking him down but then had another idea. He scrolled through his contacts and found the one he wanted.

"Hello?" said the voice on the other end.

I must have woken him up.

"Hey, it's me," he said into the receiver. "I need a favor."

THIRTY-TWO

Owen leaned back in his seat and rubbed his eyes. It was late. Turnberry sat on the other side of the desk. They were alone in a back office of the sheriff's department. Two glasses of some pretty decent scotch sat untouched in front of them. They didn't feel much like celebrating. Even though they had their man in custody, a heavy cloud hung over them.

There was little reason for them to be so glum, aside from the fact that their killer had been right under their noses and was an integral part of the investigation. He'd zeroed in on either Heim or Frank as potential suspects over a week ago, but he had continued to harbor the hope that the perp would turn out to be someone else in the local medical field, someone he hadn't worked with before or even known. It was a tough pill to swallow when the collar was someone you actually used to like. The funny thing was, even when Maureen pointed to the room that the killer was standing in during their experiment, he'd have put his money on the younger doctor. He'd made a slight error in judgment, he now realized. He should have separated them to make sure, but he had figured at the time that doing so would tip them off to the fact that they were part of the experiment just like Tyce and the other doctors he had chosen to be present.

Navarro broke the silence when he knocked on the open door before stepping into the room. "Hey, boss. This just came in from the office." He held up a thick manila folder stuffed with papers.

"What's that?" Owen asked.

"It's the background search on Dr. Frank."

"Why are we just getting this now?"

"Office said that once we arrested Heim, they put it on the back burner, but they still kept at it just in case. It came in a few minutes ago."

"Give it here." Owen was a little perturbed that he was just getting it now but was too tired to make a big deal out of it.

Navarro sat down next to Turnberry. Owen pulled out another glass and poured him a couple of fingers. They each took a drink and sat in silence for a moment. Owen's finger began to mindlessly trace abstract designs on the folder cover as he sat in thought.

"You going to look through the folder," asked Turnberry, "or are you just going to sit there and pet it?"

"What?" said Owen, snapping out of his thoughts.

"I know that look," Turnberry replied. "You're thinking there's more to this whole thing, and it's bugging you. You had us looking into Frank and Heim and half a dozen other local medical professionals even before Maureen did her little experiment. And now you're sitting there with info on our other prime suspect, so what are you waiting for? Let's have a look!"

Owen nodded and flipped the folder open. There was the whole life's history of the younger doctor laid out before him: notes on the family; high school, college, and med-school transcripts; financial information. The boys at the home office had been thorough.

"It's funny," he said out loud to the other agents, "I would have put my money on Frank if you'd asked me a couple days ago."

"I know what you mean," said Turnberry. "I keep thinking about what Lowdon was saying about how he couldn't keep up with the guy he was chasing that night at the motel. And about how you mentioned that Maureen had told you that the person who dumped Lynn Sandburg's body didn't seem to have much trouble carrying it down that bank to the riverside."

"Eh, you never know," said Navarro. "Dr. Heim might be one of those old-man-gym-rat types. Like Professor Freeman was. You'd think he must look pretty decent with his shirt off if he roped in a woman like Lynn Sandburg. Not for nothing, but I've seen other pictures of her from before we had her on the slab, and she had all the hallmarks of a total cougar."

"Grow up, Rick!" Owen chided.

"Apologies, boss. But it doesn't make my point less valid. What gets me is the guy leaving that hair on her body and not dunking it."

"Sentiment," said Owen.

"Yeah, maybe," said Turnberry. "But if it was just sentiment and the doctor simply couldn't bring himself to put someone who he had an emotional attachment to in the water, why did he leave that hair for us to find?"

"Maureen said she felt like he was taunting us," Navarro said. "I'd tend to agree."

"But, Steve's right," said Owen. He was beginning to get

angry with himself that he hadn't thought this hard about it all before. "The two acts don't sync. If you really think about it—the hair, the spying on Maureen at the motel—it's almost like he was testing out her abilities."

"Because she'd be a prime candidate for his next target if she really were a psychic," Turnberry finished for him.

A knot formed in Owen's stomach. "Where is she?"

"I saw her at the motel this afternoon," said Navarro. "She was heading into her room when I left to come here after I got the notification that Frank's workup had been e-mailed."

"You don't think . . ." Turnberry began.

"I don't know," Owen replied, shaking his head. "But let's get over there and make sure."

He gathered up the papers into the folder. They left their scotch glasses on the desk and hurried through the halls of the department and out the door. Navarro and Turnberry took their usual spots in the driver's and passenger seat, and Owen sat in the back and began leafing through the file on Dr. Frank as they sped toward the motel.

It felt like hours before they pulled into the parking lot. From the car, Owen could already see that Maureen's room was dark, but that wasn't the sight that gave his stomach a sour feeling. The parking lot lights didn't give much illumination, but even through the dimness of the night, he could see two men at the door of his room, knocking earnestly. It was Ranger Tyce and his scum-sucking brother-in-law, Gabriel Lowdon.

"He took her," Tyce said as Owen and the other agents approached.

"Why didn't you call me?" he demanded.

"We tried," Lowdon piped up. "We couldn't get through to you. Figured you guys would be here."

Owen snapped his head to look at the reporter. His instinct was to tell the man to shut it, but his voice was devoid of the usual antagonism. Lowdon was genuinely concerned about whatever was going on. Owen pulled out his cell phone. He had three missed calls from the ranger and one number he didn't recognize. It had a 720 area code, though, which obviously meant it was from Gabriel.

"Shit," he mumbled under his breath as he put the phone back in his pocket. "I must have been in a dead zone at the sheriff's department." He pushed past the two men, unlocked his door, and went inside. "Tell me everything. Quick."

"I was following Allerton tonight, trying to take another shot at getting her story," the reporter began. Owen frowned at him, but Lowdon didn't register it and kept on. "She and Al headed into *The Lookout* around eight-ish. I decided I wasn't going to get my interview in a crowded bar, so I waited. Al came out around nine thirty alone, hopped in his truck, and drove away. I figured once she came out, that'd be my chance, so I waited. Little while later I saw two people come out, a guy and a girl. The girl was swaying like she was wasted and then she fainted. I caught a glimpse of her in the streetlight and was sure it was her."

"Did you see the guy's face?" Owen pressed.

Lowdon shook his head. "I followed them to a little side alley where he had his car. He put her in the trunk and drove north out of town. I followed him. Didn't think he made me, but on the state highway north, he pulled to the left, dropped level with me, and ran me off the road. Blew out a tire, so I called Al for help. Told him the story on the phone, and he came to pick me up. He said he tried you twice on the way to get me and then he and I both tried on the way back here."

"How long have you guys been here?" Navarro jumped in.

"Only a couple minutes," Tyce replied before Lowdon could speak.

"And where did he run you off the road?" Owen asked the reporter.

"I'd say maybe two miles from the climb into the mountains?" He looked at Tyce as he spoke. The ranger nodded in agreement.

It made sense. That was the area where Maureen had her first dream and the area identified as the likeliest dumping site for the older bodies.

"Okay," Owen said, looking down at his watch. "So that puts her abduction at, what, half hour, forty minutes ago tops?"

"Sounds about right," said Lowdon.

"What kind of car?" asked Turnberry.

"Black Beamer. Four door. Colorado plates. Last number is a two, and the letters I'm pretty sure were C-W-P."

"Pretty sure?" Owen glowered at the reporter.

"As sure as I can be with the light I had to deal with," the reporter shot back. "I made the last letters an acronym so I'd remember: chicks with pri—"

"All right, I get it!" Owen stopped him. "Rick, fire up the computer, run the partial, and let's see what we get."

The room was silent except for the tap of Navarro's fingers on the keyboard. Owen paced, Turnberry leaned on the windowsill, and Tyce and Lowdon sat on the bed with their hands folded. No one looked comfortable.

"All right," said Navarro after a few minutes. "I did get one hit, but it looks like a dead end."

Owen came over and stood behind the younger agent and looked down at the screen. "Stolen?" he asked.

Navarro shook his head.

"What is it?" asked Turnberry.

"Car's registered to a Brigitte French," said Navarro. "Eighty-eight years old."

"Is the address along the river in the direction they were going?" Turnberry leaned on the desk.

"Nope. Timber Drive, opposite direction."

Tyce rose from the bed and walked over to the computer. He looked down at it for a minute before shaking his head. "That's not a real address."

"How can you tell?" Owen asked.

"The house number is in the 2300s," the ranger replied. "I grew up on the next street up. Both are dead ends, and the house numbers stop in the 2200s."

Owen thought for a moment before grabbing the folder off the table. He began leafing through it.

"What are you looking for?" asked Turnberry.

"Brigitte," Owen replied, continuing to look through for the paper he was looking for. He found it and held it up. "Family history. Eldon Frank had a grandmother named Brigitte Frankreich."

"Same first name," said Lowdon.

Owen frowned at the man's stating of the obvious. "Same last name too." The rest of the room stared blankly at him. "More or less."

"How could you possib—" Turnberry began.

"Two years of middle school German. Frankreich is how they say 'France.' And there's more." He slammed a few more papers on the table and spread them out. "Brigitte Frankreich came to the country in 1947 with her three-year-old son. They were granted citizenship a few months after their arrival in New York and moved to Springfield, Illinois, before settling in Colorado Springs. Never married. And here's the kicker: there's no death certificate for her, but there's also no trace of her for the last fourteen years."

"Says here she was checked in through immigration in New York under the name Brigitte French," said Turnberry, picking up one of the papers.

"You noticed that too." Owen picked up another paper and began to pace again. "So we have a twenty-five-year-old woman who immigrates alone to America just after World War II under an English version of her name and promptly changes it back. What's that say about her?"

"She was a Nazi." They all turned around. The voice that spoke was Lowdon's. "What? You don't become an expert on government conspiracies and not know that we brought over dozens of Reich scientists during the war and that afterward, thousands of POWs stayed in America—not to mention that just as many people fled Germany and were also given citizenship, both civilian refugees and high-ranking Nazis. Being that she was a young woman on her own with a child who was born around 1944 or 1945, it's entirely possible she was part of a government program called—"

"Lebensborn," Owen and Turnberry finished for him.

"There's more." Owen continued shuffling through the remaining papers on the table. "It seems that the son, Ernst, had the family name legally shortened to Frank in 1969. I would make a guess that, if Lowdon's theory about his mother is true, he didn't agree with her ideals. Or maybe he was just trying to fit into American society. In either case, it seems his son took hold of them. Where can we find Frank's parents?"

Turnberry read through a page at the bottom of a pile. He looked up with an open mouth, and a pained look crossed his face. "We can't," he said quietly. "They were reported missing eleven years ago and declared legally dead a little less than four years ago."

"Did they have property along the river?"

Turnberry looked back down at the paper. His eyes moved rapidly back and forth. "They did. But with no will, the house went into probate. Eldon rescinded his claim on it, and the property was sold—"

"Damn," said Navarro.

"—to a Ms. Brigitte Frankreich," finished Turnberry.

"Mount up!" shouted Owen. He didn't need any more information. They'd been completely misdirected by the young doctor, and he wasn't going to let that slide. If he had Maureen, he wouldn't miss the chance to cut her up, even if he felt like there was heat coming down on him. "Navarro, you stay here and get me the local deputies as backup! Then you're going to sit here, get me every last stitch of information on the life of Eldon Frank, and find out why in the hell it took so long to get me this!"

With that, he threw the papers in his hand at the young agent and rushed out the door. Turnberry, Tyce and Lowdon followed at his heels.

"Give me the keys," he said to Turnberry.

The other agent cocked his head as though trying to remind him who the better driver was.

"Now's not the time to argue. Give! And you two"—he turned to the ranger and the reporter—"don't even think of following us."

"Fat chance on that." Lowdon snorted. Tyce just crossed his arms and nodded.

"Fine. It's your funeral. Don't come crying to me if you get hurt." Owen jumped into the driver's seat. He turned the key and barely got his seat belt buckled before he put the gas pedal to the floor and sped away.

"Keep cool, boss," said Turnberry, gripping the dashboard. "We're going to get him."

"That's not what I'm worried about." He tightened his grip on the steering wheel. He was confident they were going to get their man. Whether it would be before or after he had another body on his conscience, that was another matter.

Hang in there, Maureen.

THIRTY-THREE

Maureen opened her eyes to find herself staring up at a ceiling of smooth concrete. As she became aware of her body, she was able to determine she was sitting in a reclined position on a plastic-covered chair with her arms elevated at her sides. Her mouth was bone dry, and she found it hard to swallow. Her vision was still a little blurry, but she could identify a single light source coming from somewhere on her left. Her stomach churned. She was certain that she had been drugged.

Maureen worked to remember everything before the lights went out. She'd had a few drinks with Ranger Tyce at a bar on the edge of town. She was drinking whiskey and soda. Tyce had left, and she'd started a conversation with Dr. Frank. He was distraught over his mentor being a demented killer. She'd gone to the bathroom and had come back for one last drink, still deciding whether or not she was going to take a roll in bed with him. That was when the room started to spin, and everything went fuzzy. The last thing she remembered was being helped out of the bar by who she thought was the young doctor and him saying something.

"I can't wait to examine you," she mumbled out loud, echoing the doctor's words. "Oh, Christ!"

Maureen understood her danger. There was no way to tell how long she'd been out. Her adrenaline took over, and she found a reserve of strength to try and thrust herself out of the chair and find a way out of wherever she was. Her torso rose several inches off the chair, but her wrists were held fast by a pair of restraints, and she flopped back against the plastic cushions. She dropped her chin to her chest to examine her bonds. They were stitched-canvas straps fastened with a buckle. They were tight, and the buckle loop was on top of her wrists. It would be difficult to slip them, but if she had enough time, she might be able to do it. The straps were not attached to the chair, so all she had to do was maneuver the buckle within reach of her fingers.

It was easier said than done. Maureen clenched her fists and wriggled her forearms, trying to get enough slack in the strap to try and maneuver her hands into a position where she could undo the buckle and free herself. At first, it didn't seem to work, but after several minutes, she managed to work the buckle of the strap about an inch around her left forearm toward the underside of the armrest. There was some hope but still a long way to go.

Her head was beginning to clear enough for her to take another look around the room. Most of the walls were in shadow. There were shapes along them, but she couldn't make them out, except for a long metal table along the wall to her left that was covered with all sorts of medical supplies: scalpels, syringes, forceps, and more. The light that she was seeing was coming from a lamp on the table. It shined coldly off the objects.

"What do you think of my laboratory?" a voice came from the darkness.

Maureen turned her head toward the sound. Across the room, a tall silhouette filled the doorway. It took a step into the room and flipped on a light switch on the wall. A single bulb above her head came on. She squinted as her eyes adjusted to the change in brightness. As her eyes became accustomed, she could see that the shapes she had seen in the shadows were shelves and jars filled with blue-green liquid. The jars were each labeled, and though she couldn't read the writing at that distance, she could see what appeared to be different organs suspended inside. The trophies of a killer.

The sound of approaching footsteps filled the air. The face of Dr. Frank passed in front of the light and hovered over her. He wore only a subtle grin on his face, and if it weren't for the wild look in his eyes, she could mistake it for his gentle bedside manner. As it was, all she could think to do was spit at him.

"That was impolite," he sneered softly, wiping his cheek.

"Some people would consider drugging and tying down another person a worse offense."

Dr. Frank nodded absently and turned away for a moment. Almost nonchalantly he pulled a chair away from the table and dragged it next to her. Its legs screeched along the concrete floor. The doctor sat backward on the chair and leaned his chest on its back. He traced a finger up her arm before twirling it in a loose strand of her hair. The feeling of his touch made Maureen's skin crawl. She couldn't tell whether it was a reaction to the moment or to the idea that she had ever harbored ideas of sleeping with him.

"You don't see how special you are." His voice was soft, almost comforting, but his face remained unchanged and emotionless. He seemed to be talking at her, not to her. There was a faraway look in his eyes.

"Yeah, just special enough to cut up and throw in the river, huh?" She didn't know what else to say. Somehow, she just knew that she had to keep him talking.

"It amazes me that you can see through my eyes and still not get what I am doing here." Dr. Frank shook his head and pushed himself up from the chair.

"What's there to get? You're a creep who likes to kill people and play around with their bodies. You think you're special?"

"I think," he said, clearly fighting to keep his tone calm through gritted teeth, "that I'm a scientist."

The doctor began to pace the room, his hand to his lips. He seemed to be trying to work out exactly what he was about to say. Maureen felt a tingle in the back of her neck. She had seen this before, eleven months ago in a small church in Missouri: he was about to snap. And that made him dangerous. Regardless, she was trapped.

"You and the rest of the investigation team really oversimplified everything from the Lebensborn program and especially their concept of eugenic science. Demonized it, really. Sure, men like Himmler and his followers believed that the Aryan race was superior and that selective breeding was the key to a pure population. But they missed one important thing: the Aryans weren't real. It was the *idea* behind eugenics, that notion that we can create a population of perfect humans, that was worth pursuing.

"Imagine finding the secret to why certain individuals are highly intelligent or naturally athletic. Imagine knowing the physiology behind a person's ethical codes and then coupling it with advances in genetic research, stem cells, and gene therapy. Everything about a human being can be broken down into the simple and unique arrangement of a few basic proteins. Once that secret is discovered, we can give mothers the opportunity to ensure that their children will be the smartest, strongest, and longest-living versions of themselves."

"You really are insane."

"*I'm* the crazy one?" Dr. Frank spun around and stared at her. "This idea goes back much further than me. It wasn't even the Reich's idea, though they at least had the wherewithal to aggressively pursue it. The pursuit was founded on some poor scientific reasoning, but it was a start regardless. I find some of their methods quite useful in my work, actually. But of course, you've seen that, haven't you?"

Maureen set her jaw and stared back, a trick she'd noted from watching Manny, Layton, and Samuelson interrogate witnesses. She had him talking, seeking some kind of acknowledgment. He'd keep going if she stayed silent. The doctor seemed to take the bait. He stalked back over to the chair, sat backward on it again, and this time leaned in even closer.

"I wasn't sure about you," he said in a lowered voice. "Then you came back, talking about your visions of Lynn tied up in this very room. I was impressed, but as a scientist, I needed to test you further."

"The hair."

"Neat, huh?" He smiled. "It was then that I knew you were the real deal. After that, it was easy to manipulate you."

"Obviously, you set up Dr. Heim."

315

"He's been so trusting for years." Dr. Frank ran his hand along her cheek, excitement beginning to grow in his eyes. "I've had my plan in place for a while, in case I needed to leave in a hurry. Can't have anyone looking for me. Heim never realized I'd found out about his little affair with Lynn Sandburg. He wasn't nearly as careful as he thought. She gave me the final piece I needed. Sadly, I haven't had as much time to examine that heart of hers as I'd like, thanks to you and your little experiment." He raised himself up and smirked, shaking a finger at her. "That was a good one. I didn't anticipate you coming up with something like that."

"How did you get Dr. Heim into the morgue?" She hoped his pride would take over.

It did. "It took a moment and some luck. After you were out but before the monitors indicated that you had hit stage four, I leaned over to him and whispered something about what a shame it was that Lynn Sandburg died so far away from any of her loved ones—something simple to tug at the heartstrings. I then pretended I got a page and excused myself. I figured you'd be inside my head by then and headed over to the morgue. Judging by the information you'd given in Samuelson's ridiculous war room sessions, I took a guess at how long in real time you tended to stay within a dream and did my best to time things.

"I guess I did a pretty good job because I managed to close her back in the vault and get inside the supply closet before I heard Heim come in and reopen her drawer. It was just a minute or two later when I heard the arrest. I knew that you didn't see where I went when they didn't find me. It was almost too good to be true!"

"Why you chose this path is beyond me." She shook her head. "You're so brilliant. If all of this is really out of a pure desire to improve the human race, why not just get yourself one of those grants? People donate their bodies to science all the time."

"You shouldn't talk about things you know nothing about," the doctor snapped. "I refuse to jump through all those bureaucratic hoops. I was taught to never allow anyone to get in the way of my goals, no matter what."

"Your parents must be so proud," Maureen said dryly.

Dr. Frank actually laughed—not the evil chuckle of a madman but the hearty chuckle of someone who was truly tickled by what they'd just heard. "Ah, yes, them," he said after a moment, wiping his eyes. "Sadly, it wasn't them I was talking about. I share no core beliefs with them. My grandmother, on the other hand, she was one who would have understood."

"Do tell," Maureen said in her best mocking tone.

"My grandmother was just a young woman in Bavaria when she answered her country's call to create the next generation. She was a true believer in what they were doing and was such a picture of Aryan perfection in the eyes of the doctors who ran the facility. My father was the product of her and an SS officer. I don't think she ever really figured out which one—she was with quite a few before she got pregnant—but she was proud. When the Reich fell, she knew that the public would turn on her, so she applied for asylum in America and came here when my father was three. She kept her past private, intelligently so, but she shared it all with me—despite my father's objections.

"Sadly, it was also her death nearly twenty years ago that showed me the flaws in the science. If she were truly a genetically exceptional person, she'd still be alive. It's one of my deepest sorrows that I was never able to examine her remains. Cremation, you see. I was more fortunate with my mother and father."

Maureen felt her eyes widen. He was more of a monster than she had thought. "You mean, you killed your own parents?"

"Is that what I said?" He smiled, putting on an air of false ignorance. "Too bad you'll never know for sure."

Dr. Frank took a large syringe from the table and filled it from a glass bottle. He set it back on the table and stalked over to her, removing a rubber tourniquet from his pocket and tying it around her left arm. He turned back and reached for the needle again.

"You're not even going to rub any alcohol on my arm?" Maureen blurted. She felt her heart rate begin to quicken. She had to find another way to distract him.

"Cute, Ms. Allerton," he sneered. "Very cute." He moved next to her. The needle was getting closer to her skin.

"There's one thing I have to know." Her words made him draw back. "A last request?"

"Of course." He waved her to continue.

"I read it right, didn't I? Professor Freeman was one of yours, but you wrote *Frohman* in your experiment binder."

Dr. Frank smiled. "I never took any of his classes at Boulder, but there was an intramural kayaking club that he headed that I belonged to for two years. He confided in the members that his father changed the family name when he came over from Germany during the war. Apparently the family was wanted by the Nazi High Command. Rouge Jews, you see." The doctor took a long breath and stared wistfully into the distance as if recalling some special memory. After a moment, he looked back over her and leaned down. "So yes, Ms. Allerton. You can rest assured you were not mistaken."

Maureen felt the pinch of the needle entering her arm. A cold sensation began to flow through her veins. Her body thrashed in anger the moment Dr. Frank withdrew the syringe.

"It's no use," he said to her, putting on his bedside voice again. "You'll just speed up the inevitable if you fuss like that. Why not just lie back and relax? You might find the experience quite pleasurable as you slip away."

"You're not going to get away with this, you asshole!" It was an idle threat and she knew it, but it was all that she could muster.

"I'll be back in a few minutes," he said and then, with a casual nonchalance, he leaned down and kissed her lips. He pulled away and licked his own as if savoring some pleasant flavor. "Mmm, almost makes me wish we had a little more time for other things."

Maureen would have chewed her own arm off at that moment if it meant she could get a chance to take him down. Instead, all she could do was scream at the top of her lungs. Every filthy thing she could think to call him, she did. Dr. Frank sighed and produced a handkerchief. He rolled it into a strap and stuck it in her mouth, tying it behind her head.

"I didn't want to have to do that," he said. Then he turned back to the table and picked up the scalpel. He held the instrument in front of him, testing the edge with his thumb as he began to make his way out. "You need some sharpening."

Maureen's desperation rose with each step he made toward the door. She continued to struggle against her restraints and scream into the cloth lodged in her mouth. The doctor turned back just before crossing the threshold.

"A fighter to the end," he mused. "That's surprising. I took you for more of a quitter. Oh well, you learn something new every day. Well, goodbye, my dear Maureen. I can see I'm going to enjoy this examination." He began to close the door behind him. "You know," he added, sticking his head back through the opening, "I've never taken anyone's eyes before. There has to be some correlation between them and your second sight. I think I'll be taking them in addition to your brain."

Dr. Frank's head disappeared, and the door slammed shut. Maureen felt tears begin to well up in her eyes. To think, Father Patrick had saved her life from one madman just for her to be killed and mutilated at the hands of another. The horror, the anger, the fear at facing down death, bound, gagged, and alone, was too much. Perhaps it would be best to take the doctor's advice and just slip away.

The effects of the drug were starting to become more irresistible, and yet—through the waves of euphoria washing through her head—another feeling pushed its way to the surface. Determination. Maybe it was Father Patrick's voice ingrained in her mind. Maybe it was the hand of God Himself reaching down into her dungeon and offering her a ray of hope. Whatever it was, she made the decision then and there that even if she were to die that night, she would not go quietly.

The entire time Dr. Frank had been talking—whenever his back was turned for long enough—Maureen continued to try and quietly maneuver the buckle on the strap holding her right arm down. She hadn't been successful at loosening it enough to slip her hand out, but she had managed to move the buckle farther toward the underside of the armrest. Now she twisted in earnest, keeping her breathing calm in order to stave off unconsciousness for as long as possible. After some time, the buckle was where she thought she wanted it, but when she tried to curl her hand around the end of the armrest, she found she couldn't reach it to unlatch it.

So much for that brilliant idea.

Another wave of dizziness flowed behind her eyes. She shook her head and took a deep breath, centering her mind again. She inspected the strap again. It was thick fabric, but it was cross-stitched together with a very thin thread, and the thread was beginning to fray. Maureen craned her neck to look along the underside of the armrest. Her instincts paid off. The pad of the armrest was held on by two screws drilled into the underside. The closest screw head to the strap was about two inches toward the rear of the chair and had, over time and perhaps driven by the straining of other victims struggling against their bonds, become loose enough to stick out just a few millimeters from its hole. It might just be enough to saw through the strap. It was a long way to pull it, but she had to try.

Her writhing had given the strap just a little slack. She gritted her teeth and curled her hand back. She yanked her elbow backward. The strap slid back less than a quarter of an inch. But it was something. Maureen yanked again. And again. After nearly a dozen tugs, she felt a different type of resistance. A stray thread had caught in the grooves of the screw.

Maureen began to tug her arm from side to side, trying to create a shearing motion along the screw head. Nothing seemed to happen. She rocked her arm harder. At last, she felt the strap loosen just a bit. She pulled again to try and get the strap to loosen more, but the threads had slipped off the screw head. It would take her forever to get them back on—if she even could. She found she could roll her wrist under the strap more than before, so she gritted her teeth, flattened her hand, and pulled her arm back. The flesh on the back of her hand scraped along the coarse fabric, but she was thankful for the pain. It kept her head clear. With a last effort, her hand jerked free.

Maureen paused to take a deep breath. Her vision had begun to blur, akin to a long night of whiskey. She had enough experience functioning in that state, thankfully. She flexed her right hand to get the feeling back in it and reached across to undo the buckle holding down her left. Once both arms were free, she tried to stand. It was only at that moment she discovered her legs were bound in a similar fashion. With everything else, she had failed to notice. Maureen cursed and bent over to set her legs free, wondering how she was going to get out of the room if the doctor had locked it like she suspected he had. She didn't have to wait for an answer. Outside in the hall, she could already hear the sound of returning footsteps.

The door pushed open as Maureen slowly rose to her feet. She pushed the effects of the drug aside and focused with all of her strength on the middle and clearer of the three identical images of Dr. Frank as he strode into the room, now clad in a white hazmat suit. He pulled down his surgical mask with a gloved hand to reveal a look of surprise at finding her standing. She felt her knees wobble as she faced him, and his look changed to a confident, sadistic grin. Even out of the chair, he believed she was easy prey. She knew that she didn't have much time.

Dr. Frank held the scalpel in his right hand and stalked forward, holding the blade in front of him. The moment he was within striking distance, he slashed at her. Maureen instinctively brought up her left arm to block, just as Avery had taught her on the farm. She felt the shock of the blow pulse through her shoulder and the sting of the scalpel blade as it sliced into the back of her hand. She managed to deflect it enough to throw Dr. Frank off balance, however, and found just enough space to connect with a hard right across his jaw.

The strike hurt her knuckles, but it appeared to hurt Dr. Frank more as he staggered back. A thin stain of blood formed on his lower lip. He must have bit it. He still held on to the blade, though. Maureen took a deep breath through her nose and took up a proper fighting stance, picturing the doctor as the punching bag hanging in the Wyoming barn and trying to remember everything she'd learned from Ernest during their sparring sessions.

Dr. Frank rushed forward impatiently and slashed at her with the same slicing blow he tried the first time. This time, Maureen ducked, pivoted, and hit him with three more snapping punches as he sped by. Dr. Frank gritted his teeth as he turned back to face her. He was emotional and was going to keep making mistakes. The problem was, Maureen could feel that her adrenaline rush was beginning to wear off, and soon she wouldn't be able to defend herself. She needed to end the fight now.

The doctor tried to stab at her with the scalpel, giving her the chance she was waiting for. Utilizing a maneuver she'd picked up from Iggy, Maureen grabbed the wrist of the hand holding the blade and used his momentum to throw him over her hip. Dr. Frank landed on his back with a groan of pain. Maureen kept hold of his wrist and twisted as he fell, sending the scalpel sliding behind the chair. Maureen stomped on Dr. Frank's arm as she ran to pick it up, trying to give herself an extra moment. The decision backfired, though, and she lost her balance, falling forward on all fours. The room blurred again, and she felt her limbs get heavy. She shook her head violently and crawled along floor, which felt like a heaving ship deck under her.

Maureen reached out and finally felt the cold metal of the scalpel in her palm. Her fingers just closed around it when she felt a pair of arms wrap themselves in a vise-like grip around her. They pinned her own arms to her sides and lifted her off the ground. Maureen kicked her legs but could not get free. Dr. Frank's arms held her like steel cords. All the life seemed to drain out of her at once, and she felt as helpless as a rag doll being flung through the air. A part of her wanted to give up. She was tired. She'd fought hard. And she would lose soon enough.

No. Not like this.

With that thought kindling the dying embers of her spirit, Maureen flung her head back and into the doctor's face with all the force her neck could muster. She felt the top of her skull connect with the bridge of his nose, and the sickening crunch rang out behind her ears. The arms let her go, and she found herself falling, almost in slow motion, to the ground. Maureen knew that she still held the scalpel in her hand. As she hit the floor, she turned her body to face Dr. Frank and stabbed with everything she had. The blade pierced his inner thigh, and she dragged it down an inch before it pulled free from his flesh. Instantly a stream of crimson blood began to pour from the wound. The doctor screamed in agony and fell back, clutching at his leg.

"You bitch!" he screamed. "You fucking bitch!"

Maureen stumbled to her feet and shakily, step by step, made her way toward the open door. The opening seemed to change positions with every step she took. She looked back at the doctor on the floor. He was crawling behind her, dragging his paralyzed leg. She turned back and tried to speed up her pace. She reached the outer hallway. The doctor's shouts of "bitch," "slut," and "whore" grew fainter. Her legs were jelly, and she fell down to her knees and crawled to the base of the stairs. She dropped the scalpel and reached up to catch hold of the railing. Step by step, she began to pull herself up the stairs, trying to keep moving, as the drug continued to course through her veins. It wouldn't be long before it would do her in.

She was only halfway up the staircase when she realized she could go no farther. A warm sleepiness had begun to take hold, and it was too intoxicating, too comforting to ignore. If this were how she was going to go, then best to let it come.

A crash of wood overhead and multiple voices shouting roused her and kept her eyes from closing. On instinct, she hoisted herself up one more step as several beams of light hit her face.

Flashlights.

"Maureen," came a voice out of the darkness. It belonged to Agent Samuelson. "Are you all right?"

"Bastard pumped me full of Special K," she found herself answering, though her voice seemed far away. She looked up to see the agent, along with Turnberry, Tyce, and a half dozen uniformed officers, rush down to where she sat.

Tyce knelt down next to her and kept her from falling to the side. "Maureen, you're going to be fine. Stay with us."

"Where's Dr. Frank?" asked Samuelson, leaning down behind the ranger.

"Down there," Maureen mumbled, gesturing with a floppy hand in the direction she had come from. "Better hurry. He's bleeding out pretty bad."

"What happened?" the agent asked.

Maureen felt her face break into a rueful grin, and she leaned her head back against the wall. "He had an accident with a scalpel," she said as the darkness rose up to swallow her.

THIRTY-FOUR

Owen put on his best face as he stalked the long hallway of the sheriff's department, not wishing to betray the roiling tumult surging below the surface. Some dozen yards ahead, in the last room on the right, sat a man whose neurosis and poisoned beliefs had led to the deaths of four people—four people that he knew of; he was devious, conniving, and cold, so there were probably others. This was one interrogation he was looking forward to.

The agent reached the door and took a deep breath before entering. Dr. Frank was seated in a chair in the middle of the room, chained around the wrists and ankles. Owen had specifically asked for the table to be removed. He didn't want anything for the doctor to lean against. He wanted him as uncomfortable as possible. It was strategy but also a touch of personal vengeance.

The doctor wore a blank stare as he turned his head at the sound of Owen's entrance. Upon recognizing the agent, a chilling grin broke out on the man's face. His eyes stayed dead. Owen had never seen that look from Frank before. The pleasant, gentle demeanor of the man he'd gotten to know had been replaced with a ghoulish mask. It baffled him how he or anyone else hadn't been able to detect the monster inside.

"Agent Samuelson," Dr. Frank greeted him in a soft tone, far removed from his bedside voice.

"Doctor," Owen said, nodding as casually as he could. He pulled another chair over and sat down in front of Dr. Frank, legs crossed. He folded his hands in his lap and stared at the other man for a few brief moments before continuing. "How's the leg?"

The chains on his wrists rattled as Dr. Frank ran his hand slowly down the inside of his leg. His face stayed even. "Your officers did a satisfactory job stopping the bleeding. I'll have to thank them for that. That little hellcat of yours barely missed my femoral artery, and there's a good bit of nerve damage, but it seems I'll be able to live a normal life. I trust she made it out alive?"

"She survived." Owen wasn't about to give him the satisfaction of knowing that Maureen had only just pulled through and was still in the hospital ICU under observation.

"You will send her my regards?"

"I have half a mind to let her back in here to finish the job." His remark only made the sick grin on the other man's face broaden. "I understand you've waived your right to an attorney," he continued, refusing to let his expression change. "Are you sure that's wise?"

"Should I be concerned? Are you taping me?"

"Do you see any cameras?" Owen pointed around the room.

There weren't any, and Dr. Frank was smart enough and had been in the room by himself long enough to know it. There was no reason for them; Owen wasn't looking for a confession. He simply wanted to look the bastard in the eye and understand.

"What is it you want to know, Agent?" Dr. Frank asked, sitting up in his seat and holding his head up with a mocking air of regality.

"These four weren't your first, were they?"

Dr. Frank lowered his gaze and looked at him out of the tops of his eyes. He said nothing, but his right eye twitched.

"I might have guessed," Owen said. "So who else?"

"I haven't murdered anyone." He leaned as far forward in his chair as the chains would allow.

"Don't protest innocence with me, Doctor. We have you dead to rights."

"You have me for kidnapping and drugging your little psychic friend." Dr. Frank smiled. "We'll just see about the rest."

Owen felt the corner of his mouth twitch. The doctor was toying with him, dancing around the point. Frank was going to give him everything. Eventually. He wanted to show off his genius. He wanted validation. Owen would give him some rope and wait for him to hang himself.

"Tell me about your grandmother," he said.

"She was my inspiration," Dr. Frank said simply.

"And by that, you mean in the matters of Lebensborn."

The doctor's icy chuckle sent a prickle down his spine, in spite of Owen's resolve to keep his emotions under control. "Agent," he said as if chastising a small child, "you clearly don't comprehend any of this. The operations of the Reich were merely a means to an end. And besides, do you even know where they got their ideas about eugenics from?"

329

"Enlighten me."

"From this very country," Dr. Frank intoned triumphantly. "Think of it: at the turn of the last century, more than half the states in the Union had laws on the books allowing for the sterilization of inferior people: the cognitively disabled or those with hereditary diseases. Cultural icons including Carnegie and Rockefeller donated huge sums to this cause. And then, just because someone like Himmler and Hitler decided to take the program to the next step, America throws the blanket over its own history. Think where this country would be if someone had the foresight to keep pushing forward."

"If there were more people like you?"

"Exactly."

"That way, the Aryans like you still have a chance at controlling the world."

"Don't flatter me, Agent. The blue-eyed, blonde-haired Aryans were no more than a propaganda tool, and I know I'm not the epitome of humanity. It's not about race; it's about perfection, and it's science that will perfect humanity. I'm intelligent, sure, and strong, but I'm not the product of perfect specimens. Sadly, my father didn't share my grandmother's pride in being one of the chosen. He wasn't even three when they came to this country, and in spite of her protests, he decided to marry an asthmatic with a family history of autoimmune disease." He paused for a moment and inclined his head as though a pleasant thought had just come to mind. "Of course, they did prove to be a very interesting study in family genetics."

"They disappeared about eleven years ago," Owen said, staring as hard at the other man as he could.

"Tragic, isn't it?" Dr. Frank raised a chained hand to his chest. "It took all of my strength to allow them to be declared dead."

"And take possession of that little home on the river in which to build your kill room."

"Please, Agent. Lab."

"What about Professor Freeman?"

"Ah, he was an intriguing man, wasn't he? A man of his age staying in that kind of shape? And on top of his intellectual accomplishments? Especially for a Jew. He needed to be studied."

Owen filed the comment away with all the other things the doctor had said that he'd make him pay for and pressed forward. "And Lindstrom and Niemann?"

"A male and female subject from the same National Guard platoon: a wonderful opportunity to compare genders."

"Lynn Sandburg?"

"Legacy study. Think about it: an exceptional woman who is almost a carbon copy of her parents who are exceptional in their own right? Absolutely fascinating."

Owen shook his head. No words from the other man's mouth could convince him that he had all his faculties. The problem was, a jury might agree. And a lifetime in a mental facility as punishment for all that he had done did not feel like justice. He may not be recording anything, but the agent was making mental notes so he could give his insights on the witness stand.

"You do realize, Doctor, that you're basically confessing to multiple homicides, right?"

"You haven't been listening, Agent. I haven't confessed to

anything. Except to being an enthusiastic scientist eager for a discovery that will benefit all mankind."

"You're a goose-stepping psychopath with delusions of grandeur and a god complex," Owen said in a measured tone. He consciously kept his voice low to make Dr. Frank listen. "If I had the power, I'd find myself some that Zyklon B gas and give you a taste of what your heroes did to millions of innocent people. I have more than enough evidence in that little bunker of yours to put you away without a confession."

"You have body parts in jars labeled with last names only. You have my notes on my subjects, but they say nothing about killing them. For all you know, they were participating in my studies of their own volition."

"That's bullshit, and you know it. We'll be testing the DNA of the parts in the jar. And besides, I have a survivor who can establish your method of operation. That's premeditation and murder one."

"You're free to test away. But I'll caution you, Agent. Those body parts are stored in formaldehyde, and let's just say that samples taken from those jars might yield unreliable results. Any good lawyer would call those results into question. And as for your other witness, how do you think the jury—or the public for that matter—will feel about the prosecution's case when they hear that the FBI is using psychics to help solve their cases? Seems to me that's a public relations nightmare just waiting to happen."

Owen leaned back and pondered the man's words. It took him a moment to figure out what he was doing. Dr. Frank hadn't asked for a lawyer, but he was discussing potential outcomes of the case and defense strategies. Their eyes met.

The doctor's eyes flashed with excitement; he knew that Owen had figured out his game plan. A squeamish feeling rose in the pit of Owen's stomach at the prospect. The bastard was planning on a trial, and he was going to defend himself.

Just like Ted Bundy.

"No lawyer could possibly represent me the way I deserve," the doctor said, answering the question before Owen even asked it.

"Or let you read into the record the things that you surely want to," Owen continued for him.

"Very perceptive, Agent."

"Makes perfect sense. Why else would you risk conviction in a trial instead of seeking the insanity plea if not for an ulterior motive."

"It is a wonderful podium to inspire the next generation of science and turn the country back onto the path it should be on."

"Except we can ban all media from the courtroom. No one will hear your poison."

"You underestimate the media. There's nothing that the papers and cable TV love more than a sensation—just ask your friend Lowdon. They'll find their way to me. I'll be giving interviews on the networks within a year. The jurors will sign book deals. There will be movies. My message will never die. My story will be told. There's nothing you can do."

Owen calmly got to his feet and placed a foot on Dr. Frank's chair, between his legs. He leaned over so that his nose was within an inch of the other man's. Hundreds of things he could say rushed through his head. None seemed right. Instead, he leaned his weight into the chair and pushed the two front legs slightly off the ground. He held it there for a moment, keeping his eyes fixed on the doctor, before lowering it back down. Whatever he was feeling inside, he'd be damned if he let this psycho push him to lose control. And he wanted the other man to know the difference between what he *could* do and what he *would* do.

Owen turned calmly and made his way toward the door. His hand had just touched the knob when the doctor spoke again.

"You're a special one, Agent. I'm sorry I never had the chance to get you into my chair. I wonder what I'd find inside you."

Owen paused momentarily, his mind turning toward his sidearm. His hand twitched. He could make sure that this monster never saw the inside of a courtroom. Instead, he took a deep breath and allowed the foolish notion to pass. "I hope you enjoy your time at Florence," he said quietly. "I'm sure you'll have lots of new friends just waiting to share their feelings about your beliefs with you. There're a few people I've put in there myself who might pay you a visit. See you again at the arraignment."

With that, Agent Owen Samuelson opened the door and freed himself of Dr. Frank.

For now.

THIRTY-FIVE

Blackness lay across her vision as the rest of her senses began to awaken. It was no dream; Maureen could tell she was in her own skin. It was her own head she felt pressed against a pillow. The mechanical beep of some medical machine was echoing in her own ears. The smell of rubbing alcohol and other hospital cleansers snuck past the rubber tubing and invaded her own nostrils. Slowly, painfully, she pulled her eyelids apart.

The stark white walls of the hospital room hit her pupils hard. Whoever decided to turn the lights up as bright as they were now needed to get smacked upside the head. Maureen swallowed. Her mouth was bone dry. The desire for water drove her to try and sit up.

"The doctor said you shouldn't get up yet," a voice across the room sounded.

Maureen turned her gaze toward the voice and was met by the sight of Ranger Tyce sitting cross-legged in a chair with his hat resting upon his knee. He looked haggard, as if he'd been awake for days. She leaned back and swallowed hard. Tyce got to his feet and came over to the bedside.

"They said you could have ice chips when you woke up." He grabbed a Styrofoam cup off a nearby table and handed it to her.

"Thanks," she replied and tipped the cup into her mouth. The chill of the water sliding down her throat as she crunched the ice was a huge relief, and she soon found talking easier. "How long have I been out?"

"Nearly three days," the ranger replied.

"Jesus, man! I hope you haven't been here the whole time."

"Nah, I know you're tough. But, just the same, I've been coming to look in on you when I've had the chance. It was pretty touch and go there for a while from what I understand."

"How bad did it get?"

"Well, you didn't officially flatline if that makes you feel any better," another voice chimed from the other side of the room.

Maureen turned to see Samuelson, arms folded, leaning in the doorway. His face wore an expression of satisfaction and relief. Maureen was surprised at how little it bothered her that he was there, despite the vulnerability that she felt with both him and the ranger seeing her in the state she was in.

"But your blood pressure and pulse dipped dangerously low," he continued. "And you had a seizure. Even after they administered the drugs to counteract it, you still had two more and slipped into a coma. They say that the amount of ketamine in your system would have killed a person twice your size. The tox screen showed that he used a powdered version as a roofie in your drink and then injected you with a concentrated dose. Yet somehow, your vitals stabilized while you were out. The doctors have no explanation." He pointed a finger up in the air. "Someone up there must sure like you."

Maureen felt her mouth curl at the implication. *Father Patrick better not hear about this, or it will be all "God's plan" this and "divine protection" that.* "Remind me to donate to a kid's charity or something as a thank-you," she said aloud.

"You probably don't remember, but you did come out of it for a bit yesterday. You were so groggy and incoherent that they gave you a sedative to put you back to sleep. But you did mention something about owing *me* specifically. Something about repaying me for saving your life." Agent Samuelson smirked at her.

"You're right, I don't remember any of that. Even so, I call BS. But at least you weren't the one who told them to put me under this time."

Samuelson came into the room, taking a seat next to her. "What is the last thing you remember?"

Maureen thought for a moment. So much of that night was a blur, but soon she found that if she focused hard enough, clearer pieces began to show themselves. "I remember stabbing that bastard. I guess I got him pretty good, didn't I?"

"Sorry to say, he could have bled out if we hadn't been such noble individuals," the agent replied. "He should even have full use of his leg in a few weeks."

"I should have aimed higher—done some damage that he couldn't recover from." It was a playful lamentation, but not without an air of truth to it.

Samuelson seemed to catch the bitterness behind her levity. "We'll make sure he suffers plenty for what he's done."

"What about Dr. Heim?" she asked, remembering more of the things Dr. Frank had said to her. "Dr. Frank made it seem like he was just a patsy in all this."

"Well, if Heim *did* have any suspicions of Dr. Frank, he never mentioned them," Samuelson told her. "As far as the e-mails from his address to Lynn Sandburg, the matching IP address was the big hit against him. It took our boys in forensic IT a while, but they managed to unscramble the code. Frank managed to hack in from his own computer and made it look like Dr. Heim was sending those e-mails from his."

"How did he manage that?" Maureen crunched on some more ice chips.

"We finally got around to digging through the good doctor's college records. In addition to being pre-med at CU, he also minored in computer science."

"Of course he did."

"Something else interesting," the agent continued. "Our Dr. Frank helped pay for his undergrad by joining the National Guard. He went IRR once he got into med school and was retired out around the same time that Shelly Lindstrom and Chris Niemann joined his unit."

"So that's how he knew them," Ranger Tyce said.

Samuelson nodded. "That must be the tie-in."

"And Professor Freeman? They were at the university at the same time, sure, but did Frank take any of his classes?" Tyce asked.

"Kayaking club," Maureen said. Both men turned and looked at her like she had just spoken Greek. "Dr. Frank is a big talker when he thinks the person will be dead and won't be able to say anything," she explained.

"Well," said Samuelson, "I guess that's a wrap on that."

"Seems so," Tyce echoed, stuffing his hands in his pockets and rocking from foot to foot.

An uncomfortable silence filled the room. The two men exchanged glances. There was something they knew that they didn't want to tell her—that was painfully clear. Maureen frowned. It chaffed her when men didn't think she could catch their tells.

"What is it?" she asked.

They both hesitated.

"Maybe it's not the best time," Tyce said after a moment. "Not with you on the mend and all."

"Just shut up and tell me."

Samuelson cleared his throat and leaned forward in his chair. "Dr. Frank is planning on taking this thing to trial. He's risking a conviction on all counts and a death sentence to get a public platform to spit out his rhetoric."

"The guy's crazy," Maureen said.

"Maybe," the agent agreed. "But he knows what he's doing. He already showed his hand to me. He's going to try and use your involvement in the case to sow the seeds of doubt in the minds of the jury and the public."

"You can't let him do that!" Maureen shouted.

The monitor at her bedside began to beep loudly, and a nurse poked her head into the room. Samuelson held up a hand to indicate that everything was fine.

"You need to relax, Maureen," he said once they were alone again. "You're not recovered enough to get excited like that."

Maureen settled back and crossed her arms. "I don't see how I'm supposed to relax when I'm likely to be put on display for the whole country to see."

"The FBI is going to do everything it can to block his attempts to bring you before the jury," the agent said reassuringly. "We'll need a deposition from you when you're ready, and that will be entered in as evidence for the prosecution.

As far as the law is concerned, you're nothing more than a consultant—hired to work up a criminal and psychological profile—who was abducted and held by the defendant. Your role in the direction of the investigation outside of that has to be kept strictly confidential, or else much of our case might be called into question. So you see, keeping you out of the spotlight is best for everyone."

"What about that reporter, Lowdon? He's going to print his story regardless."

"I wouldn't worry about him," said Tyce.

"How's that?" she asked.

"Because he's going to get his exclusive," said the voice of the reporter, who had appeared at the door. "With the cooperation of the FBI. As long as I play by their rules."

Maureen turned to Samuelson. "Okay, I'm lost."

"As much as I hate to admit it"—the agent sighed—"Lowdon did help out in your rescue. A little. And I found the best way to reward him was to give him the exclusive rights to the story of the FBI's investigation and capture of Dr. Frank."

"With your anonymity intact, of course," Lowdon said with a flourish of his hand and a bow of his head.

"And, just maybe," said Samuelson, "it'll give Mr. Lowdon the break he's been working for so he can stop with the sensational journalism."

"I'll never stop being a patriot for the truth," the reporter declared. Samuelson gave him a look. The reporter got the message and began to back out of the room. "Right. So, I'll just wait out here for you."

Samuelson shook his head as the reporter disappeared. "I can't believe I'm allowing that man to interview me," he scoffed. Then he shrugged his shoulders. "But, better the info comes from me rather than Navarro."

"What do you mean?" asked Tyce.

"Lowdon's source in the FBI?" he explained. "It's Rick. I figured it out when I saw them talking by the car on the morning we discovered Ms. Sandburg. I finally got a chance to confront him yesterday. He didn't cop to it, but he didn't deny it either."

"Why don't you do something about it?" Maureen asked.

"I don't see the need to destroy a man's career. Especially one who's as new to the job as he is. He knows I'll be watching him, and I doubt he'll risk stepping out of line again. Well"— he drew in a deep breath and, lightening the look on his face, nodded toward Tyce—"maybe it's time we let Maureen get a little more rest. I'll be back tomorrow to get your statement, if you're up for it."

"Gotcha," she replied.

Ranger Tyce put his hat on his head and touched the brim. "First round's on you next time you're in town?"

There was more meaning to his words, but that was all she needed to hear. Maureen clicked her tongue and nodded her agreement. The two men made their way out of the room, but just before Samuelson crossed the threshold, he paused and turned back.

"There's one more thing that I need to know. Dr. Frank is a lot bigger than you. How did you manage to win that fight?"

"It was like instinct," she told him after a moment of thought. "Back at the farm, I exercised with Natalie's son and his friends almost every day. They did a lot of boxing and wrestling, and I joined in. When I managed to get myself out of the chair and Frank came after me, I remembered everything I'd learned. I hadn't realized up to that point that I could use any of it in a real fight."

Samuelson nodded and rubbed his chin. He looked deep in thought, as though he were unsure if he should say more. He did. "I think you owe someone a big thank-you."

"Well, yeah, of course," Maureen replied. "I owe Avery and the guys big-time. I'll find some way to say thanks."

"That's not what I meant."

"I don't get it."

"Your friend Father Patrick cares deeply about you. We know a lot about the folks looking after you on the farm. They're all ex-military who grew to have their disagreements on the way the government does things. We never paid them any mind since they were all honorably discharged, they basically keep to themselves, and they don't show any signs of starting trouble. We simply figured that he left you with them because he trusted them to protect you. Seems like he had even greater reasons for leaving you where he did. Just food for thought."

Agent Samuelson turned and left without another word. Maureen stared at the door for a long time after he'd closed it behind him, pondering what he said. She looked down at her left arm, resting on the comforter. A line of a dozen or more stitches ran from the base of her middle finger to the top of her wrist. The skin around it was a sickly yellow and purple.

One more scar for the collection.

Her thoughts were interrupted by a knock and the reappearance of the same nurse from before. She came over to the bed and checked the IV bag hanging on the hook next to it.

"Good news," the nurse said. "The doctor says now that you're awake and your vitals appear stable, you can have some Jell-O and broth for dinner tonight."

"Sounds exciting," Maureen mumbled.

"Don't worry. If you keep that down, it's likely that you'll be able to have a real breakfast tomorrow."

"And how long do I have to stay here?"

"Lucky for you," the woman said with a smile, "your stay is on the government's dime, so there's no rushing you out. We'll want to take a good few days, if not a week, of observation before you're discharged."

"What the hell am I going to do for a week?"

"Rest and recover. Leave the rest to us." The nurse picked up a controller attached to the bed and put it in Maureen's lap. "The red button calls the nurse on duty, and the other buttons control the bed and TV. Do you want me to show you how it works?"

Maureen shook her head. There would be plenty of time for television in the days to come. Her mind was far away, thinking of an ornately decorated church on the main street of a small town and of a brick house not far away where her life had made a hard left turn.

"Is there anything I can get for you now?" the nurse asked.

"Well, there is one thing," Maureen replied slowly. "If I asked for paper and a pen, could you help me mail something?"

EPILOGUE

Dear Father Patrick,

I've been going back and forth for a while as to whether I should respond to all of your letters. I know I'm not the type of person to show it, but you know I appreciate everything you've done for me. You didn't need to do any of it, and sometimes I still wonder why you did. You'd probably tell me it's what God would want you to do. I still don't know much about all that, but that's a whole other thing, and I won't waste any more paper on it.

When the FBI came to get me, they told me that it wasn't too hard to find me, that you were good, but they were better. It got me thinking. How did someone with so much counterintelligence experience leave any evidence as to where I was? Then it hit me. You wanted them to eventually find me. You kept sending me letters even after I was out of prison, sent them to a PO box that was in a building with surveillance, and Natalie always came herself to pick up the letters. If you'd wanted me to stay hidden like you said, you'd have found another, less traceable way to keep in touch

344

with me. You wanted me to get pulled back in because you still think that my abilities need to be used for the greater good.

Well, it worked. You'll probably hear about the Colorado River Killer (or whatever the press decides to call him) on the news soon enough, and you'll wonder whether I played a role in bringing him down. And of course I did—even if I didn't want to and even if it came at great risk to my own life. You'd probably say that God allowed me to bring him down and come out alive on the other end, but I can't see it in this case. When he goes on trial, this man is going to get a public platform to spout things that would make the stuff Father Preston said to me last summer seem like romantic poetry. Wherever God is, He wasn't in that basement that night. I'd say that I'll be reliving it all in my dreams for years to come, but we both know what my dreams are really like. Who knows, they might prove to be my only refuge for a time. Isn't that a pleasant thought?

Agent Samuelson assures me that there will be no mention of my involvement in the investigation, and I hope he's telling the truth. The last thing I need in my life is to become well known for this stuff. I'm not sure what comes next, but I do plan on returning to the farm for the time being. I realize now that I'm not going to get out of the deal I struck to keep you out of jail, so I might as well go along with it. It's only two and a half more years of my life, and who knows, maybe they'll actually start paying me for sticking my neck out the way I do. (Fat chance!)

I'm not happy with you for helping the feds find me, but I can't pretend like I won't forgive you one day. Just don't expect any more letters from me. I'm not particularly keen on writing this one, but I suppose I owe it to you. You may have left me out in the middle of nowhere on false pretenses, but the people you left me with taught me a few things that actually ended up saving my life. I don't believe that was an accident, so for that, I guess I owe you my life. Twice over. Which means that one day, I'll have to find a way to repay you.

I know you won't stop writing to me even if I ask you to for a while, so I won't bother. Just know that you don't have to continue the covert mission. The feds know where I am, and I'm not going anywhere. You can just send whatever you want to send me to the farm. You can even think of it as my lifeline to the world if it makes you feel better.

I'm sure that one day our paths will cross again, and when they do, I'll buy the first round. Until then, just know that I'm doing my best to behave myself, and maybe I'll actually become a good person like you'd hoped.

Sincerely Yours,
Maureen

Father Patrick folded up the crinkled paper and placed it back in the envelope that had contained it when it arrived at St. Mary's rectory a little over a week prior. He'd read it over a dozen times at least since then. He didn't begrudge Maureen the frustration she had with him. It was clear to him that over thirty years out of the game had left his skills rustier than he realized. The technology of the younger generation was quite the foil for his jungle counterinsurgency training. If he were guilty of anything, it would be of simply getting old. Well, that and of being overly sentimental. It was those feelings that made him keep writing to her.

He was glad to hear that she was beginning to embrace God's plan for her. She may not be fully there yet, but he felt confident that before all was said and done, she would be. And he himself felt grateful that he could do something to bring about her transcendence. A bit of a grandiose thought for a humble priest, he knew, but at least he was not enough of a hypocrite to blatantly deny his own human nature.

Father Patrick put the envelope back in the top drawer of his office desk and rose to his feet. He was grateful to not have anything on his schedule for the remainder of the day. After Preston's death, the diocese had asked him to rescind his retirement notice and continue on in his ministry in Sycamore Hills. It was necessary for the congregation to have a stabilizing force after the horror of what the younger priest had done to the community. He agreed wholeheartedly despite feeling a certain amount of trepidation in continuing in his role when he was the cause of his successor's death. It might have been considered a righteous kill—more righteous than anything the twisted mind of Father Preston could come up with to justify his own crimes—but in the mind of the old priest, it made him no better than the dead man. And it didn't help that the ensuing months had revealed more questions about the younger priest. He had few solid answers, but he had enough to come to believe that the motives for Preston's actions were not a creation of his own.

The old priest turned and looked at the wall behind his desk. Several of his favorite biblical passages were artfully painted on thick canvas and, framed as pictures, hung on the wall. They were a delicate reminder of not only the poetry of Bible prose but also of the tenants that formed the pillars of his faith. Father Patrick walked close to the one that hung directly behind his desk chair. It was John 3:16. It was a rather obvious choice, even for those with barely a layman's knowledge of catechism, but he smiled nonetheless as he brushed his hand over the picture's dark, wooden frame. There were powerful secrets in that passage.

He turned back to his desk and pulled out a sheet of letter paper and one of the many envelopes preemptively addressed to Maureen. In the upper-right corner of the paper, he wrote the number three and circled it before flipping the sheet over.

Then, ever so carefully, Father Patrick began to pen a most important letter.

author notes and acknowledgments

As Maureen's life resets itself after the events in *Unholy Shepherd*, I wanted to place her as a bit of a fish out of water for her first case working with the FBI—especially since she is operating without Father Patrick and Manny as her support system. Knowing that I was going to place Maureen's new home far off the beaten path in Wyoming, setting the crime scenes in and around Rocky Mountain State Park seemed like an obvious choice. The area has enough of a history of unexplained disappearances—referred to as 411s—and bizarre body recoveries to give a writer the opportunity to explore all sorts of the seedy explanations for a loss of life. The themes of conspiracy theories and Third Reich atrocities run strongly through *A Perfect Victim,* but in early concepts of the book I briefly toyed with the idea of some initial theories espoused by the character who eventually became Lowdon to include alien abduction (to which some conspiracy theorists attribute the aforementioned 411 disappearances) in addition to the theory expressed in the book of government experimentation.

The choice to make the villain of this novel as a descendant of the German Lebensborn concept came from some of my own personal interests. I am a lover of both Continental and Anglo European History, everything from World War II and before. It never fails to both fascinate and sicken me the levels of barbarity that some people were capable of inflicting on their fellow man and, moreover, how they could find ways to justify said actions. Often in writing, at least for me, exploring the inner mind of someone capable of such gruesome acts can be an outlet for the anger and outrage that they inspire. The prime example in this case is, of course, Dr. Frank. Even as his creator, I still cannot say for certain if he truly believed in the Nazi cause and eugenics as a whole or if he used them as a convenient complement to justify his own psychosis and homicidal tendencies. I did model him on two of the more infamous perpetrators of such heinous experimentation during the Third Reich; Josef Mengele, the so-called "Angel of Death" of Auschwitz (where he engaged in his deadly human experiments under the auspices of anthropological and heredity research while at the same time being a member of the team that selected those who were to be sent to the gas chambers) and Aribert Heim, who, as noted in the novel, was notorious for his work in discovering new ways to kill, most notably injecting various chemicals and other caustic materials directly into the hearts of the Jewish people confined at Mauthausen. He was also known to remove organs from inmates without anesthesia, resulting in hundreds of deaths. Both of these men escaped justice and lived out their days in South America and Egypt respectively. I suppose that bringing their narrative avatar to justice at the end of this novel was my small way of finding some kind of catharsis and righting this wrong, if only in the fictional world.

While I have researched things such as *Star-Gate* and *Operation Paperclip*—respectively, the CIA-ran remote viewing and psychic program of the 1970s and 1980s and the government operation to secretly bring over sixteen hundred German scientists, including the eventual father of the space program, Wehrner von Braun, to America during and after the Second World War— more than most laymen, I do not hold myself out as an expert on many of the topics touched on in the novel. All of what I know was put into the mouth of Gabriel Lowdon, which is to say, enough to sound authoritative without having to dig too deeply to weave a good story. Though, whereas the fictional Mr. Lowdon uses this information as proof of salacious and shadowy dealings within the US Government, I look at these events simply as an interesting part of world events which do not, in the long run, affect the lives of average Americans (aside from putting us on the moon and winning the race to create the atomic bomb).

As always, I'd like to thank my family and friends for their love and encouragement, as well as my support team at Ten16 Press and my ever-present editor and collaborator, Leslie Stratinger. In some ways, a sequel is so much harder to write than the debut novel, but we got there eventually. Maureen has finally begun to understand what her life is and has made the hard choice as to which direction she must take it in. Only time will tell how deeply she will commit to using her abilities for the ultimate good.